Even Villains Play The Hero

LIANA BROOKS

HEROES AND VILLAINS
Even Villains Fall In Love
Even Villains Go To The Movies
Even Villains Have Interns

OTHER WORKS
Find other works by the author at
http://www.lianabrooks.com

Even Villains Play The Hero

LIANA BROOKS

Inkprint
PRESS
www.inkprintpress.com

ISBN-13: 978-0994523853

www.inkprintpress.com

National Library of Australia Cataloguing-in-Publication Data
Brooks, Liana 1982—
Even Villains Play The Hero
        444 p.
ISBN-13: 978-0994523853
Inkprint Press, Canberra, Australia
1. Superheroes 2. Supervillains 3. Science Fiction 4. Romance
Fiction

First Edition: July 2015

Printed in the United States of America.

Cover Artist: Victoria Miller

LIANA BROOKS

EVEN VILLAINS

FALL IN LOVE

HEROES AND VILLAINS

A SPECIAL THANKS TO:

The Slackers, Dreamers, and Tweeps who helped me get this far. My four ice cream minions whose antics inspire me daily. My husband for always being my hero.

CHAPTER ONE

I knew the first time I saw my wife that I wanted her naked. Of course, seven minutes later I wanted revenge. It wasn't that she had handed me my first defeat ever or ruined my chances for world domination that year, it was the way she kissed me good-bye. She sent my head spinning, then walked away as if I were the least important person in the world.

It was once my arm healed, I stole some new equipment, and cloned some new minions that I felt a little different.

I wanted revenge with a side order of naked.

ACROSS THE DINNER table, Tabitha devoured him with dark ocean-blue eyes. She put a bite of lettuce in her mouth, full lips pursing around it. Eating salad never looked so good. Her tongue darted out to lick away a stray drop of dressing. She winked at him, promising with every move to do the same to him. "It's almost bedtime," she said, her voice husky and luscious.

"I don't wanna go to bed!" one of the quads screamed.

"What about cake? Don't we get birthday cake?" another asked.

Evan winked back at his wife from the far side of the table, separated by a few feet and four precocious just-turned-five-year olds, all as stunning as their mother with big, round eyes and hair that fell in loose curls meant to trap hairbrushes and sticky substances alike. He had to peek at the eyes to see who was talking. Maria had green eyes, Angela's eyes were blue like Tabitha's, Delilah's were brown like his, and Blessing—their stillborn who miraculously survived—had purple eyes. The waif in question had blue eyes.

"Angela," Evan said, "after dinner it's pajama time, and then story time."

"Mommy doesn't have a bedtime!" Angela wailed.

Tabitha winked at him again. "Tell you what, tonight Mommy will go to bed the same time you do. Right after we eat cake." She leaned over to give Angela a hug.

All Evan could see was the deep V plunge of her tight blue shirt. Oh, yeah. Crime didn't always pay, but altering someone's moral compass sure put the O's back in the bedroom.

The cake was split into fourths, equal parts purple, white, green, and blue so each girl could have her favorite color in the cake. Baking four cakes was unreasonable; there weren't any grandparents left to celebrate with, and neighbors had an annoying habit of asking uncomfortable questions. Saying little things like, "You look just like Doctor Charm! Do you remember him? Whatever happened to that guy? Do you know how hard it is to put together a good Villains vs. Heroes fantasy league without him?" made for awkward evenings.

So they had a quiet family party. Cake, then presents, after which he hurried the girls off to bed so he could read Dilly Duck's ABCs in record time before rushing to the bedroom, hoping to catch Tabitha still in the shower.

She was already out and wearing a blue satin robe that caressed her skin in exactly the way he wanted to. Rose-scented candles cast sensuous shadows on the walls.

Tabitha turned, lips curved in an inviting smile. Long fingers twined with the sash of her robe. She tossed her honey-blonde hair in the way she always did when she was about to argue, posing with feet apart and one hand casually resting on her waist. "Sweetie, we need to talk."

Evan wiped grease-stained hands on his jeans as he forced a smile. "Sure, babes, anything you want."

"Really?" She slunk forward, all sinewy limbs and doe eyes. "Promise?" Tabitha nuzzled his nose. One hand flirted up the back of his neck to play with his hair. The other traveled downward, right to his zipper.

Oh, yes, the little Morality Machine in the basement was working just fine. Another thirty, maybe forty years of this and he'd consider retiring. Or turning the machine down so his wife wasn't quite a sex kitten every day of the week. Maybe only days with Y in them.

"Sweetie?" She nibbled his ear. "I want to go back to work."

"What?" Evan actually pushed himself away from her, something he wasn't sure was possible in any other circumstance.

Tabitha tucked her chin and pouted.

"Tabby-cat, I love you, but work? I've got my... stuff... in the lab. I'm busy. And we can't afford daycare for the girls. We're barely making ends meet as it is. Do you really want to go back to being Zephyr Girl? Crime fighting is a game for the young, baby. You're not nineteen anymore."

"I'm twenty-nine. A very"—her hips pressed against his tight jeans just so—"very healthy twenty-nine."

He shivered at her touch. "You're cheating."

"I want to do this, Evan." She ground against the thick denim.

"You can do me all you want, baby."

She stepped back, frowning. "I'm serious."

"So am I." Evan sighed, reaching for his wife. "Sweetie, I love you, but what's the point in being a superhero? The government stipend barely covers the dry-cleaning bill. If it's money you want, write another tell-all superhero book. The Spanish Mask sold his third last month."

Tabitha crossed her arms. "I don't want to write another book just for royalties while you're between jobs."

He waved a finger at her. "I'm not between jobs. I work freelance in the computer business. I'm self-employed. That's not the same as being between jobs."

"Between paychecks then."

"We will have a solid income. This project I'm working on, Tabby-cat, it's going to set us up for life. We're never going to worry about money again. I promise. Give me a couple of weeks and everything is going to be perfect." He caught her hand and pulled her into his arms. The faint scent of her spicy perfume left him dizzy with need.

She rested her head on his chest. "I want to save the world. Have you seen the news, Evan? An entire town in Kansas held hostage for a week by a bomb scare before a superhero was able to get in to defuse the situation. A week! I could have that done between grocery shopping and paying the bills. Ten minutes, no pulling punches."

"I know, baby. No one is better at this stuff than you. But I need you at home, Tabby. Having you out there scares me. I'm terrified I'd lose you. Why don't you wait until I finish this project? I'll be done by the time the election rolls around. Two more weeks. Once I get paid we'll look at this again. I have that armor design for you, I just need some time to put it together."

Tabitha sighed. "You've been saying that since we got married."

"Well, my nights are busy." He nibbled her ear as he tugged her sash loose. "Are you complaining?"

Tabitha stretched against him, sending a delightful frisson of lust up his spine. "I thought you gave up the super villain schemes."

He twitched. "I did, baby. Of course I did."

"But you're keeping me here. Isn't that a little selfish? Just a teeny-tiny bit super villain-ish?" She slipped her hand between his pants and his skin.

"Ah!" He caught her hand so he could think clearly. "Not selfish. Necessary. Like oxygen or sex."

"Don't you mean water?"

"No, definitely sex." Evan slid her robe off and tossed it into a corner. "Come here, Tabby-cat, I'll make you purr."

She tugged at his shirt, pulling it up. The shirt joined the robe on the other side of the room. "What are you doing down in that lab?" she asked as her hands drew lazy circles on his back.

Ten seconds, that's all he'd need to get her panties off. Three more to drop his pants. "What was the question?"

"What are you doing in the lab? What's this project?"

"Oh, computer stuff. I told you. To help tally everything on election night. I'm trying to make the process run smoother so we don't have to worry about recounts."

"Hmmm." She gave him a dubious frown.

Tabitha was built like a supermodel and had a superhero name straight from Campy Comics, but her brain was Mensa all the way. "And this computer program has nothing to do with world domination, or get-rich-quick schemes?"

Evan contrived to look wounded. "Tabby-cat, how can you ask that?"

"Because you spent ten years as a villainous criminal mastermind?"

"I wasn't a mastermind, I was a super villain, there's a difference. Masterminds are just thugs with money. My crimes had artistic flare. I was practically Robin Hood! Robbing from the rich and scandalous, and giving to me."

"Robin Hood gave to the poor," Tabitha said with a laugh. "You were never poor."

He caught her hand, pulling her close. "Poor is relative. Besides, I'm reformed now. You showed me the error of my wicked ways. Although"—he leaned in for a kiss—"if you'd like to remind me why I gave up a lucrative life of crime, I have the evening free."

CHAPTER TWO

Someday, I know the kids are going to ask for the story of How I Met Their Mother. Every kid asks; it's a rite of passage like losing a tooth or learning to ride a bike. I just don't know how to tell them without losing their respect.

The truth is, Tabitha broke into my lab and kicked me and my minions clear into the next time zone. She can move at sonic speeds even when she's not flying. She blew past my machines like they weren't even there. Embarrassing, of course, but that wasn't the worst part. No, the part that will make my daughters lose all respect for me is how, while their mother was kicking my rear, I couldn't take my eyes off hers. Not when she wore a skin-tight white bodysuit and bustier on the verge of a wardrobe malfunction. Any man who can think straight when confronted by that must have a wonderful boyfriend at home, because I've seen drag queens hand in their Prada kitten heels for a shot at Tabitha.

EVAN WOKE UP relaxed and ready for another dose of marital bliss. Let the bachelors have their one-night stands, lost to the alcoholic haze of the weekend. Married life meant getting lucky three or four times a day, when dentist appointments and world domination didn't demand his full attention. He rolled over and reached for Tabitha.

She wasn't there. "Tabby? Babes?"

"In here!" she called from the closet. He relaxed back into the Tabitha-scented sheets. "What do you think?" she asked, stepping out of the closet in her white Zephyr Girl bodysuit: reinforced leather leggings, gloves, and bustier. Knee-high, steel-capped boots and a sky blue cape completed the outfit. Tabitha hovered, the air around her seething with the aurora borealis that always accompanied her use of super powers.

"You look amazing." She'd looked like that first time he'd seen her. "Come here."

She flew to him, settling over the bed before dropping the last centimeter. "It still fits."

"I know." He caught her lips, tasting her.

"Do you know where my trench coat is?"

"In the hall closet." He reached for her hair, but she was already gone. A breeze slammed the bedroom door open and shut. Tabitha cinched the belt to her white trench coat around her tiny waist with a smile. She sauntered away with her hips swaying to pull her purse out of the closet, along with a pink scarf.

He shook his head as she slipped past him to the door. "Wait! Tabitha, where are you going?"

She froze in the act of putting on sunglasses. "Work, remember? We talked about this. I'm going to work; you're going to take care of the kids. Right? Good. I'll try to be home by seven. Make sure dinner is ready."

The front door slammed shut on Evan's bewildered expression.

Tabitha swung the door back open. "Sweetie? Get the lawn service out here, the yard looks like a jungle, and hide the crayons. The girls found where I was keeping them yesterday. I don't want them coloring on the walls again."

Shut. Open. "Love ya!"

"Um..." Evan followed to the front lawn and watched his wife leap into the sky, flying away to save the day like any good superhero with a deadline. This was not good.

Back inside, Evan scrambled to find jeans in the mountain of unfolded laundry.

"Daddy?" Delilah said through a yawn.

"Yes?"

"I want breakfast."

"Breakfast?" He stared at his daughter. "Um, let's see what Mommy left."

The other three girls were waiting in the kitchen.

"I want Mommy!" Delilah said.

Blessing sat at the table with an expectant expression. "Pancakes?"

He peeked into the cupboard. There were boxes of things neatly stacked with matching lids. That probably meant something profound in the secret language of women, but he wasn't even getting a mixed signal.

"Daddy?" Four judgmental scowls looked up at him. "Can you cook?"

"For a given definition of cook." He closed the cupboard door. "Give Daddy a minute." Evan ran through the garage to the door to his basement lab. "Hert!"

His warty toad of a minion climbed up the stairs, six-knuckled fingers dragging on the floor. "You bellowed, Master?"

"Do you cook, Hert?"

"I wasn't programmed to, Master."

He'd forgotten that. Hert was his original minion, a summer project cooked up from the DNA of animals he'd been able to find in his backyard when he was fifteen and had nothing better to do with his life. Back then, Mom had cooked. In college he'd had the meal plan. Tabitha did the cooking once they got married. Back in the bachelor years between college and marriage... "Girls! Get dressed. Daddy's going to take you to McDonalds!"

Angela put her hands on her hips, posing just like Tabitha. "Fast food is very unhealthy for you. Mommy said so."

Evan looked at his warty minion for help.

"Never hurt me," Hert said, shrugging.

The girls wrinkled their noses in unison, a move worthy of the synchronized snob team at the country club he didn't belong to.

"I don't want to look like him," Maria said.

"Daddy survived on fast food before he met Mommy." Evan dropped his head. He was arguing in third person with five-year olds, a sure sign of senility. "This is not part of the plan," he muttered to Hert.

Tonight, the Morality Machine was getting a tweak. It might mean some extra late nights in the lab after Tabitha fell into a satisfied slumber, but sex would keep her home. Although spending eight hours a day making love wouldn't actually get the kids fed. "Everybody to the car."

The girls watched him with intent glares.

"There will be toys."

CHAPTER THREE

Superheroes were new to our world when I met Tabitha. No amount of theorizing, wild supposition, or unethical research revealed to science where their powers came from. Even I couldn't figure out what twist of genetics or fate controlled those powers, and believe me, I tried.

My interest in Tabitha may have started out as one hundred percent lust. I couldn't forget her kiss, the taste of her on my lips. Eventually, the lust dissipated a little and three percent of my fascination was with her power. I didn't care about the rest of the superheroes. I just wanted to know how Tabitha worked.

She can fly. She moves faster than any human should be able to. And she makes the world glow. Maybe I'm biased on that last one. When she's with me, everything seems brighter.

"WE CAN'T DO this, Hert," Evan told the minion as he tried to pull the lab door closed. Maria pushed her foot between them as she tried to peek down the stairs.

"I don't see what else we could do, Master," his minion answered. Two warty arms stretched across the opening to keep the girls at bay. The girls were a little taller than his favorite minion, and didn't seem too worried about the closet monster who'd eaten breakfast with them.

"I'm not programmed for nurturing or care-giving, sir," Hert reminded him. "It's not in my DNA. If you give me a week, I could work out the sequence to clone a nanny."

"We don't have a week. Not a week's notice to clone a minion, and not a week I can sacrifice in work time. It's almost November."

"We could slow time," Hert suggested. His foot bounced up to keep Delilah from crawling under his arm.

Blessing tugged on Evan's pant leg. "Daddy, can I go downstairs?"

"Now, sweetie, what does Mommy say about going to the lab?"

Folding her arms, she pouted. "Not unless Daddy's with you."

"Right. Is Daddy in the lab, sweetheart?"

Blessing tilted her head to the side in an exact imitation of her mother. He needed to win the election; if nothing else he needed the Secret Service guarding his girls before they went to school.

"Daddy?" Blessing asked. "Will you go to your lab? Please?"

Evan groaned in dismay. "That's cheating!"

"We could put them to work, Master."

"There are child labor laws," Evan said. "Even if I ignored the laws, what could they do?"

"Sort widgets," Hert said promptly. His daughters danced around him.

"Fine. Girls? We are going to Daddy's lab. Only touch something if Daddy says it's okay. Understand?"

"Yes, Daddy!" they chorused before rushing Hert like the offensive line at the Pro-Bowl and charging down the stairs.

"Hert?"

"Sir?"

"Keep them away from the machines."

"Yes, sir."

"And the knives," Evan said as he hurried down.

"Yes, sir."

"And the blow torches."

"Yes, sir."

"And the screw drivers."

"Yes, sir."

"And the electrical outlets."

"Yes, sir."

"And the drafting pencils."

"Yes, sir."

"And the lasers."

"The lasers are out for Minion Field Day, sir."

"Hert?" Evan said as the girls ran into his lab and stopped next to the Agree-With-Me Ray with appreciative 'oo's' and 'ah's.'

"Sir?"

He looked at a lifetime of notations on a collection of whiteboards, lines of meticulously maintained tools for his engineering projects, and glowing vats waiting for his next minion. "Keep the girls away from everything."

"Yes, sir."

Evan took a deep breath of the cold laboratory air and all his neurons began firing. Here, surrounded by diagrams and machines, he wasn't the geek caught flat-footed who didn't know the answer or how to make pancakes. In the lab, he reigned supreme, ready to mete out swift judgment and tackle everything.

On the far side of the room, nearest to the subterranean exit, sat his new machine: the Election Ray. The Agree-With-Me Ray's older, better-looking brother, the Election Ray didn't need close proximity to work, it just need waves of some form. Airwaves, electric waves, radio waves, and cell phone waves all worked to project a single message throbbing into the unsuspecting minds of humanity.

Early results were promising. For the first test, he'd sent a message encouraging everyone to buy purple Banala Babes Dolls. Stores had sold out, but only of red and blue. People had bought the dolls in pairs and hadn't touched the purple. Fine-tuning was in progress.

The rebuilt Agree-With-Me Ray sat in another corner under bulletproof glass. He had fond memories of that machine, but the original was too bulky for use as anything but a museum piece. A smaller version shaped like an obsidian statue of the Greek goddess Nike sat beside the first, also under glass. Three industrious minions were working on the latest version as per the specs he'd drawn up the day before—all the power of the original Agree-With-Me Ray streamlined to fit into a stylish wristwatch.

"Daddy?" Delilah ran to him. "What's a widget and when can I sort one?"

"Hert!"

"Master?"

"Give them something to sort."

"Yes, Master." Hert obediently found a jar of mixed screws and nuts, dumped it on the concrete floor, and sat with the girls to help them sort the contents.

Evan watched for a moment before heading to his favorite invention: the Morality Machine with its ability to adjust one fine-tuned aspect of the personality. After all, he didn't want Tabitha as a slobbering monster with no morals. As a villain, she'd be downright scary.

Love was a complicated thing, a complex process in a constant state of flux. Most people didn't understand how to perfect the three-part harmony of lust, attachment, and commitment that produced true love. He was ahead of the game there: lust had fueled Tabitha's first kiss. Even now, the memory was enough to make him harden with need. Any villain of moderate intelligence could whip up a basic love potion to produce lust—a combination of adrenaline, dopamine, norepinephrine, and serotonin. But, like any bad cocktail of drugs, there was a time limit on chemical mixes. The body eventually adjusted and then love faded.

Third-stage love involved free will and commitment. He couldn't take away Tabitha's free will without risking her mind entirely. Driving down the street, she might need to swerve suddenly to avoid a deer or oncoming car. Without free will, she wouldn't be able to protect herself.

So he'd focused the machine on the second stage of love: attachment. Mad lust kept the bedroom games fun, but attachment made sure she only wanted to play with him. His machine focused magnetic waves on the glands that controlled production of vasopressin and oxytocin. A second magnet sent a pulse wave that triggered memories of their time together. It was as good as staring into her eyes for hours at a time. Tabitha lived in the soft glow of fond affection, always thinking of him.

If it weren't for the Morality Machine, their first kiss would have been their last. Tabitha would have found some other man, someone she didn't instantly write off as beneath her. She would have found love the old-fashioned way, and he would have died of a broken heart.

The core of the Morality Machine winked at him under the spotlight. Such an elegant machine. The black matrix around the crystal looked like a spider web laid out by MC Escher. The crystal heart shone translucent blue and showed the perfect moment: Tabitha kissing him.

The image wasn't part of the machine, more a screen for what the machine did. Tweaking it would be hard. With the proper fix, he could boost her sex drive, tinkering with the first stages of lust. If he did that the crystal image would probably change to one of their more erotic forays into emotional expression, and that would leave Tabitha panting with need every hour of the day.

Who was he kidding? He wouldn't let her out of the bedroom like that! Super powers be hanged, he'd find a pair of cuffs and... Evan took a deep breath. Later.

Election Ray first. Sex later. If he turned it up right now she'd come home, and he needed to get some work done.

"Daddy?"

Evan jumped out of Angela's way. "Yes? Why aren't you sorting widgets?"

20

"Is that Mommy?" She pointed at the crystal.

"Yes, it is. Isn't she pretty?"

"Why do you have a picture of Mommy in the crazy spider web?"

"Because I love Mommy, and I want to think about her while I work," Evan said as he steered his precocious child back to the pile of unsorted screws.

"Where's my picture?"

"What?"

"Mommy has a picture. Where's my picture? Don't you love me?"

The other three girls gasped.

"You don't love us, Daddy?" Blessing asked.

"Of course I love you!" Evan knelt down as his brain raced to dig himself out of this hole. They were too much like their mother. Far too perceptive for his peace of mind. "I didn't have the pictures I want of you," he said slowly, constructing the lie as he went. "Why don't you girls color Daddy some pictures and we can hang them up for me to see every day?"

Maria clapped. "Can we decorate?"

"Sure, why not? Hert, do we have a decorating minion?"

"We have several programmed for color awareness and spatial reasoning, Master. Those are useful tools for programming."

"Great, bring one of them over." Evan plopped Delilah in his lap while the girls showed him the funny shaped things from the jar—mostly scrap metal—until Hert shuffled back over with a black-and-purple polka-dotted minion. Like Tabitha's canisters upstairs, the color codes had made sense at one time, but now he couldn't remember why he'd programmed the genes for polka dots. Maybe he'd been drunk at the time.

"Master, this is Fishy Thing."

"Fishy Thing? That sounds like one of my high school projects."

"Yes, Master. You programmed Fishy Thing during your senior year."

Purple and black. That's right, he'd meant it to look like the homecoming game with everyone in school colors. "Great. Fishy Thing, my girls want to decorate. Help them out and keep them away from the machines and anything else dangerous. Understood?"

"Yes, Master," Fishy Thing answered.

He checked on Agree-With-Me the Third, then went to work fine-tuning the Election Ray. The plan was the epitome of simplicity. Everyone knew the president of the United States was the most powerful person in the world. Power, influence, acclaim, wealth, attention... Everything Evan had ever wanted rolled into one. But becoming president meant close public scrutiny, lying on a daily basis, and a year of hard work as he tried to build support for his lies. Unless, of course, everyone happened to want to write his name in the box for president on Election Day.

Evan would win by a landslide. One hundred percent of the vote without rigging the system. There couldn't be an argument because everyone would want him to win. The Election Ray ensured they would justify why they voted for him. He merely needed to fine-tune it a little bit, and keep Tabitha from finding out.

Bad timing on her part. Did she really need to go back to superheroing now? Not that she would leave him, the Morality Machine kept that from happening, but she'd be upset. And then he'd feel guilty.

But really, he thought as he started dismantling the wave device to adjust the controls inside, this would put her out of a job. Everyone would agree with him. Everyone would obey the laws. Everything would be just the way he wanted.

CHAPTER FOUR

There are days I miss being Doctor Charm. I loved the attention and the challenge of being a super villain. Any thug with a fist can rob a little old lady in an alley. That doesn't take talent or brains.

But I was never a thug, or a don, or a mastermind. Small-time wasn't my style. I didn't want to be another fish in the pond, even if I was a big fish. I wanted to be the apex predator of the hemisphere. And I was.

EVAN PATTED HIS Election Ray. "We'll test this first thing tomorrow." If the calculations were right, he was one speech away from the Oval Office. Stretching, he turned to see the rest of his lab covered in pink and purple streamers. Crayon-scribbled graph paper covered most of the wall. Good thing no superhero was likely to stop by for a midnight battle of good versus evil, or they'd have died laughing. He lifted a multicolored paper chain off his computer. "Girls, Daddy's fortress of evil looks different."

"We decorated!" Angela said happily. "Now you have pictures of us so you can love us." She shoved a piece of paper at his knee.

Like a good father, he inspected the balloon-headed, noodle-limbed figures and pronounced it a masterpiece. Tacking the picture over a diagram of a magnetic shield he'd been meaning to build, he smiled at the girls. "Let's get some dinner going."

"What are you making?" Maria asked.

"Reservations," Evan said.

"Pizza!" Delilah squealed. Her sisters wasted no time picking up the refrain.

"In that case, I'll make a phone call." Evan shooed them upstairs, then headed into the kitchen to scrub the machine grease off his hands as he told them to turn on the TV.

"Daddy! It's Mommy!"

He turned to see Zephyr Girl smiling for the camera. She hovered inches off the ground, her hair in a ponytail, auroras ribboning around just like they had this morning.

Evan licked his lips. Tabitha had worn her hair like that last week while they worked in the garden. Her shirt had clung to her glistening skin. He'd tangled his fingers in her hair so he could run his tongue along her neck. He remembered how she shivered, her sweet coo of anticipation, the oak's rough bark scraping against his back when he pulled her close...

"Why did you come back?" a reporter asked as she shoved a microphone in Zephyr Girl's face.

"I thought it was time. There was no real reason behind this, simply a desire to do good."

The reporter pulled the microphone back. "And with your return, do you expect to see the return of your arch nemesis Doctor Charm?"

Zephyr Girl laughed. "I don't think anyone needs to worry about Doctor Charm. I handled him the last time we were together." Only Evan knew to look for the slight tweak in her smile that meant Tabitha was talking to him. She'd handled him all right. She handled, he'd gone down, they'd both hit their peaks. Maybe tonight she'd be interested in the fondle variation, or a replay of the events in slow motion.

"And what can we expect to see from the new and improved Zephyr Girl?" the reporter asked.

"Me at my best, saving the world!" She tossed her hair, mugging for the camera and fueling a thousand adolescent dreams. With a wink, she shot off in a cloud of sparks.

"Why does Mommy get to fly?" Blessing asked.

"Because Mommy is special," Tabitha answered from the front door. A breeze fluttered her white cape.

Evan smiled. "Hello, beautiful."

In a blink, she was in his arms, warm and safe. She stood on tiptoe, kissing him as she had the first time. "I missed you," she said. He caught her hand, keeping her from turning away as the girls tugged at her cape and peppered her with questions.

"I'll go make dinner," he whispered in her ear as he watched a bead of sweat pearl on her neck and slip down her cleavage. He wanted to run his tongue down her neck after it and then head lower. His jeans tightened.

Tabitha stretched. "I'm out of shape. I forgot how much work it takes to fight."

"Sore?"

"Everywhere!"

"I'll give you a rub down tonight."

Blue eyes went wide with desire. "Promise?" she nearly purred.

"Promise. I'll rub everything."

By the time Evan returned from tucking in the girls, amber and amethyst candles lit the bedroom. He locked the door and watched candlelight dance across his wife's bare skin as she lay on the black satin sheets, like an offering to some ancient god. Golden hair flowed like a molten river over her pale skin. Evan slipped onto the bed and kissed a thin white scar on her upper arm. Flying glass in the lab had cut her the first time they'd fought. He'd realized then that he could never win against her. Every bruise on her body tore him apart.

Running his fingers down her back, he savored her scent and her quiver of anticipation. Evan smiled and leaned down to whisper in Tabitha's ear, "Do you really want a back rub?"

"To start."

Taking a bottle of lavender oil from the nightstand, Evan warmed it in his hands and massaged the knots from her back. She hissed in pain and he lightened his touch. "What did you do today?"

"Git Kraken was terrorizing Key West with his latest genetic constructs."

Evan chuckled. "Really?"

"Truth is stranger than fiction. Apparently he was offended that he wasn't invited to host a drag queen beauty pageant."

He caressed her, basking in her presence like ancient man worshipping the first goddess. "This is the man with tentacles, isn't it?"

"That's the one. He has tentacles and ego, but not much else." Tabitha rolled to the side and stretched a long leg onto his lap. "My hip is sore."

He obediently focused on her hip, watching her body melt in pleasure.

With a languid sigh, Tabitha rolled to her back. "Mmmm. Evan, I was thinking of something this morning."

"So was I," he said, his voice low and smoky.

"Really?" She pushed up on one arm. "Have you thought about where to go?"

"I was going to start here." He moved one hand inward of her hip. "Then work my way down—"

She swatted his hand away. "I meant a job, Evan."

He frowned. "You went to work today, sweetie, what else is there?"

"I want you to get a job!"

"I have a job."

Tabitha rolled her eyes. "You lock yourself in the basement and fiddle with a computer."

"It's a job."

"I want you to get out of the house. You need friends."

"I have friends."

"Minions don't count."

"If I can watch movies with them, they count."

Tabitha propped herself on her elbows. "Look at me." Her nipples peaked in the cold air, begging for his attention.

"I am."

"You're wasted in the computer field. Why don't you go work at the university? You'd make an amazing teacher."

He lifted his eyes to her face. "Would you stay home with the girls if I went to work?"

"Is that the only way I can get you out of the basement?"

"Yes."

"Why don't you want me at work?" Tabitha asked with a frown. She sat up and crossed her arms.

"I don't want you hurt." He traced the scar on her arm. "Do you remember this?"

"It was a scratch."

"You don't heal fast, Tabby-cat, and I can't risk losing you. You have too much of me. Without you I would fall apart."

"No you wouldn't. You're a handsome man, you'd find someone else." She flopped back in the bed with a sigh. "All you have to do is smile and women trip over themselves to have you. Last time I let you go grocery shopping someone wrote her phone number on the minivan with shoe polish."

He chuckled. "There's only you, love. Always and forever, only you." He leaned down and kissed her. "As I recall, it took more than a smile to catch your attention." He nudged her over so he could finish her backrub—and think. "Would you really give up Zephyr Girl again?"

"Until the girls start school. If you taught morning classes, you could be back by the time school was out."

He fingers found a subtle dent in her skin where stretch marks had left their tracks during pregnancy. She'd hated the eighty pounds she gained carrying quads, but he'd loved her full form, almost missed it some days. That was an idea. "What if we want another baby?"

Tabitha laughed. "No."

"A little boy?"

"Couldn't we adopt?"

"We could, but I'd miss the libido boost from the second trimester."

"Tell you what," Tabby said, flipping over. "Take your clothes off and I'll fake it."

With a grin, he unbuttoned his shirt. "You have to fake it with me?"

"Every day," she said, putting a dramatic hand to her forehead as she laughed. "It's an absolute *chore* trying to fake all those orgasms."

"I hate to make you work. I'll let you off tonight." He dropped his shirt and reached for his pajamas on the nightstand, still folded from the day he'd bought them. Eventually, he'd actually wear them.

Tabitha caught his hand, pulling him down to the bed. "Kiss me."

CHAPTER FIVE

At fifteen, power was my first love. It promised me the world—if I could only break the shackles of a wholesome middle-class upbringing where ambition came second only to defying the home owner's association in terms of evil.

Ambition was my fatal flaw. Sometimes good ideas got ahead of me. A plan would come together and I would be in the middle of everything before I stopped to ask if this was right or wrong or even possible.

I tinkered with the Agree-With-Me Ray for years. It was a toy, really. Something I pulled out when I needed things to go my way. That changed when I saw the report about the millions of dollars in stolen, embezzled, and otherwise illegally obtained cash floating around, and realized, "It should be mine."

I turned the Agree-With-Me Ray on high and started making phone calls. A quick, amiable conversation and the thief bundled the stolen money in an envelope, sent it to my house, and forgot any of the above had happened. A perfect plan—until I cold-called a superhero.

For some reason, I never learned to regret that mistake.

MANICURED FINGERNAILS DRAGGED up Evan's spine. He arched, rubbing against satin sheets, and rolled over to capture his wife. "I thought you were going to work."

"Nothing is going to happen before eleven," she promised. A wicked smile curved her lips. "At least, nothing bad." She darted forward, teasing him with her tongue before retreating. Pale morning light played across her skin, throwing luscious curves into shadow and highlighting her golden tresses.

"Tease." He pulled her close so he could feel the heat of her body on his. "How do you know nothing will happen?"

"How do you know a piece of coding will work?"

He traced the curves of her body, committing every soft, sensuous turn to memory. "I just do."

"That's how I know." Tabitha's naked body rubbed him in all the right ways as she arched into his touch. "That's also how I know what I want right now."

He nipped her ear. "Right now?"

"Two or three times."

"Only three?"

"Maybe a few more in the shower if the girls don't wake up."

"And one for the road?" he asked hopefully.

"Maybe. If you're up for a marathon."

He chuckled and rolled onto his back, pulling her on top of him. "Staying up for you will never be a problem."

Tabitha flew away at a quarter after ten, leaving Evan feeling limp and hungry for more. Science liked to prove that the average man possessed only limited abilities. That was probably true, but Tabitha had a voracious sexual appetite, and he'd learned to keep up with her.

He lay on the bed, watching the ceiling fan turn slowly, thinking about his long to-do list. For some reason, images of Tabitha stretched out under him kept invading.

He wanted her against a wall tonight while she was wearing that pair of high heels he'd bought her last month. And then they could take a bubble bath. Mmmm, slipping his hand across her body in the water was always fun. A touch of his finger and she'd be begging for more. He could tease her until she was incoherent with need. And then—

"Daddy!" Blessing screamed from the living room.

Evan rolled off the bed and pulled his clothes on. His jeans were easier to put on without Tabitha around. Not to mention the lust killing effect small children had on him. "What is it?" he asked as he tripped over a fluffy unicorn.

"Daddy, I'm bored," his youngest announced in funereal tones from the middle of a sea of stuffed animals and building blocks. "Delilah locked me out of the toy place."

"The toy place?" He kicked a path through the disaster and sat on the old blue couch, confused.

"Your toy place."

Evan looked across the living room to the garage door. "You mean my lab?"

"Yes!"

"The door was locked." The door was always locked. It kept minions from running across Tabitha's path. If too many showed up Tabitha might start wondering why he needed all those minions.

"Not for Delilah," Blessing said.

That was not a good thing. He rushed the stairs and found that the door was unlocked. "Delilah? Sweetie?"

"Daddy!" She bounced at the bottom of the stairs, squeezing a furry, red minion like a stress ball. "Can we decorate more?"

"Sweetheart, how did you get the door open?"

She shrugged. "It wanted it to open. I went click"—she snapped her fingers—"and it opened."

"Click?"

"Uh-huh. Watch!" She sauntered over to his locked cabinet of power tools. "Click!"

The door swung open.

"Oh, boy." Evan stared at the door for a moment, letting all the implications sink in. His eye twitched. "Let's not tell Mommy about that little trick. Okay? Just in case we need a back-up plan for college funding." Evan grabbed her hand. "Look at me, sweetie. Do not click locks unless Daddy says so. Do you understand?"

"Okay."

Evan ran his hand through his hair. "Well, on the bright side, you have a future as a locksmith, or a super villain. I'm not sure Mommy is going to like that."

"I'm going to be a superhero," Delilah said. "Just like Mommy, 'cept my suit's gonna be purple."

He frowned. Keeping the villain aspect of his life secret from his family made sense, but there were moments he felt he ought to spend a little more time corrupting the children. Doctor Charm, father of four superheroes? He'd be the laughingstock of the super villain underground.

"Daddy?" Delilah patted his arm. "Can we have pancakes?"

"Sure." Even super villains could make pancakes. If a former mafia don could get his own cooking show, Evan could make pancakes. They came from a mix. Just add water—like sea monkeys. Although the last batch of sea monkeys he'd made hadn't turned out well. Pancakes were easier, he assumed. Less prone to eating red sports cars, for one thing.

He chased the girls upstairs and shouted over his shoulder for the minions to start putting combination locks on everything.

Two hours later, he had everything under control to the point where he could go back to the lab.

"Master?" Hert said, a clipboard clutched in his claws.

"Yes? If this is another request for a Caribbean cruise, the answer is still no. If you get one, Tabby will want one. If Tabby goes, I need to, and then the girls will want to come. I'll never hear the end of it."

"The neighbors took their dog on a cruise," Hert pointed out, a touch offended. "But that wasn't why I needed you. I have the latest popularity polls, Master."

"Excellent! Is everyone still failing?" he asked eagerly. "Anyone with over 50 percent of the vote might give me problems. I need my win to look plausible to our international neighbors; a popular candidate would ruin that illusion."

"A failing you've mentioned several times, Master," Hert said as the lab door squeaked open.

"Yes." Evan perused the Gallup Polls. "Good. This is good. I think we're still on track."

He glanced up as Delilah and Blessing approached the Morality Machine. "Girls! Stay away from that! Hert, go look after the sprouts, please. I need to get the machine calibrated. Are we getting any results from this morning's test run?"

"Nothing positive, Master," he said as a second minion ran up with the purchasing results. They were less than promising. Ideally the Election Ray would focus the victim's thought on one particular object. His tests had sent them after dolls, or shoes, or newspapers. On Election Day, he would persuade the voters to focus on his name so they would write it on the ballot, because no matter what people said, crime never paid as well as politics.

"Master?" The blue minion who'd brought the results quavered at his feet. "I have some correlating data that you may find intriguing."

Evan gestured for it to continue. "By all means, intrigue me."

"The results of the ray are more pronounced when they side with an observable trend."

"So it's working better when people are already thinking positive thoughts about the subject?"

"Yes, Master."

"Good to know, but not helpful."

"You could make a large donation to a charity on TV the night before election," the minion suggested. "Or perhaps save a bus full of children."

"I don't make public appearances. Too many people want me for questioning. And buses never are in danger when you need them to be."

"We could arrange for the danger, Master. Such a small matter..."

Evan glared at it. "None of that! I'm charming. I persuade people to give me what I want. I insinuate myself into their lives. I don't threaten them. Threatening is for thugs."

"Yes, Master." Slumping, it slouched away.

"We'll find another way," Evan said. "All I need is for them to have one thought: Evan Smith for president. Once we can transmit that message, the rest is taken care of."

Hert pursed his pale lips. "We could change the output from persuasion to pure suggestion. It wouldn't be as subtle, but we could loop the message."

"Distance hypnosis?" Evan drummed his fingers on the worktable. "I'd need to switch the tertiary capacitor to handle the energy load, but it could be done." He nodded. "Let's break down the machine and see if the magnet can handle the phase change."

CHAPTER SIX

Tabitha bewitched me. I dreamt of her, pursued her in a way I'd never chased after a woman before. Usually, women came to me. Even villains have standards, and no one can boast about forcing a woman. Brute strength doesn't have the delicious flavor of well-performed seduction.

The Morality Machine didn't compel, it just lowered her inhibitions. A superhero in bed with the villain? I can think of few things more taboo. Under the influence of the Morality Machine, Tabitha was perfectly herself—utterly confident, always in control—but living with the constant suggestion that she wanted me in every way possible.

EVAN BENT BACK over the Election Ray. "Hert! I need a hand over here!"

"At once, Master." Hert hurried over.

"Help me get the logistics box out. I must have something moving on the wrong frequency. It's days like this I wish we lived near a college. What I wouldn't give to have a live test subject from the correct demographic nearby."

"Do you wish me to unlock the Wi-Fi again, Master? I'm sure some geek will wander by to borrow it."

"Tempting—"

Glass shattered on the far side of the room. Evan moved before he'd even processed what had happened.

"Girls?" He grabbed Delilah's hand, looking for blood. "Are you okay? What did you do?"

Tears trembled in Blessing's eyes. "I wanted to see Mommy!" Blessing cried. "I smashed Mommy!" She clung to Evan's leg, sobbing at his kneecaps.

Evan pulled Delilah and Blessing close, away from the busy minions sweeping up glass, as he tried to process what happened. The Morality Machine was broken. Pieces of the miracle that made sure Tabitha loved him were scattered at his feet. Conductive fluid, red as blood, seeped from a slashed tube.

He licked his lips. Words escaped him. Not sure what else to do, he picked the two girls up. They were real, solid, something that would ground him in the here and now. No matter what else happened, Tabitha would never leave the girls. But still, he'd never turned off the machine. Even with the girls, he'd considered it too risky. There were too many variables for him to accurately calculate the possible results.

Theoretically, Tabitha wouldn't change much. She'd be frostier. Inhibited perhaps, inattentive, less forgiving and more likely to question what he did in the lab. Superheroes were defenders of the right; they adhered to a strict moral code. One that didn't involve villains.

She thought Evan was reformed though. That might buy him some time. As long as she didn't find out what he was doing in the lab, she might not notice he'd lied to her about his day job. Oh, sure, the sex might taper off for a few nights, but nothing too drastic. All he needed to do was fix the machine. This was a minor setback, a few hours of work. Nothing he couldn't fix.

Taking a calming breath, Evan walked in a circle around the broken Morality Machine. He couldn't even tell what had happened. For destruction this catastrophic, it didn't compute. There were safeguards, redundant features. He'd had the minions try to destroy the machine before he originally turned it on. The thing was built like a tank.

"Sweetheart, what did you do?" he finally asked. Scaring little girls was what super villains did, not the loving husbands of superheroes.

"Blessing tried to pick it up," Delilah supplied. "But it got stuck."

He looked at the little girl in his arms. She was tall for her age, but not tall enough to reach the crystal focus that floated in a magnetic field six feet off the ground. "How did you try to pick it up, sweetie?"

"I thinked about it, Daddy. Like when I want water. I think about it, and it comes to me."

"Uh-huh." Evan set Blessing on the ground. "Can you think something else over here? A pencil maybe? Or a cup?"

Blessing nodded with a stoic look on her face. She scrunched her eyes shut and Hert's clipboard floated toward them, hovering to a halt inches from his nose.

"I see." He rubbed the stubble on his chin. "Telekinesis. That's going to make life fun. Later, Daddy will show you how to pick up all your toys by thinking." As soon as the election was over he was going to dedicate himself to finding out the genetic mechanism for super powers. What he wouldn't do for telekinesis!

"That's not fun!" she protested, and the clipboard clattered to the floor.

He smiled. "Cleaning never is, but it still needs to be done. Now, Delilah, how did the crystal get stuck, and what did you do?"

"I clicked it, Daddy."

"Clicked it?" Evan frowned at her. "I thought we agreed you weren't going to click anymore. Clicking is bad."

"But Blessing wanted to see Mommy!"

"Then you should have asked Daddy. I have other pictures of Mommy." He took a moment to center himself and refocus. The idea that the Morality Machine might break had never invaded even his worst nightmares.

"Daddy?" Delilah asked, tugging at his sleeve. "Are we in trouble?"

He studied his broken machine. There were probably worse things that could happen, like an asteroid the size of Mars crashing into the Pacific Ocean, but on a scale of one to ten this was a thousand. "Just a little bit."

The anguished wails of the unjustly accused began again. Delilah sobbed, clinging to his knee like a limpet. Blessing's lip trembled.

"Everyone upstairs!" Evan ordered. "Hert, salvage what you can, then send a cooking minion upstairs."

"Do you still want me to lure in a test subject, Master?"

"No, that's on hold for now."

"But, sir! Your deadline!"

"A few hours won't hurt anything," Evan said, as much to himself as Hert. He needed to fix his Morality Machine, but first he needed to figure out exactly what the girls could do. Plans boiled in the back of his mind. It was like opening the cupboard and finding a gold mine. Super powers might turn out to be the magic wand that could fix everything.

Of course, the ethics involved with using children as evil minions was sketchy at best. It probably went against child labor laws. But that was neither here nor there. All he had to do was wait for them to hit their teens and order them to not rob the bank. Kah-ching!

Upstairs, Evan lined the girls up on the couch and paced. "All right, ladies, it has come to my attention that you've been keeping secrets from Daddy. Now, as a super villain—*former* super villain—I can understand your need for secrecy. In some cases, I will applaud it. For example, I will never need to know what partially digested food looks like, so kindly don't regurgitate on me.

"However, I do need to know if you are developing any skills that might make your kindergarten teacher scream next fall. This is very important. Delilah can click things open. Blessing has telekinesis." He raised an eyebrow at the other two. "Any more surprises for Daddy?"

Maria looked at the ceiling, then the floor.

"Maria? What do you want to tell Daddy?"

"Sometimes, I make stars."

"Stars?"

She cupped her two little hands and light pooled into her palms. As she pulled her hands apart a trail of sparkling stars the size of quarters strung out in front of her.

"May I see?" He held out a hand, but waited for her to nod. Evan reached gingerly for a star. It burned hot even a hand's width away. "Do they burn things?"

"Only if I forget them, Daddy."

Oh, goody. His daughter was a firebug. "That's going to make camping trips exciting. Don't play with stars in the house. Angela?"

"Angela knows what we're thinking," Delilah offered.

"I do not!" Angela shouted. She stood up with her hands on her hips, looking exactly like Tabitha in a fighting mood. "Delilah knows everybody's secrets! Not me!"

"What do you do?" Evan asked Angela.

She shrugged a thin shoulder. "Sometimes I know when people are sad. Sometimes I make them happy."

His inner evil genius squeed like a manga fangirl at her first Comic-Con. "You influence people's feelings?"

"Only a little," Angela said. "It makes my head hurt, and my tummy gets all wavy."

"Queasy you mean?"

She nodded.

"So one telekinetic, one pyrokinetic, one mind controller, and one locksmith." Evan frowned. Three high-level mutations and one limited focus telekinetic. Why didn't that sound right?

"One of these things is not like the other. Delilah?"

"Daddy?" She looked up, the picture of innocence.

"Do you do anything besides click?"

"No, Daddy."

"You're sure?"

"Yes, Daddy. I don't do nothing but listen. Sometimes people tell me funny things."

"Like?"

"Like everything, Daddy. Mommy told me what she bought me for my birthday, and the man at the store told me how to get his money from the machine."

Probably a form of mind control. Uncontrolled mind control. The tiny part of his brain responsible for self-preservation and putting the brakes on really bad ideas curled into a corner, gibbering in terror.

"She does puzzles quick too," Angela offered.

"Puzzles is easy," Delilah confirmed. "They're just like locks. They want to be in order."

They weren't even in school yet! Maybe he could talk Tabitha into sending them to a private boarding school. In the Swiss Alps. With nuns. And absolutely no boys.

He patted Delilah's head. "This is something Mommy doesn't need to know about. She's stressed. She's had a long day at work. Let's keep all of this to ourselves until the time is right."

"When is the time right?" Maria asked.

Ten weeks after never. "When she's calm. I'll get her a trip to the spa, some flowers"—*lots of champagne*—"and tell her then. For right now..." He mimed locking his lips and throwing away the key.

The girls mimicked him.

"Good. I want you four to stay upstairs while I clean the glass up. Stay right here. Do not open the front door. Do not color on the walls. Do not move things, start fires, or hit each other. I am not explaining black eyes or ER visits to your mother tonight." Or any other night while the absence of the Morality Machine kept her stuck in the rigid black and white world that superheroes loved so much.

40

CHAPTER SEVEN

Superheroes make the average person jealous. The superhero mutation is the full package of charisma and power. Stunning good looks are standard, and exceptional strength and stamina are often included. Everyone wants to be special; it's ingrained in the human psyche. But there's a dirty little secret that everyone leaves out of the pep talks: for you to be special, everyone else needs to be average.

Special is just another way of saying freak.

I have no super power of my own. I don't fly. My bones break as easily as the next person's. But I do have a highly evolved brain, a certain touch of arrogance, and a naturally persuasive nature even when I'm not augmented by machines.

I've never needed anything else.

EVAN SENT HERT and two other minions upstairs to watch the girls while he worked on the broken Morality Machine. Whatever Blessing had done, she'd done it well. The crystal focus lay shattered into a few billion pieces, the tubing hung in shreds, and the magnet that did most of the work had cracked down the center. He'd spent weeks hunting down the right size magnet to trigger serotonin and vasopressin production in the female brain.

Fine-tuning the thing for Tabitha had taken the whole three-week honeymoon. Death by sex only sounded like a good idea. In practice, there was too much of a good thing.

Especially if you were out of practice because the only woman in the world you were interested in was the one who walked away.

"Hert!" he bellowed.

There was a flap of webbed feet on concrete and his chief minion stood at quavering attention by his side. "Yes, Master?"

"Do we still have the plans for the original Morality Machine? I need a list of supplies."

"We can have most the supplies by the end of the week, Master. I'll need to check the specifications for a few things, and the crystal will take at least two weeks."

"We don't have two weeks, Hert. We may not have two hours." He rubbed the bridge of his nose. An almighty migraine was coming on. "Who owes us favors?"

"Sir?"

"Is there anyone we could have pick a fight with Zephyr Girl today? Challenge her to hot dog eating contest or something?"

Hert's eyes bulged in shock.

"Scratch that. Get some minions upstairs. The house needs to be spotless. Everything she's been asking for in the past month, find it and get it. New dresses in the closet, new shoes, go steal a new car if you have to."

The minion cleared his throat. "Don't you think, perhaps, that stealing might make her angrier?"

Evan sighed. "Right. Superhero morals. Wrong, right, black or white, no happy medium ever. I hate superheroes. Tabby excepted," he said before Hert could cut in. "I can do this. I can do this. Tabby doesn't know I'm still working as Doctor Charm. Maybe she won't notice." He looked at the shattered image of him holding his wife. "Let's pray she doesn't notice."

Four hours later, he was sitting in the corner of his lab, desperate for a long cool drink of something strong. He wanted Tabitha home, wanted her in his arms and kissing him, but he was terrified of what would happen when she did. He'd already packed a bag with the essentials, in case she gave him his marching orders.

"Daddy!" Blessing screamed from upstairs. "Mommy's in a fight!"

Evan whipped around. "Hert?"

"We didn't schedule anything, Master."

He took the steps three at a time. "What's going on?"

"Mommy's in a fight," Maria repeated calmly.

Picking up Maria so he could claim a spot on the couch, Evan watched as Zephyr Girl whipped around a giant lizard thing, the unholy offspring of Barney the dinosaur and Godzilla. Zephyr Girl darted in, pulling a trip wire past the reptilian legs and dodging a heavy fist. His heart skipped a beat. Right after Election Day, he was finishing the body armor he'd planned for her. It hadn't seemed necessary when she was a stay-at-home-mom, just kinky in a fun way.

A heavy green claw swiped downward, and Zephyr Girl didn't move fast enough. She bounced off a building, her neck snapping back.

"Mom!" Delilah rushed to the TV screen. Tiny fingers fanned over the live image of Zephyr Girl plummeting toward the ground.

"Move back!" Angela ordered, pulling on her sister's shirt. "Let me see Mommy."

"Move, Tabby. Move, baby," Evan whispered. He hugged Maria tighter. The TV needed to be off. Now. The girls shouldn't watch their mom die. He shouldn't watch his wife die. Anger burned through the fear. Whoever created that abomination was going to pay.

Zephyr Girl somersaulted. A burst of auroras buffered her feet from the hard cement and she shot back up. Vivid blue lights burned the sky.

"Yay!" Maria clapped as she bounced on his leg.

Zephyr Girl did a barrel roll to dodge another wide-armed punch. In a flare of light, she twisted, swung around, and punched the monster at supersonic speed. The creature staggered like an ancient redwood. Buildings shook with its fall and Evan laughed in relief. How would U.S. Geological Survey classify that kind of earthquake?

The girls clapped as Zephyr Girl waved for the cameras. "Nothing to worry about," she said with a radiant smile.

Voices overwhelmed the TV and the news crews all tried to ask questions at once.

"Mommy punched a lizard!" Delilah giggled.

"Zephyr Girl!" The Rainbow Dane ran up to the scene in a sparkling pink cape. "You're injured!" He posed dramatically.

Evan rolled his eyes. "Okay, girls. Enough TV. Let's go get dinner ready. Mommy will be home soon."

"Is Mommy hurt?" Blessing asked, trying to peek around his arm to see the TV as he moved to shut it off.

He glanced at the screen where The Rainbow Dane was wiping blood off Zephyr Girl's arm. Right next to the scar he'd left on her. That armor was getting built tonight. She'd never be hurt again.

"Mommy's fine," he promised, flicking the TV off. "The Rainbow Dane is helping her out. He'll wipe out the scratch, put a smiley face Band-Aid on, and send her straight home. He's a good guy, that's what he does."

"Who is The Rainbow Dane?" Delilah asked.

"Someone who is never coming to dinner," Evan muttered. He stalked off to the kitchen planning to reheat the spaghetti sauce from the freezer. On an afterthought, he went to check the Band-Aid supply. It was not a manly, hero-ish supply, but bravery was certainly involved. Any adult who could walk out the door with a Pinky the Silly Goose Band-Aid on them without dying of shame was braver than he.

A quick search of the depths of the bathroom cabinet gave him three plain bandages of the no-name, store-brand variety. Much better. Not that anyone would see the bandage because by tomorrow Zephyr Girl was going out to fight evil in full body armor. Possibly with flying minions behind her to mop up the leftovers and deal with tabloid reporters trying to get a shot of her panties.

He bit his lip. Armor. Morality Machine. Election rigging. What he really needed right now was a way to freeze time. Or a twenty-eight-hour day. Or three of him. As the spaghetti burned, he doodled out a cloning idea. Three Evans, no, better make it four. Someone needed to take care of the house. He sniffed. What was—oh. "Girls? Does anyone want pizza?"

CHAPTER EIGHT

Crime really doesn't pay. At least, not in a regular weekly paycheck fashion. When I married Tabitha, I convinced her that I had reformed. She believed me. The Morality Machine helped matters along, but I made sure I didn't give her any reason to be suspicious. That meant finding a job. Or, since it was simpler, creating a shell company that laundered the money from my various persuasion schemes and sent me paychecks out of the accrued interest until that well ran dry.

I freelanced, scaling back my plans and running a scheme only when our funds dipped into the danger zone. Little cons that never came up on the radar.

The bank run in China? Not my fault. And I will deny to my dying day any involvement with that one bribery scandal in D.C. Although it was a clever job, wasn't it?

TABITHA ARRIVED HOME as Evan dished out the delivery pizza. He smiled anxiously, not sure what reception he would get. "Hey, Tabby, how are you?"

She ran her fingers through wind-tangled hair, jerking it nervously. "Why does everyone keep asking me that?"

"Because you took a tumble today?" He reached to help her with her cape.

Tabitha jerked away scowling. "Don't touch me. Why is everyone trying to touch me today?"

Evan stepped back with his arms raised. "Sorry. Do you want me to get you some food?"

"No. I want a shower, and some quiet, and... space. I just need some space." She stalked into the bedroom. The door locked behind her with an ominous click.

He ate dinner with the girls in silence. Tabitha stayed behind the locked door, coming out in jeans and a tight T-shirt with a college logo only after he'd sent the girls to get in pajamas. The T-shirt wasn't one he recalled seeing in her wardrobe.

"Here's your dinner." He set the plate down in front of her, leaning in for a kiss.

She turned away, still close enough for him to feel the heat of her skin, but obviously uninterested.

Evan slid into the seat beside her, resting his elbows on the table and surreptitiously checking her for bruises. "Are you wearing a different perfume?" Whatever she had on wasn't her usual blend of floral notes.

"Does it matter?" she asked grumpily. She took a bite of pizza and regarded the slice with disgust. "What is this? It tastes awful."

"It's the pizza we usually get." Evan picked up her discarded piece and nibbled. "It tastes fine to me."

"Why are we eating pizza? I can't live on junk food."

"I burnt the spaghetti," Evan said. "Pizza was easier than trying to make a new batch tonight."

She dropped her fists to her lap with a glare. "You burnt spaghetti? How? What kind of idiot burns spaghetti sauce?"

He leaned back in his chair. "Tabitha?" Name-calling was new. Even before the Morality Machine, she hadn't lashed out like that when she was angry.

The look of disgust transferred to him. "Tabitha what? What excuse are you going to make this time? I'm sure it's perfect. Choreographed and rehearsed. Everyone always has excuses, and you know what that means? More work me. Why are you doing this to me?" She slammed her chair back, rocking the table as she stood up. "Every time I turn around there's another lie. Tell me, was anything you said true? Ever?"

"I love you."

Tabitha stood up, tears in her eyes. "No. You don't." She fled into the bedroom, locking the door behind her again.

Angela peeked around the corner, a stuffed cat clutched in her arms. "Daddy?"

Pulling his emotions under tight control, Evan turned to his daughter. "Hmmm?"

"Why is Mommy yelling?"

"She's just tired," Evan said with a sigh. "She'll feel better after a good night's sleep."

"Are you going to ground her for yelling? You ground me," Angela reminded him helpfully.

"Mommy's a little too big for grounding. I'm going to..." He looked around. "Do the dishes. Mop the floor. General cleaning type things. Are you girls ready for bedtime stories?"

"Yes, Daddy."

He put the girls to bed, cleaned, and after he was sure the children were asleep, tapped on the bedroom door. Tabitha answered it wrapped tight in her bathrobe, the bright overhead light they rarely used making the room cold and unwelcoming. "What do you want?"

"Can I come in? Can we talk? Please?"

She held the door open. "I don't see what we could possibly have to talk about."

Evan took a deep breath as he stepped into the bedroom. This was the tricky part. She hadn't actually accused him of anything outright, and he didn't know how much she knew. "I thought I could explain." He closed the door gently behind him.

"Explain?" Tabitha snarled. "I put my life on the line and all the thanks I get is cold pizza and burnt spaghetti?

That's how you take care of me? Like I'm some stray you let in from the cold?"

"What? You like pizza. I've seen you nibble a frozen one!" Granted, she'd been seven months pregnant, and it had probably been the cravings talking, but still.

"I hate pizza," she said coldly, crossing her arms.

"Since when?"

"Since now." She swaggered up to him, arms wide. "You got a problem with that? You want to fight with me about this? Maybe tell me what I like to eat a little more? Do you read my mind or something?"

"No, I..." He fumbled for the right thing to say. Groveling looked like the only option. "I was mistaken. I apologize. Do you want me to make something else for you? A sandwich or some soup?"

"Wow," she said in a flat voice. "You really know how to show a girl a good time."

Evan fell back on the tried-and-true. He gave her a sexy smile. "I never said I was a cook, baby. But I always give you a good time when you want one."

She went rigid, shoulders back, eyes narrowed, just as he had feared she would. "Don't touch me. I don't want anyone to touch me."

"I won't," he said, holding his hands up in defeat. "Not without an invitation." He gave her a smoldering glance that worked eleven times out of ten. Nothing. "Look, Tabby-cat, I want to—"

"Don't call me that. That's not my name." She turned away, rubbing her temples.

"Tabitha, is your head hurting?" Was sudden aggression a sign of a concussion? He couldn't remember.

Her hands dropped to her side, fisting as she pivoted. "There is nothing wrong with me!"

He sucked in a deep breath, pushed his temper back down, and tried again. "I know I made a mistake."

"You bet your butt you did."

LIANA BROOKS

"But we have something I don't want to lose. We've had good times together. We're happy together." He smiled at her. "Think of all the good times."

The bed creaked as she sat down. "I don't remember any of that. All I remember is lies." She pulled her knees to her chest and looked at the floor, tears welling in her eyes.

Evan froze, torn between rushing to her and respecting her request not to be touched. Cowardice won out. "I'll go get my, uh, watch. I left my watch in the living room. I assume I can still sleep in the bed? The couch is a little short."

Her lips curled in a sneer. "I couldn't get paid to care what you do."

Ouch. "Be right back." He closed the door gently behind him and ran for the lab.

"Hert!" He looked around the disaster zone. Minions were carefully labeling and sorting the remnants of the Morality Machine, but his minion-and-chief was absent. "Hert?"

"Master?" Hert's bulbous head appeared from behind the bulk of the machine's base.

"Do you have everything for the Morality Machine sorted out? Can we fix it yet?"

"Not yet, Master, but the continuing tests on the election machine are going very well. I have some promising data." Hert scuttled to grab his clipboard.

Evan brushed the clipboard away. "Not right now. Is the Agree-With-Me Ray running?"

"No, Master."

"Turn it on full blast. Aim it for my room."

"Sir?" Hert frowned in puzzlement.

"It might work on Tabitha long enough for me to fix the Morality Machine. I just need to convince her to give me a second chance. She fell in love with me once, it can happen again."

50

Hert frowned. "It's only meant to handle simple yes or no statements, sir. I don't know if it will have the desired effect."

"I don't want desire. I want her to agree to forgive me until I get the Morality Machine fixed. Turn it on." He grabbed the watch that contained the smallest version of the ray on the way out of the lab.

The lights were already out in the bedroom and he tiptoed across the carpet. Evan could feel the faint pulse of magnetic waves. Tabitha's scent struck him in the dark—a lush promise of fantasy fulfillment. He wanted nothing more than to slip under the sheets, hear her giggle, and feel her naked body wrap around him. With a strangled groan, he dropped into bed. Tabitha moved under the covers, the sound of cotton on cotton telling him she wasn't naked at all.

He leaned over her in the darkness, put his lips to her ear, and whispered, "I love you."

She didn't answer.

CHAPTER NINE

I proposed to Tabitha the second time we met. I had spent the intervening months stalking her, searching for a weakness, and making sure she didn't already have a boyfriend. For the life of me, I could never explain why she didn't. I can only assume every other sentient being on the planet thought themselves unworthy of her attention.

They were right. Superb doesn't begin to describe my wife. She is the pinnacle of feminine creation: intelligent, generous, giving, virtuous, funny, beautiful. I dreamed of telling her about my day, conquering the world and laying it at her feet. All I wanted was her by my side, sharing every moment of my life.

TABITHA LAY BESIDE him, resplendent and peaceful in a pair of faded gray sweats. He brushed a loose hair from her face, longing to reach those last few inches and kiss her, hold her, lock her to him so the terrible fear would go away. But he couldn't, not until she gave him permission. The look of disgust she'd given him the night before had cut him too deep. Somehow, he had to erase that look.

Evan rolled away with a sigh. Nearly a day without sex. Somewhere in the murky depths of Life-Before-Tabitha he'd gone weeks without sex, months in some cases. Sometimes he'd even been too busy to smile at pretty girls, let alone seduce them.

Now he was hot, tight, and hungry in a purely physical way. Lying next to her without touching might kill him. Or qualify him for sainthood. Wouldn't that be awkward? Doctor Charm canonized by the Pope for not touching his wife.

With a longing look back at her, he headed for an ice-cold shower. The water managed to freeze his libido—barely. Evan stepped out with his teeth chattering and fumbled for a towel. He pulled the last clean one out from under the sink and knocked over a set of black and gold T-shirts. A too-sweet floral scent wafted up. Not Tabitha's normal perfume at all. This was the kind she would gag over when the lady at the perfume counter attacked.

He cinched the towel around his waist and held one of the T-shirts up. "Baby? Where'd you get these shirts?" He walked into the bedroom with the shirt in front of him.

Tabitha opened her blue eyes and screamed.

Evan spun around, looking for something wrong. "Tabitha? What? What's wrong, baby?"

She scrambled away from him on the bed. "Get away from me!"

He froze. "I'm away, I'm away. What's wrong? I just wanted to know where you got the T-shirts."

"Give me that!" she ordered.

He tossed it on the bed and she pulled it close like a teddy bear, breathing deeply. "Don't touch my stuff."

"Sorry. It fell out when I went to get my towel. I didn't mean... anything." How did he get into this mess? "Are you going to punish me for everything now? 'Cause if you are, may I suggest a whip and handcuffs? We've never tried that."

She swept past him with a haughty look, slamming the door in his face.

"Tabitha, my clothes are in there."

A minute later, a pair of jeans and stained white shirt hit the bed.

"Thanks." He dressed and waited for her to change.

Tabitha stepped out with her hair pulled back in a ponytail that he wanted to free her hair from, her new college T-shirt tight enough to taunt him with everything he wanted to touch, and soft, faded blue jeans he knew felt as good as they looked.

Everything about her begged for him to touch, to worship the body of his goddess. "Tabitha..." It was a prayer.

Her eyes went wide and she froze. "What are you doing here?"

"Waiting for you."

"Why?"

"I wanted to talk to you." For a given value of talk, that was true. He wanted to use his tongue on her. That was almost the same as talking.

"No, I mean what are you doing here in this room?"

"Waiting to talk to you," Evan said slowly, patiently enunciating each word.

She turned slowly, studying the room. "Why am I here?"

"Because this is your bedroom?" he guessed as his patience frayed to one last thread. "Let's sit and talk, yes?" The Agree-With-Me Ray was still pumping vibrations through the floor. It was a yes or no question. All she needed to do was not fight him.

Tabitha hesitated, then shook her head. "I'm leaving."

"Tabitha, no! Don't go. We can work this out."

She grabbed her purse and frowned at him. "I don't even know you."

Evan stared at the closed door, lost.

"Daddy?" Maria walked over and slipped her hand into his. "Why is Mommy slamming doors?"

The truth was impossible. Evan couldn't even articulate the idea. "Um, she was in a rush, sweetie. A big project." He ran a hand through his hair and choked back tears. Tabitha... He couldn't... This was a nightmare. Some horrible dream brought on by too much pizza and stress. He would wake up, roll over, and his wife would be smiling at him suggestively. If he closed his eyes, he'd be stretched next to her beneath the sheets. He'd go exploring, reconquering familiar terrain as though for the first time...

"Daddy?"

He blinked. "I need to get dressed. Get your sisters up, it's playgroup day."

"What about breakfast?"

If he saw the pot of burnt spaghetti, he'd throw up. If he saw the bottle of wine from their honeymoon, he'd break it open and drown himself. "We'll buy donuts."

"Okay." Maria ran off, shouting for her sisters to get up.

He locked the door and found himself sitting on the bed hugging Tabitha's pillow. It smelled like her, a mix of floral notes and spice and something exotic that was all Tabitha. A scent he'd know anywhere. He sniffed again. And something else. Different. A sharp sweetness that turned his stomach.

He held the pillow to his face, trying to name the elusive scent. The perfume she'd worn last night. A new scent, but that was no surprise. People liked giving superheroes presents. She'd probably stopped by a college town for lunch, and someone had recognized her and given her the perfume along with a stack of T-shirts. With a sigh, he dropped the pillow.

The sound of the girls chattering in the living room told him they'd finished getting ready for the Mommy's Day Out playgroup. A hundred dollars a head and some nice ladies from the local churches would watch your kids in a moldy basement for three hours so you could keep your sanity. Evan really wanted to spend the three hours forgetting yesterday ever happened. And this morning. And maybe tomorrow.

He hit his face, trying to slap himself back to intelligence.

Tabitha was angry. Good. Fine. He knew that might happen. The Morality Machine was a calculated risk. There had always been a chance the calibration would fail, or that her basic chemistry would change. Even he couldn't build a flawless machine, although he'd never had a complaint before. Still—Evan took a deep breath—he could see why she objected. Leaving her aroused for seven years was a little unfair. He'd always meant to slowly turn the machine down and lull her into happily married life.

But that carried the risk of losing her. What if she didn't like him anymore when the machine turned off? What if he wasn't her type? Or she met someone else? Losing her was the one nightmare he couldn't face.

And now she was gone.

One of the girls banged on the door. "Daddy!" Blessing hollered. "I'm hungry! I want a pink one!"

"Hold on," Evan said. "Let me get my socks." Even in the bathroom chilled by his cold shower, her perfume still lingered. Tabitha's ring twinkled beside the sink. Evan picked it up, running his thumb over the smooth white gold. Tears blurred the shape of the diamond. He'd bought it for her before they'd eloped to Australia. She'd been wearing an ocean blue skirt over a tiny white bikini, the diamond sparkling in the sunlight. Three carats of flawless marquise cut shining over Byron Bay as they said their vows. It fit perfectly.

She loved that ring. She'd loved him. For seven perfect years, she'd loved him.

The ring cut into his clenched fist. It hurt, but not as much as watching her walk out that door. The look in her eyes, disappointment and betrayal, hurt most of all.

What sort of idiot burns spaghetti sauce? *Oh, Tabitha, love. That isn't even the important question. What sort of idiot can't make his wife love him?*

Somehow he'd known all along she didn't really love him. Oh, there had been lust at first. An initial spark of interest that made everything the Morality Machine did possible. But he'd known in his heart-of-hearts that a woman like her could never love a man like him. He could have her body, but he could never have her admiration. Women like her wanted perfect men. Super men. Heroes, not villains.

It didn't matter. He pulled on a clean shirt. Today he'd fix the Morality Machine, and tracking down Tabitha would be a simple matter of watching the news. He'd find her, turn on the machine, and fix this mess.

When Election Day rolled around, it wouldn't matter that he couldn't cook. He'd be president of the United States. If a computer geek who worked freelance out of his basement wasn't good enough for her, the president and de facto leader of the free world would be.

He pulled on his jacket out of habit and froze, captivated by his reflection in the mirror. The jacket, custom-tailored black Dior, had been off-limits since the wedding. It always hung in the closet, a laughable reminder of life before her. The jacket radiated warmth, like a favorite blanket. It hugged him, promised him security.

"Daddy!" The scream at the door was accompanied by a ruckus that would make a zombie horde proud.

Toddlers and Dior didn't mix. The jacket went back in the closet. Today was a grease and gears day. The jacket could wait.

"You girls ready?" he asked with a big, fake smile as he opened the door.

CHAPTER TEN

I can count on one hand the number of times I have cried in my life. I cried when the doctors told us Blessing would live. I cried when we buried my parents after a drunk crossed the yellow line. Then Tabitha left me, and I learned what true sorrow was. There is no pain like losing the woman you love.

"MASTER?" HERT SIDLED up to the worktable cautiously.

Evan's gaze slid sideways to the paper Hert held, probably another calendar revision reminding him of the week he'd lost to the depression. "What?"

"We found her, Master." The minion held a paper out, quivering in terror.

"Give me that." Evan snatched it away. "I am not that scary," he shouted as Hert flinched.

The minions all ducked.

From across the room, Angela frowned at him from her throne of stuffed animals. He'd spent sleepless nights waiting for Tabitha to come home, clearing part of the lab and turning it into a kid-safe play area complete with ratty couch, old TV, and movies on VHS. The girls were fascinated by the ancient technology. Black ribbons of cassette tape hung from the ceiling like paper chains designed by Death.

He glowered back, and his daughter's eyes narrowed, making her look painfully like her mother.

A wave of happiness hit him. The gears spread out on the table looked like dancing daisies. Pink clouds floated past. Evan shook his head, but the pink clouds persisted. A small rainbow burst in front of him. "Angela?"

"Yes, Daddy?" she asked in a smug tone that was an exact replica of Tabby's when she'd just won a fight.

"Stop it, or you're grounded."

The pink clouds vanished, melting into the dungeon gray of the basement. His own dark feelings of self-hate and fear returned. "You should never manipulate people's emotions, Angela. That's what super villains do."

She unwound her blanket and walked over to his workbench. "Is that what you do?"

"What?" He looked up in alarm, then picked up a gear and made a show of studying it.

"You're a villain aren't you, Daddy?" He tapped the gear slowly on the tabletop.

"Of course not."

"Then why do you have machines and minions?"

Evan glanced at Hert. "They're cheaper than cats and dogs."

Angela crossed her arms. The other girls were paying attention now, cherubic faces peeking out of their blanket fort. "You make people agree with you."

"Obviously not," he growled, "or we wouldn't be having this argument."

"You're a super villain."

"Would your mother marry a super villain? She's a superhero. Everyone knows superheroes don't marry villains. There are rules."

Tears filled her eyes. "You tricked her! That's why she left us! You tricked her!"

"What? No! Sweetie, no." Evan scooped her up in a hug as guilt twisted in his gut like a knife. "No, Angela, no.

Mommy knew I was a bad guy. I gave that up so I could be with her. I didn't trick her. I love her."

"But you are a villain," Angela said.

"Only as a hobby." He patted her back and rocked side to side like she was still three months old and easily calmed. He glanced at the paper Hert had pushed at him. "Girls? How would you like to go to Colorado?"

CHAPTER ELEVEN

Pick up and leave home? Home is where the heart is. Tabitha is the soul and center of my world. I could no more willingly live apart from her than I could will myself to quit breathing.

EVAN WATCHED FROM the foyer of the university biology building as students walked through the pine-studded campus. Tabitha stepped out of the library wearing jeans and a conservative T-shirt. His breath caught. She looked amazing. His heart raced as he waited for her to turn and smile. He needed that smile more than anything in the world.

"Mister Fascino?" The dean of the biology department opened his office door.

Evan tucked the cuff of his Dior suit shirtsleeve over the miniaturized Agree-With-Me Ray then turned with a smile. "Dean Lang, it's so good of you to see me at such short notice."

The giant of a man laughed heartily. "Trust me when I say, Mister Fascino, that I would rather speak with prospective teachers than the prospectus committee again. Drink?" he offered, motioning to a decanter of amber liquid sitting on a low side table near oversized windows.

"No, thank you." Evan took a seat and smiled at the dean. "I've found it's dangerous to accept unknown liquids from the biology department. Biologists have such a quirky sense of humor."

Dean Lang laughed. "We have more petri dishes filled with strawberry Jell-O on April Fools' Day than real specimens. That's eighteen-year-old Glenlivet whiskey, if you're interested. A gift from the family when I took the job." He settled his comfortable bulk into a dark leather chair. "So, you're interested in teaching here?"

"Yes, sir," Evan said, stepping away from mental calculations of how much the dean had spent on office furniture. "Professor Buckley mentioned there was an opening as an ethics lecturer. I've wanted an excuse to move to the area, so I thought I'd apply."

All of that was true. Since finding out that Tabitha had enrolled as a mid-semester transfer last week under the name Zinnia Perl, he was more than a little interested in moving to the foothills. Finding the aging Professor Buckley and persuading him to take an early retirement had taken all of ten minutes, in which time the professor had mentioned someone would need to fill his post as the ethics teacher—a class Tabitha took four days a week.

"And, have you ever taught ethics?" the dean asked.

"Not as such, sir. I hold dual degrees in genetics and mechanical engineering. I'm very familiar with the ethical quandaries of science. I've attended a number of ethics classes and symposiums." Mostly true. He'd tested out of a number of ethics classes, which was practically the same thing.

Evan adjusted the mini Agree-With-Me Ray clipped to his watch. "Why don't I start today?"

The dean blinked at him with an expression of bovine confusion.

Being in that class was essential to life. If he couldn't see Tabitha soon he wouldn't survive another day. He needed something from her, a look, a gesture, something to give him hope.

She'd have no way to ignore him. Angry as she was, she wouldn't miss the chance to ask about the girls. Maybe threaten him. It didn't matter. She could break every bone in his body if it meant she'd consider forgiving him. He tapped the watch again. "Class starts in a few minutes. You want me there."

"Ah," said the dean, shaking his head. "Are you... Are you quite ready to teach? I could have someone else fill in."

"No need. Professor Buckley was kind enough to give me a copy of his lecture notes. I know the material."

Dean Lang rubbed his temples. "Well, if you're quite sure. I suppose I could, um... Ah."

"Write up my packet and finish the paperwork," Evan suggested. "That would be perfect. I'll come by and sign everything tomorrow."

"Right." He shuffled paper. "I'm sorry, did you already send your credentials over? I don't recall seeing them."

"I'm sure you saw them. You complimented me on the thesis paper I wrote." Evan arched an eyebrow. *Stubborn old man. Agree-With-Me!*

"Quite. Yes, of course I remember now. Age and all." The dean gave him a weak smile.

Evan stood up. "Thank you so much for the job, Dean. I look forward to working here."

He ran to the classroom, a small lecture hall on the far side of campus, featuring orange plastic chairs and fake wooden desktops. He scanned the crowd, but couldn't find Tabitha.

Taking a deep breath, he walked down to the teaching podium and pretended to busy himself with the papers. The material wasn't all that interesting, only a review of free market eugenics and the synthetic life form *Mycoplasma mycoidesJCVI-syn1.0.*

The classroom door opened, bringing the smell of dying leaves and something a little too sweet for pleasure. Tabitha's new perfume.

He looked up, drinking the sight of her in as he tried to prepare an argument for the coming confrontation. He wasn't following her; he was here for the job. She'd said something about finding work, hadn't she?

Tabitha took her seat, glanced at him with an easy smile, and then looked away as if he were the least important thing in the world. Again.

Somehow, Evan managed to stumble through the fifty-minute class without begging Tabitha's forgiveness. Her sweet smile dominated his thoughts as he rambled on about medical testing and... something. There were words, he strung them in sentences, none of that mattered. He felt fifteen again, lost in a hell of shame and fear. Finally, the lecture ended and he could say, "Time's up. Make sure to study chapter twelve for the quiz on Friday."

The students filed out. Tabitha collected her books as she chatted with a friend, then turned to look at him with a pretty, pink blush on her cheeks.

He licked his lips as she walked down the aisle between long rows of stadium seats. A wiser man might have run, but he couldn't. He'd do anything to see her again, take any abuse just to be near her.

She trapped him with her smile as surely as any cage. "Doctor?" she asked, an innocent note of hesitancy in her voice.

"Mister Fascino, for now." He smiled. "I'm still waiting to defend my thesis." Wrong answer. He cleared his throat. "Evan works best." *Or Love, Lover, Sexy, Husband, any of those.* It didn't matter what she called him. If she spoke, he would listen.

"Evan." Her mouth curled around his name the way it did in bed when she begged for release. A prayer, a charm, a promise—on her lips his name became a many-faceted thing. "Are you coming to the department mixer tonight?" she asked.

"Um, what?" He'd been lost in memory.

"The mixer. It's not quite a dinner, but they usually have pizza and punch, store-bought cookies. You know the drill. We all come and socialize."

"You like pizza?"

"Love it!" She laughed, the way she always did when they were alone together, and happy.

What was that supposed to mean? There was no hand signal, no hint of what she was thinking. Just Tabitha clutching her books to her chest and looking virginal as the day they married. "Um, I don't know. I wasn't planning on going."

"You should come," she said. "We graduate students have to stick together."

"Right."

Her hand reached for his, a butterfly's touch. "I'd like you to come."

If she'd asked him for the moon, he would have found a way to put it in her hands by supper. "I'll be there."

She walked away. No backward glance. No significant eye gesture to signal she'd left a note. Nothing.

Evan checked under her desk, under his desk, and by the door. Not even a pencil shaving.

It didn't make sense. She stormed out of the house furious, and now she acted like she couldn't wait to see him at dinner? Dinner? Was there some sort of coded message? A cryptogram spelled out in pepperoni?

There had to be a rational explanation for all of this.

He fiddled with his watch and froze. The Agree-With-Me Ray? It wasn't supposed to work like that. He should have been able to persuade her to listen, but it wasn't the Morality Machine. Not by a long shot. If it worked like that, everyone from Dean Lang to Tabby's new BFF would be offering to show him their private leather-and-lace collection.

He grabbed his phone and dialed. "Hert?"

"Yes, Master?"

"How are the girls?"

"Watching a movie, Master. There is popcorn everywhere."

"Fine. Did you get the video feed of Tabby?"

"Yes."

"And? What was the signal? What did she do? Did she do something at super speed I didn't see?"

"We're still analyzing, Master, but I don't believe she did anything except invite you to dinner."

Evan chewed his lip for a minute. "All right. New plan. Find out where this mixer is, get a team in to bug her apartment, and pick some minions to watch the girls. It looks like I'm going to have a late night."

CHAPTER TWELVE

There should be some background story about my awkward youth or how I was teased as a child, or even how my parents never loved me. I could write that story, but it would all be lies. No one pushed me into a life of crime. I've never tried to excuse my behavior that way. I've never tried to excuse my behavior at all.

As a boy, I was precocious. As a teen, I was handsome. I never wanted for attention or adoration, but I always wanted more. Intelligent people often take up challenging hobbies to pass the time. I took up the idea of world domination and, unlike all the Goth aficionados in black lipstick, I didn't sit around paying lip service to the idea. I chased my dreams until the day my dreams changed.

That happens sometimes. Even the best plans need reconsideration when a better offer comes along. When my choice came down to having the world or having Tabitha, I wanted her more.

EVAN SCROUNGED AROUND the makeshift lab in the rented house. The small, four-bedroom brick Tudor near the university wasn't much; the only real selling points were the partial basement for his lab and the fenced yard for the girls.

While his minions were still busy trying to unpack all the toys, he worked like a maniac on the Morality Machine. "Hert, did we find that part?"

"The crystal focus, Master? Yes, we have one left."

"Only one? I need a second one for redundant back up. Using only one focus was my mistake the first time."

The minion shuffled his webbed feet.

"What?"

"The other is in the Election Ray, sir. I would have to cannibalize that—"

"Never mind." Evan turned back to the Morality Machine with a glare. "It'll work. Start running the tests so we can get this calibrated. I need to go get dressed."

Hert frowned at him as he hurried upstairs. Evan pointedly ignored the look. There were hundreds of things he needed to be doing this week. Chasing down Tabitha hadn't been on the agenda, but he couldn't put it off another day, not even another hour.

"Daddy?" Angela walked over to him clutching her stuffed dog. "Where is Mommy?"

"You said Mommy would be here," Blessing reminded him.

Maria and Delilah joined their sisters. Four pairs of eyes watched him with innocent expressions of hope.

Time to lie. "Mommy is working undercover to stop something bad. I'm going to go meet with her tonight, and find out how long this project will take."

"I want to see Mommy," Delilah said.

"And I promise, Mommy wants to see you. Maybe she can sneak out to see us tomorrow." He made a mental note to arrange that. "I'm going to get changed real quick, okay? Are you girls all settled in? Do you like your new rooms?" They nodded. He settled them in the living room where they could watch a movie with Hert and the other minions could guard them.

Tabitha wanted to see him. That put it all in perspective. She'd come to talk to him. Obviously, there was a plan. He'd go to the mixer and get a clue. Who knew, maybe he hadn't lied about her being undercover. Maybe the whole mess the other morning had been an act.

Evan made a mental note to have the minions check for bugs and began pulling clothes from a hastily packed box. He didn't know what to wear. A classy tux? No. Mixer. What did people wear to mixers? He pulled some faded jeans and a white T-shirt from the box. He hated the generic, blue-collar look, but Tabby loved it. Something about a man in jeans worked for her, and never failed to get him laid. He needed a 'No Fail' plan just now.

The mixer was held in the biology department building's main lecture hall. The maintenance staff had cleared away the chairs. Sad crepe-paper flowers in school colors lay amid the greasy pizza boxes like the tattered standards of a lost legion.

Evan tugged needlessly at his shirt, turned his mini Agree-With-Me Ray to full, and stepped into the room with a confident smile. He'd been to parties before; this wasn't one. On the scale of entertainment, it ranked somewhere between filing taxes—something he never did—and attending a birthday party with clowns and thirty crying toddlers.

Finding Tabitha was a matter of finding the largest crowd of stuttering males. They surrounded her like Neanderthals worshiping a sun goddess.

Across the semi-crowded room, their eyes met. Blue eyes sparkled like sunlight on the waves. He'd never get tired of that come-hither look.

Evan raised an eyebrow, a silent commentary on her crowd of admirers, and walked to the buffet table to score a cookie. Doctor Charm's arsenal included flirting. Running to her would only rank him alongside the rest of her adoring sycophants. Husband or not, he had to follow the rules of the game.

When she was ready, she'd break free.

And she did. Evan nearly spit punch all over the white linoleum when he saw her walking toward him with an easy smile on her face. She didn't look angry. One corner of his mouth lifted in a half smile. That body... All those curves, the satin-soft skin... He was in lust all over again.

"You broke away from the crowd," he said, sipping his drink to keep from claiming her lips. The memory of her taste turned the sweet punch sour. "Is it always so lively?"

Tabitha shrugged, blushing. "We're a department of people watchers."

"Maybe we should hire someone to party while we watch." He kept her gaze.

Tabitha licked her lips. He almost bent down to chase her tongue and coax it out to play. She giggled, a sweet sound that promised beautiful things.

Maybe he needed to find a dark corner and see if she was interested in a fast anatomy lesson. No. Focus. Wife. "So..." Evan cast around for a topic. "Are you here with anyone?"

Why are we here? was an even better question, but she'd told him to be here, so the answer to everything was here. *Give me a hint, Tabby-cat.*

"Oh." She tucked a loose strand of hair behind her ear. "I'm just here with my roommate, Hilary. There's..." She giggled again and looked at the floor. "There's no one." Blue eyes looked up at him. "Are you seeing anyone?"

Evan took a breath. Deep cover was not a comfortable place to be. Swirling the punch around his cup, he shrugged. "It's complicated."

"How can it be complicated? You're either with someone or you aren't." Her hands went to her hips, the flirt gone. "So, status?"

"It depends."

"On what?"

"Do you love me?"

She blinked, caught off guard.

"Zinnia! Zinnia, there you are." A blond man built like a rugby player cut between them. He looked vaguely familiar.

70

"There you are, Z-girl. Sorry I'm late." He gave Evan a passing glance. "Who's your friend?"

"Evan Fascino, the new ethics professor."

"Ethics professor?" Rugby laughed. "You ever get laid, or are you, like, the fifty-year-old virgin?" He grabbed Tabitha's arm and she winced.

"Are you all right?" Evan asked Tabitha, blocking Rugby with an upheld arm.

Tabitha looked confused. "I'm fine. I hurt my arm falling down some stairs."

"Stairs?" The fight. He hadn't even asked her about the fight. "Let me see."

"Dude, I got it." Rugby pushed him back. "I do sports medicine."

More likely he did anything too drunk to object.

Rugby pulled out an alcohol wipe, rolled Tabitha's sleeve up, and peeled back the bandage. An angry red gash ran parallel to the scar he'd given her.

Evan felt his heart skip a beat. This was all his fault. And now some chump was pawing his wife. "Can I help?"

"No, I got it," Rugby said, waving the wipe past Evan's nose. A sharp, super-sweet smell assailed him.

Evan sneezed. "What is that?"

"This? Just a homeopathic recipe my grandma used to use, mostly lotus blossom. Way better than alcohol. Doesn't smell bad either. Right, Z?" He shoved the wipe toward Tabitha's face.

She grimaced and turned her head. "Better than alcohol, I guess."

"Thane!" someone shouted from the other side of the room. Rugby frowned. "Be right back. Z, you wait for me."

"I'll wait for you," Tabitha said as her smile faded. When she turned back to Evan her expression was vague, disinterested.

"So, that's your boyfriend?" Evan felt himself losing his grip on reality as the storm of emotions swept him away.

His wife. His. *Wife!* And she let some strange man patch her up. "Is he why you're here?"

"What? I'm here because he asked me to wait." Her face filled with confusion. She rubbed her temples. "I'm sorry. Sometimes I get these headaches. What were you asking?"

Evan unclenched his jaw to say, "I was asking if you and Rugby were an item."

"Thane and I?" She shook her head. "He's like that with everyone. He's a super... a super protective person." Her eyes lost focus again. "He wants what's best for everyone."

"And that means bossing you around?" The temperature of the conversation continued to plummet.

"I'm here alone. My parents live in Wisconsin. I'm not a city girl. I feel out of place here. Thane's a real friend."

Evan stared at her. "Wisconsin?" Tabitha's parents owned a condo in Miami. She'd grown up in West Palm. So why did Wisconsin sound so familiar? He stepped back, not sure what was happening anymore.

"Evan?" Tabitha touched his arm lightly. He raised an eyebrow, not sure how to go on. "Have you ever met someone that you trust implicitly from the first time you see them?" She sounded so hesitant. Fearful.

"A few," he admitted grudgingly, letting her soft touch reel him back in.

A warm smile brought life back to her blue eyes. "I feel like that with you. I don't believe in past lives or anything, but I feel like I know you." She squeezed his arm. "I'm so glad you're here. We're going to be great friends."

He stared at her. *'I don't even know you,'* she'd said as she walked out on him. The words reverberated through his head. Gently, he lifted her hand to his lips. "You can trust me. With everything."

"Ready to fly, Z?" Rugby Thane butted back in. "We've got kicking dinner plans."

Tabitha turned to Thane, the smile falling from her face. "Sounds great."

CHAPTER THIRTEEN

I should probably say a word about my competition. There is none. As far as you and the rest of the world is concerned, I am the pinnacle of creation, and I have a machine that will make you nod your head in agreement as I say that.

There are other super villains, of course. They tend to crop up like mushrooms in the wake of every major disaster. I consider them useful. They keep the superheroes occupied and out of my hair while I take over the world. Some of them are even good enough to become reoccurring headlines. But they aren't as good as me.

Seeing Tabitha with another man, seeing her smile and leave with another man, was a punch to the gut. I'd give up major limbs before I let another man have my wife, but what could I do? She acted like she didn't know me. Like seven years of marriage never happened. I couldn't compete with that.

If Tabitha wanted me, I'd fight to the death for her. But when she walked away of her own free will, I was lost.

EVAN STRODE OUT of the building, ready to kill someone for the first time in his life. She didn't know him.

She didn't know him, and she was going to dinner with another man.

He dialed the lab. "Hert, I need perfume samples. Lots of them. And I need the Morality Machine dismantled now. Now! There's something wrong here. What? What girls?"

His girls. He was already going to hell for not belonging to any of the right religions, stealing money, and being a super villain. Compared to that, forgetting his daughters for a few minutes while his life fell apart was... He took a deep breath. Unforgivable. No wonder Tabitha didn't love him.

Rubbing his wrist, he took the mini Agree-With-Me Ray off. It hadn't worked. Maybe it even hurt her. He sucked in the pine-scented night air and tried to focus.

Evan could think of two possible explanations why Tabitha didn't remember him. The first, and the most obvious, was that the Morality Machine had affected her memory and personality more than he'd anticipated. She still seemed attracted to him, so had he been breaking down her memories all this time, rather than her morals?

The other option was that something else had stolen her memories. A head injury in the fight? She hadn't hit her head on the ground, but maybe she had a concussion from the creature hitting her? Or she was so angry with him she'd blocked him out of her memory? Or... He dug through his mental file of possibilities.

The smell of Thane's homeopathic treatment bothered him. Maybe because her shirts reeked of it when she came home from the fight. Evan looked up at the cold starlight. The smell, the T-shirts, and a tall blond man.

He'd never paid much attention to superheroes and their identities. Some villains dedicated years to researching a nemesis. A few went as far as fixating on superheroes, but that was too creepy-stalker-freak for him.

Superheroes came, and after a polite chat, they went away. Except Tabitha. He'd been too spellbound to speak before she broke the Agree-With-Me Ray.

But the big, blond Thane, he looked... Evan slapped his thigh. Time for the professor to do a little homework.

At home, Evan pulled out all the reference material he'd amassed on superheroes, super villains, and the unsolved crimes of the last century. Most of it he'd stolen, some of it had been compiled from court records and newspaper printouts by the minions, and none of it was alphabetized.

Blessing snuggled on his lap as he flipped through the reports on superheroes unmasked. Delilah and Maria helped the minions sort the Morality Machine parts, and Angela thumbed through a thick book.

"Here we go," Evan said, shifting Blessing to his knee. "The Rainbow Dane, also known as Thane Mitely, raised by a single mother named Ava Mitely. It's rumored that his father was the Roaring Thane, and that's where his name came from." He set the papers down. "I don't remember the Roaring Thane."

Hert tilted his head. "I've read about him, sir. He was one of the early superheroes. Super strength, if I recall correctly."

"Who did he fight?"

"Everyone, sir. He fought any and all crime. If he saw a wrongdoing he'd roar, hence the name, and attack."

"So, what, drug dealers and hippies? Corrupt cops? What was his MO?"

"Anything, sir. Jaywalkers, clerks giving wrong change, people who ran stoplights. He said once that he could tell someone was going to commit a crime before they acted."

Evan shook his head. "Sounds psycho to me."

"The police objected as well, but he helped enough that they were hesitant to stop him. He was killed in a fight with the Magenta Fox, who in turn was killed by the Roaring Thane's mother. She called herself Lady Grimoire and her super skill, if you call it that, was potions."

"Interesting."

"When the superheroes first appeared in the public they weren't under any code of conduct with the government. The only thing separating a villain from a hero was media perception," Hert said.

"I can't say the registration card scheme has changed that." Evan drummed his fingers on the floor.

"Daddy?" Blessing asked. "What does this say?" She pointed to a caption under a black and white photo of a little girl on a swing in front of pine trees.

"Zinnia Perl, age four, near her childhood home of—" Evan gasped, taking the book away from Blessing. "I'd forgotten all about this. It's in her book, the one we wrote the year she was pregnant. Some news reporter kept calling to demand the official story of her life, so she finally wrote the autobiography just to keep people from asking questions. It was her tell-all book!"

"Daddy?" Blessing pulled the book back. "Is this Mommy?"

"Yes. Her parents took her to Aspen for Christmas that year. It was a generic snow picture." He had sorted hundreds of old photos trying to find the ones that didn't have enough detail to unravel her false history. Evan snapped his fingers. "Hert, listen. I have two theories."

"Very good, Master."

"The first is that the Morality Machine breaking somehow caused Tabitha to lose her memory of everything that's happened since I turned it on."

"A possibility, Master. Although an unlikely one."

"Right. The Morality Machine shouldn't show precise brain damage like that. Maybe it would affect impulse control, but not memory. My second theory is that someone has taken, or suppressed, her memory."

His minion frowned. "I haven't heard of anyone working on memory, sir."

Evan sighed. "Yes, that's where it falls apart."

Angela walked over and sat in his lap. "When do we get to see Mommy?"

He studied the girls for a minute. "How does tomorrow sound?"

Their eyes lit up. "Really? Tomorrow? Promise?" The cacophony of four piping voices drowned out his reply for a good minute.

Evan waited it out. When they finally fell silent, he smiled grimly. "Daddy needs more data so he can prove his theory. Do you want to be my ice cream minions tomorrow?"

Maria raised an eyebrow in an exact copy of his favorite cynical pose. "What's an ice cream minion?"

"It means I pay you in ice cream cones to help me follow Mommy." The clapping started. "One ice cream cone per person. Not multiple cones per kid," he clarified.

The clapping stuttered away.

"Go upstairs and get pajamas on. Tomorrow we are stalking a superhero!"

He waited for them to go upstairs before turning to Hert. "Find out Tabitha's schedule for tomorrow. It's a Saturday. Maybe see if you can lure her to a park or something. I think that once she sees the girls, she'll remember them at least. No woman forgets her children after twenty hours of labor. If this is some joke she's playing on me because she's angry..."

He took a deep breath to steady himself. "She won't pretend that she doesn't know the girls. It doesn't matter how angry she is with me. She wouldn't hurt them."

CHAPTER FOURTEEN

I can only recall one instance before this where I truly felt nervous: the night I waited to see Tabitha the second time.

Expectation was pure torture. Every breeze that brushed past the warehouse door made me turn. Every noise made me jump. I'd put everything into this one gamble, wagered everything on getting my machine right the first time.

In retrospect, I could have tried the Morality Machine on any number of victims. But at the time, it never occurred to me. My entire focus was on winning Zephyr Girl for myself.

When she arrived, words failed me. She was beautiful. Beyond beautiful. She put Helen and her thousand ships to shame. She made springtime seem dowdy, and long summer days plain. Zephyr Girl landed lightly and sauntered toward me, an unfathomable expression on her face. "Hello, Doctor Charm. Or should I say Evan?"

I hesitated, holding the control for the Morality Machine and drinking in her beauty. "I knew you wouldn't stay away."

She laughed, the sound of angels. "Do you know why I'm here?"

I looked away then, wishing the burning kiss she'd left me with would lead to more without mechanical intervention and knowing it wouldn't. "I can guess." And just like that, I flipped the switch that changed her life.

When I looked up, her eyes had filled with erotic hunger. "I want you. Against the wall. On the table. I want a blistering hot love affair that will keep the tabloids talking for decades."

"Really?" Vivid images filled my mind. I'd never brought a girl

home to the lab before her, but it was years before I could look at some of my machines without picturing her stretched over them wearing nothing but her thigh-high boots.

I remember, now, that I fumbled for the ring. It was the first time in my life I felt truly sinister. I was taking something I knew no woman as beautiful as Tabitha would ever offer me.

My hand shook as I held the ring box out. "Why don't you marry me instead?"

She froze, and I swallowed a curse, certain the Morality Machine wasn't strong enough.

And then she was wrapped around me. Fingers tangled in my hair, her lips teasing mine. Torso... Well, a gentleman doesn't divulge all the details. Suffice it to say, I thought my conquest was complete.

CHASING FOUR STICKY children around a strange city on an unbelievably warm October day counted as a torture more cruel than even the most depraved super villain could devise. Pitchforks and eternal damnation had nothing on whiny, tired children who just wanted their mother. Evan collapsed into a park bench as the girls tore into their third ice cream cone each.

Delilah looked up at him with a huge smile ringed in blue. "I love you, Daddy!"

"Love you too, pumpkin."

"Can we have cookies when we get home?"

He raised an eyebrow at her. "I thought you girls weren't going to give Daddy a heart attack until you turned sixteen and started driving. All this sugar is killing me."

Delilah frowned at him. "I don't remember that."

"I remember it distinctly. Right after you were born you signed a contract."

Her eyes narrowed and she turned to her sisters. "Did we sign a contract with Daddy?"

"In sparkly purple pen," Evan added. "I distinctly remember the ink was sparkly purple."

The girls fell into earnest discussion, giving him a moment to breathe. Across the park, something caught his eye. A familiar silhouette in the afternoon sun. Tabitha.

Blessing gasped. "Mommy!"

"Wait!" Evan caught her arm before disaster struck. "Mommy is undercover, remember?"

"Ooooo." Four innocent, ice cream-smeared faces turned to him.

"We're going to go play catch, and Mommy is going to give us a sign. But you have to pretend you don't know her. Okay? We don't want the bad guys to find out about Mommy." He looked each of the girls in the eye. "Do you understand?"

"Yes, Daddy," they chorused.

"Good." He watched Tabitha for a moment, heart in his throat. This was the only way to know. Even if she was angry with him, Tabitha wouldn't ignore the girls. If the Morality Machine had erased her memory... Well, that was a bridge he would burn later. "Come on, girls, let's go play catch."

They played with an over-sized pink softball. Delilah tossed it to Angela, Angela tossed the ball to Maria, and Maria tossed to Blessing, who tossed it to Evan.

Tabitha sat down in the grass, talking animatedly with her friend while she flipped open a psychology textbook.

A few more times around the circle and Evan growled in frustration. "New plan!" he told the girls. "Let's make teams. Blessing and Maria against Delilah and Angela."

"Whose team are you on, Daddy?" Angela asked.

"I'm going to be the monkey in the middle. If I catch the ball I get to throw it anywhere in the park."

Delilah put her hands on her hips. "Anywhere?"

"Anywhere. Even up a tree!"

"Not fair!" Maria protested.

Evan shrugged. "I suppose you better keep the ball away from me then."

They threw the ball around him, rolled it between his feet, and once Angela threw it so hard he had to duck or risk a serious head injury. All the while, Tabitha talked blithely on as if her four beautiful daughters weren't mere feet away.

Desperate for some sign, Evan jumped after the ball. He grabbed it, twisted away, and rolled the softball so it bumped against Tabitha's foot.

She looked down at the pink ball in surprise, then smiled brightly as Blessing went running up. "Is this your ball?"

Blessing stared, and finally nodded. "Uh-huh. Daddy bought it for me."

"What a nice Daddy you have," Tabitha said. She handed the ball to Blessing. "Here you go."

Blessing moped back to the circle. She looked back at Tabitha. "Daddy, why didn't Mommy say she loves me? She always says she loves me."

Tears and fear choked him.

"She's undercover!" Angela said in exasperation. "Weren't you listening?"

Blessing nodded. "I forgot. I thought she was going to wink at me."

Evan struggled to find his voice. "Undercover agents don't wink," he lied.

They played ball for a few more minutes, but the girls had lost interest. They wanted their mommy. The one that didn't recognize them anymore, thanks to him. Eventually, Evan caught the ball and steered them away from the park.

Back at the rental house, he served a dinner of ramen noodles and grape juice. Everything reeked of failure. He read the girls their bedtime story, tucked them in, and slunk off to the improvised lab.

Hert looked up as he entered. "Good evening, Master. I have excellent news."

Evan raised an eyebrow as he collapsed onto an up-turned crate.

"The latest Election Ray results are very promising. I believe we have the calibration 95 percent perfected."

He nodded wearily.

"Sir?" The minion looked confused. "Isn't that good news?"

"What about the Morality Machine, Hert? Where do we stand with that?"

"Um." The warty minion checked his clipboard. "Not finished, sir. We've inspected all the components and run all the tests you specified. There is nothing conclusive."

Evan covered his eyes, aware that he was too exhausted to move, but unwilling to give up. Failure wasn't something he could accept. There had to be a way to fix this.

Hert cleared his throat. "If I may say, sir, it would help immensely if you were in the lab during the day."

"I can't be in the lab! The girls need me!"

Hert gave him a flat stare. "Sir, I am genetically programmed to point out personal inconsistencies that hinder your work. Sir, you did nothing today."

"I took the girls to see Tabitha."

"No, sir. You walked around the city eating unhealthy amounts of frozen non-dairy concoctions mooning for a woman who left you."

Evan surged to his feet. "She didn't leave me. Tabitha wouldn't leave me. She wouldn't leave the girls. She... forgot who we are."

Hert cleared his throat again. "Sir? The Morality Machine doesn't work that way. I can think of no way the Morality Machine could affect a person's memory. The magnetic waves specifically target the posterior pituitary gland to excite production of vasopressin."

"She's a superhero. No one really knows how their body chemistry works. It's a mix up. It's just... Just..." He paced in the tiny rat-trap of a basement. Swallowing back a lump in his throat, Evan took a deep breath. "I need some fresh air. I need to think. Watch the girls."

He walked out of the garage, not quite sure where he was headed. While his mind swirled with all the possibilities and implications, he found himself walking under the looming shadow of the university library.

A few late lights dotted the campus buildings. The students were off partying, or sleeping, or visiting family. Anything but studying, if he remembered college correctly.

A chill wind stirred the pine trees, bringing the first scent of winter. How had it all gone so wrong?

He had a timetable. He was supposed to be a few days away from the single greatest achievement any American could have. The world should be unfolding at his feet. Nothing on the timetable mentioned Tabitha storming out, or—the word he'd danced around—divorce.

With a sigh, he collapsed onto a bench, staring into the darkness as he waited for an answer.

CHAPTER FIFTEEN

I can't recall a time I truly felt guilty. Even when one of my minions ate all of Great-Grandmother's fine china my senior year of high school. Guilt was the same thing as getting in trouble, and I could always talk my way out of trouble.

The only person with any measure of control over my actions was myself. I think that's true of everyone, although most people will deny it. There is no angel or devil sitting on your shoulder telling you what to do. Laws are there as pleasant reminders of the consequences that await the foolish, but in the end the only authority a person can rely on is their own.

And you know what? You can't sweet talk yourself. There was no rationalization for what I had done. Not a single thing I could say that made the situation better. I'd had the perfect life, and I'd lost it being stupid.

I could bend the will of anyone I met to suit my needs, but I could never force them to give me the one thing I always craved.

Even with the Morality Machine, I couldn't force someone to love me. I tricked Tabitha into love, but the emotion was tainted. Seven years of lust with never a moment of true love. It was the one-night stand that never ended, until the machine broke and Tabitha walked back to her life with nary a backward glance.

WIND RUSTLED THROUGH the pine trees, bringing the scent of wood smoke and car fumes. Evan sat back in the park bench with a sigh, watching the sun sink low over the mountains as he replayed the afternoon's encounter in his mind. This wasn't the end. He wouldn't let it be the end. Somehow he could find a way to get Tabitha back. If he couldn't, what was the point of going on?

The girls, obviously. They needed a parent, although a stuffed zucchini would probably do a better job than he was at this point. Tabitha's laugh broke through his misery. He looked around and spotted her walking into a large, square building across from the park. He ran to catch the door as it swung closed and stepped into what looked like an unused gymnastics center, complete with a sad pair of rings hanging off to one side over a cracked mat. He could smell the faded sweat from glory days long past.

A large woman in tight blue spandex walked past, completely ignoring him. The door shut quietly behind him as he took in the rainbow array of spandex suits. Apparently Tabitha had joined an aerobics class for the middle-aged and balding. One violently yellow suit with red zigzags on the far side of the gym caught his attention—The Rolling Shock. Evan looked around trying to find other familiar faces.

Once he knew what to look for, he could see the old gymnasium was packed with the full roster of superheroes he'd defeated. He stepped into the shadows, weighing his options. The Rainbow Dane was there, standing on the far side under a spotlight in earnest discussion with Hempman and The Rolling Shock. All three a good reason to leave. But Tabitha was there too, still dressed in her jeans and T-shirt, holding court with Angler Girl, The Buxom Boss, and The Starlit Starlet near a table of snacks.

Had Tabitha left him for this? He'd been searching for the complicated answer, but what if the simple one had been right all along? What if all she wanted was to be with her own kind? Evan watched her as he leaned back against the door, casually preventing any more heroes from joining the party.

Tabitha had bags under her eyes, and her gestures were agitated. At a glance, she looked like a woman under extreme stress. He'd never seen her miserable before—one point in his favor despite everything—and now that he knew what it might look like, he knew he'd never be able to bear the real thing. Starlit grabbed a cookie and noticed him; his buttoned down shirt and slacks didn't help him blend into the crowd. Starlit straightened, preening and smiling in an inviting way that would have worked if he were still sixteen, single, and had never seen Zephyr Girl. Really, the other superheroes should have kicked Tabitha out years ago for being too beautiful for their collective good.

Starlit said something, and the other women turned. Tabitha's eyes widened. She excused herself from the others, and made a beeline for his position by the door.

"Professor," she hissed, grabbing his arm. "What are you doing here?"

"I was taking a walk when I saw you come inside. Is this another department shindig?"

Gore Smasher walked past and Evan stopped to stare at the layer of flab jiggling in purple spandex. "Was I supposed to wear a costume? Halloween isn't until tomorrow, but I'm game." Bemused and befuddled professor was as good a cover as any.

"No. This is a private party." Tabitha was pushing him to the door. "Professor, please, you need to leave."

He caught her hand, warm and soft. Evan couldn't look her in the eyes. If he did, he'd be lost. He'd fall right there, kiss her, steal her away. "You don't look like you're dressed for this party either. Why not come with me? We can grab a late snack."

"I... I can't." She tugged at her hair nervously. "I'm sort of..." She rolled her eyes. "I'm playing hostess. My friends really feel strongly about this, and we're trying to get more people involved."

"Oh, so this is a political thing?" Evan kept the anger in check.

Tabitha snuck a look over her shoulder at The Rainbow Dane. "Sort of. It's almost political."

Starlit did a wiggly finger wave and motioned for him to join them.

Evan hit the small Agree-With-Me Ray on his arm. "Look the other way," he said, just loud enough for it to carry.

As everyone else turned away, Tabitha turned back to him. "You really don't belong here."

"The question is, do you belong here?" He squeezed her hand. "You don't look happy. To me, that's a good indicator that you don't want to be here. So why not leave?"

"I can't!" Finally she looked at him, blue eyes blazing. "I can't leave. We have a deadline. This is important. Our group is trying to stop villains. Super villains."

"And?" Evan asked with deceptive casualness.

"Some of us want to aim for the younger villains." The color drained from her face. "They want to stop them before they can hurt anyone."

A cold chill ran up his spine. "There's a lot of wiggle room in that statement. How young are your friends thinking of aiming?"

Tears glistened in Tabitha's eyes. "As soon as we can find them. A child of a superhero becomes a superhero. A child of super villain..." She choked.

Evan pulled her into his arms as she started to cry. "You don't want to do this, do you?" he whispered in her ear. Against his shirt, she shook her head. Hot tears melted through the fabric. "Shhh, it's okay. You don't have to do this."

Tabitha pulled away. "I have to make the world safe. I have to stop villains before they hurt anyone. It's who I am. I... I don't have a choice. We start tomorrow. The Rainbow Dane says we can't wait any longer."

"Correct me if I'm wrong, but a person can't be a villain until they do something wrong. Innocent until proven guilty and all that."

Tabitha shook her head. "That's not what—"

"Who in the blue blazes are you?" The Rainbow Dane roared grabbing Tabitha's arm and pulling her away. "Zephyr, get over here. Who is this schmuck?"

"He's... he's my ethics professor." Tabitha wiped away a tear.

"Shock!" the Dane shouted. "Get Zee a drink, she's not feeling like herself."

"I'm fine!" Tabitha protested. She tried to step away, but The Rolling Shock grabbed her, stunning her still and forcing a drink to her lips.

Evan knocked it out of his hands. "The lady said she wasn't thirsty."

The collected superheroes stared at him as if he was a fuzzy bunny that had suddenly turned into a carnivore.

"I don't know what sort of games you're playing," Evan said. "I see the costumes, and I don't know the rules, but I do know that when a lady says no, she means no. Now, let Miss Perl go."

The Rainbow Dane chuckled. His laugh rolled like thunder, and soon the whole room joined in. "Oh, Pops, we ain't at the university anymore. This is real life, and around here, we don't play games. Shock, show the nutty professor here the door."

The Rolling Shock grinned maliciously as he strutted toward Evan.

Evan pressed the Agree-With-Me Ray just in time. "I'm not here. Nothing happened."

The Rolling Shock froze mid-step. The entire party turned, acting as if nothing had happened.

Evan rushed back to Tabitha. "Sweetheart, can you hear me?" The sickly sweet smell that had clung to her since the fight assaulted him. He picked up the cup she'd dropped.

Not perfume, but this. The same smell as the homeopathic lotus wash the Thane had wiped her cut with.

Cut. Blood. Drug. Blood stream.

Gingerly holding the edges of the cup, Evan wrapped it in a napkin and tucked it in his pocket. "Hold on, Tabby-cat. I'll be back for you."

CHAPTER SIXTEEN

What is the difference between a villain and a hero? I never thought to ask. As I walked away from Tabitha that night, I knew one thing: even if she never loved me, I was going to save her. Tabitha was trapped. My children were threatened. This meant war.

EVAN TUGGED AT the cuffs of his tuxedo. "Hert? How do I look?"

"Charming as ever, Doctor." The minion ran a rag over the toe of his shoe. "There, sir. Quite ready to take over the world."

"That plan is on hold," Evan said as he glided into the garage.

An owl cried mournfully in the distance as the minions stilled to look at him. "On hold, sir?"

He hit the assembly with the megawatt smile he hadn't used in years. "I've declared war on the superheroes."

A purple minion with a yellow Mohawk fell backward in a faint.

Hert clicked his tongue. "War, sir? Alone? Against how many superheroes?"

"All of them. Except Tabitha, of course."

"Of course." Hert set down his clipboard with delicate care. "Sir, are you quite sure you're feeling well?"

He tossed the cup to Hert. "That's what they're using to poison Tabitha. I think it's a derivative of the lotus flower, but double check anyway. I want an antidote by morning. The Rainbow Dane stole my wife and he wants to kill my daughters because they are the children of a super villain." Evan's eye twitched just a little. "He will not have that opportunity."

"Understood, sir." Hert clutched his clipboard again like a long lost teddy bear. "I think I can find other super villains, if we have a few days time."

"We don't have days. I'm going in alone—"

"Daddy?" a sleepy voice asked from the doorway.

"Angela? Why aren't you in bed, sweetie?"

She rubbed sleepy eyes. "You were being loud. Is Mommy home yet?"

"Um." He bit his lip as he scrambled for a plausible lie.

Angela looked at his Dior suit. "Where are you going, Daddy?"

"To deal with a very bad man, Angel."

"Are you going to hurt him?"

"That's a possibility."

She yawned. "Can I come?"

Evan's eye twitched again. "No, sweetie. You are going to stay here where it's nice and safe." In his mind, a vivid image of The Rainbow Dane attacking the girls while he rushed to rescue Tabitha bloomed in Technicolor. The minions would do their best to keep the girls safe, but he hadn't engineered them for violence. One by one, his projects would fall, and then his daughters would die.

"On second thought, maybe you can. Go back to bed. I'll have a surprise for you in the morning."

CHAPTER SEVENTEEN

What kind of father takes his girls to war? This one. Call child services if you like, but first tell me where my daughters would be safer when a superhero was hunting them. I wasn't letting my children become the nightly news.

"HERT! I NEED another crystal focus." Pre-dawn light refracted off the necklace in Evan's hand. Sweat stained his previously flawless suit.

"Sir, we don't have any other crystals. Not even small ones."

"Then break the one in the Election Machine!"

There was a little gasp.

Evan turned to his minion. "What?"

"We'll never find another piece of holmium that size by next week, sir, let alone calibrate it in time."

He stilled as his mind raced. Everything he had ever wanted dangled in front of him, but now the road forked. He could have the world, or he could have Tabitha. Evan looked at the purple bulb of serum on his worktable sitting next to the four necklaces with magnetic shields meant to protect the girls. There were five people in the world who truly mattered. Losing even one of them would kill him. "Break the Election Machine down. We don't need it anymore."

Hert's bulbous eyes squelched as they blinked. "Yes, Master," he said in a doubting tone.

The door to the basement squeaked open. "Daddy?" Blessing walked down the stairs. "Daddy, what is that?"

"This is a little machine that's going to keep you safe." Evan pushed back from his worktable with a smile.

"Safe from what?"

"Crazy people, flying trees, dropping houses, speeding bullets. Anything with mass. I meant to give one to Mommy, but since she's working, I decided to make one for each of you girls first."

Four miniature pieces of defensive technology lay in a row on the worktable. If he did decide to give up a life of crime, he could probably sell the prototypes to the US military for a reasonably-sized fortune.

"They aren't very pretty, are they?" his daughter asked.

"No, not really. I haven't gotten that far."

Blessing poked at one. It scooted away from her finger before she could touch it.

"Magnets," Evan explained. "Once you have it on, it should repel everything away from you. Right now, they're repelling everything away from the table. I need to find a better power source." Kinetic energy was his first choice, with a backup battery of some form.

The other three girls wandered into the basement, joining Blessing in giving his work skeptical looks.

"Why do we need this?" Angela asked.

Evan sighed. He put his tools down and tried to find an answer. There wasn't a good one. "Mommy is undercover."

"We know that," Maria said.

"And she's run into a little trouble."

Angela smirked at her sisters. "I told you so."

"Daddy is going to help Mommy out. While I'm doing that, I need to keep you girls safe. I'm making you some shields. You will wear these while the minions watch you and Daddy helps Mommy."

"I want to help Mommy," Maria said.

Evan smiled. "That's very sweet of you, but this is grown-up stuff."

Maria's eyes narrowed. Little sparks of solar heat coalesced around her. "I want to help Mommy!"

"We can be superheroes too," Blessing said.

"Uh huh." Evan nodded. "Except the people Mommy is having trouble with are, technically, superheroes." The girls stared in shock. "They've gone rogue," he explained.

Delilah wrinkled her nose. "Then we can be super villains."

"Not a good idea!" Evan sprang to his feet in alarm. "It's not safe. Very, exceptionally, really not safe. I can't begin to describe how not safe that is." He took a deep breath and looked down at his little girls. They were children. Little children. "Shouldn't you be playing with dolls?"

Maria rolled her eyes. "We won't get hurt, Daddy. You'll protect us. You never got hurt as a super villain, did you?"

"Um..."

"See? We'll be safe."

Delilah raised her hand.

"Yes?"

"Can we have costumes?"

He was blindsided with nowhere to run. "Sure. I'll have a minion get right on that. You do realize that if I let you near a fight, your mother will kill me. She will skin me alive. Literally. This is a very bad idea."

"Mommy doesn't like you leaving us alone either," Maria said.

"Minions don't count," Angela added.

Hert gave him a sympathetic look. "I'm afraid the genetic programming on these specimens is flawed, Master."

Evan collapsed back into his chair with a sigh. "Control models, Hert: they never do what you want them to."

CHAPTER EIGHTEEN

In the end, the minion programmed for color and spatial coordination was given an hour to watch What Not To Wear, *a credit card, and free run of the local sewing shop. The girls talked dresses, designed costumes, and I changed the defensive shields to match Locke, Rage, Strike, and Curse, the newest super villains in the world's pantheon.*

Delilah was my perfect walking Lock-pick, all jazzed up in a Victorian suit of copper and black. We added ruffles to the sleeves, and a little top hat. I turned her shield into a watch and she was ready to unlock every secret in existence.

Angela, who could manipulate emotion, chose Rage as her name. She could make people happy, but as a villain, she was going the other way. I dressed her like a young Harry Dresden in a black leather duster, a black fedora, and armed her with a small walking stick. Instead of the pentagram Harry wore, I gave her a heart inscribed in a star for her defensive charm.

Maria became Strike, a dark princess with velvet gown, puffy sleeves, and a choker that held a black gem covering the shield. Very much what I pictured Galadriel wearing if she'd taken the One Ring.

Last of all was Blessing, who changed her name to Curse. We went for a mystic-in-the-desert look with a red robe and hood, except we split the skirt and gave her tennis shoes so she could run.

I never believed in impractical body armor, despite how much I love it on Tabitha.

THE GIRLS RAN around the small backyard, throwing fire at the minions and practicing shielding against water balloons.

Evan held up his last trinket against the setting October sun: a dark gray handgun. The Neanderthals who called themselves superheroes would never realize the true threat the weapon represented—at least he hoped not. Feeling a twinge of fatalistic ennui, he loaded everyone into the minivan. Hert strapped himself into the passenger seat.

"Are we clear on the plan?" Evan asked.

"Yes, Daddy," the girls chorused. At least it was Halloween. They didn't look too out of place.

Yet. He glanced at Hert.

"Yes, Master. The minions are in place. The area has been fully explored and we've set up the 'distraction' for local law enforcement."

Running a hand over the lump in his pocket, Evan took a deep breath. "Very well then. Ladies, let's make this a night to remember."

The twenty minute drive to the warehouse district where the minions had tracked Tabitha to lasted just long enough for Evan to regret everything he planned to do, but not long enough to think of an excuse to back out. He parked across the street and adjusted the cuffs of his Dior suit. "Hert, send in team one."

With a curt nod, Hert sent the outer perimeter team of minions scrambling into place.

"Ladies?" Evan twisted in his seat so he could see the girls, their costumes squashed by their booster seat straps. "You stay with Hert. Move to the upper deck, and locate Mommy. Blessing—"

"Curse," she corrected from under her red hood.

"Of course, excuse me. Curse, you take this, and drop it on the floor in front of Mommy." He handed her a round sphere of purple glass with the antidote to the lotus poison. "The fog from that should clear Mommy's head. Then I want Strike to lay a line of fire between everyone in the building and Mommy. It's okay if I'm on the other side. Rage?" He looked over at Angela. "Keep them confused. And, Locke, you keep the doors open. Once Mommy is with you, get back to the car. Don't stop for anything. I'll go in and keep them distracted."

And it would probably hurt. But how else could a man prove his love? He stepped out of the car, snagged his sunglasses, and gave himself one last look in the side mirror. Devastating. Doctor Charm, dressed to break hearts. "Give me five minutes to get their attention, then start the fireworks. Hert, keep them safe."

"Yes, Master."

Striding across the empty road, Evan tried to remember the logic behind this insanity, if there'd been any in the first place. Save Tabitha, keep the girls safe. At least the goal remained beyond reproach. Alas, noble didn't mean *actionable*. So he was winging it. Taking it on the fly. And really hoping he'd get a chance to punch The Rainbow Dane in the balls.

The door swung open with ease. All the super-heroes had assembled, dressed in full costume this time. To an outsider it probably looked like a regular Halloween party—if you ignored the fact that the punch smelled of lotus flowers, everyone looked tense, and the conversation was less than convivial. Phrases like, "Kill them all, it's doing the world a favor," floated past and made his blood boil.

Angler Girl nodded to him vaguely, as if she couldn't quite place his face. Rolling Shock scowled in confusion and whispered something to The Rainbow Dane.

Hempman pivoted. "Doctor Charm? Where?"

Evan smirked. They deserved everything he was here to dish out.

The Rainbow Dane turned around. "You?" he roared. "What are you doing here?"

"Me?" Doctor Charm asked with an easy laugh. "I was in the neighborhood. The Peerage asked me to stop by to welcome you to town." He held out a hand to The Rainbow Dane.

The Dane scowled at him. "Who are the Peerage?"

"Why, my dear boy! The Peerage are the criminal royalty. The movers and shakers of the underworld. I must say, we are all very impressed with this scheme of yours. So original. One hundred percent shock value. I, myself, am merely a plotter. I don't do the violent crimes. I find it ruins your suits. Blood stains on Dior? You can imagine the dry cleaning bill. But this? Dane! This is perfect. Deliciously evil. You are to be congratulated." Doctor Charm mimed doffing his hat as he gave the Dane an elaborate bow.

The Dane wrinkled his brow. "I don't know what you're talking about."

"Why, the murder of all those innocent children. Quite ingenious. You'll be the most wanted man for decades to come." Doctor Charm turned to a passing super-heroine in a frighteningly short skirt. "I say, old chap, are all of these delicacies for your enjoyment, or would you mind if I took something home with me?"

Starlit Starlet, stunned by his boldness, stopped to gape.

Doctor Charm lifted her hand to his lips. "*Enchanté*, madam. May I have the pleasure of your company this evening? Do say yes." Overhead light winked off his watch.

"Y-yes," she stammered.

"Charming, absolutely charming." He tucked her arm into his. "Have a fabulous evening, Dane. Remember, the Peerage is only a call away if you ever need some advice."

The Rainbow Dane stamped the floor, enraged.

Time was running out. The superheroes were stunned now, but in a few moments they'd shake off the stupor and attack. "A tip, gratis: the name will have to go. The LGBT community has never fully embraced the villains of the world and you don't want a lawsuit from them over the use of the rainbow when you start murdering children. Come to think of it, I suspect the Danish will be highly incensed when you start portraying them as wanton killers. A name change will do you a service all round. If nothing else, you need to let the public know that you've changed sides."

"I am a superhero!" the Rainbow Dane screamed.

Doctor Charm laughed. "Naturally. Naturally. A super-hero who murders children. Isn't he a gem?" he asked Starlit.

The Rolling Shock pushed forward. "We aren't murdering innocent children."

"No?" Doctor Charm smiled. "That's not what I heard."

"We're stopping the children of super villains, and super villains themselves."

He laughed. "The children of super villains? Oh my. Do you know how many super villains have children? Anyone?" He scanned the crowd for an answer. "Anyone at all? No, and rightly so. Super villains don't have children. It's called a condom. We keep things under wraps. Now, superheroes? *You* have children."

There was a gasp from somewhere in the crowd.

"All those adorable little tykes dressed up this evening as they go begging door to door. I suspect there's even one or two dressed as Doctor Charm. They'll make easy targets for the Dane here, and you have no way of knowing who they belong to."

"Super villains have children!" the Rainbow Dane shouted.

"Really?" Doctor Charm caught the hand of another passing heroine. "Stay with me, darling," he whispered.

Zephyr Girl stepped closer. She'd added a small blue mask to her costume, but otherwise looked unchanged.

He tried not to show how much it hurt to look at her.

"The Rainbow Dane is leading us on a noble quest."

"Zephyr? Is that really you?" Doctor Charm leaned forward. "Not so girlish anymore. A bit of weight gain? A pregnancy or three perhaps? I hear you have a boisterous husband back home, or was that a rumor?"

Tabitha's back went stiff.

"She doesn't have any family," the Rainbow Dane said. "She has—what in the blue blazes is that?" He pointed up to the ceiling. Doctor Charm cocked his head at the lights, ignoring the floating purple glass. "Light bulbs. Invented by Thomas Alva Edison in 1879. They turn electric energy into light waves. Really quite an ingenious design, but not new. You've never noticed them before?"

"I meant the purple bulb, you frakkin idiot!"

"Frakkin?" Doctor Charm laughed. "You need to stop watching science fiction shows. I don't see any purple dots. Perhaps it's time to get your eyes checked? Ladies, shall we leave? I fear our host is less than Charming."

The women hanging on his arms tittered appreciatively.

The Rainbow Dane roared, ready to charge, and the anti-lotus bomb dropped. Purple smog filled the air around Tabitha.

"Zephyr Girl! Get away!" the Dane shouted.

Tabitha coughed, but started moving backward, her heels dragging on the floor.

Time to move the party to the next level. Evan was wondering when Maria—Strike—would lay down the cover fire when a voice boomed out. "You stole my mommy!"

Rage and anger made his blood boil. He wanted to break heads, rip the stone from the foundation. He shook his head and focused on not listening to Angela's mental suggestions.

Overhead lights burst, falling from the ceiling as sparks of flame encircled the room.

"Time to leave. Ladies, it was a lovely thought. Another time perhaps?"

"Who are you?" the Dane demanded.

Evan turned to see him pointing at the girls. Frozen in terror, he barely noticed Hempman closing in on him.

"I'm Rage," Angela said.

"Strike."

"Curse."

"Locke," the other girls said, all posing. "You stole our mommy. You want us dead. Now, you face your choices."

Terror swept the room like a living thing. People dropped to their knees crying. Burning embers rained down at Strike's command, sending people shrieking as they batted at singe marks in their polyester costumes. Doors opened, and people babbled nonsense as Locke let loose.

The Rainbow Dane shook it off and charged. "Abomination!"

Evan dove to intercept, but Hempman knocked him to the ground.

"No!" Zephyr Girl rose up, punching the Dane and sending him flying.

"Those are monsters, Zee," the Dane growled.

"Those are my daughters. The only monster here is you." She wavered on her feet, not fit for a fight.

Evan pulled his arm back sharply, slamming his elbow into Hempman's nose. With a twist, he broke free and had his gun pointed at The Rainbow Dane. "Don't move."

The room stilled.

"Or what?" the Dane mocked. "I'm a superhero, what are you going to do? A bullet won't hurt me."

"This isn't loaded with bullets. One shot, and you're a normal human being. No super power. No abilities. No protection."

Dane rushed him, and he pulled the trigger.

Sneering, Evan side-stepped the enraged superhero. "You'll never touch anyone again. You're normal now. Average. There's nothing heroic about you."

The Rainbow Dane floundered. He staggered forward, and fell to the floor gasping in panic.

The Rolling Shock jumped him. He pulled the trigger. "Join your friend. Be average. Be nobody. Be forgettable."

Evan risked a glance at the causeway above. Tabitha and the girls were gone. "Superheroes and heroines of varying sizes, it's been a delight to thwart you all this evening. Please remember me for all your future vanquishing needs, because—if you touch my family again—there won't be a single superhero left in the world." Doctor Charm bowed. A swirling opera cape would have added a nice touch.

Silence met his threat. Doctor Charm walked away, confident as only a super villain holding all the cards could be.

After closing the warehouse door, Evan sprinted across the street to the van. Hert was helping the girls buckle. All four were slumped in their seats, barely interested in their bags of Halloween candy.

Tabitha leaned on the side of the van looking lost and confused. "What happened?"

"You were given a lotus serum. It interrupted communication between your synapses and blocked your memory." Evan brushed a loose hair from her face. All his fears fluttered away. Tabitha was back.

"And the fog?" she asked, taking off her mask. Turning it over in her hands, she dropped it to the ground.

"A clarifying agent. It'll pull the lotus serum out of your blood stream. You'll probably have to pee like crazy in an hour, and you might get sick, but your memory will come back."

"Everything seems like a dream. I can't remember what's real and what isn't." Tabitha rubbed her arm, shivering. "Are you real?"

"Always."

Evan helped his wife into the car. She was thinner than he liked, and purple bruises under her eyes marred her perfect face, but she was still beautiful. If only he knew if she was really coming back to him. He kissed her forehead.

Glancing back to make sure Hert and the minions were loaded, he sighed. "Let's go home."

CHAPTER NINETEEN

What's it like to fight a superhero? Picture an enraged bull with the intelligence of a monkey and the survival skills of a cockroach. Then think of a way to defeat them. The only option is to outsmart them. That's what I did. A room full of superheroes and I was the only one with my brain turned on.

There is no Peerage, so don't go looking for them. Super villains are self-centered as gyroscopes. We don't play well with others. We don't cooperate. If we did, we'd run the world.

There is no cure to being a superhero. No one knows what makes one person a hero and another an ordinary person. Obviously super strength and flight aren't average skills, but in the grand evolutionary scheme of things, are they that impossible to accept?

And even if we knew what caused the abilities, would I have any right to 'cure' someone of being who they are? That's like saying I have the right to 'cure' a person of being Irish, or African, or religious, or gay. You don't have to like what a person is to accept them as they are.

I hate superheroes, and for a moment I even considered killing The Rainbow Dane. He stole my wife. He tried to murder my children. But who am I to say who lives or dies? So I left the gun with bullets in my ankle holster and shot him with an extra strong persuasion ray. Nothing changed physically, he was just hypnotized into believing he's average. It's such a simple lie, one almost everyone believes.

Maybe someday I'll start shooting people with the persuasion ray and telling them they're heroes.

THEY STOPPED TWICE, once so Tabitha could pee, and the second time so she could throw up. Somewhere in the middle of Oklahoma, she woke up and stared at him.

"Feeling better?" he asked.

"A little." She rubbed a hand over her shoulder. "What happened to the girls?"

"They grew up. Full into superpowers. Just like their mommy." Evan tried to smile, but there was too much tension. He drove in silence, waiting for her to tell him what she was thinking.

Tabitha cleared her throat. "I don't remember what I did."

"It doesn't matter."

"It does to me."

He let her fall back asleep. The memories would return. It would take time, patience, but they would come back. They rolled into the driveway as the morning sun started to pink the sky. He carried the girls in one by one, tucking them into their beds with a kiss on the forehead. Then he carried Tabitha to their bed. She didn't move as he laid her down, and he dampened a desire to check her pulse. She was breathing. She was home. For now, that was enough.

It should have taken fourteen hours to get from the college campus back to the house. The real house, with a good lab and the broken Morality Machine. Evan did it in five. Tinkering with a minivan's engine was not illegal, although the speeds he reached probably were. But the police had more interesting things to do with their time, like figure out why every car on the road from Colorado to Texas decided to pull over for a few hours.

Evan stretched out beside her as light filtered through their dark blue curtains, washing the room in deep jewel tones. This might be all he had, this moment of peace with her. When she woke up in the morning, would she love him? Old insecurities wrapped around him tight as a boa constrictor. Could she love him? Could anyone love him?

Tabitha sighed, rolling in her sleep so her head rested on his shoulder, an arm casually flung across his stomach.

It didn't matter if she loved him. He loved her. He always had. He always would. Content, Evan settled beside his wife and fell asleep.

* * *

A shriek and the sound of glass breaking in the kitchen woke him up. Tabitha sat up in bed beside him, still wearing her Zephyr Girl costume under a faded T-shirt he'd found wadded up in the back of the van.

"Morning, beautiful."

She raised a skeptical eyebrow at him and scooted away. "Tabitha!" His plea came out too desperate.

"I feel like I haven't showered in days. It tastes like something died in my mouth. Lemme get a shower before we talk."

He sighed. "I don't want to talk," he muttered as she walked away, hips swinging. Grumbling, he kicked himself out of bed, sent the girls to watch TV with a box of cereal, and cleaned up the broken bowls.

When Tabitha came out with wet hair, dressed in old sweats and a T-shirt he'd bought her as a joke when the girls were born that read, 'I make milk, what's your superpower?', the girls were asleep in front of the TV, still worn out from their late-night adventure. It was a perfect opportunity to slip back to the bedroom and make up for lost time.

If only she were willing.

Her face was emotionless, no repelling glare, but no come-hither smile either.

Evan's shoulders slumped and he turned away. At least the minions would talk to him.

"Where are you going?" Tabitha asked.

Wondering why she would ask the obvious, he stopped by the door. "Downstairs."

Her hand rested light as a butterfly on his arm. "Are you angry with me?"

"No. Why would I be?" He caught her hand, horrified that she would even think that.

"Because I ran off with another man?"

He shook his head, emotions churning in his stomach. "You were kidnapped. It's not the same thing."

"Then why won't you look at me?"

Evan lifted her hand and gave it a gentle kiss. "Do you want me to look at you?"

She pulled away. "I'm not sure anymore. I'm..." She sighed. "I'm not sure who I am. I'm not sure what I did."

Anger boiled back up from the depths of his psyche. "Did Thane touch you? Did he force himself on you?" Making The Rainbow Dane believe he was average would be enough to protect Tabitha and the girls, but if the Dane had hurt her, Doctor Charm would expand his repertoire beyond basic conniving to outright murder.

Tabitha stared unseeing at the wall for a moment, then shook her head. "No. He stole my memories, he confused me, lied to me, but he didn't..." She trailed off waving a hand. "Thane locked a part of me away, and now I don't know who I am." She sat down, watching the sleeping girls. "I think I need some time to sort it all out."

"I'll go down to the lab then, give you some space to think. We can talk later." Evan let her hand go. If he couldn't make the world perfect, at least he could give her the space she wanted.

"Do you think space is what I need? Evan, I'm adrift." She walked over to their daughters and tucked a blanket lovingly around Maria's shoulders. "What kind of parent forgets they have children? Can a good wife really forget she's happily married? I'm a superhero! And..."

"And you lost. It happens. We all lose some days." Evan kept his voice flat. Admitting he was out of his depth and lost wouldn't change anything.

"I did something wrong," Tabitha hissed. "*Wrong.* How can I keep going from there? How do I know I'll make the right choice next time? I don't know how to live with doubt. I feel empty inside. Everything I was is gone." She stood in the living room looking small for the first time. "I'm empty."

"We'll work it out." He headed for the lab again, and Tabitha followed him down.

"What do you think is down here that will make me better?" she asked as she picked her way through the mess of stuffed animals and destroyed cassette tapes.

He hesitated. Time for truth. "This." Evan pointed to the Morality Machine. "It, ah, tweaks your normal levels of uprightness and makes you a little more, um, horny. For lack of a better term. Sex fixes everything?"

Tabitha ran her hand over the broken machine. "I love your lab." She smiled shyly, and then it turned sly. "Minions, out!"

The multicolored minions peeked out from their various hiding places, large eyes bulging in confusion.

"You knew about the minions?" Evan demanded. They ate grass clippings and occasionally nachos, so there wasn't even a food bill for them. "My mother doesn't even know about the minions!"

With a giggle, Tabitha rolled her eyes. "I met Hert the same night I met you."

"Yes, but I told you I got rid of them!" he shouted over the sound of a hundred flapping feet.

"Lock the door on your way out!" Tabitha called after them. She gave him a patient, one-eyebrow-raised look. "You are charming and sincere, but not a very good liar, dear. Little things are noticeable. Like the perfectly trimmed lawn when we don't have a lawn mower. Not to mention the actual minions all over the building last night. They don't blend in with the scenery as well as you think."

Huffing, Evan folded his arms. "I told you we had a lawn service."

"Yes, dear, and I'm the one that pays the bills. I know I'm an adult who wears spandex in public, but that doesn't mean I can't add two and two together to make four."

There was an ominous click from upstairs as the last minion filed out and locked the door.

Tabitha turned to him with a sultry smile. "From the first time I saw you in here, all I could think about was having sex on one of the machines. I thought I'd lost my mind."

"Um..." He looked at the Morality Machine. Had the minions fixed it overnight?

"How does this one work?" Tabitha asked as one elegant hand caressed the machine.

He scrambled to form coherent sentences. It was almost impossible when she smiled like that. "Ah..."

She hit him with her best come-hither look. "Is it magnets like the rest?"

"Ah, mostly." Evan nodded, grateful for the easy out. The room was suddenly a lot warmer than usual.

Tabitha laughed. "You're right. I feel better."

Evan blinked. "What'd I miss?"

"It's a magnet, love."

"Yes. An effective one at that. Remember the second time you came to my lab?"

"Vividly."

"I turned this on, and instead of you breaking me into pieces we eloped. And had wild sex six times that night."

"Seven."

"Which is almost the polar opposite of killing me."

"Evan? For a smart man you really are remarkably dense sometimes. I told you I came to have wild sex and start a scandal that would keep the tabloids talking for decades."

He nodded. "After I turned on the machine."

She shook her head. "How do you think I fly? I use magnetic power all the time. I'm immune to your machines. That's why I could fight you when no one else could."

Evan blinked. "Um... You wanted to... with *me*?" The possibility that Tabitha wanted him for himself had never crossed his mind.

Tabitha's eyes went wide. "Who wouldn't? Evan, you're gorgeous! You're on posters. You have a fan club. Have you never read the fan fiction? I used to read it and laugh. Until I met you." She sighed dreamily. One delicate hand touched his face. "How could I not want you, Evan?" She pressed against him.

He held her there as he fell in love all over again. "Because you're perfect? You deserve someone as wonderful as you are."

"And I have you, don't I?" Tabitha tilted her head back, begging for a kiss.

"Always." Leaning in, he captured her lips. She tasted soft and sweet and exotic. She was everything he'd ever wanted, and everything he'd been missing. And they made love on the broken machine that he'd never needed at all.

Evan Smith (Super villain, RET.) teaches ethics and genetic engineering at the University of Colorado. He lives in the foothills with his beautiful wife, four daughters, and is currently expecting his first son.

LIANA BROOKS

VILLAINS

GO TO THE MOVIES

HEROES AND VILLAINS

For the unsung heroes.

CHAPTER ONE

Dear Mom,

New York is everything I hoped it would be. I love this school! Last semester alone the students showed a marked improvement over the previous year. And, so far, we haven't had a single senior drop out. This might be our highest graduation rate ever.

I'm really excited by all the improvements. It makes me feel like I'm actually doing something useful. I'm in control of myself, and it's wonderful.

The date with Simon was less exciting. He's... um... 'Dull as a brick' might be the right term. You'd think it would be easy to find someone who could carry on an intelligent conversation in New York, especially with Internet dating. It's 2032! But, no, this hypothesis has been proven incorrect yet again.

Give my love to Daddy, Gideon, and the minions. If Maria stops by, tell her I'm worried about her. Delilah and I talked about staging an intervention. I'm not sure, but Delilah thinks Maria will calm down once the shock of losing Martin is over. It may be just a phase.

Oh, and Blessing wrote me. She's in South Africa and loving it. She sent the most hideous picture of a giant bug ever. I forwarded it to Gideon. And I told her not to bring it back no matter how much she adores its fangs.

Your loving daughter,
Angela

APRIL IN NEW YORK City. Angela could almost taste the coming summer. She'd even rolled the car windows down to take advantage of the first warm day while she drove back from lunch. Summer would be bliss: eight weeks kid-free that she planned to fill by maxing out her tourist quota and hitting every landmark in a day's drive. By the time her second year as a teacher began in August, she would know more about New York than any native-born city slicker.

Angela parked her car and rolled the windows up. The school was experiencing an unprecedented surge in academic reform, but that didn't mean she needed to tempt the alumni with an easy steal.

A police siren screamed in the distance, echoing the fear and despair radiating from the school. It felt like the first edge of trouble, a nudging headache that made her want to snarl despite her good mood—but New York was like that, the underlying anger of the citizens scraping against her nerves until she was emotionally raw.

Public School 84 was hers though. Angela had been there long enough that she'd been able to slowly shift the mood of the school from fearful resentment to an amiable interest in learning. It was probably just a schoolyard punch-up, nothing to worry over too much.

Sipping on her smoothie, Angela headed for the impressive security array that divided the outside world from the inner sanctum of PS 84. Outside there were guns, drugs, and chaos. Beyond the arch of metal that scanned for everything from weapons to lethal viruses, there were regimented schedules, dusty dead-wood copies of Shakespeare's sonnets, and young minds ready to argue over every word she said.

One of her favorite students had spent an hour debating the merits of shoelaces. You couldn't buy that kind of doublethink.

The security guard wasn't at her usual place in the main lobby, but Angela knew the drill. She swiped her ID, scanned her fingerprint, and headed for the lunchroom where there was undoubtedly a fight emerging.

As she neared the cafeteria, however, fear washed over her like the noxious smell of a skunk in the dark. Angela tossed her unfinished smoothie in the trash and thought of pleasant things. Bluebonnets on the Texas prairie, the smell of hot apple cider on a crisp winter night, the laughter of her baby brother, the love of her parents... She took it all, wrapping it into the idea of what her school should feel like.

At first, the collective mind of the students fought back. They were scared, and fear was a familiar friend. But she pushed, and they swayed under her will. Manipulating emotions was right up there with the ability to generate polka dots on a wall in terms of usefulness; unless she wanted to turn people into mindless slaves, there was very little she could do as far as the government was concerned. Besides, brute force wasn't her style.

Influencing things was different though. *This is different*, she told herself. She turned the corner into the cafeteria and almost jumped at the sight of Travys Freeman—top student in her AP calculus class—holding a gun.

The security guard had her Taser out and was trying to talk Travys into handing over the weapon. Terror so thick it was almost a physical force rolled off Travys. There was no way he would hand over anything to the guard. He wanted to turn it on himself. He just hadn't worked up the nerve. Yet. Waiting would be fatal for someone.

Angela cleared her throat and pushed on the mob. Everyone turned, even Travys. She smiled winningly. "This isn't about the quiz yesterday, is it?" she asked, weaving between the tables.

Travys made eye contact. Big mistake. Eye contact meant she had his full attention, and once she had that, he was hers.

"Travys, I asked you a question."

"It's not about the quiz, Miss Smith." The gun wavered, not quite dropping, but he wasn't sure where to aim.

Angela laid a comforting hand on the security guard's arm. "We don't need an audience do we, Travys?"

He shook his head.

"Miss Netley, why don't you get everyone to class? The bell is ringing," Angela added as the bell marking the end of lunch rang out. The crowd stayed frozen, spellbound by the same power that kept Travys from pulling the trigger. It was risky, but she refocused, encouraging everyone to hurry away. "Everyone go to class. Not you, Travys. I want a word with you."

The security guard shook herself out of her stupor. "Come on people, get to class. What are you gawking at?"

Conversation hummed to life around her and Travys sagged. The terror that had buoyed him was gone—only crushing despair remained.

Angela took a seat across the cafeteria table from him as the students and teachers filed out. Some of them tried to stay, or shout, or intervene, but she kept them all walking.

Travys peeked up at her, brown eyes filled with tears. "I'm sorry, Miss Smith."

"Guns don't solve anything. You know that."

He was getting ready to kill himself. She could feel it. The desire to stop the pain overwhelmed him. Angela tried to bleed it off, taking some of the despair herself. It hurt.

"What happened? You can tell me, Travys." She pushed thoughts of safety towards him. He wanted to believe, but Travys had no memories of safety. When they'd first met, he was a failing student, a scrawny sixteen-year-old who flinched when anyone raised their voice. Her power allowed her to create a sanctuary in the classroom, and in that sheltered place, he'd bloomed into a brilliant student.

"Did you get a college rejection letter?" she asked. It seemed the most probable answer.

He jerked his head to the side as if he'd been slapped. "Chris came home."

She sucked in air so fast it whistled past her teeth. "I thought he was doing twenty to life?"

"He got off on a technicality." Chris Freeman was his son's worst nightmare. He was a dealer with an anger problem who saw his only kid as a punching bag. Angela had never met the man, although she'd wanted to rearrange his brain after meeting Travys's mother, a sweet woman who was the poster child for domestic abuse.

"What's your mom doing?"

Travys's eyes dropped to the floor. "She didn't come home from work."

Which made her smarter than Angela thought. "Maybe she didn't know he was coming home."

"She knew."

And crueler than she'd guessed: she'd abandoned her son to a monster. "I'm sorry."

"I'm not going home," Travys said. His thoughts turned back to the gun. Angela could feel his longing for an escape.

"Shooting yourself won't make anything better."

He startled.

"Give me the gun. We'll make other plans for tonight. You won't go back home to him."

Travys hesitated.

"Give me the gun, Travys." She seized at his mind, making him want to please her. The desire for her approval was false—Travys was too strong-minded to need outside approval—but it worked. His arm lifted slowly, like he was fighting gravity.

"You can trust me."

"Nobody move, NYPD!"

Angela jumped. She'd been too focused on Travys to feel the approach of the police. In a split-second decision, she released her hold on Travys and reached out for the minds of the police before they could ruin everything.

It was the wrong decision.

Travys screamed in pain. His hand convulsed around the gun, pulling the trigger, and sending a bullet through the flesh of her upper arm.

Still trying to grasp the collective mind of the police, everything blurred and Angela found herself standing near the main office in the arms of a strange man in bright green spandex.

"Travys! Hold still!" The police were moving, too focused for her to grasp; they'd stunned and cuffed Travys before she could even figure out what had happened.

She tried to brush the man aside. "Let me go." Angela released Travys's mind and focused on herself. The man in bright green held her.

"We need to get you to the doctor," the man said.

Angela realized he wasn't holding her as much as trying to hold her arm. Blood seeped between his gloved fingers. She blinked at it. The pain was secondary to the emotional savaging she'd taken from Travys's mind.

"Stay calm. An ambulance is on the way," the man repeated. He was trying to make eye contact. She didn't cooperate with him.

"I'll be fine. I'd like to check on my students now."

"If I hadn't rushed to your rescue, you would be dead." Confusion tinged his voice, as if he was waiting for praise.

She glared at the team hustling Travys out of the school. "If the police hadn't burst in here screaming, Travys would have handed the gun over and I wouldn't have been shot." She pushed him away. "This is your fault."

"No," said a crisp, authoritative female voice. "This is your fault."

Angela turned to look at the newcomer, an older woman with salt-and-pepper hair and a grim expression, which she recognized from a picture. Katrina Bocks, de facto government employee and chief of the United Nations Council for Superhero Control.

Not a friend.

"Miss Smith, please let the EMT examine your arm, and then I have some paperwork for you to sign."

"What sort of paperwork?" She wouldn't qualify to sign with the teachers' union until she'd worked a full school year, and she doubted the school board was prepared for this kind of situation. Besides, the chances that The Company was involved with something as benign as arranging medical leave were astronomically low. She'd sooner believe in love at first sight.

Katrina gave her a bitter smile, her emotions colored by hate and anger so violent it was almost a physical aura around her. "How long have been aware of your superpowers, Miss Smith?"

Angela played innocent. "Superpowers? I'm a teacher, but that's a generous compliment. Though some days I can't imagine anything harder than twisting these young minds around calculus." She widened her eyes, the very picture of an innocent southern belle.

Katrina wasn't buying it. She held up an old-style thumb drive. "I have papers saying you are a superhero with the ability to perform psychic manipulation."

"I don't believe anyone can do that."

"I also have evidence that you and the young man were in a very unprofessional relationship. When he came to his senses and realized how he'd been used, he came to school to kill you. The public will be incensed to hear you lived." Satisfaction edged Katrina's words. She thought she had Angela pinned in a corner.

The woman had come far too well-prepared. Angela looked over at the EMT hovering behind them. Time for a quick getaway. "I think I need to see the doctor now."

"I'll wait with you," the man offered. "For your protection."

Right, he was her well-meaning bodyguard, another concerned citizen fighting for truth, justice, and the

American way. Angela moved to walk past Katrina, then stopped. "How long have you been tracking me?"

"I learned several months ago that a mind-raper was in the area. I didn't know who it was until today."

Angela nodded. Considering they didn't know the name of their target, they had certainly put a plan together quickly. Daddy was not going to like hearing about this. There was always a risk of The Company stumbling across her path this close to headquarters, but things had been so quiet lately she'd been sure she was flying under the radar. "I'll meet you at the hospital, I suppose?"

Katrina smiled triumphantly. "Yes. There's some very simple paperwork you need to fill out. And then we'll discuss more of your future after your surgery."

Her arm stung at the reminder. "I don't think I need surgery, just stitches."

"And I don't think a mutant should be allowed to breed," Katrina said. "Fortunately, the government sees my point of view. A quick snip-snip and you'll be safe to release into the wild."

Angela turned to follow the EMT, teeth clenched hard enough to hurt. There were so many things she wanted to say. None of them would help. Training took over, memories of summer drills under the hot Texas sun. The Company could come at any time. There was no hope of fighting them, so you had to evade, dodge, run.

She let the EMT load her into the back of the ambulance and waited until they'd hit the first stoplight before she dialed the only number that mattered. "Mom, they found me. Come pick me up."

CHAPTER TWO

Dear Mom,

The doctor says I can get the stitches out in a few weeks. There's going to be a scar, but that's what happens when a bullet takes a bite out of your arm. I might need physical therapy after the stitches come out, but it will have to wait until I can get a job here. Maria was able to sell my bike for a reasonable price so I have rent money for a bit and a new name. AJ David; it sounds like something out of a buddy-cop movie. Any minute now some burly old guy will break in and tell me he's two days from retirement.

Anyways, yes, I'll be able to find a job here. Just not teaching, for obvious reasons. Is it wrong to pray that your former boss will accidentally drop into a pit of lava?

It's L.A.—you'd think there'd be jobs everywhere but I can't find anything. Teaching is out until The Company backs off, and apparently blonde waitresses are a dime a dozen. I'm seriously tempted to cheat and force someone to hire me. I tell myself that I couldn't live with that in the long run, but every night I eat ramen noodles I seriously consider world domination. It's so easy. People want to do what I say, if I want them to. And... Well. I'll think of something.

Tell Daddy I say thank you for the allowance. I know he said it was my birthday money a little bit early, but since he'll send a birthday gift too, it's a loan. I'll pay you guys back when I get a job.

Love,
Angela

LOS ANGELES WAS ON the short list of places Angela had hoped never to live. Now, staring at the criminally beige walls of the cheapest apartment she could find, she listened to the L.A. traffic and an argument in Spanish from next door. A door slammed, and with a resigned sigh, Angela grabbed a plate of cookies. She stepped into the communal hall to see which one had retreated.

Luiz, single mom and neighbor, grimaced. "Sorry."

"Cookie?" Angela offered.

Luiz grabbed one and took Angela's unspoken invitation to step inside. They sat at the white plastic table Angela had found on the roadside as Luiz chewed her cookie angrily. "It wasn't supposed to be like this. We came out here to get away from my ex, be near family. My brother and I started a stunt company. We've got a good reputation, but the past few months." She shook her head as she stared at some personal nightmare. "Mikey said he had a big job, something that would set us up. He quit showing up to work, and now he's been arrested on a DUI. I'm so stressed and I'm always yelling at Mia. She's right. I'm a horrible mom."

"No, you aren't." Angela reached over and rubbed her shoulder. "She didn't mean that. Mia's a good kid, she loves you."

"She's failing classes."

Fights between Luiz and her daughter Mia revolved around two things: Mia's grades, and Mia's string of good-for-nothing boyfriends. Angela had heard every single fight for the past week. "Is she not doing the homework, or does she not understand the subject?"

"She says she doesn't understand." Luiz wiped tears from her face. "I just want something better for her. I don't want her to wind up like me."

Angela took a cookie. "Do you want me to tutor her?"

Luiz studied her suspiciously.

Being the only blue-eyed blonde in an area heavily populated by Latinos, Angela had gotten used to the looks of suspicion and contempt. She'd gotten the same response when she'd gone to high school in Laredo while her dad taught at the university for two years. She'd also picked up enough border-style Spanish to make the fights all too easy to understand.

"I can't pay you," Luiz finally said.

"Let me borrow your bike so I can interview for jobs a couple times a week. That would be payment enough."

Luiz mulled it over, grabbing another hot cookie. "You can ride?"

"I have an M1 license, but I sold my bike when I left New York." It was sell the bike for cash or tell the school, and thereby The Company, where to send her last paycheck. She'd opted for selling the bike and twisting Delilah's arm until her sister used her security firm mojo to produce a new life for her under the name Angela Jane David.

Luiz's eyes narrowed. "How long have you been riding?"

"Since I was eighteen. Mom wouldn't let me have a bike when I was living at home." She shrugged.

Luiz drummed her fingers on the table. "If I can get you a job, you'd tutor my daughter so she doesn't fail classes?"

"I can tutor her so she understands what she's doing in class. Failing and passing are up to her. I can't magically make her a perfect student." Angela saw a mother's fear in Luiz's eyes. It rose off the heat of her skin like a perfume. "I'm a good tutor. I've done it before to pay bills."

"I know something you can do. The pay isn't tops, but it'll cover your groceries for the week." She stood. "I'll pick you up at seven. Wear riding gear, black if you have it. Try to act tough."

* * *

Arktos landed on the roof of the US Bank Tower in a corona of cold blue fire as the sun sank into the Pacific Ocean. He was late, again. He wanted to run his hand through his hair in frustration, but the mask he wore, the one that lent him better night vision and kept his features hidden while he worked, covered his head. The thieves had pulled off another jewel heist last night, and he wasn't any closer to tracking them down.

He walked to the edge of the building, looking down at the City of Angels from over a thousand feet up. People scurried around, wrapped in their own worries, insulated by their private fears and precious egos. Somewhere in that mess were the three people he wanted.

They were getting better.

The first heist had been badly executed, and it was only because the police hadn't called The Company for help that he hadn't caught them then. It was frustrating that a set of amateurs who couldn't plan ahead enough to take care of a silent alarm were still smart enough to wear masks and gloves.

Their second heist had been better planned. The woman had acted as a distraction. A car wreck, an armored car blocked in traffic, and then the fire bug in the group had bombed the truck, grabbed the cash, and they were gone. His only hint had been a flash of blonde under the woman's USC Trojans baseball cap.

A blonde woman with the ability to influence emotions fit the description of the mind-raper who'd escaped The Company in New York. It wouldn't be the first time a rogue had teamed with a villain, and it wouldn't be the last. And if they had kept to hitting stores and trucks, he wouldn't be so worried. Last night's heist though—that had been different. The mind-raper had held an entire restaurant in thrall while the heist team robbed them blind.

That twist left him with a sick feeling in his stomach and the urge to freeze the criminals in their tracks. His fingers tingled as frost settled around him. Even in the spring heat, he was cold.

Arktos leapt from the building, letting the rush of air strip away his worries. On the edge of thought, he could feel the tug of an idea. A vision appeared, a hazy overlay of the city, and he saw the studio.

With a chuckle, he barrel-rolled in the sky, switching directions high above the streets and heading for home. Sometimes his premonitions let him see something that was about to happen, like the first heist that he'd called in to the police. And sometimes it acted like an alarm clock to make sure he got to work on time. A subtle reminder from his subconscious that he needed to get to work if he wanted to get paid.

CHAPTER THREE

Dear Mom,

L.A. is even weirder than I thought it would be. I miss Texas, but I have a job...

Love,
Angela

HOLLYWOOD MAGIC CREATED A strip of alley wide enough for a motorcycle gang to roar down in the middle of a giant room that seemed to be mostly places for lights and cameras to hang.

Angela took off her helmet and wiped sweat from her eyes. Fog roiled around her feet, giving the impression of a winter chill, but the glaring lights were hot. At the far end of the alley, two men argued over something, a camera angle maybe. She glanced at Luiz for direction.

Originally she'd thought she was coming along to play Luiz's assistant, make a coffee run or three, but Luiz had introduced her as the stuntwoman AJ David. She'd flashed a couple of cards and told Angela to sign all the paperwork as fast as she could. Angela made a mental note to make sure she had all the proper licenses, permits, guild cards, and union paperwork done by morning. There were rules in Hollywood, and she was certain she'd broken about fifty unwritten ones. Hopefully Daddy could fake a California accent long enough to play her agent if anyone called.

"They're going to make us do it again," one of the men said. Angela thought his name was Dyfed, but she wasn't sure. Luiz was riding as the gang leader, doing tricks that made Angela's heart stop. Dyfed and Michael were a set of twins who did jumps. Angela was paired with a woman named Raina who had told her their only job was to gun their motors and look fierce. Or as fierce as was possible with a helmet on.

Luiz glanced at her. "Welcome to show biz. It's a lot of hurry up and wait. They're trying to get the angles and lighting right before the talent shows up."

"Talent?"

"Movie stars," Raina said. "Try not to swoon like a girl."

Angela frowned but couldn't think of a decent reply.

"Glee!" the man on the other end of the set yelled.

"Patrick Swendon," Luiz said. "He's the director. If he tells you to do something, you nod and say, 'Yes, sir.'"

"Got it."

"Glee!" Swendon yelled again. "What are you doing there?" He was pointing at the 'gang'.

Angela turned around to see if anyone had joined them. It was just the five of them in black leather and a morass of confusion.

"You with the blonde hair!" Swendon shouted. "Earth to Glee! Get over here?"

"Um..." Luiz said.

Angela pointed to herself.

"Yes, you!"

She coasted her bike across the set, stopping just in front of a lean man who was on the wrong side of fifty and red from anger. "Yes, sir?"

"You're supposed to be riding with Tyler, remember? We went over that yesterday. Why are you down there with the gang?"

Angela bit her lip.

Luiz coasted up beside her. "Mr. Swendon, this is AJ David. She's one of my stunt riders."

The director glared at Angela. "Get off the bike and come over here." He turned and yelled at someone in the shadows behind him. "Get me my glasses! Where are my glasses? Thank you." After putting them on, he turned back to blink at Angela. "You're not Glee's body double?"

She glanced at Luiz, who shook her head. "No, she's just a rider."

"We need to get her hair covered. It's almost a perfect match for Glee's wig." His eyes narrowed. "How tall are you?"

"Five ten," Angela said.

He sighed in disappointment. "Too bad. You would make a perfect body double if you weren't so tall. Glee's at least four inches shorter than you."

"They're probably the same height if Glee's in her heels and AJ's wearing flats," Luiz put in helpfully. *Job*, she mouthed to Angela.

The director nodded. "How are you with mouthy, temperamental women who like to rage at the world?"

"I have sisters," Angela said. No regular human being could ever match Maria throwing a tantrum. Normal humans couldn't throw lightning and turn enemies to piles of ash when they were in a bad mood.

"Good enough. Where's Tyler's body double? What's his name?" The director stormed off into the shadows.

A motorcycle pulled up beside her, fire engine red and ridden by a tuxedoed man. Jet black eyes matched jet black hair. He had a strong jaw and dark skin, but not the right bone structure for a Latino. He was disconcertingly familiar.

She tipped her head to the side trying to decide where she'd seen him before. At the store maybe? Or on TV?

"Tyler!" Swendon huffed. "We aren't ready for you."

"I'm done with makeup, there aren't any lines, and all you need is a shot of me rolling down the alley with a blonde hanging on. Why don't we shoot this and call the scene done?"

Angela tried to remember if she'd ever heard of an actor named Tyler. It didn't ring any bells.

"Glee said she wanted to do this," Swendon argued.

"Glee's still in her trailer trying to memorize her lines for the next scene." Tyler gave Angela a look usually reserved for cockroaches right before they became a smear of entrails on the kitchen floor.

Angela shrugged it off. The big, muscled types were all the same: lots of bulk and no brains. He'd probably played football in high school, and she knew enough football players to gag at the thought of ever spending another night watching men run around in tights.

"Fine," Swendon said. "We'll get the lights in place. Roll down the main drag with the body double. Somebody go find Glee! Tell her she has five minutes!"

Tyler scowled down at her. "Well? Are you going to ask for an autograph?"

Several snippy rejoinders came to mind, but instead Angela smiled. "Naturally, as soon as I see an actor I like."

He blinked.

Angela stopped herself from rolling her eyes. "Where am I supposed to be?"

He got on his bike and looked at her over his shoulder. "Hop on."

She climbed on behind him, carefully avoiding the name of the position she was in. There might not have been the Fear of God in her house growing up, despite being in the Bible Belt, but there was certainly the Fear of Grandmother Meredith. As in, "What would your grandmother say?!?" or "Your Grandmother Meredith must be rolling in her grave!" Although Mom had stopped using that when Dad had snapped back, "All seven of them."

Dad had never thought highly of Grandma Meredith, and she'd died before Angela had ever met her, but the specter of the proper southern woman lived on. Southern Ladies did not say Certain Words.

Angela settled in, flipped her hair, and held the bike seat on either side of her thighs. It was that, or wrap her arms around tall, dark, and stupid.

"You're supposed to hold on," Tyler said.

"It's a test shot." She didn't move to grab him.

He revved the motorcycle, driving faster than necessary, weaving between barely visible marks on the floor that Luiz assured her would vanish in post-production. On his mark, Tyler pivoted the bike with precision control, and she had to grab his waist to keep from falling off.

"Told you so." He smirked.

Angela growled and flipped her hair again, aiming for his eyes. Tyler dodged. She slid off the bike and walked over to the camera crew. "Was that good enough? I'd rather drive myself."

The woman behind the camera nodded. "It's good. All we need is Glee and we can do the actual take." The woman gave her a conspiratorial grin. "What did you think of Tyler Running Fox? Does he smell good?"

"Tyler... Running Fox?" Angela looked over her shoulder at the biker who'd tried to hurl her to her death. "He's the one who ruined *Hamlet*? I didn't recognize him without the goatee."

The camerawoman choked on a laugh. "You didn't like his Hamlet? He won an Academy Award for that!"

"The screenwriters butchered Shakespeare's play. They didn't even get the 'To be or not to be' soliloquy right. It was painfully bad," she said as she became aware of someone looming over her shoulder.

Tyler Running Fox—Hollywood hero, Academy darling, the highest-grossing and most popular Native American actor ever—glared down at her.

"I don't like the way you drive, either," she said before she flounced back to her bike, well aware she wasn't going to act in Hollywood ever again.

CHAPTER FOUR

Dear Mom,

Tell Gideon I'm proud of him for getting into MIT. My alma mater won't know what hit it! I've already sent an email to my advisor warning her that my baby brother is on his way. She said she'd consider taking early retirement if he wants a math degree. On the other hand, she said that if he goes for an engineering degree like Dad she'll stick around just to watch the havoc. Apparently, Dr. Trenbel in engineering gave her a hard time while I was there and she would like, and I quote, "To let him try and handle a Smith!" I'm sure she means it with love.

I had a job for about eight hours, but I don't think I'll have a second shift. I'm trying to get worked up about it, but it wasn't anything more than riding a motorcycle. I miss teaching.

Have you heard anything about Travys? I tried to find out what happened while I was at the library, but I can't find a mention of him in the system. Could The Company bury a trial like that?

Love,
Angela

"OKAY, THAT'S WHERE YOU'RE wrong," Angela said as she leaned over Mia's shoulder to scrutinize her homework. "A squared plus B squared is C squared, and you forgot to take the square root of the total." She reached over and put a little square root sign over the number sixteen. "See?"

"I can't do math!" Mia flopped forward like a marionette with her strings cut. "When will I ever use this? Tell me when I will ever need to calculate the lengths of the side of a triangle."

"When you're a famous architect designing the next great skyscraper?" Angela suggested. "Or when you're an artist working on proportions. Everything involves math. Here"—she scribbled the Pythagorean Theorem on Mia's paper—"this is fun. It's super easy, plug-and-play math."

"Math is not fun," Mia grumbled.

"It can be."

"It really can't."

"What if I add one chocolate chip to the cookie dough for every answer you get right?"

Mia eyed her homework. "Make it three, or we're still going to have chipless chocolate chip cookies."

Angela nodded. "Three per correct answer. I'll take one away for every one I have to help on." She stretched her legs out and basked in the California sunshine. The AC was wheezing inside, but outside a nice ocean breeze cooled the city streets. A nice something breeze, at any rate. The fog had lifted, the city buzzed around them, and Angela felt safe dipping into the public mood for a minute to check how her neighborhood was doing.

It was a little like gardening. She didn't need to pay attention to everything that was going on all the time. Like checking the flowers and pulling the occasional weed, she checked on the general mood of the area every few days to ensure everything was running smoothly.

Today the area was happy. Spring sunshine and a clear sky were enough to perk up anyone's mood. There were a few hints of anger, and one of deep despair, but they were close enough that she could touch them at a distance and alter them, turning anger to patience and despair to humor. Later, she decided, she'd go for a run and check on Despair. It felt like a severe case of postpartum, but she couldn't remember seeing any new mothers in the area.

Not that this was a friendly neighborhood. Nothing like the little town in Texas she'd spent most of her time in. On the lakes of LBJ there was a quiet retirement community, a few young families, and typical Southern nosiness. Between her father's charm, the novelty of being a quad, and her own forceful personality, she'd known everything about everyone.

LA had tabloids and gossip, but it all centered around the same handful of people, as if the only measure of worth was money.

She leaned her head back, soaking up sunshine and the blissfully carefree life of the unemployed who had money for rent and groceries. Tomorrow, she'd be worried again. For today, she would patiently coax Mia into appreciating math and maybe hit the cupcake place to celebrate payday.

Splurging on cupcakes meant a ten-mile run, but what was the point of running if not to eat cupcakes every now and then?

Luiz bounced down the apartment steps. "AJ, what are you doing? We need to leave."

"What?"

"We have a night shoot, remember? We need to be there by five to start blocking out the fight scenes." Luiz was already wearing her riding gear—tight black faux leather pants, a tight yellow shirt, and a faux leather jacket cropped short, her helmet dangling from her hand. "You signed the contract."

"I insulted the 'talent' last night too," Angela said, miming the air quotes. "I don't think they want me back."

"Did someone call you and tell you not to show up?"

Angela raised her eyebrows. "No phone, remember? I'm broke."

"Then get your gear on and get unbroke by getting your lazy self to work. You're worse than my brother."

"Oooo." Mia pretended to bite her nails in mock fear and then smiled. "You better go. She's serious."

Angela ran upstairs, stuffed her leathers in a backpack, and grabbed her helmet. She pulled the jacket on over her T-shirt that read 'Fight Like A Girl—Zephyr Girl.'

Luiz was waiting on her bike.

"I really need to buy my own transport," Angela muttered. "I hate holding on to people."

"Yeah, but holding on to Tyler can't be that much of a chore. I've seen his body. If he didn't look so much like my ex I'd make a play for that." Luiz revved the engine and sped into traffic before Angela could respond that the last thing she wanted to do was make a play for Tyler Running Fox.

They left black skid marks in the parking lot, but made it inside on time.

"We're doing the setup, not shooting," Raina said when Angela asked for a place to change. "You don't need to be in costume for that."

Their set was outside, a miniature city skyline with a scaled-down helo pad. Luiz started them out on some wrestling pads, working on stunt throws. "Have you ever danced, done karate, anything like that?"

"I had a blue belt in karate, but all I remember are the basic self-defense moves." Having her mom kidnapped when Angela was four by people who had wanted to murder them all had put her family on the defensive. Her sisters had done better with martial arts, Delilah going so far as to pick up a couple of extra disciplines, but Angela hadn't ever needed it. People didn't attack her. Anyone coming towards her got hit with a heavy dose of regret that sent them straight to their knees.

Luiz frowned. "Have Raina do a practice throw with you." She tugged at her black braid. "I wish my brother was here. He's always been the one up-front for stunt fights. Dyfed! Come 'ere."

"It's easy," Raina said. "Stand like this and pretend you're holding my arm while I flip."

Angela rested a hand on her and Raina somersaulted in the air, landing flat on her back. "Are you okay?"

"AJ, it's a stunt, I'm supposed to land like this."

"Right."

Raina stood. "Let's try throwing you. When I touch your back, I want you to fall forward like I pushed you hard. Ready? One, two, three..."

Angela felt the light tap of Raina's fingers on her back and flung herself at the mat. "Oww."

"A little less enthusiastic next time."

Luiz whistled. "Everybody take ten minutes and get water, stretch out. I'm going to block out the fight scene with the director."

"I thought it was blocked," Raina said. "Didn't we go over this last week?"

"There's been a change."

Angela wandered over to the sideboard full of food. As she shrugged on her leather jacket someone said, "Nice shirt. I like Zephyr Girl."

She turned. A handsome, dark-skinned man faced her, giving her elevator eyes. Her shirt must have riveted him, because his gaze never got above her neck.

"I'm a fan of hers," Angela said as she pulled her jacket all the way on and zipped the front. It was too hot for a leather jacket, but she didn't like his stare. A little standoffish body language was in order.

Luiz swore loudly in Spanish and stalked over. "I swear on my mother's grave, I am ten seconds from quitting this contract and calling it a day. This is not the only studio in Hollywood, it's just the most—" She stopped and scowled at the newcomer. "What are you doing here?"

He picked up a donut. "I heard you had the good food."

"I thought principal shooting was done for you guys."

He shrugged. "We had an emergency meeting to discuss issues." He gave Luiz a wicked grin. "Want to hear some good gossip?"

Luiz grabbed a flimsy plate and piled it high with potato chips. "Lay it on me."

"The TV show *Fractured?* It's getting canceled."

"What?"

He held his hands up in a shrug of surrender. "You heard it here first. Carla didn't show up for her promo scenes yesterday. This afternoon she called to say she's buying herself out of her contract. No Carla, no Pacifica, no *Fractured.*"

Angela watched the exchange with morbid fascination. It was like discovering a new continent. All the words were ones she should understand, but the dialect was foreign.

Luiz must have seen her befuddled expression because she laughed. "AJ, this is Jacob Kapsimolis. He's a superhero."

She took an involuntary step backward. "Really?" A Company employee in Hollywood was not what she needed.

"I'm the Red Death on *Fractured,*" Jacob said. He flung his arms forward. "I'll have my revenge!"

Angela's heart skipped a beat, and then she realized he was acting. "Oh. That was... was good. I've seen the show a few times. I like it," she added lamely. She'd seen half an episode in the airport and it hadn't been horrible.

Jacob looked pleased, then shrugged. "Except, as of tomorrow, I'll officially be another unemployed actor begging for coffee money. Who are you?"

"She's the new stunt double," Luiz said.

"I heard about you." A grin lit up his face. "The one who hates *Hamlet*, right? Sweet! I can't stand Shakespeare."

"AJ David, stuntperson." She held out her hand. "And I do like Shakespeare, but not the way Ty—"

Jacob bulldozed over her introduction. "Speaking of stuntpeople, where's your brother, Luiz? I was hoping he could help me drown my woes."

"He got a DUI while on probation," Luiz snapped. "I ain't paying the bail, so he's rotting in the clink." She took a drink from her water bottle. "Do you ever feel like this studio is a breath away from collapsing in on its own stupidity? Studio Sluts will be the death of us all."

"Studio Sluts?" Angela asked.

"Glee was a Studio Slut," Luiz said. "She got her first part because she was sleeping with the owner, his latest bit of tit. The movie should have tanked, but she was perfect for the part and stole the show. The studio signed her on a six-year earn-out contract—she had to star in a movie which grossed a certain amount, or continue acting in the movies until she hit that point. This is her third and the contract's up in six months; the only way it will gross anything is because Tyler is here."

"Carla is Glee's replacement," Jacob said. "When Glee's second movie tanked, her sugar daddy dropped her and picked up another young thing. He's the one who bought out her contract with *Fractured*, I guarantee it. Carla has never had that kind of money."

"And now Glee has decided she won't be shooting any of the stunts because she's afraid of heights." Luiz rolled her eyes. "Two weeks ago she threw an almighty tantrum because Swendon brought in a body double. Now she's flip-flopping, tonight's shoot might get canceled."

Angela picked up a water bottle. "Maybe—OW!" She flailed as someone pulled her backward by her hair.

"Give me the wig!"

Angela rounded on the woman tugging at her hair. "What on earth are you doing?"

CHAPTER FIVE

Dear Mom,

Don't worry about sending money. I've found a job and my first paycheck comes before the end of the month. If Delilah calls to ask you about a Rembrandt, tell her you're not interested. There's a new exhibit coming to the museum and she was going to go birthday shopping for you.

Remember the da Vinci she picked up for you when we went on that trip to Paris our sophomore year? It's going to be like that all over again.

Your law-abiding daughter,
Angela

ANGELA RUBBED HER SCALP, scowling at the woman who'd yanked on her hair.

"I need Glee's wig if we're going to film this scene," the pinched-faced woman said with a puckered glower.

Luiz batted the woman away. "That's her real hair, Kerry. AJ, this is the wardrobe director for this disaster. Kerry, AJ, she's filling in for my brother."

"No, I don't have a blonde you can borrow from me." Patrick Swendon stepped around the corner mid-argument with a slightly shorter, bald man. "Kerry, where's the wig?"

"I don't need a wig," the other man argued. "I'll take your coffee girl. I just need someone who can pose in a white catsuit."

"Sweetie, you have a casting director, go ruin his day. I have enough problems."

The bald man put his hands on his hips. "You are so sleeping on the couch tonight!"

They both came to a stop in front of the buffet table. Swendon looked Angela up and down. "Can you jump off buildings?"

"Yes, sir."

"Good, you're Glee's new body double for stunts. Kerry will get your costume."

"Jacket off," Kerry ordered.

Angela obligingly unzipped the jacket and noticed the bald man's eyes fixed on her shirt. She resisted the urge to take a deep breath.

"Have you ever considered being a superhero?" Baldy asked.

Angela smiled shyly as she shook her head. "Not really."

"She's a fan of Zephyr Girl," Jacob said with a wink.

Swendon stepped in front of her. "No. Mine."

The bald man gave him a limpid-eyed look. "Oh, come now darling, you know you like threesomes."

Panicking, Angela turned to Luiz for help.

Luiz leaned over. "That's Patrick's husband, Geoff. He's also the producer and director for *Fractured*. Rumor has it that he's obsessed with the superheroes, especially Zephyr Girl."

Jacob was nodding eagerly, Geoff Swendon was already fawning, and Patrick seemed resigned.

Angela smiled shyly. "What do you need me to do?"

"All I need is a few days of filming, so we can edit Carla out and put you in as the superhero Pacifica. It's a blue and white catsuit, you'll look amazing," Geoff said with his hands folded in prayer.

"I need you to do Glee's stunts," Patrick said. "But it's mostly night shoots at this point."

Luiz held a hand up. "AJ is already under contract with my company. Patrick, if you want her you're going to need to call her agent and set up a separate contract for her. Right now she's here as a stunt rider and background character. Geoff, she can do some test shots with you tonight, but then you need to write up a contract."

Both men nodded eagerly and Angela sighed. Daddy was going to have way too much fun with this. And she was willing to bet that sleep wouldn't be in either of the contracts.

* * *

Arktos woke with a scream. A cold sweat covered his body as he fought off the nightmare that had woken him. A beautiful, red-haired woman approached a door, the door exploded, and her body was found in the cold dawn light. Again, and again, and again, the scene had repeated itself in his dreams until finally he'd fought to escape sleep.

After taking a deep breath, he climbed out of his oversized bed and pulled on a pair of jeans. He went downstairs where a light was on in the kitchen.

His little brother Aaron looked up in confusion. "I thought you said you didn't have anything to do tonight."

"I couldn't sleep. Bad dreams."

"About Mom?"

Arktos shot his little brother a look that would have chilled the blood of most men. "No. It wasn't about anything real." He rooted around in the kitchen until he found a pitcher of lemonade. "What are you doing up?"

"Studying." Aaron sulked.

"You need to sleep too."

"It's only ten. I'm going to finish the practice worksheet for math and go to bed." Aaron worked in silence for a few minutes, portraying the Good Student with a skill that never went as far as the classroom. "I'm not going to get kicked out this time," he said when he caught Arktos watching. "My grades are good. I've even got a tutor."

"A tutor?" Arktos raised an eyebrow. "The last 'tutor' you had couldn't add two plus two."

"This one's different." He hesitated a moment. "My friend Mia has a tutor. She said I could come over and study with her this weekend."

"We'll see," Arktos said. He'd take Aaron over on his bike and see if there was an adult in the area before passing judgment. Taking a sip of his lemonade, he stared out the window to the dark garden and wondered if he should go for a run. Sleep wasn't going to come back easily and sitting in the kitchen held no appeal.

He turned to tell Aaron he was headed out when the vision caught him. It was an alley outside a conference hall that he knew. And there, the red-haired woman pulling up on a motorcycle. She parked the bike and sauntered down the alley, fully confident of her safety. She touched the door handle, and he felt the heat of the blast.

"Are you okay? Hey!" Aaron jumped out of his chair. "Are you okay?"

"I've got to go. There's going to be a problem downtown. Get to bed. I'll be back before you leave for school." He kissed Aaron's head before running out the door. "Get some sleep."

CHAPTER SIX

Dear Daddy,

The next time you suggest to the director that I replace the star of a show, I will drop scorpions in your Dior suit. Do not play innocent with me. There are rules in Hollywood, and one of those is that unknown girls who fill in as motorcycle stunt riders don't get offered jobs as lead actresses within twenty-four hours of getting their first job. Don't think I don't see your hand in all of this.

What I'd like to know is: Where did you hide the minions?

They're in the studio, aren't they? Lurking like the little monsters they are in the shadows? Are there minions at my house, Dad?

The minions can't eat intruders. This isn't Texas. California doesn't have the same home defense laws, and I really don't think your genetically altered minion is the same as a dog. That's going to be very hard to prove in court.

I love you, Daddy. I know you just want me to be happy. But can you please call the insane producer back and tell him I can only work one job at a time? I can't be Glee's stunt double and shoot the new episodes they need for Fractured *at the same time. I need sleep!*

Your very busy daughter,
Angela

ANGELA TOSSED THE RED curls of her wig and parked Luiz's bike in the alley behind the conference center. She hadn't put on her Rage getup since arriving in L.A., but tonight the mental screams of terror echoing from the center warranted the kind of investigation that would attract questionable attention.

Tight black jeans, a bright red tank top that matched her hair, and a leather duster that was too heavy for the L.A. heat were a start. She'd added a black domino mask that obscured the shape of her nose and cheekbones when she'd moved to New York, because no one needed to see their favorite schoolteacher beating down the local thugs. The heart and star pendant around her neck—a little invention of Daddy's that would shield her from most things—completed the outfit.

The 'most' still worried her some days.

Terror radiated from the building, escalating until the headache tearing into her brain was a living fire. Whatever was happening, she would hit back. Hard.

Checking to make sure the alley was empty, Angela sauntered towards the back door and hoped someone inside had been kind enough to leave it open. More often than not the people hired to cater at these places would stick a rock in the door to keep it from locking every time they slipped out for fresh air.

If not, she could always pick the lock. Angela sighed. The whole point of moving away from her sisters was to avoid a life filled with crime and superheroes.

Angela reached for the door and someone hit her. A breeze ruffled her wig and she found herself on her back in the alleyway, staring up at a masked man. No hate tainted the aura around him; nothing that suggested that he was dangerous except that he was bigger than her.

She raised an eyebrow. "Hello?"

The man took a deep breath. "Hi." He smelled like mint.

"I'm new to the area, so I'm not familiar with the protocol when you're jumped by a masked man in an alleyway. Is there a secret handshake or something?" she asked sarcastically.

"I'm here to save your life."

Angela looked around for signs of danger. The man was the only thing in the alley, and he was cradling her, hand cushioning her head, muscular arm suspending him in a pushup so his body weight wasn't resting on her.

"Right. What danger am I in, exactly?"

"The door is going to explode and kill you," he said in a very serious tone.

She lifted her head to peer over his shoulder at the door. It was a mistake. The movement meant gyrating under him in his spandex suit, and she caught a whiff of cologne, soap, and clean sweat. His emotions shifted, becoming tinged with desire and arousal.

Angela cleared her throat and lay back down, trying to put space between herself and her captor. "Mmhmm. Tell you what, let me up and I'll help you find your doctor. I bet someone is very worried about you missing your medicine."

The man shook his head insistently. "I had a vision and saw you killed."

"And I had a vision where I won an all-expenses-paid trip to Fiji. That doesn't mean anything is going to happen. Let me get up, please."

"No. It's not safe."

Her patience frayed as the terror inside amped her headache up another notch. "I'm not lying here until I die of starvation because the door might—"

The door exploded.

Blue ice surrounded them like a shield, then, as the last piece of shrapnel fell to the ground in a smoldering pile, the ice receded, leaving frost patterns on the pavement.

"I told you so," the superhero said as he pushed himself up. He was taller than she was and his black costume had jagged blue lightning strikes crossed over it.

Angela smoothed her wig out. "Fine. You have visions. Are they anything useful, like winning lotto numbers?"

"It doesn't work like that."

"It never does." She eyed the smoking wreckage of the doorway. "Care to clean this up?"

"What am I, your maid?"

"And my nanny." Angela stepped towards the door.

"Who are you?"

She pointed. "Cool the hallway off, and I'll tell you."

The hero shot a jet of icy cold air down the wall. Melting metal cracked under the arctic blast.

"Very nice," Angela said, turning her back on him and studying the remains of the door. "Very nice indeed."

* * *

"Who are you?" Arktos repeated. Nothing in his vision had hinted at the fact that the woman would be another superhero. Or quite so... attractive. With their bodies pressed together he'd been far too aware of lithe muscles under him and the subtle spice of her citrus perfume. It clung to him like a phantom hand, stroking his libido.

She gave him a come-hither smile. "I'm Rage."

"Rage?"

"Because I manipulate emotions and enrage people?" She waited with an expectant smile. "It's sort of a joke."

"I've never heard of you."

"Under the circumstances I'm sure I can find it in my heart to forgive you."

He stretched an arm across the doorway, blocking her from stepping into the hall. "You need to go home now."

She patted his cheek. "You're so cute. How long have you been in the business? Three years? Four?"

"Six."

"I've been in it for over twenty, so let's pretend that I know what I'm doing and you're the newbie who still needs training pants. M'kay? Good. I'm glad we had this little talk." She fluttered her eyelashes at him before brushing past, trench coat swaying as she walked.

He stared. "No one has been with The Company for over twenty years. None of the talent, at least." Most heroes didn't survive four years. It was a rough life and he'd only made it so far because he was cautious. He had Aaron to think about.

She threw him a glance over her shoulder. "I didn't say I was with The Company. I said I was in the business."

"Rogue."

"I prefer the term freelance." She shot him a coy smile. "The pay is nothing to write home about, but I set my own hours."

"And what's your talent?"

"I can sense emotions."

He waited for her to add something. When she didn't respond, he jogged along the hall to catch up. "What else do you do?"

"Nothing," she said, resuming her brisk pace.

Arktos's eyebrows went up under his mask. "Do you even know what's going on in there?"

"I hear people screaming in pain and the door was booby-trapped. That's enough for me. It's giving me an ever lovin' headache."

He caught her shoulder and pulled her away from the balcony door. "I don't hear anything."

She didn't flinch under his gaze, or try to pull away. "I hear emotions like you hear words. Most people are just whispers; I can sense their emotion if I really try, but usually it's drowned out by the noise of my own thoughts. This is like having a rock concert under my bedroom window when I have a migraine. People in there are terrified. It's a sustained group emotion and getting worse. Something has them trapped, and some of them are about to die. The human body isn't capable of sustaining stress reactions for prolonged periods of time. It's damaging. Now, is this door going to explode?"

"I don't think so," Arktos said slowly.

"Good." Rage pushed the door open with exaggerated care and peeked inside. "Looks like a concert crowd. Maybe a benefit show of some kind?"

"Henry West was giving a speech here. It's not campaign season yet, but he likes to make the rounds to keep the donors interested."

Her smile was a little cruel. "Lots of old people with money?"

"That sounds about right."

"I see two people on stage. One of them's an emotional manipulator, but I can't tell which, they're too close."

Arktos leaned in, aware he was brushing against her body as he peeked inside. On stage was a blonde in a stunningly short red dress. Next to her stood a man wreathed in flames.

"I think the blonde's the mind-raper. I want to talk to her. She won't be able to manipulate me."

"Because you're special, right?"

He glared at her, trying not to smile when she didn't flinch. "Yes, because I'm special. See if you can get the pyro to hold still while I talk to the blonde."

"I have a better idea." She pulled her jacket off, revealing an angry red wound on her arm with fresh stitches. "Hold this." Tossing her red curls so they caught the light, Rage stepped into the room.

Arktos wasn't sure what he was expecting her to do, but as she moved he was hit by the overwhelming desire to stare at her. Rage fascinated him, the way the light caressed her fiery curls, the graceful curve of her hip. He imagined what her hand would feel like as it stroked him. How soft would her lips be when he kissed her?

He shook his head and refocused on the thieves. One of them was missing. There were always three: the blonde, the pyro, and the bagman who wore a mask. Where was their bagman?

"Attention, ladies and gentlemen! Hello!" Rage waved.

Everyone turned to face her, including the criminals. Arktos eased his way into the shadows by the door and headed for the mind-raper on the stage. Katrina from the head office had sent him a detailed description of the woman who'd molested a child and injured a police officer escaping from Bugman. He hadn't expected her to come here, but he wasn't surprised either. California attracted all sorts of freaks.

"Boys and girls, I hate to break up such a fun party, but Mommy and Daddy need some alone time now. Sweet cheeks"—Rage pointed at the blonde with her Prada bag, no doubt filled with stolen jewelry—"It's not Halloween, you shouldn't be trick-or-treating. Put it down."

The blonde dropped her bag of stolen goodies.

Arktos grabbed it. "Can you get the people out?" The pyro was shaking; if he lost control people would get hurt.

"Show's over!" Rage said.

A strong desire to head for his car washed over Arktos. Then fear, which was buffeted by lust, and followed by terror. The emotions grabbed at him, worse than any childhood night terror, pulling away his focus. Rage and the pyro stood toe-to-toe, staring at each other.

He edged toward the blonde, not quite able to take his eyes off Rage.

Fear made his mouth go dry.

Rage moved without warning, bringing her knee up and dropping the pyro with ball-aching accuracy.

His head cleared and he made a grab for the blonde, but she was already racing off through the crush of fleeing people.

The pyro groaned a curse. "I'm going to kill you."

Rage tilted her head to the side. "So sweet. We've just met and you're already offering me death threats. It's adorable."

"I'm not adorable!" The pyro lunged at Rage.

Arktos moved without thinking, diving between pyro and rogue and throwing up a shield of ice. It steamed.

Something dug into his shoulder. He rolled sideways to see Rage poking him with a booted foot.

"Are you always this overdramatic?"

"He was trying to kill you."

"So throw an ice cage over him, not me!"

"I was trying to protect you."

She rolled her eyes. "How adorably antiquated."

Arktos stood, brushing imaginary dust off his uniform. "I thought the pyro was adorable."

"The pyro is getting away."

He pivoted in time to see the pyro launch himself skyward. Arktos followed, chasing his quarry into the clouds and losing him high above the L.A. skyline. By the time he returned to the crime scene, Rage and her bike were gone.

CHAPTER SEVEN

Dear Mom,

I wish I could come home for the barbecue this weekend, but there's a thing I need to attend for the TV show I'm now acting in. I need a dress, if you have any that you think would fit.

Ever busy,
Angela

SCROLLING THROUGH THE SEARCH results on her phone was a less-than-ideal way to research. Angela bit into her apple and tried again to find anything about the superhero she'd bumped into, but the best she could find were references to a Roman legend about a centaur and the Greek word for 'bear.'

Arktos had darker skin, and maybe black hair—she thought she'd seen it curl out from under his mask. Dark skin, dark hair, a Greek name...

Jacob Kapsimolis winked at her as he swaggered off the set. "They're almost ready for you, gorgeous."

Angela rolled her eyes and finished her apple.

"Are you reading something dirty?" Jacob tried to peek at her screen.

She turned the phone off. "Just playing a game."

He sat beside her on the table under the shade of a tree. "No need to give me the cold shoulder. I'm being friendly." He bumped her knee. "Want to get more friendly?"

"I'm not looking right now."

Someone waved, her red costume fluttering in the slight breeze. "Jacob! And, hi, you must be the new Carla."

"I'm AJ."

"AJ, this is Amarilla, she plays the Scarlet Starlet. The good version of my Red Death," Jacob said.

Amarilla dropped beside her. "I've heard all the gossip about you. Now, give the good stuff." Her eager smile was slightly off-putting.

"What do you want?" Angela asked.

"Why are you here? Who are you with? How'd you get the job? All of it. Oh, and is it true you and Tyler Running Fox had a fling?"

Angela felt her cheeks heat with a blush. She brushed a strand of hair back from her eyes and began inventing wildly. "I, um, I'm from New York. I was... in a relationship, and things went bad. Really bad. So I decided a change of scenery and some time single was the cure. I came to LA, and voila! Here I am."

Amarilla leaned on the table. "Confirm or deny, you are The New York Girl?"

Angela frowned. "What do you mean The New York Girl?"

"Tyler left New York a few years ago," Jacob put in. "All the tabloids said it was because his one true love had spurned him for another man. Now you're here, a girl from New York, and rumor has it he was ignoring Glee for you."

"Oh! No!" Her blush deepened. "No. Um, no. Tyler and I, we, ah, we aren't... aren't anything, really. I think he hates me, actually. We're not friends. At all." She shook her head. "I'm not that girl."

Amarilla leaned in closer. "Who burned you in New York?"

"You probably wouldn't know him," Angela said. She tucked a stray hair behind her ear and tried to remember what Delilah's fictional history said she did. "I was on stage. Strictly chorus stuff, background frippery really. There was scenery with better billing than me."

"And the man behind the heartbreak?"

"Chris," Angela said without thinking. Chris Freeman and his temper were to blame.

Jacob whistled under his breath. "Wow."

"What?"

"Christian Sajemel and Tyler Running Fox were best friends before The Girl." Amarilla bumped her shoulder against Angela's. "I guess Christian's kinks weren't enough to keep you from Tyler's powerhouse." She winked.

"It's not like that at all!" Angela's face burned with more than the hot California sun. "Let's talk about something else. Jacob! Tell me about you. All about you."

Amarilla scooted closer to Angela. "He's named for a bed sheet."

Angela waited for one of them to start laughing. Neither did. "Okay. Now I want you to tell me she's lying."

"She's not," Jacob said. "My mom was a Twihard and obsessed with one of the characters."

"Tell her!" Amarilla urged, clapping. "It's gross!"

Jacob rolled his eyes and grinned in a sheepish way. "Promise to still go out with me after I tell you?" He hit her with a smoldering come-hither look.

Dark eyes? Check. Dark hair? Check. Shameless flirting? That was a new twist. "I didn't promise you a date at all."

He gasped dramatically. "I haven't won you over with my stunning physique yet?"

"Nope."

Jacob sighed. "If you must know, my mother's high school bedroom was decorated entirely with the face of a certain character from the Twilight series who shall remain nameless. I was conceived on sheets bearing his likeness."

"Ewww!" Angela laughed. "Wow."

"That's not the worst part." Amarilla poked Jacob. "Tell her the rest!"

"My mom kept the sheets, and my nursery had the same decorating scheme until I was thirteen." Jacob hissed through his teeth. "Yeah. It's embarrassing."

Angela and Amarilla fell into a fit of giggles.

"Jacob!" someone shouted from the studio's dark interior.

"And that's our cue to go wow them. Do you think you can toss your hair around in the wind?" Jacob asked, holding out a hand.

Angela hesitated.

Jacob stuck out his bottom lip in a pout. "No?"

"It's not you," she hurried to assure him. "It's... I was hurt, and I'm not ready to jump back in the ring." Not to mention that the chances of a rogue and a superhero finding true love were one in a million, and her parents had used that one chance up. On her way to the studio, she tossed her apple core in the outdoor compost bin. Jacob was a perfect Arktos she decided as she watched his movie-worthy rear end saunter off. But was it her imagination, or had he looked bulkier the night before?

She tried to remember being in his arms, the curve of his biceps blocking light and shrapnel from the explosion. Yup, definitely more mass. She'd have to tease him about padding his suit later.

There was a loud crunch behind her. Pivoting slowly, she scanned the empty courtyard. Not even a squirrel managed to get through studio security.

There was another crunch, like something small and warty eating an apple core out of boredom. She knew that sound. Leaning sideways ever so slowly she peeked behind the compost bin and saw the unholy offspring of a frog and a water balloon. It looked like an escapee from a kid's cartoon, a rounded squarish body with spindly arms and legs, bulbous eyes, all in eye-searing orange with blue polka dots. A second-generation minion.

Daddy had sent shock troops.

Of course he had. She grabbed the minion and squeezed. "How many of you are there?"

It tried to squirm out of her hand.

"Tell me, or you're confetti."

"Five!" the minion shouted. "Just five!" Its twiggy arms were surprisingly strong, or would have been if she hadn't been arm-wrestling minions since she was four for pennies.

Angela loosened her grip.

"Can I go now?"

"Oh, you're going all right." Straight back to Texas in the first box she could find. Her father was an excellent man in many ways, but he was a super villain and had been using minions since he was sixteen. Was there such a thing as rehab for minion abuse? *"Learn how to communicate without spies!"* or *"Six steps to not taking over the world and mowing the lawn yourself!"*

Not that she really wanted him to change, she assured herself as she snuck into the wardrobe room and dumped a two-thousand-dollar pair of black sandals onto the floor. It was just hard to maintain cover when hideous mini-monsters started stalking you on set. She stuffed the fussing minion in the shoe box with a sigh.

"AJ?" Jacob's voice filtered through the wall of the dressing room.

"I'll be right there!" She wrapped the box with a belt from the communal dressing table and shoved the minion in her locker to deal with later. The Hollywood promotional machine stopped for no man, woman, or minion.

* * *

Angela's eyeballs were fried. Hair billowing in the breeze sounded like a wonderful concept on paper, but the reality of staring into a fan with an open mouth and enough lip gloss to drown a goldfish wasn't a sexy one.

Jacob winked at her from his chair by the door.

"I thought you were done an hour ago," Angela said.

"I had time to wash the makeup off. Want to go get some dinner? There's this great little Greek restaurant on West Third that you'd love. The dolmades are to die for."

She scuffed her shoe on the cement floor of the studio. "I wish I could."

"But?"

"I'm still filling in as Glee's stunt double and there's another night shoot today. Tonight. Whatever." She rolled her eyes at her own rambling. "I need to take a quick shower and get down there. They still haven't found Glee's wig so I've been standing in for all sorts of random things."

"Why don't they just buy another wig?" Jacob asked as he picked up a black leather riding jacket.

Angela shrugged. "Search me."

He stepped close. "Is that an invitation?"

Angela's heart skipped as she remembered strong muscles cradling her. But she shook her head. "Not tonight." Or any other night. Not between them.

She risked opening herself up to catch his emotions. Frustration and excitement emanated from the next lot over, where Glee's action movie was filming. Jacob seemed quiet, although she caught a whiff of lust and dominance. Jacob brushed her arm with a finger. "I could wait for you to finish."

She stepped away. "That's sweet, but by the time I finish whatever it is I'm doing for Glee, I'm not going to be good company."

"Tomorrow night?"

"You're persistent, aren't you?"

Jacob crowded her again, his body heat making the small hall connecting the studio lots uncomfortably warm. "I always get what I want."

Angela's pulse quickened again, but this time it wasn't pleasant. "Good for you," she said, turning to walk away. "But I just left an abusive relationship and I'm enjoying some quality Me Time. When I'm interested in adding a man to my life, I'll give you a call." Angela left, walking just a little too fast, hoping the brush-off would be enough to cool Jacob down.

He caught up. "I don't get it. I'm good-looking. I'm a nice guy. I'm the friendliest person you've met in LA. Why won't you have dinner with me?"

"Because I'm working two jobs, and I don't want to have dinner with anyone?" Angela shrugged. "This isn't about you. Relationships are a two-part harmony and if one part isn't playing along you can't have a relationship."

Jacob pursed his bright red lips, the remnants of the photo shoot giving him an almost clownish appearance. "I'm a nice guy, but I guess it's true what they say about nice guys finishing last."

Anger mounted. "Real Nice Guys don't pressure girls into dates, guilt-trip them over dumb things, or take someone saying that they don't want a relationship as a personal rejection. If you delivered pizza and I never asked for pizza, couldn't pay for pizza, and didn't want to eat pizza, would you be upset that I didn't take the pizza when you showed up?"

"Did you just compare sex to pizza?"

"Yes." She was practically running as she reached the door to the studio. The stage was set for another motorcycle scene and then some fancy dress party that Tyler was supposed to crash, probably with Glee in tow. Once again, Angela wondered if she could find a script. "Do you see Luiz?" The studio doors were open to the outside, a dingy alley with blue lighting bleeding into the sound stage with two sweeping staircases, a chandelier too glittery to be real, and the pompous air she expected from a library in a Disney movie. "Um..."

"Jacob!" Glee waved from her dressing room door. "Come here, baby!"

"See? She wants my pizza!" Jacob stuck his tongue out and then strutted toward Glee.

"Bless your heart," Angela muttered. Luiz's sharp whistle cut through the air. Angela turned around, looking for someone in black leather riding gear.

A hand tapped her shoulder. "Over here," Luiz said.

Angela frowned as she pivoted. Luiz was wearing a skimpy purple gown with a violent lime green stole. "That's not riding gear."

"The Talent are the only ones on bikes today. And Glee, of course." She snickered at her own joke. "The rest of us are playing Menacing Uninvited Guests at the museum party."

"Oh, the set is a museum?"

"You haven't read the script yet?"

"I keep meaning to do that."

Luiz pushed at her back. "Go get showered and into a makeup chair. And be grateful that they filmed the hot make-out scene already."

Angela shook her head as she retreated. "I really need a script."

CHAPTER EIGHT

Dear Mom,

I know normal people sometimes juggle two jobs, but I don't think they ever juggle two jobs like these. I spent all afternoon staring into burning hot lights with an industrial fan trying to whip my eyeballs out, took a thirty second shower, peeled myself out of the white banana suit, and pulled on a black silk negligee pretending to be haute couture.

I did finally get a script. Without breaking any confidentiality laws, I can firmly say that the writers watched way too many Indiana Jones and James Bond films in their youth. Ty is playing Indibil Riberio, a Brazilian archeologist who is also an agent for Interpol. There's a criminal biker gang, a girl on the run from trouble, and more motorcycles than I ever needed to ride. Tonight's scene involves a bike wreck (onto very soft mats—I checked), a kissing scene in an alley (because Indibil Riberio can't keep his hands off a semi-naked woman—at least that's believable), and then they break into the museum charity ball to steal the Thing! The script doesn't say what the Thing is, but I keep hoping that they're there to rescue a rock-like superhero. Probably not.

And tell Daddy that I sent him a box. It took me all morning to find the minions, but I found four of them and shipped them home priority. Hopefully they won't eat the box and give anyone a scare.

All the love from your very sleep-deprived daughter,
Angela

SHE SENT THE EMAIL as Tafi, the makeup artist, finished turning her into a stunningly edgy beauty her own mother wouldn't recognize. Angela tried standing in the boots wardrobe had provided. "I'm going to break my ankle if I run in these."

Tafi winced. "Boots? With this dress? Wanda? Why is the body double wearing boots?"

"No one will see her legs!" Someone, presumably Wanda, shouted from behind a row of gowns.

"Did you *see* the skirt? They're *supposed* to see her legs!"

Angela stood, tugging the dress down in an attempt to cover her panties. "My legs and everything else. This slit is indecently high." Apparently tonight's shoot called for wearing haute couture's sluttier cousin.

The stylist walked in, pink curls bouncing around bright red, cat-eye glasses. "Lose the panties. She needs to go commando. Find some strappy heels. And somebody paint her toenails red. Glee has red nails. Her body double needs red nails. Think continuity people!"

Tafi gave a put-upon sigh. "Why isn't Glee doing this? I already did her makeup twice for this scene."

"She doesn't ride motorcycles," said the stylist.

"Or run in heels!" someone else shouted.

"Or film," muttered Tafi.

Angela wanted to lay her head down, but Tafi would kill her if she messed up a single curl before the shoot. Never mind that bullets would bounce off her shellacked hair. Tafi and Wanda held a quiet conversation. Fred, the shoes guy, was consulted. Finally Kerry, the lead stylist, was pulled in. Several black dresses that appeared identical to the one she was wearing were held up. She cringed when Tafi held up a strappy black nightmare left over from a BDSM shoot. At least haute couture's slutty cousin had a frill pretending to be a sleeve on the left side. It covered her stitches nicely.

Tafi returned with some strappy black shoes. "These cost more than I earn in a year. Do not break the heels."

"I'm going to break my ankle!"

"Ankles are replaceable. These are not."

Angela sighed mournfully. "I feel so loved."

Tafi shook her head. "Love is for headliners. You are a body double." She strapped Angela's shoes on. "Stand up. Turn. Good. You look like Glee."

"Which isn't the same as beautiful?" Angela guessed.

"You will look beautiful in the movie. Now. Go out there. Shake your shapely self. And pretend to be Glee so we can turn a profit on this. More profit means more rent money."

Angela rolled her eyes. "You're just my pimp, aren't you?"

"Work that money maker!" Tafi ordered as she pushed Angela to the set.

Blue filters covered the lights and Swendon's favorite smoke machines worked overtime to fill the false alley with fog. A motorcycle roared beside her. She jumped, then saw the crew playing with the sound effects panel. What she couldn't see was Swendon, Luiz, or whoever was working as Tyler's body double tonight.

She crossed her arms and waited for direction. A bright light flashed on, making the fog glow, and a motorcycle purred up beside her. The rider had a helmet in place. She smiled. "Let me guess, I need to come with you if I want to live?"

The rider's head shook slowly from side to side. "Get on," Tyler said, his voice muffled by the helmet.

"Why don't you have a stunt double?" She'd grabbed his waist just before he popped a wheelie and spun the bike around. "I hate you."

"Tyler? Tyler?" Swendon swam through the fog. "There you are. Mark, turn off two of those fog machines, this is too much. Okay. We've done the closeups already, but I need a good night shot of you racing away. AJ, do you see those green mats off on the right?"

She nodded.

"Good girl. When Tyler hits his mark, I want you to throw yourself at the mats. He'll slow down enough for you to jump, but he won't stop. Have you done something like this before?"

"Not dressed like this," she said honestly.

"Don't scuff the shoes. They're expensive."

She tightened her grip on Tyler's waist as Swendon walked away. "I know I'm not as important as the shoes, but try not to kill me."

Tyler revved the engine in response and tore down the alley, weaving between marks. As they drew near the mats, he jammed on the brakes.

Angela jumped, throwing herself at the mat and landing hard as she rolled. "Good times," she muttered, climbing to her feet.

"You need to tuck and roll," Luiz said as she held out a hand. "Get it right quick, or we'll be shooting all night."

"Right. Just like gymnastics." She tried to remember the last time she'd jumped off a moving object to save her life. Probably when Blessing decided to drive and wanted to see if a car could fly. She'd thrown herself out of the car into the lake as her sister went off the edge of the pier. The car had flown fine, though the shocks hadn't survived the landing. She walked back to the starting point.

Tyler pulled the bike up beside her. "Want a ride?"

"No. You like to throw me off your bike. Walking's much safer."

"Riding's quicker. Some of us need our beauty sleep."

"I hate to break it to you, Ty," she said, quirking an eyebrow, "but you'll never sleep enough to be pretty."

He gunned the engine and went to wait for her.

She climbed on and he was moving before she could grab his jacket. The bike slowed, barely, and she jumped. With a midair twist she managed a splashy landing on the mats and skidded across them.

"Perfect!" Swendon yelled. "Set up for the next shot. AJ, you're going to be in silhouette. Somebody show her the mark. Only one fog machine. Lights for the scene!"

The lights flickered, changing to illuminate a stretch of wall with a dozen cameras aimed at it. It was like being on the wrong end of the target range. Angela trudged over, leaned against the wall, and tried to ignore the throbbing in her arm.

Tafi dashed forward and fixed the hem of her dress.

Swendon wrinkled his nose. "AJ, try lifting a leg. Good, just like that. Now, breathe hard. You've just run from the bad guys, jumped off a bike, and you're alone and desperate and scared." Swendon clapped and turned to find other prey. "Tyler, stalk through the fog, throw the helmet to the side—not so hard this time—and go over to AJ. I need you to talk, we'll dub in the conversation we recorded this morning. Ready? Set? Action!"

Angela laid her head back on the fake brickwork, hoping it wouldn't crush Tafi's hard work. There should have been footsteps echoing. In the movies there always were. In reality, well, they probably added the sound effects after the filming. All she could hear was the sound of her own breath and the faintest whirring of cameras just past her elbow.

Fog swirled as a backlit hero approached. Pity it was Tyler. She watched him throw his helmet offstage towards the coffee pot. He swaggered toward her, all exaggerated gyrating hips and swinging shoulders. He stopped in front on her, leaned forward. The smell of mint toothpaste and his cologne filled the air between them. For a brief moment she regretted not putting on perfume. He was larger than life; she was a cowering mortal seeking safety.

"Talk!" Swendon screamed from deep in the fog. "Cut! We need lips moving! AJ, say something when he walks up, anything! No, nothing people will lip read easily. Again!"

This time she closed her eyes. Morpheus tempted her to the realm of Hypnos. Sleep... Wonderful, promising, revitalizing sleep.

When she heard the helmet crash she lifted her head. Lips moving... "Would you like to play at questions?"

"How do you play that?" Tyler's voice was as deep and dark as his eyes. If he hadn't butchered *Hamlet*, she might have liked him.

"You have to ask a question."

"Statement." He put a hand on the wall beside her head and leaned in. "One-love."

She shivered in the cold air. "Cheating."

"How?"

"You always end in a Jade's Trick," she shot back, switching to Shakespeare because she couldn't remember the next line of Stoppard's play.

Tyler leaned closer, angling his head so his lips were a breath away. "I haven't started yet."

"I wonder that you're still talking, Signior Benedick. Nobody marks you."

His smile was devastating. It lit up the dark alley and promised to do wicked things until morning light.

Her pulse trilled and she knew she'd forgive him *Hamlet* if he kept smiling like that.

"What? My dear Lady Disdain? Are you yet living?"

"Is it possible Disdain should die while she hath such meet food to feed it as Signior Benedick? Courtesy itself must convert to disdain, if you come in her presence." Giving in to the invitation in his smile, she arched away from the wall.

Tyler rested his hand on her hip, urging her closer. "You and I are too wise to woo peaceably."

Lips near his ears, she whispered, "That's not the next line."

"Cut!"

Reality slammed back full force as Tyler turned away.

Angela stumbled back, gaping at the camera in shock. They'd been alone—at least, it had seemed that way.

Angela shook her head. Obviously the lack of sleep was causing hallucinations. There was no way she'd just zoned out and flirted with Tyler Running Fox, the butcher of *Hamlet*. Nope. Grandma Meredith would roll in all seven of her graves if that had happened. Proper Southern Ladies did not flirt with men who couldn't recite the 'To be or not to be' soliloquy correctly.

"Do you see that smile?" Swendon asked the world at large as he shook Tyler by the shoulders. "That will make us all very, very wealthy men. Why couldn't you smile like that earlier?"

Tyler held up a hand and chuckled.

Angela stared in horror. Heaven forfend, as Othello would say; he chuckled? He was human?

He hit her with another smile, warm, welcoming, the kind of smile that made panties drop. "AJ was seducing me with Shakespeare."

Swendon narrowed his eyes at her. "What?"

"We had a Shakespeare quote-off. I wasn't seducing him. I was... teasing." She nodded. That sounded believable.

A chorus of groans rose up from the cast. "Glee doesn't know Shakespeare," Swendon whined.

Angela smiled sweetly. "Sometimes I don't think Ty does either."

Tyler glowered down at her, but mirth danced deep in his dark brown eyes. "Let's reshoot the scene. I think someone wants to hear the 'To be...' speech from *Hamlet*."

"Done right," Angela confirmed, smirking.

"On your own time," Swendon said. He brushed Tyler's arm. "Where's special effects? Where's Yandel? Why does Tyler have blood on him in this scene?"

Tyler pulled his jacket off in confusion. "It's not mine. He glared at Angela. "Are you bleeding?"

"Um, I shouldn't be? I didn't have any of the special effects blood on me." But her arm hurt. She risked a quick glance. Blood seeped from under a torn stitch.

Tyler brushed her arm, his fingers cold on her pale skin. "What happened?"

"I must have popped a stitch out when I landed."

He motioned for Swendon. "Our stunt lady was improvising."

"AJ!" the director wailed. "Was any of that in the shot? It was such a perfect shot."

"Her arm was away from the camera," Tyler said quickly. He turned his attention back to her. "Why didn't you tell anyone you'd hurt yourself?"

"How did this happen?" Swendon demanded, pushing Tyler aside.

"I cut myself moving into the new apartment. I'm cleared for stunt work. Look, it's only a little blood. There isn't much. It just smeared. I'll pay to get the jacket cleaned if that helps."

Tyler shook his head. "You really are new to Hollywood. The Talent never pays for anything."

Angela glared back. "Then I guess I'm not The Talent. My parents taught me to take responsibility for my actions."

His eyes narrowed into angry slits. "Must be nice to have a couple grand to spend on a jacket."

"A couple grand?" Her voice squeaked.

"That's how much it will cost to replace the jacket." Tyler shrugged. "But you're a pretty white girl. I'm sure Daddy can pay for it. If not, there are plenty of people searching for their next porn star."

Angela rolled her eyes. "Grab a baby wipe from your Whine and Cheese bag, Running Fox. It's just a little blood."

CHAPTER NINE

Dear Mom,

Finding an all-night ER in L.A. isn't hard. I managed to get there and was only lost for, like, five minutes. Eight days in my new city and I've been to the ER! I think that's a family record of some kind. Do I get a trophy?

I'm okay. I ripped my stitches doing a stunt. It's not a big thing. I'm sore and exhausted, but hey, the Cupcake Shoppe was open when I drove past at four in the morning, so I grabbed one. With any luck, I'll be able to sleep until noon without interruption.

Your still tired daughter,
Angela

ARKTOS FOCUSED ON CHILLING the buildings around him so the pyro's fire wouldn't bring the block down and wished for approaching police sirens. This end of town was a victim of the last depression, home to nouveaux rich who had fled during the housing crisis, leaving empty buildings that had slowly filled again with vagrants. Though at least the street people were smart enough to run and hide when a flame-covered maniac attacked.

Another fireball blossomed in Arktos's face. He shot spines of ice at the pyro. The idiot capered backward, letting his heat melt the ice so he was merely splashed instead of skewered. Arktos tried throwing a cage of ice around him. It began steaming immediately.

Gravel crunched behind him.

Arktos pivoted and only instinct kept him from catching a baseball bat with his nose. It grazed his head, leaving his ears ringing. The blonde. Of course, he thought as he jumped to the side. He thought he'd been lucky finding the pyro alone.

Fire roared like a living beast, filling the alley behind him. He fought the fire with ice, but that only produced steam. He turned, trying to focus on putting up a thick glacier wall to cut the pyro out of the fight, and took a bat to the ribs for his inattention. They gave way under the force of the blow and he dropped to his knees.

The blonde swung again, slamming into the side of his knee.

Arktos swallowed a cry of pain and rolled to his back as he entombed himself in ice. He was a triple threat; able to fly, manipulate cold and ice, and heal rapidly, but he still needed time to heal in. If the blonde knocked him out, the pyro would turn him to a charred corpse before he could recover.

The fire outside his blue ice tomb dimmed. Two shadowy figures leaned over him and he felt heat on his back. Wiggling so he had some elbow room, he hit his knee, forcing the joint painfully back into place. He tried breathing and choked on blood. Broken rib. Wonderful. At least he'd be able to run in a few minutes.

His head spun as terror gripped him. This was it. He was going to die. Some dim corner of his mind shouted at him that this feeling wasn't his, that the terror was alien, but the fear flared higher, consuming the voice, consuming everything. He clawed at the ice, desperate to escape. He couldn't die like this. Wouldn't. Aaron needed him to come home.

A third person walked into sight. The ice distorted his view, warping the image so he could only see rippling lines, but even through the ice, he could make out the black and red costume—and the sudden drop in his terror levels—that had to mean Rage.

Arktos slammed his fist into the ice, punching his way free. She wasn't a triple threat and there was no way he was going to let some unprotected empath try to take down the pyro alone. He fought the pain and fear and ice until a swell of peace blanketed him.

Exhausted, he let his head drop back to the ground and saw the fleeing pyro burning bright as his ice cage melted away. "This was not the plan." His ribs scorched. He turned to his good side and saw blood.

"Tell me about it. I hate having my beauty sleep interrupted." Rage bent over and picked up something silver that glittered in the pre-dawn light. "Cinderella left us a present."

She walked the battle lines looking for more loot before coming over to him and dropping to her haunches, dangling the silver earring above him. "Beautiful little trinket, isn't it? Silver or platinum, custom-made, expensive... I think I'll keep it."

Arktos winced as he tried to sit. "Give me the earring."

"I have contacts who can find out who made this and who bought it. I doubt you do. But, if you're very nice to me and keep talking, I might be persuaded to share my information."

He grinned through the stabbing pain in his side, panting only a little as bones shifted. "Are you going to scribble your phone number on my hand?"

She tossed the earring up, caught it in her gloved hand, and tucked it away in her pocket. "Do you know that little ice cream shop up on the Pacific Highway? The one near the overlook?"

Taking a shallow breath, he nodded.

"I like to drive up there at nights, watch the waves without the city all around me. I'll be there Friday. Maybe we can bump into each other, if you're out of the hospital."

"De nada. It's all good. I'm healing. Give me fifteen minutes and I'll only be sore." He reached out a hand. "Give me the earring."

"Not happening."

He coughed and winced again.

She raised an eyebrow. "That's a convincing impression of a pierced lung you're doing."

He smiled up at her. "For someone who missed her beauty sleep, you look great."

"And a concussion? Are there any other injuries I should tell the EMTs about when I call the ambulance?"

"Give me fifteen minutes." Arktos forced himself to sit upright, his muscles burning. "It'll hurt like hell, but I've had worse."

"When?"

"I was twelve..." He gasped and pressed his side. "I was twelve and my mom decided that taking a baseball bat to my head was a good way of reminding me how much she hated parenting me." Any other time he might have shrugged it off, but right now he couldn't work up the energy to move. "After lying on the floor overnight I woke up with a headache and the munchies. I blamed it on a bad dream until I saw the blood. This is better. I'll be hungry and sore, but that's it."

"Well, if I'd known this was just a midnight munchie run I would have brought cupcakes."

"I hate cupcakes. Your choices are either vanilla or chocolate and I hate both."

Rage leaned over him, crimson lips drawing his attention. "Blackberry-lime cupcakes."

Arktos chuckled, regretting it instantly as bone sawed at the muscles on his side. Definitely broken. "Why does 'blackberry-lime' sound like a pick-up line?"

"Because you're a male under age eighty. I could probably say 'antidisestablishmentarianism' and make you think about sex." She took his hand. "How about I stay here for a bit, just to make sure you recover enough to get yourself home."

"This isn't a death watch," he said through gritted teeth. Super healing. What a bad idea! Instead of letting a doctor pick out the organic shrapnel while he slept, his body pushed it out like an infection as new bone grew on the rib. His world narrowed to a point of shining light on the roofline where the first rays of dawn hit the metal trim. Pain swallowed him down into the darkness.

And then he felt suddenly light, like floating on a warm, lazy river, drifting away from the world.

"I'd worry less if you were talking," Rage prompted.

Arktos focused on the woman beside him. She was lovely, in a violent kind of way. The black leather trench coat had to be hot in sweltering L.A., but the humidity made her red silk cami cling in all the right places. Deep summer-sky eyes studied him intently. His hand shook. She'd come out here, alone, to save him. The pyro could have killed her—she had to have known it was a risk—but she'd still come to his rescue. The irony was enough to kill him.

He laced his fingers with hers. "What's your name?"

"What's yours?"

"You first."

Her smile turned seductive. "Statement. One-love."

He blinked.

"It's from *Rosencrantz And Guildenstern Are Dead*. The Question Game?" She waved her free hand airily. "At the university we made a game of reciting it to see who knew it best, but don't worry, most people don't know it."

"I know the play," he said. "I just don't expect beautiful women to start quoting Tom Stoppard at me instead of giving me their names."

"Ah. Well then." Her smile was wry, flirting but mischievous at the same time. He could get used to a smile like that.

"And I don't know the next line."

Rage grimaced. "I'm not sure I remember it either. Let me think." She muttered a few lines under breath, casually rubbing at her ribcage.

He tried to disentangle his hand when he realized what was happening. Rage could make people feel things, and she could feel other people's emotions, and now it seemed she could take some of it away. The same pathways in the brain that registered emotion would respond to pain, wouldn't they?

"Let go," he whispered, not wanting to see her hurt. He tried harder to pull his hand away. "Stop it. I know what you're doing."

Rage arched a delicate eyebrow over her domino mask.

"You're taking—" The need to breathe cut him off.

"That's right." The pain ebbed away into nothingness. "I just took one year of your life away."

"Don't play the coy ingénue and quote *The Princess Bride* at me. You're going to kill yourself doing that."

"Kill myself by exciting your serotonin receptors? Somehow I doubt that."

"Empaths are like fire bugs, they can overload. Go insane. Burn out." He stared at the city lights reflecting off the smog overhead. "That's what's wrong with the pyro. He's about to burn out. If I can't get him in an isolation ward soon he will do his best impression of a firework and leave chunks of burned pyro all over the city."

"Graphic and unpleasant details that you should have mentioned sooner."

"Uh huh." He closed his eyes.

"Hey now! Stay with me here."

"Why?" He meant to ask why she was helping him but it was too hard to form the words. So easy to fall asleep.

Everything would be better tomorrow.

Her thumb caressed the sensitive skin on the palm of his hand. "Don't leave me. You're the only man who's made me laugh in years. You're kind."

"Says the woman who's known me for how long?"

"I can read emotions. It's there, all of it. Your worry for people, all the drives and concerns, all your insecurities. Simmering away just beneath the pain."

"Is that supposed to make me feel better?" he asked, voice rasping.

"What do you want to talk about?"

"Not me or my bare-naked emotions!"

"Do you want to talk about you being bare-naked?"

He opened an eye. Rage smirked, waggling her eyebrows in a suggestive way made famous by silent film. "No."

She sighed dramatically. "As you wish. Would you like to play at questions?" She held on tighter. "The next line is, 'What's your name when you're at home?'"

Arktos quit fighting. "What's yours?" Another cough shook him, but the pain was minimal.

"When I'm at home?"

"Is it different at home?"

"What home?" Rage shot him a triumphant smile that dared him to keep the game up as his muscles spasmed around the break.

Pushing himself into a sitting position, he asked, "Haven't you got one?"

"Why do you ask?" Rage stood and brushed dirt from her black jeans.

He stood too, wincing as he tested his knee. "What are you driving at?"

"What's your name?"

He smirked back. "Repetition. Two-love. Match point."

Rage stepped closer. "Who do you think you are?"

"Rhetoric. Game and match." He took her hand back. "A kiss for the winner?"

"I don't remember that part of the play."

"I'm improvising." Arktos brushed a stray hair back from her eyes. It felt like a wig, and the too-blue-to-be-true eyes were probably contacts. He couldn't bring himself to care. She'd been there to defend him. He traced her jaw line. "A kiss for the winner."

"Who won?"

"Does it matter?" he whispered, leaning forward.

She met him halfway.

Arktos slid his free hand behind Rage's neck as she pressed against him. He ran his tongue across her lips and they parted, inviting him in.

Her hands rested on his shoulder, fingers kneading the muscle as she pulled him deeper into the kiss.

Arktos slid his hand under her jacket, feeling the sweat of the hot night and the thin layer of silk between him and her skin. He slanted his mouth, taking more. Demanding more.

She tasted of lime and vanilla, an exotic confection meant for him alone.

With a little gasp she pushed away. Her eyes were wide, her breath coming rapidly, cheeks flushed as if they'd done more than kiss. She shook her head to clear it, then came back to him.

Her kiss was desperate and raw, as though she could steal his soul and all the secrets of the universe with a touch of her lips.

Arktos leaned against the hot bricks behind him and lifted her, needing to feel the weight of her. Their tongues met again and this time he felt her control slip. It started as a strange warmth on his arms where skin touched skin, gliding over him until he was caught in a torrent of emotions. He felt her hunger for more, loneliness mixed with lust, desire warring with fear.

He pulled her tight against his chest in an attempt to comfort her. The need to protect her and drive away those fears was almost stronger than the need to know every inch of her. Almost.

But not here. They had to go somewhere quiet. Somewhere private. *Not home*, he thought as she bit his lip and slipped out of his hands.

Cold surrounded him as she withdrew. "Rage?" He held out a hand, inviting her back.

She stepped farther away, shaking her head. "No. No. It ends here."

"Ends?" He pushed away from the wall and pursued her. "What do you mean it ends here? It's only just started."

"This... Us? We are a bad idea. This can't happen." She wiped the back of her hand across her mouth. "We can't be together."

"I don't understand. Why not?"

She licked her lips, eyes drowning him with regret. "You can't give me what I want."

All the air left his lungs. You aren't what I want. His mother had used those words again, and again, and again. Go away. I don't want you. A rhythm as familiar as his own heartbeat. "What do you want?"

"A family. A husband, some kids, maybe not the white picket fence or a farm, but I want a family and you work for The Company. I can't be with you for the same reason I can't sign with them. I'd have to give up all I ever wanted, and I won't." She tugged at the edges of her trench coat, wrapping it around herself. "I'm sorry."

Arktos stared, trying to bring his defenses back up. "Kids? Isn't..." He took a deep breath, feeling his muscles mend and his heart break. "You know you can't, don't you? That's why it's part of The Company contracts. All superheroes are sterile. The same mutation that allows me to fly makes it so I can't father children."

She rolled her eyes. "What utter bunk."

"Bunk?"

"Southern Ladies don't swear."

She took a tentative step toward him, hand reaching out to caress his arm. "Superheroes can have babies."

He caught her hand and brought it to his mouth for a kiss. "I wish we could, but every one who's tried has died or been unable to conceive."

"That's not true."

"Do you have proof?" Every nerve was alive with the need to remove the space between them and kiss her again.

"I have proof."

Rage kissed him, and he tasted the salt of her tears. He let her go.

"My name is Angela. I'm the oldest of five children, and my daddy is a super villain."

CHAPTER TEN

Dear Mom,

What did Maria do? I've read your email twice and I think you let Gideon encrypt it because there's no way Maria has given up being the evil overlord of South America to work for the U.S. Forestry Service. Things like that don't happen in the rational world. Granted, my world has been less than rational lately, but that's because I gave up all pretense of having a brain and moved to California to work in Hollywood!

That came out wrong.

I'm happy here, really. Everyone is very friendly and the job isn't bad. There are worse jobs. I miss teaching. I miss feeling like I contributed something good to society. But I pay my rent and, for some reason, I have fans. I hope they're normal people and not... Well... Never mind. Least said soonest mended.

Your daughter who would prefer not to be a sex object,
Angela

SOME FLIGHT OF INSANITY had suggested that a run after Angela woke up would make everything better. Never mind the heat index of 105, or the ninety percent humidity, or the fact that she was supposed to be shooting night scenes for *Fractured* all week and should sleep until five.

No, she'd woken up at eleven and gone for a run.

At least the cop car that had been trailing her had finally turned off. The poor officer was probably worried that she was going to get heatstroke, which wasn't actually that farfetched an assumption, Angela thought as sweat dripped down her face. But half a mile ahead she could see the twinkling gem that was her destination: Cupcakes, a teeny tiny little building with a vacant lot next door that had been turned into an urban garden. It was the home of blackberry-lime cupcakes and worth the five mile run each way.

Angela put on one last burst of speed as 'I Am Not That Girl' by the Brutal Cheerleaders started. *I am not that girl. I can't be the one you want. I'll never fall that far. I am not that girl.*

Reaching Cupcakes, Angela paused to wipe the worst of the sweat off her face with her shirt, then opened the door and walked into the arctic chill of the bakery. The sharp contrast from the heat rose goosebumps on her skin, and tempting vanilla scented the air. It was a little piece of heaven, and for the moment it was all hers; the two small tables near the front window didn't exactly invite customers to linger. Angela pulled out her earbuds as the bell over the door jangled again. "A blackberry-lime and some water from the tap, please," Angela told the girl at the counter.

"Blackberry-lime and ice water," said a deep voice from behind her.

"Right." The girl stared past Angela, fingers suspended over the register.

Angela turned and looked up at Tyler Running Fox. He glanced at her and dismissed her without recognition. Angela suppressed an eye roll and turned back to the shop girl, still frozen in place. "Cupcakes?" Angela prompted.

"Uh-huh." The girl blinked rapidly. "Is that Tyler Running Fox?"

"No, it's Harry Dresden," Angela snapped. "Can I have my cupcake, please?" She rubbed at the goosebumps that still prickled her arms.

"Sure." Abruptly, the girl remembered how to use the cash register and rang them up as the same order.

Angela tried to catch her eye to say something, but the girl was staring open-mouthed at Ty again. Grudgingly, Angela slapped a twenty down. "Keep the change." Not that there was much. They were not cheap cupcakes. She could probably make a batch for the price of one if she wanted to, but that would require complicated equipment like muffin tins and a citrus zester. Cookies were easier.

Tyler stood by the door, staring out the window but not seeming to look at anything in particular. The area was full of tiny bookstores, art galleries, and eateries started by people with a bit of seed money and whole lot of dreams. It was hard to picture Tyler in that crowd. If he had dreams, they were the kind where he debated what country he wanted to buy when he filmed his next movie.

"Can I have my water?" Angela asked. The girl blushed and hurried away. Angela picked up the spare cupcake and walked over to Ty. "Here." From her earbuds the Brutal Cheerleaders crescendoed into the chorus: *I am not that girl. I am not the woman in your dreams. I am not the one holding on. I am not that girl.*

He glanced down at her with a frown.

She rubbed her arm again as she waited for him to match her face to the one he'd almost kissed on the movie set.

"Thanks." He nodded at her earbuds. "You've got good taste in music."

"Um, thanks." Angela wasn't sure what she'd been expecting. Maybe a, "Hi, AJ." Or a smile. Recognition, at least. Shaking it off, she grabbed her water and stepped back into the all-embracing warmth of the L.A. sunshine and smog. Heat kissed her skin.

Basking in the warmth, she sipped her water and devoured her cupcake. Angela tossed the wrapper into the little garden next to the shop, where the seeds pressed into the paper lining would become another round of cheerful, heat-resistant flowers. The orchids were her favorite.

After one last sip of water, she dumped the rest over her head and tossed the cup in the recycling bin. A stray thought tickled her senses; someone was watching her intently. She looked around, but saw only Ty, standing in the window, completely absorbed with nibbling at his cupcake. Weird.

By the time she arrived home her legs were shaking and the cupcake just a memory.

Mia and Aaron glanced up from the front step of the apartments where they were reading their textbooks. "Hey," Mia said. "How was your run?"

"Good." She sat down next to them. "Homework? Isn't school out yet?"

"Two more weeks," Mia said.

Aaron grumbled, "Finals."

"Can you help us? The teacher told us to read chapters seventeen and eighteen because they're on the final, but we haven't covered them in class yet."

"It makes no sense," Aaron said. "All I see are letters."

Angela nodded. "Yeah, let me get a quick shower."

"Real quick," Aaron pleaded. "My brother's coming in an hour."

She nodded again. "The fastest shower ever."

And it was. The water heater was broken for the third time this month but the pipes weren't well buried, so the water was still warm enough. She raked a brush through her wet hair, pulled on the first shirt and shorts she could find, and dashed back downstairs.

Mia giggled. "Nice shirt."

Angela glanced down at the white tee that had ZEPHYR GIRL emblazoned on it in sparkling blue letters. "What? It was my mom's. I like it."

"Help!" Aaron shoved his book at her. "What is this supposed to mean?"

They were still working on chapter seventeen when Aaron's brother roared up the street on his bike. Aaron groaned. "I gotta go. He has to work tonight. Can I come back for chapter eighteen? Please?"

"Yeah, I should be around this weekend." Angela smiled fondly at him and handed the book over. "Call Mia and she can get a hold of me."

Aaron shoved his books carelessly in his bag and put on his helmet. "Bye, Mia!"

"Bye!"

Aaron's brother waved too.

* * *

"Get a shower," Arktos said, tossing Aaron's bag against the wall. "I have work to do."

Aaron ran off upstairs as Arktos plucked old binders from the bookcase and piled them on the table. Every superhero started their career by interning at the main offices on the east coast; he'd gone to NYU on their dime and worked at the offices scanning copies and filing paperwork in his free time. It would have been mind-numbing if the subject hadn't fascinated him: the whole history of superpower mutations had been collated in the four years he'd been there. He'd read about the first superpowers, about the heroes and the villains, about the ones that got away and the ones who were laid to rest in a quiet cemetery outside the city.

During his last semester, Katrina, the Company boss, made the move to a paperless office. He'd been in charge of shredding everything. The binders he retrieved now were filled with the papers that had escaped the purge, mostly original profiles handwritten by the heroes he'd always admired. He set the last of them on the table and flipped through the binder full of villains.

My daddy is a super villain.

Males and females alike stared back at him as he turned the pages. They weren't ugly, per se—the mutation seemed to grant good looks to most of them—but none looked like the kind of person you'd call 'Daddy.'

And then there was the other thing: most people didn't introduce themselves as the oldest unless they'd grown up with their siblings. Most. It was a gamble, but something about the way Rage had said it made him think she'd grown up in a nuclear family. That was her dream after all: mom, dad, the kids, maybe a dog.

The water shut off upstairs, and he considered her accusation that The Company was lying about children. Having Aaron around was already violating part of his contract. But what else was he supposed to do? Grandma could barely take care of herself, and Aaron was always getting into fights or ditching school. Moving him off the reservation to a private school in L.A. had made sense.

At least it had when he'd moved Aaron out two years ago. Since his little brother insisted on getting kicked out of every school in a thirty-mile radius, his prospects had dwindled to a single over-crowded public school on the poor end of town.

Aaron fit in perfectly. They'd grown up poor.

And letting him date Mia seemed to be a good choice so far. Mia was a level-headed kid and her tutor...

Arktos took a deep breath and rubbed his still-tender ribs. He'd almost driven straight past Mia's house because all he'd seen were long tan legs in too-short shorts. With her hair wet like she'd just stepped out of the shower, his mind had gone from brotherly concern for Aaron to tallying up his ten best pickup lines. And then swung straight to guilt, because he was mentally cheating on Rage, who didn't want him anyway.

He leaned his head back. The stuccoed ceiling offered no inspiration for his women troubles. Beautiful blondes; there were two too many in his life right now.

Forcing the memory of Rage's kiss from his mind, he opened the second binder, full of the forgotten ones. The super villains who got away, the superheroes who went rogue, all the people who had dropped off the radar for whatever reason.

Most of them weren't even in the computer system. No one had felt the need to file the cold cases. But some of them were promising: at the very back of the binder was a model photo, a handsome man in a three-piece suit who was smiling at the camera like his career depended on how many people swooned. At the bottom of the same page, Arktos had tucked an old print photograph of a blonde woman with a warm smile and the words ZEPHYR GIRL printed across her white shirt in metallic blue.

He took the photograph out and set it to the side. Doctor Charm and Zephyr Girl were in the wrong folder. They were both dead, killed in an explosion at Doctor Charm's lab during a fight.

The smile on Doctor Charm's face drew his attention, though. Rage had the same chin, a similar bone structure. And Charm was the sort of villain someone would take as a lover too.

"Hey," Aaron said as he headed for the fridge. "What's for dinner?"

"What are you making?"

"A sandwich." Aaron stopped to look over his shoulder. "Nice job, big brother. Did you get her phone number?"

Arktos's forehead crinkled in confusion. "Whose?"

"Angela's." Aaron reached down to grab Zephyr Girl's photo. At Arktos's stumped expression, Aaron wiggled the picture. "Mia's tutor? The hot chick teaching me math? The one with the legs you were staring at?"

Arktos colored and snatched the photograph away. "That's Zephyr Girl."

"Really?" Aaron shrugged. "Then AJ is her clone. Barbie doesn't have outfits that match that perfectly."

Arktos looked at it again. "Rage said her name was Angela, and that her father was a super villain," he told Aaron as the pieces slowly fell into place.

"Did she mention her mom was a superhero? That's the sort of thing I'd mention."

Arktos flipped the pages to check the death dates of the hero and villain. "Go upstairs. Get the blue book in my closet, the big one."

"Okay." Aaron gave him a long, critical look.

"Hurry!"

Aaron ran and came back with the book. "What's in here?"

"Superhero missions. It's one of the books Katrina wanted tossed because of water damage, but I managed to find somebody who could redo the binding. Check page ninety-two, I think that's it. Operation Poisoned Apple."

"Sounds cheerful," Aaron said as he sat and turned the pages. "Here it is." He slid the binder across the table.

Arktos studied the photographs. "What's it say?"

"Ah, not much, it's a summary of an operation that was busted. Some heroes went rogue and wanted to kill the kids of super villains, but it was busted up by some heroes. Um, why can super villains have kids if you can't?"

Arktos pressed his lips together. "Good question. Are there any names?"

"Rolling Shock. The Rainbow Dane." Aaron chuckled. "Oh, here, Zephyr Girl; she's the one who broke the ring up after going undercover as a rogue."

"Year?"

"Twenty-twelve."

Arktos's heart skipped. What did this mean? He held the photograph out to his brother and caught his gaze. "Aaron," he said slowly. "Zephyr Girl died. In 2005."

CHAPTER ELEVEN

Dear Mom,

I'm trying to picture Maria joining the U.S. Forestry Service and I'm drawing a blank. The mind boggles.

By the way, do you have Delilah's work number? I asked her to look into something for me and she's refusing to answer her cell phone. I need to talk to her ASAP.

Love,
Angela

THE APARTMENT WASN'T MEANT for pacing, but Angela tried anyway. Five steps to one corner, six steps to the next—three if she didn't want to go into the kitchen—five, six... "Delilah, pick up your phone!" Picturing her sister diving for the ringing cell didn't do any good. Delilah's playback tune circled around for its second replay, because everyone wanted to spend their night listening to orchestral arrangements.

"Hello?"

Angela squeezed the phone. "Delilah! Where have you been?"

"At work."

Angela checked the clock. "Isn't it a little late for work?"

"I had to go back to the office after a funeral." Delilah sighed on the other end of the line. "Is someone going to die if I ask you to call back next week?"

"Maybe."

Delilah paused. "Someone we like?"

Angela bit her lip. "Yes?"

"Angela, what are you doing over there? I thought you were supposed to be lying low and keeping out of trouble."

"I'm not in trouble. I'm observing trouble. There's a big difference." She resumed pacing. "There's... It's complicated. I'm sorry. Whose funeral were you at?"

"Midwestern Fury's; he was the main superhero for Chicago."

"And you killed him?"

"No. I went to his funeral to see if I could find his killer. He's the second superhero we've lost this year."

Angela checked the phone to make sure she had the right number. "Why do you care? I thought you were firmly anti-hero."

"I am, but the same big game hunters who go after superheroes like to hunt my big name clients. I told you about that stalking case back in February. I think it's the same person, or the same group. Atlanta's Golden Hunt is the name the man gave me, but I still don't have enough evidence to hand the case over to the police and get them shut down."

"They hunt humans?"

"Just apex predators in general, but to join they need to kill a human, yes." In the background Angela could hear the soft clicking of a keyboard. "The stalker and I had a good chat before the police arrived. All right, I have your data. The earrings are custom work made by Jorge Fidel out of Brooklyn. He made two sets of twisted silver and platinum—good call on that. One set is still in the Brooklyn showroom, the other was sold to Tyler Running Fox. According to the gossip, he gave them to his girlfriend."

"Ty doesn't have a girlfriend," Angela blurted out. She rolled her eyes at herself and continued. "At least not that anyone's mentioned to me."

"Glee Keni? The actress?" Delilah made an exasperated sound. "Why am I the one who knows who's dating who in Hollywood when you're the one who lives there?"

Angela shrugged and readjusted the phone. "I've worked on set with both of them. If they're dating then it's a low-key relationship."

Delilah snorted. "Wishful thinking, kiddo. In the past month, a man acting as Running Fox's agent has purchased close to a million in jewelry for Glee. Rings, necklaces, lots of bracelets." More clicking followed. "Hmmm. Does Running Fox have a gambling problem?"

"Not that I'm aware of, why?"

"His net worth is a fraction of what it should be. Let me check... Good grief. He spends an estimated ninety percent of his income on charity. That's ridiculous."

"Ten percent of his income is probably more than normal people earn in ten years." Angela flopped on her couch. "So, I guess that confirms most of my worst fears."

"Oh? Am I missing some sisterly gossip?"

Angela mumbled under her breath, and then with a sigh, told her sister about the pyro and Arktos. "Both are familiar. I knew I'd bumped into them before, but this just makes it worse. The blonde dropped the earring. She and Pyro are close. I guess it makes sense that it's Glee and Tyler. And Jacob told me when we first met that he was a superhero."

"You don't sound certain."

"Jacob... He's nice. I guess. I don't know. He gives off a weird vibe sometimes. Very possessive. Very controlling. Arktos isn't like that."

"It could be that he feels like a different person in uniform. Or maybe Jacob is a superhero but isn't Arktos. Either way, you need to stay away from them."

"I know." She crossed her arms. "I told Arktos it wouldn't work. That we couldn't... anything, really."

"Good, because you can't. Not without blowing your cover sky high. He's Company, Angela. They're monsters."

She rolled her eyes. "One day that attitude is going to get you into trouble. No," she said over her sister's protest. "Skip it. What about Travys? Have you found out anything about him?"

"He's buried deep. The case never made it to public records. I'll work on it tonight after I go over the data I collected from the funeral."

"Delilah, this Golden Hunt thing. Don't try to attract their attention. Okay?"

"Would I do something like that?" Delilah asked with an air of innocence.

"Yes."

"Meh. I'll be careful. I'm collecting data in my role as a security advisor. I'll let the police handle everything. I'll call you when I have something on Travys."

"Okay. Love ya. Bye."

"Bye."

Angela stared at the silent phone. It took her a moment to realize she was holding her breath. She shivered as she forced herself to draw oxygen into her lungs. Poor Travys. Poor her. Why couldn't The Company just leave her alone? All she wanted was a normal life: a job, PTA meetings, maybe someone to go to the movies with on a Friday night.

There was a knock at the door before it swung open. "AJ, you need to lock up. This is L.A.," Luiz said as she walked in. "What are you doing?"

"Um." Angela waved the phone. "Waiting for a phone call and moping."

Luiz's forehead wrinkled. "Is everything okay?"

"Yeah. I guess. It's just... family stuff." Angela shoved her phone under the couch pillow. "What do you need?"

"Mia's school is holding a fundraiser tonight at the Salsa Bar. The whole charter school funding thing. I'm trying to drum up some support." Luiz did a quick rumba step. "Want to go dance?"

"Sure. I..." Well, why not? It was better than moping. "Yeah. Sure. How much is it?"

"Twenty-five will get you in, but all donations go to the school fund so they can buy the old building. If they can get enough by July first they can open the school after Labor Day in September." Luiz gave her a cheesy grin. "How's that for a sales pitch."

Angela smiled back. "I'll grab some cash."

"Great! I'm going to go knock on some more doors. I put flyers up at the studio but the Salsa Bar is the low-rent district and I don't think we're going to get a great turnout."

"I promise to put on something pretty and flirt with anyone who makes eye contact as I drive over. With my helmet on. Visor down."

Luiz rolled her eyes. "Very helpful. Thank you."

Angela retrieved her phone and went to raid her closet for dancing clothes. She didn't own much in the way of flirty, super-short skirts, and she wasn't going to wear a skirt on her bike anyway. Instead she grabbed tight white jeans and a shimmering blue blouse with an asymmetrical hem. If the party got really hot she could kick off the jeans and just wear the shirt as a super-short dress. She pulled it on and did a practice turn in the mirror. It covered all the important bits. Good enough.

It took thirty-five minutes to work her way through L.A. traffic to the little shack on the beach that served up Latin dance music, south-of-the-border food, and the best selection of homemade salsa in the state of California. Angela found herself checking her side mirrors the whole way, watching for a familiar black bike. But if Arktos was out tonight, he wasn't on her side of town.

Which was good, she reminded herself. They'd kissed. That was it. It was time to laugh it off and move on.

Angela parked her bike at the end of a long row, trying to make sure she wouldn't get boxed in. Mia was on door duty, smiling winningly with the line of people dropping twenties into her cash box and flirting with Aaron, who sat beside her with a proprietary air.

Mia waved when she saw Angela. "Hey! I wasn't sure you were coming."

Angela smiled. "I wasn't, but your mom dragged me out of the house. How's the fundraising going?"

Aaron grimaced and Mia's smile turned brittle. "It could be better."

Angela fished an envelope filled with cash out of her pocket. "Here, see if that helps."

Mia started counting. "Holy mother of... AJ! Where did you get this?"

Aaron took the envelope from Mia and counted. "Did you kill somebody?"

"My sister sent me some cash to help me set up a new house. I figured I have a job. I don't need handouts."

"What does your sister do?" Mia asked.

Angela looked at the envelope filled with money taken off drug runners when Maria had taken over South America. "She's in law enforcement."

"I'm going to be a cop when I grow up," Aaron announced. "This is bank."

"Will it help?"

Mia nodded eagerly. "This gets us a lot closer. Thank you." Salsa music wafted out into the sultry evening air.

"You should go dance," Aaron said, nodding toward the door. "My brother's in there complaining because no one knows how to tango."

Angela laughed. "And I'm supposed to find him how? Is he wearing his helmet?"

"Can you tango?" Aaron asked.

"I learned in college. There was a competitive dance team. It was basic stuff, but it was fun."

"Go inside!" Mia ordered. "No one's dancing. It's worse than a freshman social."

"I'll tell my brother to come say hi to you!" Aaron called after her.

As soon as she opened the door, Angela was hit by the savoury smell of grilling meat and hot chiles. All the tables had been pushed to the side to open up the dance floor, but everyone was avoiding it. Shrugging off her riding jacket, Angela worked her way through the crowd, searching for Luiz.

"AJ!" Luiz's hand waved over heads. "Over here!"

"Hey," Angela said as she pushed her way to the bar past a group of men arguing the baseball season. "You've got a good turnout."

"Everyone's paying minimum cover," Luiz said. "The Salsa Bar takes five per head, plus the cost of food, so five people make a hundred dollars."

Angela did a quick head count. "You're going to need another fundraiser."

"Don't I know it!" Luiz took her drinks from the bartender and paid him. "We staked out a table over in the corner. Here, take this." She shoved a pink drink into Angela's hand and led the way.

A tall Latino man met them halfway and took the drinks. "AJ," said Luiz, "This is my brother, Miguel. Miguel, AJ David."

He set the drinks down on a table and held out a hand. "My friends call me Mikey, but you can call me Lover."

Angela shook his hand, and he pulled her toward the table. She pushed back. "Thanks, but Mikey is fine. I'm not in the market for a boyfriend right now."

"Who said anything about dating?" Mikey asked as he let her go and opened a beer. "I just want to give you a proper L.A. welcome."

Luiz smacked him upside the head. "Ignore him," she told Angela. "And you," she said, rounding on her brother, "no more beers. You're in enough trouble."

"It's just one!" Mikey protested. "I'm not driving! Let me relax."

Ignoring the bickering siblings, Angela scanned the room for familiar faces. Jacob was on the far side of the room. He held up a drink when she caught his eye and winked at her. She waved. So. He really was a superhero after all. That was... weird. She tried to picture kissing Jacob. It didn't work. Arktos? No problem, she dreamt about that, but superimposing Jacob over Arktos's mask still felt wrong.

"Mikey!" Tyler Running Fox caught her off-guard and she almost stepped on his foot when she turned. "Luiz. AJ. How's things?"

"Hey, Tyler," Luiz said as Angela slid out of the way. "I didn't expect to see you here."

He shrugged. "I saw the flyers and thought I'd help."

"Tyler!" Mikey raised his beer. "How is my favorite stunt face?"

Tyler chuckled. "I'm good. I've missed having you on set though."

"I bet you did," Mikey said. "Who was riding for you?"

"I did my own stunts while you were gone. It wasn't a big thing." Ty's gaze slipped her way and Angela shrunk back, bumping the wall with her shoulder blades.

Mikey took the opportunity to grab her hand. "What do you think, sweet thing? Would you rather go riding with me or Tyler here?"

"Um." Angela licked her lips and tried to find a polite reply. The room was too crowded. There were too many emotions and too many thoughts, too many people sizing her up like a prize cow at the auction. Pyro. She struggled not to say it aloud as she forced the tangled emotions aside.

"AJ's been riding with me all week," Tyler said. "Consider it the perks of staying sober and employed." He picked a pretzel out of Luiz's bowl with a smile.

"Luiz!" Angela said, desperate to escape. "Do you dance?"

"Not if I can avoid it," Luiz said as another tango began.

On the other side of the room she could see Jacob eying her. The music was getting louder; all she wanted to do was run out, jump on her bike, and get as far away from L.A. and superheroes as ten bucks' worth of gas could get her.

"I dance," Ty said.

She turned, stunned. "Really?"

"Do you want to?" He held out his hand, waiting for her, not demanding anything.

Angela let her boundaries slip a little, trying to sort through all the emotions in the room. *Come on*, she told herself. *You can do this. This is small fry.* She found Tyler's emotions. He was calm, almost disinterested. She could turn him down or dance with him; neither would change what he thought about her. "Sure," she said, taking his hand lightly as her pulse evened. "Let's dance."

They stepped onto the dance floor as the tempo picked up and Ty moved away from her, circling back, a predator on the hunt. There was no choreography for this, only instinct. A tango was a primal dance, an expression of desires as old as time.

Angela shivered in the air-conditioned spotlight. A dance. It was just a dance. Taking Tyler's hand she moved with the music, a few basic steps. A twist. A dip. And then she was pressed against him, feeling the warmth of his hand on her back, the scent of his sandalwood cologne overwhelming the distant smell of the grill. The pyro hadn't smelled of sandalwood.

Angela pushed him away, moved into a more complicated series of steps that was meant to flare a skirt but still got her point across in jeans.

Tyler followed, his smile predatory. He caught her, pulled her back to him.

She gave him a sultry stare as she lifted her foot and caressed the length of his leg. *So. It's like that, is it.*

He dipped her, turning her in time to the music, and pulling her back up.

They promenaded, walking together as the music crescendoed. Tyler led her into a series of tight turns, a split, and then a final dip as her heart raced and the music came to an end. His hand slid down the length of her body, resting for a second longer than was kosher on her rear, and then he pulled her out of the dip with a wink.

Angela managed a weak smile before she retreated to the heat and darkness off the dance floor.

Luiz had both her eyebrows up. "Where did you learn to dance?"

Angela snatched up a bottle of water. "College."

Luiz shook her head in awe. "Girlfriend, that was scorching. If I weren't one hundred percent het, I'd make a play for you."

Angela scowled as she uncapped the bottle. "Try Ty."

"Nope. Still too much like my ex." Luiz grinned.

"I'm het," Mikey said, eyes hungry with lust. "Come with me. Have my babies." He dropped out of the chair onto one knee. "Marry me!"

Angela took a slug of water. "No."

"Hey, AJ." Warm arms slipped around her. "That was sexy," Jacob whispered in her ear.

"Thanks, I—" Her phone rang and she edged Jacob aside so she could pull it out of her back pocket. Delilah's number lit up the screen. Her chest tightened. "I've got to take this. Family stuff." She waved to Luiz as she hit the answer button.

"I've got bad news for you," Delilah said without preamble. "I found Travys."

CHAPTER TWELVE

Dear Mom,

Delilah found Travys, the boy who shot me. He's in jail on murder charges. There wasn't a trial. There couldn't have been a trial. I'm not dead, so he can't be guilty of anything. But The Company has something on the judge.

It's a trap. If I go back to rescue Travys I'll have to go to court, prove I'm alive, and disprove everything The Company will say about me. I checked my old TalkPlace account. All the teachers from the school have unliked me. I did a little social media stalking on RealTime, and they all think I'm a pedophile. The Company convinced them that Travys shot me because I hurt him.

I want to hurt somebody. I want to make them feel the way I feel right now. I want...

I want it all to have never happened. I want to be back at school, planning my final exams and my touristy attack on New York. I was going to go to Broadway. I was going to see my kids graduate and help them finalize their college applications. I was going to do something other than run around in a trashy plastic suit pretending to be a slutty version of you.

I want to do something good; instead I'm stuck in a cheap cosplay so Geoff Swendon can relive his adolescent fantasies.

I miss teaching. I miss being me.

Angela

"DO YOU KNOW HOW hot you are?" Jacob asked, wrapping his arms around Angela from behind as she stepped off the set. "I could just eat you up."

"Ugh." Angela tried to shrug him off as Jacob nuzzled her neck. The plastic suit she wore as Pacifica clung to her sweaty body. "I'm melting in this heat. Seriously, I'm disgusting. Let me get a shower."

He held her tighter. "Who were you texting?"

"It was an email to my mom. Please, let go." She pushed his hand away.

Jacob stepped back, arms wide. "What?" he sneered. "Holding out for Running Fox? You think he'll get your name on the A-list?"

Most of the film crew stopped to watch them.

"What are you talking about?" Angela demanded in a whisper. The crew was breaking things down for the night and after the day's tabloid headlines, the last thing she needed was a fight.

Jacob scowled. "I saw you dancing with him. You like him more than me!"

"News flash, Jake," Angela said, tossing her hair. "I'd be the same if I were dancing with Quasimodo! It's a tango. It's supposed to look like an erotic argument."

He frowned. "You liked it."

"I like dancing. That's not a crime."

"It should be the way you do it." He pouted, then tilted his head to hit her with a dark-eyed smolder. "Don't be mad. I'm just jealous. Running Fox has it all. The girls, the gigs, the money... I don't want to lose you to him. That's not fair." He held out his hand.

"You can't lose me," she said in prelude to explaining that he didn't own her, but the director walked past. "Give me a sec, Jake. Mr. Swendon!" She chased him down.

Geoff Swendon turned midstride. "AJ, sorry about the AC. They'll have it fixed by tomorrow. Thanks for being such a trouper out there."

"Can I talk with you for a minute?"

He checked his watch. "I can give you ninety seconds if you talk fast."

"Alone, please. It's about the finale."

The director went pale. "Ah..."

Angela nudged him into compliance.

"Step into my office," he muttered. "At least I have a fan in there."

It was a ramshackle little space that looked like a secondary prop room, but it fit Geoff. He collapsed into a worn, patched chair with a sigh. "I'm not killing Pacifica," he said without preamble. "The writers tossed the idea around, but everyone likes you. We won't kill you."

"I want to die!"

Geoff blinked at her and she blushed.

"I mean, I think Pacifica needs to die. It fits her character. She would sacrifice herself, and the weapon you plan to use, she's the only one who could get close. Who else would sacrifice themselves to save a villain's life?"

"Are you trying to talk yourself out of a job?"

Angela shifted awkwardly. "It fits. And I'd feel guilty if someone else left. You brought me in on a short contract to fill in for Carla. Everyone else has worked so much harder."

The director started laughing. He slapped the table. "Wow!" Wiping tears of mirth from his eyes he grew serious. "Who put you up to that little speech?"

"No one."

"Come on. Tell Poppa Swendon the truth. Little girls with Hollywood dreams don't throw it all away over a guilt trip."

Angela racked her brain for an excuse he'd accept. "I'm scared."

"Of what?"

"People." She grimaced. "Red carpets, award shows, the hordes of people. I... I just... It makes me nervous."

"Didn't you act on Broadway?"

"Only in the chorus. No one knew me. I never had to go to photo calls. I was anonymous. The idea of walking the red carpet gives me panic attacks." She forced a tear. "Please? Kill off Pacifica."

He swiveled back and forth in his chair. "I'll think about it. No promises. But you still need to be at the dinner Friday night."

"What dinner?"

"Call Jacob in here," Swendon ordered. "I know he's lurking out there."

Angela brought Jacob in and took up as much of the precious air space in front of the fan as she dared.

"Jacob, I need you to promise to stay with AJ on Friday night. She's panicking over her first red carpet."

"Happy to, sir," Jacob said as he slid an arm around her waist and pulled her in for a tight hug.

The room really was too stuffy for three people. Jacob hugging her in her sweaty suit was going to give her heat stroke.

Angela shifted away and raised a hand. "What's happening Friday?"

"The studio head's birthday blowout in New York," Swendon said. "It's the biggest party all month. Two red carpets, one for the dinner and one for the actual party."

Angela's knees buckled.

Jacob caught her. "Easy there, Peach. Don't go fainting on us."

"It's this costume. I need to change into something cooler." She plucked at her collar. "I can't go to New York on Friday."

"Why not?" Jacob asked. "Do you have a hot date?" He raised his eyebrow, daring her to admit she had something planned.

"Yes. A very hot date with a very cool guy."

Jacob kissed her on the forehead and winked. "Don't worry. I'll be there."

CHAPTER THIRTEEN

Dear Mom,

I have no idea why Delilah would say she couldn't meet you for dinner this week. That's weird. Maybe there's a man in her life.

Your single daughter,
Angela

"DELILAH, I'M SERIOUS. WHAT am I supposed to wear to this thing?" Angela asked as she dropped the pile of clothes next to her suitcase. The ancient apartment's air conditioning wheezed as it fought the heat wave. Last night she'd opened the window out of desperation, hoping to catch a night breeze, but she was still sweating.

"You need a conservative suit."

"A what?"

There was a pointed silence from the other end of the line. "Please tell me you're joking. Don't you own any business clothes?"

Angela held up a vintage Marchesa dress borrowed from her mother. The light caught on the gold leaf hidden under wispy, ocean-blue gauze. "Hollywood and Chicago have very different standards."

"I'll bring you something." Delilah said something away from the phone and then came back. "I've found the video The Company is using to blackmail the judge. It's bad. Career-ruining bad."

"Can you handle it?"

"I'm trying to see if I can make it vanish. If they have it locked down at Langley I can't waltz in and grab it. The Company headquarters are a different matter."

Angela held up another dress, this one a rich purple with strips of gem-encrusted illusion netting. It would make her look like a high-priced hooker, but it would work. "I thought you'd been to Langley."

"On official business as a guest, yes. Not after hours. They have pretty good security."

"Pretty good?"

"They aren't my level of good, but so very few people are. I have a black suit that should fit you. Do you own a blouse?"

"A what?" She tossed two sets of jeans into the carry-on and tried zipping it. Too much. Her jeans might have to stay home.

"I'll find you a blouse. No jewelry. No perfume. Can you do that?"

"Why would I be wearing either?" The zipper finally closed on her bulging bag.

"Sometimes I find it difficult to believe we're related."

Angela fell backwards on her bed. "I got Mom's genes, you got Grandma Meredith's."

"Ewww!" Delilah squealed. "That's a horrible thing to say to someone! I am not anything like her. I'm like Daddy, I enjoy the finer things in life." Something rustled in the background. "Who's the guy from the tabloids? Is that really Tyler Running Fox? Jeans? Did you really wear jeans to go dancing?"

"I rode my bike there!"

"Doesn't L.A. have cabs?"

"It doesn't matter. I didn't intend to dance. Yes, that's Ty. No, we are not in a relationship. No, there is no chance of us being in a relationship. No, I didn't enjoy dancing with him."

"Liar. He is so your type."

"Shut up." A motorcycle roared on the street below. "I gotta go. My ride to the airport is here."

"Okay, I'll see you tonight. Get to the back door of the center by nine and I'll pick you up."

Angela picked up her discarded jeans and shimmied into them. "You realize how hard it's going to be to break away, right?" she asked as a piece of paper drifted to the floor.

"Make it happen. Love you." Delilah hung up.

Sometimes having a Type A personality sister was a real pain in the B. She picked up the scrap and unfolded it.

FRIDAY 11PM—I'LL FIND YOU

Downstairs Luiz honked the horn. Who was she meeting tonight? Besides Arktos, who she wasn't meeting because she'd be in the wrong state. She took the stairs two at a time trying to think of names. She hadn't worn the jeans to work, just dancing...

The memory of Tyler's hand fondling her brought a cold flush to her skin. A hot dance. His fingers caressing a part of her body they had no business touching. The wink as he walked away.

Damn. He probably thought she'd check her pocket as soon as she left the dance floor.

"Hey, AJ," Aaron said as he passed her on the stairs.

She shook herself back to the moment. "Hey." Aaron was headed for the bike. "Where's Luiz?"

"She and Mikey left a couple minutes ago," Aaron said as he reached for his helmet. "They had to stop and see his parole officer before they went to the airport."

Angela checked the time on her phone. "I guess I'll have to pay for parking. There's no way she's going to make it back in time to give me a ride. Dang it."

"I can give you a ride," Aaron's brother said, his voice muffled by the helmet.

"Oh?" She blushed. "It's okay. You need to get him home. I'll be fine, thanks."

"It's no problem!" Aaron rushed to say. He practically threw the helmet at her. "You go. I'll go study with Mia some more."

Angela wagged a finger. "Uh-uh. Luiz would flip out if you were here without adult supervision."

"We'll sit on the front steps. Promise. It only takes an hour or so to get to the airport and back. We'll be good."

Aaron's brother sat on the bike contributing absolutely no support for her arguments. "I don't know."

"Please?" Aaron begged.

"If anything happens, I will help Luiz bury your body," Angela warned.

"You're losing plausible deniability," Aaron's brother said. "Hop on. We'll call it payback for the tutoring."

"Payment," Angela corrected automatically. "Payment is when you reimburse someone for services rendered. Payback is when you get even with them."

He held out a hand. "Payback, because when you tutor my brother I spend the whole time racking my brain for a decent pickup line. You always leave me tongue-tied."

"Have you come up with a good one yet?"

"Not yet."

"Try two tickets to the Shakespeare festival next month. They're doing *Much Ado About Nothing*." She put on the helmet and climbed on the back of the bike, her clothes secured in her suitcase-slash-backpack.

"And wilt thou have me?" Over the helmet intercom his voice still sounded muffled, but she detected a note of Aaron in there. When the kid's voice dropped another octave he'd probably be a double of his big brother.

"Aye, and twenty such."

"I'm a unique man. You might have to settle for just me." He switched lanes. "That's all you need for a weekend getaway?"

"I hope it's two dresses too much." She wrapped her arms around his waist as they coasted down the street. "Why can't people wear jeans to parties?"

"Not fancy enough," he said as they merged onto the highway.

She leaned her head down, trying not to look at the traffic all around them. "I hate not driving myself."

"You should have said something earlier." He chuckled.

It was a soothing sound. The bike was moving fast enough to create a breeze and for the first time in days she felt her skin prickle into goosebumps. Angela sighed happily.

"You're supposed to hold on."

"I am holding on."

"Hold me tighter."

She did, and they made record time to the airport.

Aaron's brother pulled up to the curb. "So, we have a date next month?"

"Do you have tickets?"

"I can have them. You'll go even though you've never seen me?" He shifted nervously in his seat. "I mean... You know."

"Aaron talks you up a lot, but if it makes you feel better, we can go as just friends." She held the spare helmet out. "Thanks for the ride."

"AJ?"

"Hmmm?"

"What if I want us to be more than just friends?"

She hesitated, then smiled. "Then we'll see how the date goes."

CHAPTER FOURTEEN

Dear Mom,

Airports... Have I mentioned how much I hate them? I managed to stuff all my luggage into a backpack so I could avoid check-in, but still, there's no food. I'm starving and everyone is looking at me like I'm a lunatic because I mentioned stopping at a restaurant before going to get dressed for the thing tonight. Dinner isn't being served until eight and we have to be ready at five for the step and repeat (whatever that is). I'm hungry now! Maybe the hotel has a minibar with candy I can steal. I can always dream.

Your ravenous daughter,
Angela

ANGELA HELD HER BREATH as Amarilla tightened the last strap of the lime green dress in place on her arm. "It's official, I'm a walking advertisement for the carnival."

"I'm wearing bright orange."

"It suits you." Angela twisted a few times. "You can't see any naughty bits, can you?"

Amarilla tilted her head. "In that dress it's all naughty, but there's no nip slip. Relax." She rested her hands on Angela's bare shoulders. "It's just dinner."

"Plus a million people with microphones and cameras."

She tried to tug the bust line up a little. "If I lean forward I'm going to fall out. This dress was not designed with any regard for my personal modesty."

Amarilla grinned and shrugged. "Don't lean forward."

"Ladies." Jacob walked into the room without knocking and spun around in his raspberry-colored suit. "Aren't we a delicious looking confection?" He winked at Amarilla and then gave Angela a once-over. "I would love to see that dress rumpled on the floor."

"So would I, but not next to your suit," Angela muttered. "Where are my shoes?"

Amarilla grimaced, wiggling a foot. "The cute white ones with the low heel?"

Angela glared down at Amarilla's feet. "You stole the only decent shoes. That's mean!"

"Here." Jacob tossed her a pair of silver T-straps with six inch heels.

"Ha." Angela threw them back on the floor. "No. Not only would I tower over everyone in those, but I would fall and break my ankle." She dumped the contents of the studio-provided shoe box onto the bed and picked through the designer torture wear. "Does anyone who designs these things actually wear them?"

Amarilla sat on the edge of the bed and held out a pair of canary yellow shoes with fake feathers. "I don't think so."

"Executive decision time," Angela said. "I'm wearing flip flops."

"You can't wear flip flops on the red carpet!" Amarilla protested.

"My skirt will cover my feet," Angela replied stubbornly. "It's flip flops or barefoot."

Jacob stroked his chin thoughtfully. "Go barefoot. If someone gets a picture they'll say you're quirky. Flip flops will get you in trouble." He clapped his hands. "We've got to go or we're going to be late."

Angela grabbed her purse. "I feel like a zoo exhibit. All we need is a parrot and my day will be complete."

They were ushered down a roped-off sidewalk into a netted pavilion in front of the conference center. Someone had done their best to turn a quarter-acre of urban environment into a flower-strewn meadow, complete with babbling stream. Butterflies flitted under bright lights.

Jacob bumped her shoulder. "Don't stare. Last year they constructed a huge aquarium so that it looked like we were under the sea."

"Lots of mermaid gowns," Amarilla added. "I'd just signed my contract so I wound up in this hideously bright pink sequined thing." She shuddered in mock horror.

Jacob took her hand and squeezed gently. "This is easy. We stop at each station, smile, chitchat with whoever is standing around, and then move to the next. When we get to the door we can go inside and relax."

"Why are we doing this again?" Angela tried to pull herself in, fighting to ignore all the emotions swirling around her. This was a noisy group, a mob fueled by obsessions and hate. Her head started throbbing. She squeezed Jacob's hand tightly. "I don't want to do this."

"You'll be fine. Amarilla and I will protect you from those mean ol' cameras," Jacob said as he put a hot hand on her back.

She pulled away from him as she started to sweat. "I don't feel so good."

Amarilla rearranged the strap covering the scar on her arm. "Fake happy. Big smiles, eyes wide open. Fake it."

Angela allowed herself to be swept along in the stream of starlets being photographed. She smiled as she burned under the lights. When the cycle of photography finally led to the main entrance, she went looking for the director. Patrick and Geoff Swendon were taking advantage of the open bar on the foyer. "Mr. Swendon?"

Both of them turned to her. Patrick, the director of *Fractured*, smiled. "Did you survive?"

"No, not at all, I feel so sick. Can I go home now?"

"Oh?" Patrick fixed a flyaway hair. "It's just dinner."

Time was ticking and Delilah was probably tapping her toes with impatience. "I have a killer migraine and—" She covered her mouth with her hand and grimaced.

Swendon frowned. "All right, we can cover for this. We'll shuffle people around at our tables a bit so no one notices a gap. You need to be back here by ten forty-five, and no later. Get changed into the gown you're wearing for the party tonight. The studio sent everyone a couple of choices."

Angela bit her tongue on her first response. The studio had sent her a hideous yellow leather corset and mini skirt for the first red carpet. It probably went with the canary shoes. "Yes, sir. I'll be back. I just need to close my eyes for a little bit. All those bright lights..." She trailed off into a shrug.

"Let's get you out of here without a fuss. There must be an activities facilitator somewhere nearby." Swendon pulled her into a back hall and scanned the crowd of tuxedoed waiters, most of whom were wearing their designer clothes better than the talent waiting to be served.

Cutting through the mob like a shark was a woman in a pristine chocolate brown suit and a conservative updo. She approached them with a tight smile. "Can I help you?"

"Miss David needs to go back to the hotel for an hour or so. Health concerns. Hush hush. We'd rather it be a discreet exit and reentry."

"Naturally," the woman said. "This way, Miss David."

Angela followed after her sister with relief. "I was worried you wouldn't make it in."

"Oh ye of little faith." Delilah eyed her up and down. "Are you shorter than me?"

"I'm barefoot."

Delilah twitched an eyebrow up in condemnation. "Somewhere in our ancestry I'm sure there's a savage who's proud you've kept up the old ways."

"Amarilla stole my shoes!"

Delilah pushed open a back door and motioned to a waiting cab. "In. You can change in the backseat."

"Won't the cabbie notice?"

"Freddie? He might, but he's my minion so it's not like it will matter."

Angela climbed in and peeked at Freddie, who was indeed a warty green minion from her father's lab. "How'd you rate a minion?"

"I asked." Delilah shoved a box at her. "Clothes. Put them on. Including the stockings, please. We'll fix your hair and makeup after."

Angela eyed the new outfit dubiously. "I have to go back to the party."

"One bridge at a time, sister mine. One bridge at a time." Delilah handed her a sheaf of papers. "The judge was taken to a party and there's video. He looks drugged, but either way the scandal would ruin his career and marriage. Oddly enough, I think it's the marriage that he's most worried about losing."

"A nice change." Angela sorted through the paperwork as Delilah fixed her hair. "What's this? The earring stuff?"

"I told you Tyler Running Fox was the one who bought it. I was able to find surveillance footage."

Angela turned on the dome light so she could get a better view. "That's not Ty," she said through gritted teeth.

"Looks like him to me. The computer made a ninety-five percent match."

Angela shook her head. "This is his stunt double."

"And you know this how?" Delilah leaned over to scrutinize. "I thought Running Fox wasn't a person of interest in your love life."

"He's not, but I've worked with him." She put the papers down. "Do you ever just run on a hunch? No evidence. No data. Just... I've got this feeling."

Delilah lifted an eyebrow in distaste. "Not if I can help it."

Angela studied the picture again. "I'll find some evidence then."

"You think Running Fox is a good guy?"

"I don't think he's a criminal." She handed the picture back to Delilah. "That's Mikey, my next door neighbor. He promised his sister that he would clean up his life. There was a new job, something big. It was going to make everything better. Luiz is dirt-poor, she's counting pennies from the couch just to make ends meet. She's saving everything she can to send her daughter to a better school. Mikey promised her she wouldn't have to anymore, and then he was arrested for a DUI.

"The same week the three bandits became the two bandits. I'm willing to bet Mikey was the bagman and the laundry runner. He's Tyler's stunt double. Someone who's only seen Ty in the movies would probably buy it, and someone coming in with that kind of cash, it makes sense." She shrugged. A nice theory, but what did it all mean?

The taxi slowed to a stop in front of a grim detention center. "Freddie, circle the block and check for watchers," Delilah ordered her minion.

"Problems?" Angela asked, shucking out of her lime green pseudo-dress.

"Everything about this screams trap. The Company has done everything in their power to draw you out. Have you checked your social media accounts?"

"I saw. Everyone hates me."

"Did you see the, 'I've known she'd do something like this for years!' comments?" Delilah asked. "You met all those people in September when school started, but their accounts say differently. Someone wanted you to come and defend your good name."

"So why are we going to a detention center instead of meeting the judge somewhere safe?" She shimmied into the pencil skirt Delilah had given her and pulled on the blouse.

Delilah checked herself in the mirror and smiled. "The judge was blackmailed into not giving Travys a trial by jury. Tricky, but sometimes sentencings don't need juries. That didn't keep The Company from presenting evidence. Travys was locked away because the judge believed he was guilty. I promised to make the blackmail disappear if he gave us a fair hearing. Presenting you as alive and well, plus the testimony of Travys, should solve everything. Off the record. On the record is a whole other mess, but I have my team working on the paper trail."

Angela frowned, pausing halfway into the suit coat. "I need minions."

Delilah handed her a makeup compact. "When we get in there, stay calm but talk fast. And don't cling to Travys. The Company made serious accusations about your relationship with him. Act distant."

Angela nodded, pulse hammering. *Hold on, Travys. I'm coming for you.*

CHAPTER FIFTEEN

Dear Dad,

How does Delilah rate a minion chauffeur and all I ever have are spies? I need minions who listen to me. Preferably, some that can blend in with a classroom environment.

Going back to school soon,
Angela

FREDDIE PULLED UP BESIDE the gate.

"Show time," Delilah said as she checked herself in the taxi mirror one last time. "Let me do the talking to start with."

The walk to the side door of the detention center was as dark and foreboding as the red carpet had been bright and forcefully cheerful. Angela followed her sister like an obedient puppy, eager to get in and be done. Travys could have his life back, she could have her life back, and everything would finally be over. She'd give The Company the slip and get back to what she loved.

Delilah held the door for her. "Any weapons I should know about?"

"I never was interested in them."

A night guard looked at their IDs and ran Delilah's purse through a scanner, but he seemed unsurprised by the late hour visit.

The judge waited for them in a small, bare room with cracked linoleum and water stains on the ceiling. "Miss Samson," he said, holding out a hand to Delilah.

Delilah took it and shook perfunctorily. "Judge Bronson, it's a pleasure to see you again. Thank you for accommodating such a late meeting."

The judge made a dismissive gesture. "I'm old. I don't need sleep as much as I need my curiosity assuaged." He studied Angela as he sat down. "Is this the evidence you said you had?"

"Indeed," Delilah said. "This is Angela Smith, the teacher Travys Freeman was found guilty of murdering."

"Hello," Angela said, braving a small smile.

"Where have you been?"

Delilah rested a hand on her shoulder. "She was recovering from the shock at her parents' home in Texas. It wasn't until my firm called her parents about the details of her burial that Miss Smith even knew there was a problem."

The judge gave Angela a critical look. "You don't watch the news?"

"My father has high blood pressure and the politics get him worked up. I tried checking online, but I couldn't find a trial date." The judge made eye contact and Angela had no problem with letting the guilt build.

He coughed. "There were problems with the trial."

"That much is painfully apparent," Delilah said crisply. "Where is Mr. Freeman?"

The judge sighed. "We have him in a holding cell in anticipation of his release. And I'm not saying I'll release him, either. This is... not what I intended. There's the whole question of why Mr. Freeman had the gun in the school in the first place. That's enough for me to keep him in jail."

"Not without trial and the benefits of counsel," Delilah said. "What you've done is illegal. That boy has a right to trial with a jury of his peers. You either provide him with that trial and have it dismissed for contempt of court, or we sort this out tonight in a quiet way that serves justice and preserves your reputation."

Judge Bronson glowered at Delilah.

She raised an immaculately sculpted eyebrow. "You are the one who created the situation, Judge Bronson. I'm simply providing a way for you to correct your error."

The judge reached for his pen, and stopped. "No. No more mistakes. I need to know why Mr. Freeman had a gun on school property. He won't tell me, but I assume you have an explanation."

"He was going to commit suicide," Angela said. "His father was abusive and Travys didn't want to deal with it anymore. He didn't shoot at me. I tried to get the gun when he shot at himself."

Delilah squeezed her shoulder. "Stop growling," she whispered. "Judge?"

Judge Bronson looked from Angela to Travys. "Do you think sending him back to that situation will help?" He held up a hand. "I understand your concern, Miss Samson. I'm not saying the boy needs to stay here, but I won't countenance sending him back to a dangerous home environment that inspired him to attempt to take his own life once. Unless you have arrangements made, he will stay here until child protective services can be called in to evaluate the situation."

"Happily," Delilah said, reaching into her briefcase, "I foresaw such an argument and took it upon myself to have our firm follow up with his mother and a sponsor." Delilah presented the judge with a small dossier. "The Bright Hope sponsor network has matched Travys with one of their patrons. Travys's mother has signed the necessary paperwork and he has been enrolled in a private school in

Virginia. He'll receive room and board, an excellent education, and the sponsor will cover the cost of his first four years at any university as long as he maintains a three-point-oh grade average or better."

Judge Bronson's brows knit together as he reviewed the paperwork. "Very thorough. Everything here was done in anticipation of his release."

"Either now or as the result of a trial." Delilah shrugged as if to say that minor detail meant nothing to her. "Travys Freeman was imprisoned and found guilty of first degree murder without trial. Standing in front of you is his alleged victim. If Travys doesn't walk out with us tonight our next stop will be a meeting with a *New York Times* journalist. Tomorrow morning, Travys will leave for his new school, or your name will be plastered over every morning talk show in the country."

The judge scowled at Delilah and Angela's throat constricted with fear. "I don't appreciate blackmail, Miss Samson."

"This isn't blackmail," Delilah replied. "You made choices, and you will deal with the consequences like a responsible adult. I won't coddle you because you're in a position of power. You aren't an infant."

The judge was still waffling. Angela focused on agreement, on his desire to do good, and a sense of right, wrapping it all up and nudging it at him.

With a heavy sigh, the judge nodded. "Fine. I'll sign the release paperwork." He looked up at Delilah. "And the rest?"

"The blackmail The Company used will be gone by noon tomorrow. I suggest sticking to public places and avoiding your phone."

Delilah paced while they waited for Travys to be released and change into his street clothes.

"Will you stop doing that?" Angela asked. "Everything's fine now."

Her sister shot her a dark look. "Let's get out of the city before we declare this a roaring success."

"You're making me nervous."

"Good." Delilah checked her watch. "Do you have your phone?"

"Always."

"Check the social networks. Keywords 'superhero' and 'Bugman.'"

Angela pulled her phone out of the little purse she was wearing and typed in the commands. "Is there a reason for this?"

"Some people track superhero sightings." Delilah glowered at the guard.

Angela snuck a glance in his direction, then hit him with the desire to sleep. Everything is fine, she whispered to his mind, relax. Sleep. He sighed, settled back, and didn't even notice when his phone clattered to the floor.

Delilah scooped it up with gloved hands. "Our friend here was texting a buddy, 'Sketchy stuff tonight. Two hotties visiting the judge after hours.'"

"That's not technically illegal. Is it?"

"Depends on who he was sending the message to." Pulling a thin wire from her pocket, Delilah connected the guard's phone to hers. "Let's have a peek at his contacts list."

Angela frowned. "Downloading information from another person's tech without consent is illegal. I paid attention to that part of my Ethics and Law class."

"Super villain!" Delilah said with a cheerful smile. She unplugged the phone as Travys walked around the corner in the same jeans and T-shirt he'd worn when he was arrested. There was a small ketchup stain on the bottom of his shirt, a leftover from lunch.

No, Angela realized with sobering unease, a bloodstain. Her blood. Heaven above, that had been close. It was almost enough to make her believe in miracles.

Travys blinked at her in confusion. "Miss Smith? They said you were dead!"

"A gross exaggeration," Delilah said. "Shall we get going? There's a cab waiting for us."

"We'll get you some fresh clothes on the way." Angela held out a hand.

Travys stepped around her as he headed for the door. "Where's my mom?"

She touched his mind too, felt the unease and despair that hadn't been addressed while he was incarcerated. He was confused. Lost in a sea of his own fears and a danger to everyone.

Angela glanced at Delilah as she bit her lip.

"Your mother is out of town, but we hope she'll be in contact with you soon."

Travys's face shut down, and then he seemed to shrug it off.

"She would have been here if she could," Angela said.

"No she wouldn't. She's always leaving, my mom. Always making plans to get the money so she could go somewhere else." He stopped at the door. "I'm not going back to live with Chris. I ain't doing that."

"You've been enrolled in a very good school in Virginia," Delilah said. She opened the door and nodded for Travys and Angela to follow. "I'll make sure your mother calls as soon as she can."

As they walked out of the detention center, Angela tugged at the curl of confusion until it straightened out. It was the least she could do. Her nerves twanged with the need to put everything right.

Travys stepped out of the detention center and took a deep breath of fresh air. Shoving his hands in his pockets, he looked up at the overcast sky with a smile. "The moon's playing peek-a-boo. I missed that. Is that stupid? I was locked up and I didn't miss TV or my mom. I missed seeing that moon. Like, it's always there when nobody else was."

"That's very poetic," Angela said.

"Poetry later, leaving now," Delilah said. "We all have places to be and—"

A plume of dust shot up in front of them. Under the weak streetlight and the peek-a-boo moon, the person who landed in front of them was recognizable as the superhero Bugman. When he smiled light glinted off his white teeth.

Angela decided to hate him on principle. Real people did not have teeth that shone in the moonlight.

"Going so soon?" the superhero asked as he sauntered forward. "Well, well, well, how cliché. The villainess, her sidekick, and the hag."

"Who are you calling a sidekick?" Delilah demanded.

"Who are you calling a hag?" Angela wished she'd left her hair down so she could toss it around as a physical punctuation to her question. Sometimes life had no sense of narrative.

Bugman pointed at Travys. "Did you really think you'd get away with this?"

Angela pulled her student back. Chin lifted, she glared at him. "Travys did nothing. He was wrongfully incarcerated. If you really represent justice"—Delilah snorted in disbelief—"you will let us walk away unmolested."

The sneer on Bugman's face was nearly as frightening as the leer she'd grown accustomed to seeing on Pyro. "Criminals must be punished. This boy shot you, Miss Smith." He dragged her name out in a mocking way better left to the playground.

"I'm not dead. Habeas corpus, sir. No corpse. No conviction."

"By tomorrow morning, you will be a corpse. And you"—he pointed at Delilah—"will be back in Company headquarters where you belong."

Delilah's eyebrows were lost under her fringe. "Which company?" she asked, feigning confusion. "My company headquarters? Yes, I'm expected there. That's the thing about reality. Those of us who live in the real world are expected to show up at work every day. And not wear spandex." Her lips curled into a grimace of horror. "Halloween is over, and padded codpieces are not in fashion."

Bugman made the mistake of looking down at his crotch.

Delilah had her gun trained on the superhero in the blink of an eye.

"Put it away," Angela ordered with an emotional shove that would have turned most people into voluntary slaves. Decades of sisterhood and a stubborn streak the size of the Rio Grande made Delilah immune. She didn't even acknowledge Angela. "Please," Angela begged. A cold breeze ruffled the loose hairs on her neck. "Please, don't do this."

"Listen to the teacher," Bugman said. "There's no way you can—" He froze midstep, wreathed in blue ice.

Angela leaned forward. "Bugman?"

She felt someone move behind her. "Aren't you supposed to be on the red carpet tonight?" a soft voice whispered.

CHAPTER SIXTEEN

Dear Travys,

I'm writing this on the flight into New York, and I hope I'll be able to hand it to you in person tonight.

First, I want to apologize for all of this. It was selfish of me to go into hiding like I did. I thought I was protecting... Well, everyone really. Myself, my family, my mom most importantly.

I know that doesn't make much sense, but if you ask me one day I'll tell you the story of the man who tried to destroy my family. He left my mother broken. It took her years to heal, and The Company supported him in what he did.

I promised myself when I was little that I would never let the superheroes bully my family again.

And in doing that I broke the promise I made to all of my students on that first day of school.

I remember how you came in, shy, and skinny, and just a little scruffy. You were hiding in the back row under that torn brown hoodie you loved so much. My heart broke a little because I could see how curious you were. You soaked in the first few lessons but I could never draw you out of your shell.

And then one day you asked a question. That was one of the best days of my life. I felt like I'd accomplished something real. I'd connected with a student and made you interested in math. That's geeky, but for a teacher it's huge.

Travys, you are such a bright, wonderful, intelligent young man. You are going to do great things. The whole world is waiting to open up for you. And I'm going to make sure you get the chance to explore it.

Sincerely,
Miss Smith

ANGELA WHIPPED AROUND AND found herself nose to nose with Arktos.

The safety of Delilah's gun clicked off. "We are behind schedule, ladies and gentlemen. Everyone I like, to the car please. All strangers in spandex get to stay here."

Arktos took Angela's hand before she could move away. "Are you hurt?"

She shook her head.

"We need to go," Delilah insisted, pulling Travys behind her and urging him toward the waiting taxi.

Angela shook her head. "Give me a minute."

Delilah flicked the safety back on. "You'll be late."

"Please? Sixty seconds."

"I promise she'll be quick," Arktos said. "Bugman won't stay frozen forever."

Angela shivered. "Did you kill him?"

"No, I chilled him, it's like stasis. He'll thaw in a few minutes and never know the difference. Except you will be gone."

Delilah put her gun away. "Sixty seconds. The clock is running," she said before hurrying after Travys.

Angela licked her lips and then risked looking into Arktos's eyes. "What are you doing here?"

A gentle smile played about the corners of his mouth. "Rescuing a damsel in distress?"

"I think the lawyer might object to being called a damsel."

He shrugged. "I kept seeing the detention center and knew you were getting into trouble. I thought you might want backup."

"Do you realize how much trouble you're going to get in for this? The Company is not going to see me as the good guy here."

His gaze became intense. "They can consider it my resignation."

Angela jerked back, bumping into the frozen Bugman. "Resignation?"

"I read the file on this case." Arktos raised a shoulder and shrugged it off. "There's no way to put a positive spin on locking a kid up because you want to use them as bait. I've got a little brother. I can't risk someone deciding he's a pawn to be played with. So I'm out."

Angela shook her head. "You can't quit."

He chuckled. "I still have my day job. You know, the one that pays the bills?"

She shook her head harder. "No, I'm serious. Leaving The Company is suicide. You can't walk away from them."

He twitched an eyebrow. "You haven't had any trouble."

Angela rolled her eyes. "I have plenty of trouble, but I also have my family. We're good at handling tough situations. Who will be there for you?"

"You?" He gave her a look like a lost little puppy.

She blinked.

The quiet night grew loud around them. "Angela?"

Her jaw dropped. "I... Um. We need to talk about that."

"Hardly." He leaned in and dropped a chaste kiss on her lips.

She didn't mean to, but she found herself following him as he pulled away, chasing down another touch.

Arktos drew her close. "You're going to be late for the ball, Cinderella." He stroked the side of her face. "See you on the red carpet tonight?"

"Yes."

He caught her hand before she grabbed his mask. "No cheating." Arktos kissed her palm. "Would you still rather hear your dog bark at a crow than a man swear he loves you? When you depart from me, sorrow abides and happiness takes his leave."

The taxi horn blared behind them. "Sixty seconds is up!" Delilah yelled from the back seat. "Get in the car or walk."

He blinked. "Charming lady."

"Did I mention I come with relatives?" Angela winked, grinning. "I guess—"

Delilah stormed up with a manila folder in her hand. "Take this." Delilah shoved the folders at Arktos as she grabbed Angela's arm. "You," she said to Angela, "are coming with me."

Angela was impressed that she made it to the car without breaking her ankle. "Was it that important to leave right now?" she demanded as she slammed the door behind her. "Really? I wanted to get his name!"

"You don't know it?" Delilah stared at her. "You told him your real name and you don't know his?"

"Um..."

"Angela Shalom Meredith Smith, you are the stupidest thing I've ever seen since Gideon decided to collect a box of rock pets and named them all Herbie." Delilah's eyes slid to Travys in the front passenger seat. "Hell, woman, there's even a witness."

Travys sat up in alarm.

"I've always used my legal name," Angela said. "Travys knew who I was all along. I talked about our family in class. I'm not ashamed of who we are."

"You never mentioned the whole superpowers thing," Travys said.

"What superpowers?" Angela asked. "Do we look like we're wearing spandex?"

"Your boyfriend does," Delilah snipped.

Angela crossed her arms and fell back into the leather seat with a hmph. "He's not my boyfriend."

"No, he's the guy you were kissing whose name you don't know. Mother will be so pleased."

Delilah dodged the shin kick, so Angela contented herself with sticking out her tongue. "I know his name."

"What is it?"

"I don't need to tell you. Not unless we're serious, and we aren't. Arktos... I was telling him good bye." She could feel the pull of Delilah's power, the subtle desire to tell her sister everything. "I won't see him again. Ever."

"Darn right you won't." Delilah pulled out another folder from her briefcase. "This is your new driver's license, state ID for Virginia, and the emails you've been exchanging with Redbrick Academy. Travys's school is hiring a new computer teacher. It's not your area of expertise, but you can fake it. 'Here's a mouse, go click. Here's a keyboard, go type.'" Delilah mimed teaching.

Travys giggled. "I could teach that class."

Angela stared at the papers. "Leave L.A.? Why... No. I can't leave L.A. right now."

"You went there to lay low for a bit. It's not my fault you started a new career!"

"You have a new job?" Travys looked at her in confusion.

"I've been acting." Angela pushed the paperwork back at her sister. "I've got commitments. Contracts. People are expecting to see me."

"What about Travys?" Delilah demanded.

"What about Mia and Aaron?" Angela shot back. "Who's going to tutor them? Who's going to step in on *Fractured*? Travys is going to be fine. He's going to a good school, I can keep in touch with him by email, and by this time next week his mom will be there."

Delilah stared at the roof of the car in her classic Counting To Ten And Praying For Patience pose. "This is about Arktos, isn't it? You're going to risk everything to play tonsil hockey with a superhero."

Angela rolled her eyes. "This has nothing to do with Arktos. I told you, we're through. This is about being a responsible adult and not leaving my coworkers jobless because suddenly there's a little risk associated with living there."

"It's not a little risk!" Deliah shouted. She took a deep breath and let it out with a huff. "Listen," she said in the voice Angela knew as Delilah Being Reasonable While Telling Everyone What To Do, "you can't honestly think going back to L.A. is a good idea. It's not. The facts are black and white. I understand that you want to be responsible, and it's a very noble ideal, but you need to check back in to reality. You are not AJ David, movie star, you are Angela Smith, math teacher."

Delilah reached over and patted her hand. "I'll make some phone calls and by morning roll call this will all be a bad dream. You'll be teaching again on Monday. Isn't that what you really want?"

Angela caught herself nodding and stopped. "Delilah! Stop messing with my head! I'm going to L.A. The end. I'm not arguing with you."

"Only because you know there is no logical argument for your actions."

"I have loose ends I need to tie up." Angela tapped on Freddie's shoulder. "Take me back to the conference center, please."

Delilah slammed back into her seat, arms crossed.

Travys grinned nervously. "I'm so glad I'm an only child."

"Don't think I'm not envious," Angela muttered.

Delilah rolled her eyes as the cab stopped outside the center. "I don't like this plan."

"Objection noted."

"I don't like Arktos."

"I wouldn't let you kiss him anyways."

"That green dress was hideous on you."

"Agreed."

Delilah huffed. "Be careful?"

"As careful as you always are."

Her sister winced. "Try to be a little more careful than that. You don't know how to get handcuffs off."

* * *

Arktos thumbed through the files as soon as he landed at the small Company safe house outside the city. No one seemed to remember it existed and he doubted anyone would look for him there. Not when he was supposed to be highly visible on the red carpet in under an hour.

Mikey's photo on the first page came as a gut punch. Glee's was no surprise; he'd wondered about that since her first wig went missing. For the pyro there were two pictures, Jacob Kapsimolis and Tyler Running Fox with a dainty scrawl that read, "Hunch?" A second, slightly neater author had written, "Not Ty." underneath.

He sat down at the ancient computer and logged into The Company's remote access portal. Katrina liked to operate everything on a need-to-know basis, but right now that suited him. He found his file, erased it. Found Angela's, erased it. Found Zephyr Girl's, erased it.

A few little clicks and everything vanished into the ether.

Arktos checked his watch: time to fly. There was a red carpet waiting for him.

Not that the cameras mattered, he thought as he changed. Omnipresent cameras were part of life in L.A. No, this red carpet was special because AJ would be there. The gem-encrusted confection she'd worn earlier had left him speechless. Tonight? He adjusted his tie. Maybe tonight she'd recognize him.

CHAPTER SEVENTEEN

Dear Daddy,

I need you to come out to L.A. and I need you to bring your Agree With Me Ray. There's... I'm compromised. That's the right spy term isn't it? When things go all fluffy shaped and everything is wrong?

There's this guy who needs to forget I exist. I think he's working up to ask me for something I can't give. I don't want to hurt him. I don't know if I could send him away. But he's such a nice guy. He can't live on our side of the tracks. He's in love with me, but he doesn't know the family. He doesn't know about Maria. And I can't let him near Mom.

He's Company.

Please, get here as fast as you can. Maria will bring you if you ask. She'll understand. People that come into our lives are in danger every second we're with them.

Please, Daddy, hurry.
Angela

ANGELA SLIPPED INTO THE sound stage's only bathroom with a working air conditioner, leaving the lights off, and locked the door. Swendon had given everyone a long lunch so he could work out some details of the script, and that suited her just fine.

The phone rang. "Hey, Button."

"Hey, Daddy." Angela slid down the door and sat on the cool tiles in the glow of the emergency lighting. "How are things?"

"Better here than there from the sound of it. Do you want to give me the whole story?" he asked with the same patient tone he'd used on Blessing after she wrecked the car for the third time.

"Not really. It makes me sound like a twitterpated idiot."

"That happens sometimes. I did incredibly moronic things at your age." She heard the sigh of leather as he settled back in his favorite chair. "Who's the guy?"

"Arktos, the main superhero for the region."

"And he's in love with you?"

"It's not my fault! I told him it would never work." Angela wiped a lone tear from her eye. "I didn't mean to break cover. There was just... The people were scared and hurt. I thought I could go in, rescue them, and get away without anyone caring. I don't dress like a superfreak, so you know, maybe I could be just a good citizen."

"Mmmhmmm." Her father's dubious tone came through loud and clear. "Sweetie, I may think you're cute as a button, but the rest of the world hasn't spent a lifetime around you and your sisters and your mom. I don't want to sound harsh, but there is literally no way I can think of aside from radical cosmetic surgery that will let you blend in with everyone else."

She rolled her eyes. "Daddy, I'm in L.A. Every other woman is a hot blonde with long tan legs. I don't have a monopoly on this look, you know."

"Are they all as smart as you?"

She stuck a tongue out at the phone before responding. "No. But no one has asked me my IQ. That would be weird."

"You're still an intelligent, down-to-earth, easygoing, beautiful young woman who is going to turn heads. I tried to talk your mother into letting me enroll you in a Swiss priory with barefoot nuns chanting hymns for this very reason. I thought I made a very rational argument. I even had a PowerPoint."

Angela giggled. "Never mind that we aren't Catholic."

Her father sighed. "Do you love this guy?"

"No."

"Really?"

"I haven't even known him a month, Daddy. Love doesn't work like that. It's not eyes-across-a-crowded room and bluebirds singing."

"Fine, so it isn't marriage-and-a-baby love. He's a horrible man troll who is threatening you?"

"I didn't say that." Angela studied at her fingernails. "It's just... We got too serious too fast. I'll take some of the blame. He's easy to like. Smart. Funny. He quotes Shakespeare all the time. You'd like him," she said without thinking.

"So you want to rip his heart out and put it in a blender because...?"

"Daddy!" Angela frowned at the phone, appalled. "I didn't say that. I said I want him to forget about me. He knows too much already and it won't be long before he figures out who Mom is. What then? What are we supposed to do when a Company superhero finds out that Mom is alive? They'll come for her and then I'll have to kill him for real. This is easier. Better."

There were heavy footsteps in the hall outside and someone tried to open the door. Angela braced herself against the sink. "Occupied!"

"Hurry up!" a man on the other side yelled.

She ignored him.

Her father coughed. "Angela? Do you remember when Rolling Shock took your mom from us? Do you remember how you felt when we went to the park and your mom was there and she didn't recognize you?"

"Yes," Angela whispered.

"Do you hate Arktos enough to hurt him like that?"

"I don't want to hurt him. I'm trying to save him!"

"Then let him decide whose side he's on. If he knows the truth about what happened and he backs The Company, we'll take care of it."

Angela's breath caught and she forced the words out in a whisper. "And what if he proposes?"

"Then we'll set an extra plate at the dinner table. It was going to happen eventually; your mother and I knew it would. Five children do not grow up and stay single for eternity. That's not how life works."

"Daddy!"

The person outside hit the door with something hard. "I gotta go, lady!"

Angela turned her back on the stall door. "I'm not ready to get married!"

"Then ask him out for dinner."

She swallowed and took a long, ever-so-slightly-shaky breath. "Love you, Daddy."

"Love you too, Button."

Angela turned off her phone.

"Hurry up!"

Grumbling, she opened the door. "Good grief, do you think it's easy to pee in this suit?" she demanded as she swept past the gaffer. It wasn't until after he slammed the door that she realized she'd have to hold it until the next break. Stupid men. Stupid phone calls. Stupid shooting schedule. Even superheroes needed to pee sometimes.

* * *

"AJ!" Jacob tackled her with a sweaty hug. "How is my most favorite lady?" A drop of his sweat fell onto her neck.

"Good. Off, now." She pushed him away and tried to focus on the script she was reading.

"We're going out for drinks. Wanna come?" Jacob asked as he played with her hair.

Angela batted his hand away. "Can't. I'm dying tonight." Swendon had decided the easiest way to pick who was getting offed in the season finale was to film everyone dying so he could put off the decision until the very last minute.

Jacob sat next to her and gazed adoringly. "Tell Swendon to cut the talk. Everyone knows Pacifica will survive. You're the fan favorite."

"You have to kill your darlings to make art," Angela countered. She hit him with a light wave of disinterest.

He ignored it. "Come on, Peach. I want some quality time with you. I feel like it's been forever since we did something together."

"That's because we've never done anything together," Angela returned, trying to keep the sarcasm from showing too blatantly. Try as she might, she couldn't make Jacob fit into the mold of Arktos. He was too short, not muscular enough, and he was always grabby. It was getting on her nerves. "Tell you what, I'll call when I'm done shooting and meet you at the bar. You aren't planning to go to bed early, are you?"

"Not if you'll keep me up late." He winked lasciviously at her.

"Great. Have fun!" With a chilly smile she hit him with the urge to walk away, a strong urge. That got through.

Jacob pivoted and zeroed in on his next victim. "Mikey! I was hoping you'd be here tonight. Let's go get a beer. I'll drive."

Angela flipped through the script one more time as the crew reset the scene and someone painted her leg with fake blood. Geoff Swendon meandered through everything, checking the lights and sound.

"Is Pacifica ready?"

"I'm ready." She tossed the script on her chair and walked into the light. "Let's kill me and call it a night."

Three hours later, Angela walked through the dark sound stage alone. While she'd showered, the place had shut down. Even the janitors were gone. It was almost ghostly. Appropriate though, she decided. This was her last day on a film stage, and she was the last one leaving. It had been fun in its own way. A learning experience. Today she was a TV star with a fan following and her picture plastered over a dozen magazine covers. Tomorrow she'd be unemployed and sending her application out to various schools.

Maybe she'd join the Peace Corps so she could travel Africa with Blessing. They could do with a nice bonding experience.

Her ringtone echoed as she stepped into the deserted parking lot. "Hello?"

"AJ, it's Luiz, are you home yet?"

"Not yet. I'll be there in a couple of minutes, why?"

Luiz swallowed a sob. "Somebody jumped Mikey. The police just called me. They're taking him to the hospital. I'm going to go meet them, but I'm onsite for the Clayborn movie and I'm worried about Mia. I don't know where they got him. Can you..." She sniffed. "Can you go make sure Mia's okay? Call me as soon as you get home?"

"Of course. Have you tried calling her yet?" Angela jogged for her bike, stuffing her nonessentials in her backpack as she ran.

"A dozen times, but she won't pick up. She's probably already asleep."

"Don't worry about it. I'll call from the house in fifteen minutes. You go take care of Mikey. I'll stay with Mia until you get home. Luiz"—she focused on her friend, somewhere out there in the city of millions—"it's going to be okay." Angela willed Luiz to believe her. "Mikey will be fine. Mia is fine. We'll make this okay."

"Yup. Good. Okay." Luiz's breath sounded ragged.

"I'm going to hang up now so I can drive. I will call you in fifteen minutes. I promise. Mia is fine."

"Okay. Thank you." Luiz hung up as Angela heard sirens in the background.

She pulled her helmet on and turned the key on her bike. Nothing happened. She tried it again. Nothing. Angela pulled her helmet back off. Leaning down, she checked under the bike. Wires were hanging loose. Someone had sabotaged her bike. What kind of punk move was that? Why would anyone mess with her bike?

A shiver of apprehension rolled up her spine.

Yeah, there were a couple people who might hate her. It probably wasn't hard for Glee to guess who Rage was; they'd been mistaken for each other enough times. Even if Glee hadn't put two and three together to get five Angela was likely on her hit list for everything else that had happened in the past month.

A car turned the corner, moving slowly like a shark on the hunt. Angela stood, holding her backpack by the straps so she could use it as a weapon if someone jumped out. The car glided to a stop in front of her and the window rolled down.

"Are you okay?" Tyler asked.

Angela eyed her bike and then the darkly beautiful actor. "I'm good."

"That's not much of a poker face, AJ. What's wrong?"

Angela sighed, muttering about gambler's chances. "My bike won't start. It's fine. I can call someone for a ride."

"Isn't Luiz working tonight? I heard Clayborn's movie has a motorcycle gang."

Well, wasn't he Mister Well-Informed? She shrugged. "Bike gangs are popular right now." She cursed at her phone. Five minutes wasted. Right now Mia could be... Her mind shut down. She didn't want to think what could be wrong with Mia right now if Mikey had been attacked at the house. She realized Tyler had said something. "What?"

"I asked if you wanted a ride." He sounded more worried than amused.

"Yes, please. I've got to get home." She opened the door and hesitated. "I'm telling you now that me getting into this car isn't a sign that I like you, trust you, or want anything to do with you. I'm not trying to seduce you in any way. I'm desperate. I need to get home. I will give you gas money."

"Understood. I am m'lady's taxi cab." He rolled the window up and gripped the wheel with both hands. "I'm so glad I went to college for this. Very good use of my degree."

CHAPTER EIGHTEEN

Dear Mom,

I'm fine. Daddy's worrying over nothing. Don't worry about it.

Love,
Angela

ANGELA SLID INTO THE soft, heated leather seats in a car interior that was chilled to Spokane Cold. "Where are you from?" Angela demanded, rubbing warmth back into her arms.

Tyler chuckled as he turned up the heat on her seat. "North Dakota."

"Which is in the arctic circle, right?"

"Only a couple hundred miles away. You're from the south?"

She settled back in her seat, letting the warmth pull the stress from her muscles. "I spent most of my life in Texas. You can move around, but it's hard to escape."

"Were you a spoiled southern princess or a cowgirl?"

"Yes." Her phone vibrated against her foot and she picked it up. "Yes?"

"Hey, Peach. Where ya at?" Jacob asked. In the background she could hear dance music.

"I'm leaving the studio. Um, about tonight—"

"That's why I was calling. Mikey and I are getting bored waiting for you."

"Mikey?" she asked, wrinkling her brow as Tyler pulled out of the studio compound onto the main street.

Tyler glanced her way, but she shook her head and he stayed silent.

"You know, Luiz's brother?" Jacob asked. "He's sitting here with me and we're both waiting for you. Even though we both know you like me best."

"Um, Jake, lemme call you back. I forgot something inside." Angela hung up in confusion.

"Something wrong?" Tyler asked as they headed for the highway.

"Jacob wants me to meet him and Mikey at the bar, but Luiz is going to meet Mikey at the hospital because he got beat up. I told her I'd go home to sit with Mia until she can come home. Why would Jacob say Mikey is at the bar if he isn't?"

Tyler switched lanes in the heavy weekend traffic. "Maybe the guy stole Mikey's ID and then got beat up. Seat belt on, please."

"Right." She twisted and a bright red car parked beside the gas station caught her eye. The number plate read JACOB-1.

"AJ?"

She buckled herself in. "It's nothing." Red cars were a dime a dozen in L.A. and there had to be hundreds of Jacobs.

The car merged stealthily onto the highway. "Do you want to talk about it?"

Hundreds of Jacobs. Especially after Twilight. "Hmm? No, not really." She shook her head, then sighed. "I'm sorry. That was rude. It's been a long day. I died. It was a surreal experience. And now this. I'm tired, and worried, and things aren't going the way I want. If

I start talking I'll start babbling. I'm already babbling. You don't want that."

They were silent as the miles vanished under wheels far quieter than Angela's thoughts until Tyler finally said, "Are you going to give me an address or am I supposed to guess where we're going?"

"Oh! Sorry. Next exit and make a left."

"That's not the high-rent district."

Angela shrugged. "I didn't have a job when I moved in."

"You could afford somewhere safer now," Tyler pointed out. "You have a job."

She glanced at the clock: 12:13. Stop talking, drive faster. "No I don't. My contract expired at midnight. I'm currently unemployed."

Tyler's eyes widened. "You're kidding me. Geoff can't possibly be planning to kill you off! Pacifica is the best character."

Angela shifted in her seat. "Why do people keep saying that? I have no lines. I stand around like the world's most awkward lingerie model."

"But your faces! You're so expressive." When she looked over Ty was smiling, one of his full-blown, panty-dropping, forget-you-have-a-lover smiles that made him oh-so-popular.

She turned away as soon as she realized she was smiling back. "It doesn't matter. Acting was fun for a bit, but it's not what I came to L.A. to do. Next right." She pointed to the street.

Ty turned on the blinker and slowed. "What did you come here for?"

"To teach. The only reason Luiz hired me was because she couldn't afford a tutor out of pocket."

"Because tutoring and acting are very similar skill sets?"

Angela sniffed. "I haven't been acting. Standing around in a white catsuit doesn't take any skill."

"Making it look anything other than ridiculous does."

She narrowed her eyes. "Do you watch *Fractured*?"

"It's allowed. Don't you?"

Angela quirked an eyebrow. "I already know what's going to happen. Why would I watch it? A left here and then stop by the second streetlamp."

"The dark streetlamp?"

"Yes."

Tyler brought the car to a stop beside the curb. "This really is not the best area for you to be living in."

"It's a poor working-class neighborhood; that doesn't mean everyone here is a criminal." She glowered at her bag as she made sure everything was in it. "What do I owe you for gas money?"

"Consider it payment for the cupcake."

"You remember? You didn't even acknowledge me!"

"I was distracted. Sorry."

He managed to look faintly uncomfortable, but Angela hmphed disdainfully and pulled a twenty out of her wallet. She tossed it on the dashboard. "Thank you for the ride."

"Which window is yours?" Ty asked as she got out.

"Why?"

"So I know you got in safe. There are open hallways and... Listen, humor me. Please?"

Angela's lips twitched in a grimace of surrender. "Second window on the left. I'll turn it on when I get in." She tried not to slam the door; it still closed with a satisfying thud. It figured that the one time she wanted a superhero to come to her rescue Arktos was nowhere in sight.

She took the concrete stairs two at a time and ran headlong into Mia.

"AJ!" Mia grabbed her arm and dragged her down toward the street. "We need to go."

Relief washed briefly over Angela as she realized Mia was okay. "Why aren't you asleep?" she asked as she shifted her backpack to the other shoulder.

"Aaron's stuck on the highway. The bike ran out of gas, and I've got to help him. He's trying to push it but it's uphill. I can't call my mom, she'd kill me! But you can take me, right? All we need to do is go on your bike, get Aaron some gas, and take it back so he can get home."

Angela bit her lip as she counted to ten. "Mia, does Aaron have a driver's license? Any driver's license?"

"Um... No?" Mia's eyes went wide. "Come on, AJ! He's got to get home before his brother does or his brother'll kill him! That's brothercide or something."

"Fratricide." Her eyes strayed to the street to where Tyler was still parked. On cue, the window rolled down. "Give me a minute," she muttered to Mia. Putting on her brightest smile and radiating a desire for goodwill and agreement, she strolled up to Ty's car. "Hi."

"Hi." His smile was warm with no hint of mocking. "Did you forget your key?"

"No, I didn't make it as far as my door. There's a little problem. Mia's boyfriend ran out of gas on the highway and he needs a rescue. Do you think you could possibly, pretty please, drive us over there? I promised Luiz I'd take care of Mia until she got home, and I owe Aaron's big brother for giving me a ride to the airport."

Tyler stared down at the steering wheel for a long moment and then shrugged. "Sure. My sleep schedule's shot anyway. Hop on in."

"Thank you." She opened the door and motioned for Mia to get in the back seat.

Mia climbed in, settled down, and then stared. "AJ?" she asked in a stage whisper. "Is that—"

"Al Capone? Yes he is."

Tyler shot her an amused smile. "I always thought of myself more as the Elliot Ness type."

"What, you're untouchable?" Angela asked as she buckled in.

He winked at her. "You can touch me all you want."

Angela gasped in mock horror. "Mister Running Fox, there is a child in the car!"

"I'm fifteen!" Mia protested.

"Fifteen and about to be grounded for life if your mother ever finds out about this little escapade." Angela glared at Mia. "Please tell me that you didn't do anything that will result in a baby in nine months."

"Ohmigosh! AJ! No! Aaron just came over to hang out. We watched a movie."

Angela raised an eyebrow.

Mia blushed, and then tossed her hair nonchalantly. "We might have made out a little. But that was it! I swear! We kept our clothes on the whole time."

Tyler made a noncommittal noise. "I can think of a couple of loopholes that would—"

Angela hit his shoulder. "Don't give the teenager ideas."

He hit back with a smoldering gaze. "Can I give you ideas?"

Angela gave him a steely glare. "Not this late at night and not when I'm this tense."

His face melted into concern. "Do you want me to turn the heater on the seat up again?"

She snuggled back into the leather. "Yes, please. Mia, what exit is Aaron at?"

"He said he can see the gas station with the green sign."

"Two miles," Angela translated. She leaned her head back and texted Luiz to let her know Mia was all right. The whole boyfriend on a stolen motorcycle bit could wait for morning.

The car accelerated with barely a sound. "There's water in the glove box," Tyler said quietly.

She popped it open without a second thought. "Thank you."

"Are you okay, AJ?" Mia asked, leaning forward.

"It was a long day. No big. I'm good. How'd your math test go?"

"I didn't get a hundred, but only because I didn't show all the steps on the last problem. Mr. Marshall doesn't like it when you combine steps." She gasped. "There he is! On the right!"

Angela swatted Mia's arm down.

Tyler flipped on the four-way flashers as he pulled over.

Angela waited for the car to stop before she hopped out, but only because Mia was in the car and she wanted to set a good example. This would be so much easier to handle with her sisters around. Or Arktos. Someone with super strength who could fly? That would be nice right now. "Aaron! What are you doing?" She heard the car door shut behind her as Aaron toed the ground. "Well?"

"I wanted to see Mia. It's no big deal. All I did was run out of gas."

"You stole your brother's bike! Aaron, what is he going to do when he gets home tonight and you aren't there? The poor man is going to have a heart attack! I can't believe you would do this to him."

"I know how to ride!" Aaron protested.

"That doesn't mean anyone in L.A. knows how to drive! It's Friday night. All it would take is one careless drunk and you're splattered all over the highway. What do you think that would do to your brother? He'd be devastated. Get in the car."

"I'll take the bike down to the station," Tyler said as he walked up beside her.

Her cheeks flushed as she realized she'd just ordered Aaron to get into a car that wasn't hers. "I've got it. I'll get the kids out and we can walk."

"Why don't you take the kids home in the car so no crazy drunks try to play hit the pedestrians? I do know how to ride a bike. Promise." He slipped his hands under hers, taking the bike away.

"I don't think it's a good idea."

"Can you drive a car?"

She stared at him in disbelief. "*Yes!*"

"Then why can't you take mine?"

"I don't want to make you do any more. This isn't your problem."

One eyebrow shot up. "Which of those kids is yours?"

She glanced over her shoulder to the car where Mia and Aaron were whispering ferociously. "Both of them."

"Really?"

"I tutor them." Angela lifted her chin and waited for him to argue her claim.

Tyler just shook his head. "You kill me. Here." He tossed the car keys at her. "I'll be back before you know it."

Angela held the cold keys, and then gave in. "Thank you. I'm sure you had better plans for the evening."

"My grandma raised me to be a gentleman."

"That was sweet of her."

He smiled, and she had to stop herself from leaning forward and kissing him. It was probably his cologne. Wasn't there some expensive man perfume that made women lose their minds? She was pretty certain she'd seen an ad for it at the back of a GQ magazine. That had to be it. With another quick smile she retreated to the car.

"Do not ruin these seats or I will kill you," Angela warned the kids. She adjusted the seat and turned on the heater before pulling back into traffic. "Why does he have the air conditioning blasting?"

"Because it's hot outside?" Aaron guessed.

"I can practically see my breath in here!" She took the off-ramp, and then did a U-turn to go home. The car moved like a dream. As they neared their exit she was beginning to fantasize about long road trips with this vehicle. "Do you think we could make it to the border before Ty noticed his car was missing?"

"He probably has GPS tracking," Mia said.

"That's a darn shame." Angela turned for home. "If I ever become filthy rich I'm buying one. I love this car."

"There's only five in the world," Aaron said.

Angela patted the car fondly. "And I'm sure this one loves me. Maybe Ty will let me adopt it."

"Probably not," Aaron said.

She gave the warm leather seats one last rub. "I know. Come on. Everybody out. We'll wait for Ty to get back and then I'll drive Aaron home." Before the temptation to run off with the lovely car became too much to bear, she put the keys on the dashboard along with another twenty from her purse. "I hope that covers the gas for tonight. I'm broke."

Mia smiled weakly at her. "I'll pay you back."

"Don't worry about it. If my bike was working, none of this would have happened. Well, Aaron being stranded on the highway might have happened, but not the whole hitchhiking with strange men thing. I don't recommend doing this ever again."

A motorcycle turned the corner with a roar, picked up speed, and accelerated before the rider popped a wheelie and slowed.

Angela gasped. "Tyler! Get down—that's not your bike to break!"

He laughed. "But it was fun."

She snatched the bike key from him. "Fun isn't the same as safe."

He leaned closer. "Lots of things aren't the same as safe."

"Your keys are on the dash," she said primly. Angela turned back to Mia and Aaron, who were sitting on the steps. "Okay."

The logistical problem of staying with Mia while taking Aaron home presented itself. Calling her mom or Maria to come babysit seemed like the best idea. Maria would be here in a flash of light if she wasn't occupied. What time was it in Brazil?

"I could stay here," Aaron offered. He sat up. "That's

good idea. Right? I'll stay here until morning when Mia's mom gets back from work. She won't mind. I'll sleep on the couch."

Angela frowned at him. "What about your brother? You've already snuck out of the house without permission, stolen his bike, and spent the night unsupervised with your girlfriend. For that matter, what will Luiz say? Mia is going to wind up in a convent under a vow of silence for this. Luiz is going to have a herd of cattle. A whole herd." She glared at both of them, young, stupid, and in love, when she heard someone laughing. "Are you still here?" she asked Tyler. "Don't you have a club to go dancing at or something?"

"Oh, no, this is much more entertaining. I'm excessively diverted." He grinned at her over the top of his car.

"I'm glad someone is happy with this mess." She turned back to the kids. "Mia, you go upstairs. Lock yourself in the house and in your bedroom and stay there until I get back. I can't believe I'm doing this at one in the morning."

"AJ, I'll take Aaron home."

"What?" She stared at Tyler in confusion. "I can't just let you... No. I'll take care of it. We've intruded on your time enough already. It's bad enough that he ran off. I can't send him home with someone his brother doesn't know."

"Angela?" Her name floated in the night air. "I'm his brother."

"Oh," Aaron groaned behind her. "I'm so dead."

Angela stared wide-eyed at Tyler. "That's one of those little details that should have come up an hour ago."

"I'm not supposed to talk about it," Aaron protested. "So I don't have weird people with cameras following me."

Ty shrugged. "You were doing such a good job of chewing him out I didn't want to intrude. Keep the bike for me? You can leave it at the studio lot tomorrow when you go to get yours fixed."

"Are you sure?"

"I wouldn't have offered if I wasn't. Aaron, get in. Angela, I'll wait until your light comes on. Thank you for helping tonight. I would have panicked if I'd gotten home and he wasn't there."

Aaron slunk to the car. Angela grabbed Mia's arm and all but pulled the girl upstairs after her. She flipped on the light, locked the door behind them, and watched as Tyler Running Fox drove away with his little brother.

"Am I really dating..." Mia started, but a look from Angela quelled her.

"Bedtime. Right now. And maybe I won't tell your mom everything. Maybe." Angela waited until Mia was out of the room before she dialed Jacob's number.

"Hiya, Peach. Ready to party?"

"I dunno, why don't you and Mikey come over to my place instead? I don't feel like the club scene tonight." She held her breath waiting for a reply.

Jacob took his time. "Mikey says he doesn't know where you live."

Liar. "Okay, then I'll meet you somewhere. How about the old warehouse we filmed on Monday? Some punk messed with my bike and that's close enough."

"Want me to pick you up?"

"Nah. You can park there and we can walk to the bars." Too many cameras in the studio lot, although she'd bet her entire paycheck that they'd not seen a thing when the wires were cut. "I need some fresh air. See ya soon!"

Mia peeked around the corner. "What are you doing?"

"Go to bed. I need plausible deniability. As far as you know, I was here with you the entire night."

CHAPTER NINETEEN

Dear Maria,

If I become a fugitive in the States will you let me move in with you? This is not entirely a rhetorical question.

Call me,
Angela

TY TOSSED HIS WALLET on the table. "So, you stole my bike and rode across town on the freeway on a Friday night."

"AJ already gave me the lecture," Aaron grumbled.

"But she's not your big brother and I am. I get to yell a little. Don't I?" He ruffled Aaron's hair. "Can't we skip the stupid teenage stunts?"

Aaron crossed his arms. "You go do stupid stuff. What happens when you get killed? I'm supposed to move back in with Grandma? Maybe go to a foster home? That's going to end well." His jaw stiffened.

"I'm not going to get killed."

"You don't know that. Every time you go out you might not come back and it doesn't matter!" Aaron yelled. "You care more about people you've never even met than making sure I'm here. I go out all the time. You've never noticed."

Ty's fists clenched. "All the time?"

Aaron took a step back. "A couple times."

"Fine." Ty took a deep breath. "You're right. I quit."

"No!" Aaron's mouth dropped open. "Don't send me back. I'll be good. Please. I promise, no more stupid stuff."

"I mean I quit superheroing. Last week I turned in my resignation. Katrina thinks it's because I took a rib to my lungs. I told her I can't breathe when I fly. I'm officially not with The Company anymore."

Aaron's eyes went wide.

"I don't have any movies lined up for the summer, so I thought we'd go on a road trip or something. Go see some national parks or something. Get out of the city."

"We could go to Texas," Aaron said.

"I guess. Why Texas?"

"'Cause AJ said she was thinking of moving back home over the summer if she can't get a job here, and I figured since you two were dating we might go see her." Aaron's face lit up with a grin. "She has a pool. I saw pictures."

"Why was she showing you pictures of a pool?"

"It was for a word problem; we had to figure out how many gallons of water we would need to fill the pool."

Ty chuckled. "Yeah, I don't think we'll have an invite to visit her. AJ and I aren't dating." He hung his car keys up on the hook and headed for the fridge.

"But, you drove her home," Aaron said, padding after him. "You let her drive your car."

"Because it was an emergency and because I trust her not to do anything to the car."

"She almost stole it."

"What?"

"She said she was going to adopt the car."

He pulled a gallon of milk from the fridge. "I think this is the first time a woman has been more in love with my car than me." Unscrewing the lid, he took a swig of milk. "I feel really inadequate."

"She likes the heater," Aaron reported. "Maybe you could offer to buy her a blanket and take her for a drive."

Of all the things he could think of doing with AJ and blankets, driving wasn't at the top of the list. "Don't get your hopes up. AJ made it clear she's not interested in me." He opened the fridge again, searching for dinner. "We need to go grocery—"

A vision replaced the contents of his fridge. AJ falling. The pyro holding AJ and dropping her. His hand clenched around the handle of the fridge so hard the plastic cracked.

"Tyler?" Aaron put a hand on his shoulder. "What do you see?"

Ty shook his head. "Nothing. It's nothing." He could see how to save her, where he needed to be... But Aaron needed him more. He'd call the police in the morning. If the pyro was arrested there wouldn't be a chance for AJ to die. It wasn't like AJ was going to go out again tonight. "What are we eating?"

* * *

Angela kicked a rock that skidded across the broken pavement and ricocheted off the brick wall of the warehouse. It was past two in the morning. Logically she knew she should go to sleep and then call the police in the morning. That would be the sensible thing to do. At the moment sensible and her weren't good friends. This needed to end.

Light from a car scraped across the rough brickwork before it fell on her, casting a long shadow. She didn't turn around as doors opened and two slammed shut. "Hey."

"Hey," Jacob said. "Why are we meeting here?" The lights turned off as he locked the car door with an audible click.

Angela turned. "Hey, Glee." The actress was wearing a teeny tiny skirt and a neon green shirt that complemented her neon pink hair. She also had a baseball bat, which brought a new level of fun to the evening's proceedings. Finally, everything felt right. "Cute toy."

"My little friend here?" Glee stroked the wood. "This is just a reminder that bad things happen when you play rough. Friendly insurance."

"Every girl should have a friend," Angela said as she sent mellow vibes out. Jacob slowed, his footsteps dragging a little as he swayed under her power.

Glee kept coming with a smile. "You're a naughty girl, AJ." She tapped Jacob's shoulder with the bat. "She's trying to influence you."

Jacob shook his head and frowned. "What? AJ? Why would you do that?"

"Why would you lie about Mikey being with you?"

"Mikey was getting ahead of himself," Glee answered. "We helped him understand his place in the food chain. Now it's your turn."

Angela flexed her hands, feeling the weight of the fingerless boxing gloves. There were still a few ways to end the evening quietly, but Glee was the epicenter of rage—full of hate and anger—nothing Angela was tossing at her was getting through.

"I used to be a scout for The Company," Glee said. "Their little one-trick wonder, kept on a leash and only allowed out for special occasions, until I met Jacob. With my ability to sense when a superhero is near and his abilities to do everything else, we figured we'd knock this town over. It was going so well until you poked your nose where it didn't belong." There was more between Glee and Jacob than simple friendship; Angela could almost see the emotional connection stretching between the two. Glee was holding Jacob back, keeping him from listening to Angela's empathic suggestions.

She began untangling the psychic knot as Jacob circled around behind her.

"I didn't ask for much, just a chance."

Glee shrugged. "But you decided to help Arktos. Between us, that was a bad choice." Her girlish giggle was out of place.

Angela shuffled backwards, trying to keep both of them in sight. "So what? I'm supposed to apologize and let you beat me senseless?" The emotional thread between her two assailants weakened.

Glee looked shocked. "What do you think of us? We're not thugs, AJ, we're entrepreneurs. Think of us as your local supernatural mafia. There are always entry-level positions."

"I'm strictly freelance, sorry." With one last burst of thought she snapped the line between them.

Jacob moved with blistering speed, a blur of hot red. He brushed against her arm. "Option two: come with me."

Glee groaned in pain. "What did you do?"

"I cut him loose." Angela grabbed Jacob's arm, trying to control his attention. "Jacob, you don't need to do this. I can help you. I can get you a new life away from The Company."

The arm under her hand burned like a stovetop.

"What did you do?" Glee screamed. "He's not stable." She rushed Jacob, clutching at his other arm. "Jacob. Jacob? Come back to me. You need me. You love me."

Angela could feel conflicting emotions of need and hate but none of them belonged to her. Jacob's arm grew too hot to touch and she let go. "What did you do to him?"

"I kept him calm!" Glee snapped. "He needs me! Jacob! Jacob, you need me." She clung to him, hugging him close.

Red and blue police lights lit up the alley. Jacob pushed Glee aside as he turned. "What's that?"

"The police," Angela said scathingly. "You thought I was going to meet Jacob alone?"

"I thought you'd be smart and bring Arktos." Anger and fear poured off Glee in a choking fog.

Flames wreathed Jacob as a car door slammed in the darkness. "Tell them to back down."

"Turn yourselves in," Angela ordered, using all her persuasive abilities to force them both to back down.

Jacob screamed and fire engulfed them.

Luck alone got her shield up in time. Angela and Glee both slammed into the wall. Only a bubble of magnetized air kept them from burning. "Jacob! Jacob, stop! You're hurting Glee!" Angela choked on the fiery air.

Jacob stepped through the fire. He held out a hand. "Come with me. Now. Or she dies."

Angela stood on shaking legs, her attention split between an unconscious Glee and the raging villain in front of her. "Do you promise to let her live?" Behind her back she turned on her phone's GPS. If nothing else Gideon and Dad would be able to track her. "You need to turn down the heat, or I won't be able to come."

Jacob swayed a little, but he nodded. The fires in the alley died, although he kept the police at bay with a wall of flame. "We're leaving."

"What about Glee?"

"She's not the one I want."

Angela nodded. "Let me make her comfortable at least. I... Please?"

"Hurry."

Kneeling, she stripped off her riding jacket and pillowed it under Glee's head. With a sharp tug she ripped her necklace off and left it in Glee's hand. Even if the fire moved toward her the shield would keep her safe. As safe as Angela could make anyone.

"Stop wasting time."

They were airborne before Angela could respond. All of L.A. spread beneath her feet. It would have been beautiful if fear wasn't overwhelming her.

Jacob's hand was hot on her wrist. Where he touched her, the skin burned.

She tried to scream, but the wind swallowed her words. In terror she hit back with the only weapon she had left. Blocking out the pain she focused on calm. On the midnight blue clouds swirling around them. On the ocean on the horizon. On happiness... And Arktos. Tyler's smile as he quoted Shakespeare. The way he was always making her laugh.

"Stop it." Jacob shook her, wrenching her shoulder from its socket. "That's not me. That's not how I feel!"

Angela slipped around his sweaty palm so she dangled by her fingertips. "Jacob!" The words fell behind them as he flew higher. She clutched his wrist with her other hand, heart racing in terror. Out of instinct she tried to connect with the necklace only to remember she'd left it with Glee.

The bitter cold of high atmosphere bit her fingers. She tried to squeeze his hand tighter, hold on somehow so she could survive the madness, but as the freezing air engulfed Angela, she trembled. Millimeter by millimeter she slid out of Jacob's grasp.

Tears stung her cheeks as she tumbled into a freefall high above the Pacific surf. The wind skirled past her ears. She shut her eyes, praying she wouldn't feel a thing past the moment of blistering pain as her body broke.

And then she was sitting comfortably in the air. The city, which had been zooming towards her, hovered below without even a breeze to indicate that she was doing anything more than dreaming. Angela twisted and saw Tyler behind her.

"I thought you were staying home tonight, Lois."

She wrapped her arms around his neck. "Get me on the ground. Please." She didn't open her eyes until she felt her boots sink into wet sand. Heart racing, she stepped back shaking more from fear than the cold ocean spray misting her as the tide came in.

"AJ?" Tyler started to step forward but stopped as she shook her head. "What happened?"

The lights of Palos Verdes twinkled in the distance. "I don't know. I thought... I needed to talk to Jacob." She rubbed the cold from her arm. "I..."

A bright light dawned on the false horizon rushing towards them. Jacob landed a few feet away on the beach, fusing the sand where he stood. A miasma of emotions poured off him.

Angela choked, drowning in the waves of bitter hate rolling off him like heat from a flame.

"Arktos, why can't I get rid of you?" Jacob asked as he stepped forward, leaving a fiery silhouette of a man behind him. Black blisters covered his arms and face; he sank as he walked, the sand beneath his feet turning molten. "I came to Hollywood to be a star and do you know what happened at my very first audition? I went in for the part of Keith Little in the new Code Talker movie. I had the looks, the dark hair, the right skin, I even studied a bit of Navajo for the part. It was Oscar bait the whole way and what happened?" The fires behind Jacob flared with temper.

Tyler's hand closed around Angela's wrist, gently tugging her back. "What happened?" Tyler asked, voice even.

"I lost the part!"

A shield of ice bloomed in front of her as the flames roared heavenward.

"You stole my role!" Jacob raged. "You took away my chance at being a serious actor! All because you were born lucky. I didn't lose the part because you were a better actor but because you were born to the right people." Jacob spat. The wall of ice steamed.

"Born on a reservation into abject poverty isn't the usual definition of lucky." Ty tugged at her arm again. "AJ," he whispered, "I can't hold him back. We need to leave."

"He's hurting." The mental anguish emanating from Jacob was burning through her mental barriers faster than it melted the thick wall of ice. Travys's pain had hurt when she'd tried to absorb some of it, but this—she staggered sideways under the assault. "Please, Jacob." She leaned against the ice. "Let me help you. You hurt. It can be better."

"No. It. Can't." He ground the words out through clenched teeth as his legs burned in the molten sand.

"You can heal. You're a superhero." She clutched at his pain, drawing it in deeper. It was like swallowing a burning knife. The self-hatred dimmed the city lights, made the fire so inviting. If she just stepped into the flames, let them consume her, all the fear and jealousy would burn to ash.

"He took everything I wanted. He stole my life."

The ice wall floated away into the atmosphere. Angela fell forward, head resting in the lava-like sand that bubbled and glowed.

Another capsule of ice appeared and the lava blackened as it cracked. "AJ. Angela. Please, we need to go."

The pain ebbed, leaving her shaking. It wasn't so bad, balanced across two people. She gasped, watched her breath turn to fog in the cold. "He's going to kill himself. He can't even... He doesn't understand he's physically hurt." Angela pushed herself to her feet. "How can I save him?"

"You can't." Tyler's sharp pronouncement made her turn.

"I have to."

"You can't save everyone. It's not possible."

She swallowed the bile rising in her throat. "I have to. I can. He just hurts. I can, can take that away. Make him happy again."

"At what cost?"

Jacob slammed a fist into the ice shield, creating a waterfall.

"Look at yourself," Tyler said. "You're burnt. You're bleeding."

She followed his gaze down to her ripped jeans. Her shoes had burned away at some point and her feet were red, blistering from the heat. There was a hand-shaped burn on her arm where Jacob had grabbed her. "I can save him."

Jacob reached through a hole in the ice and she screamed as her arm burned. Tyler grabbed her, trying to pull her away, but it was too late. She was caught in a maelstrom of emotion. Fear tore through her. Deep despair like she'd never felt before. All of Jacob's emotions, his self-doubts, and bitter self-hatred tore into her.

Tyler held her close. "Let go."

Her knees trembled then buckled.

"Angela, you can only save one life. Choose yours. Please," he whispered. "Stay with me."

She pulled her mind free of Jacob's thoughts and collapsed.

Jacob screamed, his voice rising in a deadly crescendo.

Ice covered her. And then there was darkness.

CHAPTER TWENTY

Aaron,

I'm going to be home late. Don't watch the news.

T

TYLER LEANED AGAINST THE hospital glass watching the surgeon try to perform a miracle as Jacob flatlined for a third time. The doctor in charge shook her head. "Time of death, four-oh-three ay-em."

He turned away in misery. Angela was in a room two floors down, lying in the dark alone. He'd been able to keep Jacob from burning her to death, and he'd flown them both to the hospital as soon as Jacob passed out, but it wasn't enough.

Jacob was dead and it looked like Angela was going to follow.

She lay unresponsive under a white blanket. Monitors were hooked up to her arm but that was it. The triage nurse couldn't find a reason. Psychic burnout wasn't a condition the doctors were willing to acknowledge, but he'd seen it before. When he was training there had been others like Jacob. Like Angela. People who couldn't control the mutations they were born with. People who died pushing their bodies past the limits. Humans weren't meant to fly, or burn, or freeze.

He rubbed a hand against his thigh where he'd seared himself to the bone experimenting with his own powers. The scar had long since healed, but the memory of the pain remained.

There was a soft knock on the door lintel. "Mind if I come in?" The light from the hall illuminated the face of a man in a lab coat. "I'm Dr. Smith. How's our patient doing?"

Ty looked over at Angela's pale face. "Same as she was, I guess."

"What happened?" the doctor asked as he puttered around the bed, checking the pulse on Angela's wrist, and tucking the blanket higher.

"You wouldn't understand."

Dr. Smith smiled. "Try me."

"She's... She's a superhero. She can feel other people's emotions, and she tried to take Jacob's. He's the pyro. Superheroes, superhumans maybe. They're different." Ty took a deep breath and shook his head. "She thought she could save him. I think she was trying to take his emotions away so he wouldn't lose control. It doesn't work like that." He crossed his arms. "We don't work like that."

"Well," the doctor said, "she's in good hands now. Rest and fluids are the best cure for exertion. Now, ah, what did you say your name was?"

"Ty. Tyler Running Fox."

The doctor nodded with a knowing smirk. "The one who played Hamlet? My daughter hated you in that."

"Yeah? You'd be amazed how often I hear that." A lump formed in his throat. He worked his jaw, chewing down the fear. "Will she be okay?"

"She shouldn't even be alive." Dr. Smith sighed, rocking back on his heels. "I don't suppose you had a chance to check the news, but it's bad. The island's on fire. One of the helicopter pilots dropping water brought back footage of the beach; it's glass and ceramic now. If it hadn't been for you this young lady would be a pile of ash."

Guilt weighed him down. "I didn't save Jacob."

Dr. Smith sighed again. "That's one of those things you learn in this business; you can't save everyone. You'll kill yourself if you try. Come on," the doctor said, taking Ty by the shoulder. "I'll buy you a coffee. By tomorrow morning this will all seem like a bad dream."

They stepped into the brightly lit hall and a shoe came flying from behind them, smacking the doctor in the head and bouncing to the floor. "Daddy!" Angela's outraged cry.

Dr. Smith rubbed his head as he stepped back into Angela's room and flicked on the lights. "Hello, sweetheart."

"Daddy, what do you think you are doing?" Angela sat up in the bed and crossed her arms in a pose that reminded him of Aaron throwing a tantrum.

"I thought this is what you wanted!" the doctor protested.

"I changed my mind."

The doctor made a show of sighing. "Is this what you really want?" he asked Tyler. "For the next eighty years? She's never going to grow out of it, trust me on that."

Angela watched him with wide eyes.

Tyler turned back to the doctor. Now that he knew what he was looking for, it was obvious. Father and daughter shared a nose. "Is Zephyr Girl out in the hall?"

The doctor's dark eyes narrowed. "Zephyr Girl? Why would you ask about her?"

"You are Doctor Charm, aren't you?" Ty circled around the doctor so he could be near AJ. "Angela said her father was a villain."

"And from that you leapt to the conclusion her mother was Zephyr Girl?" The doctor sounded incredulous.

"I concluded that after seeing her once. Pictures of Zephyr Girl are not hard to come by. And it makes sense. You both disappeared at the same time."

"I'm certain Zephyr Girl was reported as dead."

Tyler shrugged. "It makes sense, doesn't it? Two people from opposite sides meet, they fall in love, fake their own deaths, and run off together. It's like Romeo and Juliet with better communication."

Dr. Smith steepled his fingers. "That's an interesting theory. Why don't I buy you a cup of coffee? We can talk about your conspiracy theories and your long day and by tomorrow this whole tragic tale will be no more than a bad dream."

"Daddy!" Angela scowled. "I have another shoe."

The doctor rolled his eyes. "He's really too smart for his own good, darling. It will be much easier for all of us if he just... forgot."

Angela huffed. "You aren't allowed to play mind games with my boyfriend!"

"Boyfriend?" Tyler blinked.

"Or whatever."

"Fiancé?" he suggested.

"How long have you known him?" Doctor Charm demanded.

At the same time, Angela gasped. "Tyler Running Fox!"

"It doesn't hurt to ask!"

Angela slapped his arm.

"I lied. It hurts to ask." He caught her hand and kissed it. Her fingers entwined with his.

Doctor Charm cleared his throat. "I hate to interrupt this charming scene, but if you're awake, my dear, we should get going. Bribes and persuasion can only hold off the curious onlookers for so long, and neither of you are low profile individuals."

Angela winced. "Sorry. I just wanted to talk some sense into Jacob."

"Um..." Tyler squeezed her hand, not sure where to start in breaking the news to her.

"I know he's dead. One of the nurses here must have some latent talents because I can practically read her thoughts." Her face grew pale. "She was a big fan of *Fractured.*" A tear slipped out of her eye. "Daddy, what are we going to do?"

"Don't worry. I have a plan."

The blonde woman who walked into the room and shut the door couldn't be anyone other than Zephyr Girl. Her face was Angela's softened by age and graced with fine lines around the mouth and eyes. A few wisps of white streaked her already pale hair. "Dearest, there's a woman named Luiz on the phone demanding to talk to Angela."

"She's my neighbor," Angela said. "I was supposed to be babysitting her daughter tonight."

Tyler held out his hand for the phone. Zephyr Girl handed it over and he put it to his ear. "Luiz?"

"Running Fox? Tyler Running Fox." There was a beep. "I swear I called AJ."

"Yeah, um, she's in the hospital right now."

"*What?*" The scream hurt his ear.

"Minor accident. No big deal. She's checking out soon."

"Why are you with her?" Luiz demanded.

He turned to Angela for support. "Because? Why not?"

Luiz muttered something in Spanish then sighed. "Mickey woke up, wanted to talk to the police. He said Glee jumped him with a baseball bat. He thought someone was with her but he wasn't sure who."

"What did the police say?" Tyler asked.

"They already had Glee in custody. The officer said something about a DUI. I'm not sure. Is AJ really okay?"

"Yeah!" He held the phone out to Angela. "Tell her you're okay."

Angela tucked her hair behind her ear. "Hey, Luiz. I'm good." There was a brief pause. "Oh, no, just a really bad migraine. I felt like I was going to black out so Ty took me to the ER. No big." Another pause. "My bike broke, he drove me home. It's nothing. Uh-huh. I'll see you tomorrow."

"Nothing?" Tyler asked.

Doctor Charm started whistling. "This is going to be fun," he said to the beautiful woman snuggling with him in the doorway. "Do you remember our first fight?"

"Mmmhmm, I broke your arm."

"And then I bought you a necklace."

"You bought a computer chip being smuggled in a necklace, took the data, and left me with the hot gems."

"That's what I said."

Zephyr Girl patted him on the arm. "You're adorable."

Tyler pointed a finger at Angela. "That's where you get it!"

"Get what?" She looked taken aback.

"You told me I was adorable on our first date."

She rolled her eyes. "That wasn't a date."

"We went out in public and did things together."

"We stopped a heist together! That's not the same thing as having dinner together." She laughed and shook her head. "It wasn't a date."

He frowned. "I'll cook you dinner. Or breakfast, since the sun is going to be up in an hour."

"Today?"

He smiled at her parents. "I'll cook for all of us."

CHAPTER TWENTY-ONE

Dear Mom,

Next time I tell you I'm fine I'd prefer if you just called instead of unleashing Daddy on Los Angeles. I think that might have been an overreaction. Don't you think?

I mean, yes, convincing the entire city that the whole setup was a stunt for Fractured *and that nothing was really real was great. But I'm not sure letting Daddy use his giant Agree-With-Me-Ray on a city is wise. I think it's going to cause trouble in the future.*

Ty says, "Thank you!" for taking Aaron this week. With school starting on Monday and filming for the movie starting Thursday I didn't think we were going to find time for a honeymoon.

Love and kisses,
Angela

THE HOUSE STILL SMELLED new. Even after moving Aaron's things into his new room and finding he'd packed his gym clothes without washing them first, the house smelled like fresh paint. Ty lit a candle and looked around.

Home.

He'd never really had one growing up. There had been a string of his mom's boyfriends' houses, and then his grandmother's double-wide trailer, but there was never something he wanted to go back to. And now he had a home, and a wife, and in-laws... who were a little bit more daunting than he'd anticipated. Still...

Out by the pool he saw movement. Light from the full moon glinted off Angela's diamond ring as she walked past the pool. He licked his lips, tried to remember how to breathe.

How was it possible for a woman to grow more beautiful every day? The first time he'd woken up beside her with sunlight streaming in so she glowed like the princess from a fairytale he thought he was still dreaming.

* * *

"Hey." Ty kissed her cheek as he walked past to dive into the pool. He surfaced on the far side, treading water and smiling his panty-dropping smile. "Are you going to come swimming?"

Angela dipped a toe in the water to make sure he hadn't chilled it to an unagreeable temperature.

"It's safe," he promised.

"With you in it? I don't think so."

He swam toward her. "What's the worst that could happen?"

"I might lose my bikini again," she said as she sat on the edge of the pool, letting her legs dangle in the warm water to tempt him.

"Mmmm, I don't see that as a problem." He started massaging her calves. "I don't think you mind either." He moved up her legs and then lifted her into the water.

She wrapped her legs around him, bare legs rubbing against bare skin. "What happened to your No Skinny Dipping rule for the pool?"

"We're alone." He kissed her, tongue teasing her lips apart as his fingers nimbly untied her bikini bottom.

She kissed his neck, working her way up to the sensitive spot that made him shiver. "Dost thou love me?"

"Troth, no, no more than reason."

Angela pushed away, gliding through the warm water. "Why then, the world is deceived, for they have said you are much in love with me."

"Peace, I will stop your mouth." He caught her on the far side of the pool where they could see over the hill to the beaches below. Her top sank to the bottom of the pool. They swam in the darkness, exploring each other until the moon was high in the sky.

Eventually they moved from the water to the wide chaise longue on the lanai. Ty pulled a towel over them, taking the opportunity to kiss her once more. "I love you."

"I love you." She curled up beside him, laying her head on his shoulder. "I have ever since the night in the alley."

"When you rescued me?"

Angela shook her head. "No, before that. When I was riding the motorcycle with you, and then you came walking through the fog to quote Shakespeare for me. When you walked away and I still was waiting for a kiss I realized how fast I'd fallen."

"That was a mistake," he said, pulling her closer.

"Me falling for you?"

"No, that was genius. You should do it every day. Not kissing you was a mistake. To be fair though, I didn't realize what I was missing. Now I know better, and not a day is going to go by that I won't kiss you and tell you how much I love you."

Actor Tyler Running Fox is off the market! Running Fox wed AJ David during an intimate ceremony at her family's estate in Texas. The two have been cast opposite each other in the upcoming production of Much Ado About Nothing *produced by Twelfth Night Films and directed by Susanna Hall.*

LIANA BROOKS

EVEN VILLAINS HAVE INTERNS

HEROES AND VILLAINS

This is for the everyday heroes who save the world one day at a time.

CHAPTER ONE

December 2033

Dear Dad,

Just because Mom mentioned she liked Claude Monet's 'Grand Canal' painting does not mean she wants a copy of it for the house. I know it doesn't mean she wants the original. And telling me not to steal the piece while it's on tour at the Art Institute here in Chicago is not going to convince me to pick it up in time for Christmas. Reverse psychology stopped working when I was twelve.

In other news, you will be happy to learn that Peter Manigault, as painted by Allen Ramsay, mysteriously appeared at the Art Institute this weekend. The curator was very surprised. Personally, I think his shock was more over the two-dollar price tag left on the picture frame than the return of the old painting. It's possible I'm biased.

Locke

DELILAH WATCHED IVAN PETROVICH step toward her on the pier made ghostly by the nighttime gloom. "Don't take it personally, Miss Samson," he said, broken nose still purple from where she'd punched him a week before. "It's not that we don't like you."

"A lot," his companion added. She'd never learned his name. His file was marked 'Snail' because he was always trailing the rest of the gang. "I'd get your autograph if you weren't handcuffed."

A freezing wind whipped the snow at her feet as Delilah smiled. "Take 'em off, big boy. I bet we can find a pen."

Snail stared, confusion clouding his round face.

Ivan shook his head in frustration. "No. You stay handcuffed, we stay alive. We've been over this."

"This is overkill," Delilah said as icy spray from Lake Michigan bit her ankle. If they pushed her in the water it would be merely waste disposal. With the arctic front that had moved in, all they needed to do to kill her was to leave her outside for another hour.

"You're asking the wrong kinds of questions. Hanging with the wrong kind of people," Ivan said. "I bet your parents warned you about talking to strangers."

"Not as such, no." The shackles around her feet were making life difficult. Ivan had welded them shut before she woke from whatever drug they'd used to give her such a stupendous headache. If she wasn't careful, she was going to lose both her feet tonight. Or her life. She glanced over her shoulder at the water and tried to figure out if the heat from the broken shackles would be tempered enough by the chill of the water to escape with only third degree burns. Physics had never been her favorite subject. "I really think this is a bad plan, boys. If we go through with this, what will we have to do next time we meet? You're escalating the problem. All I want to know is what hit the street. I hate being left out."

Ivan grabbed the lapel of her woolen dress coat, pushing her back so she balanced on her Miu Miu heels. "You should have stayed out of it."

"Don't make me kill you, Ivan. You know what the dry cleaners charge. We go to the same place. Mr. Way is not going to be happy about this."

"But the boss will be. Goodnight, sweetheart." He moved to kiss her and Delilah kicked back, pulling him down into the water with her.

Cold wasn't the right word. Cold was snowflakes, or iced tea, or the look in her mother's eyes when anyone mentioned Colorado. Lake Michigan in mid-December was a crypt. Death circled, numbing her to the bone. Water poured down her throat as she reflexively gasped for air. Be a mutant freak. Try to save the world. Die of drowning.

Heat burst around her as the shackles fell away. Maybe three seconds had passed. The freezing water had numbed her soul right out of her body. She could almost see herself in the dark water, feebly trying to claw to the surface but sinking anyway because her muscles couldn't move.

Mom is never going to forgive me for this.

The murky darkness of the water became an air-filled darkness bursting with pain, cold limbs brought to warmth and burning from the change of temperature. Freezing water filled her mouth, her lungs... Air.

There was air! There was the sensation of someone holding her close, and then her knees slammed onto something too hard to be the muddy lake bottom.

Delilah choked, coughed, and vomited out polluted water onto a moonlight-smeared wood floor that bobbed up and down.

None of those words made sense. She made a living out of being sensible, politically aware, and biting her tongue. And yet the floor was bobbing at her. "Th-that's n' ri'." Her teeth chattered. So unbearably cold. Pain. Cold. Heat. Darkness. Movement. She looked up at a shadow, searching for the man it belonged to—but there was no man. No light. Only a shadow. She forced her arms to hug herself for the relief it offered. "'Elp?"

"I can get you a blanket," the shadow said.

"'Es." Hot tears burned her face. She was alive.

Anger burst through the pain. Ivan was going to regret

this night for the rest of his foreshortened life. She'd make sure of that.

Ivan. Snail. The mayor. In her mind she lined up the rogue's gallery. Dealing drugs out of rehab centers, now that took a twisty kind of mind. The city tried to reduce street crime by sending minor offenders to weekend rehabilitation instead of jail, and what did those hoodlums go home with? A nice duffle bag full of pamphlets, clean underwear, and dime bags of meth.

But something more was happening. The thriving Chicago sub-economy had gone quiet in the past few weeks, like birds before a storm. Or the jungle when an apex predator stalked past. She thought she'd finally caught a break when Ivan and Snail scheduled a meet down on West Wacker. All the evidence was on the camera... The camera!

She struggled to stand and started stripping off her wet clothes. If the camera was ruined... *Argh! Ivan you idiot, why couldn't you off me in the normal way?* His modus operandi was leaving people "drunk" and stripped in one of the parks. The cops logged it as a partygoer who'd wandered off and been killed by Chicago's infamous weather. It happened. It was a shame. No crime though. Why'd he have to change his style now?

Because you're a freak, she reminded herself. The usual drugs didn't affect her strange body chemistry.

"Um..." The man's voice was behind her. "I found a towel if you want... Should I leave?" he asked as she threw her shirt to the side and slid out of her pants.

Pocket. Fingers. Cold fingers never worked the way she wanted. Why couldn't the goons have been operating in Miami? This was it. This was definitely going to be her last winter in Chicago. In March she'd ask for the raise and a transfer to the Subrosa Securities offices somewhere warm. The French Riviera maybe. Or Spain. Or... somewhere. She wiggled out of her boots and dug her fingers into the lining where she'd slid the ultra-thin camera as soon as she'd realized someone was following her. *Hot dog!* With shaking hands she patted it dry. There. Good. Evidence. Now...

Her teeth started chattering again.

A warm, scratchy blanket was laid over her shoulders. Delilah looked down, saw a cord... followed the cord to a little green light.

"Heating blanket," the shadow said. He faded into the corner. "I know you're not a native, but we figure even tourists should know better than to swim in Lake Michigan in the middle of winter. That's why it's not posted on the docks next to the prominent 'Keep Out—Authorized Personnel Only' signs."

Delilah's fist clenched around the camera. "Th-thanks. Silly me." She sucked in cool air. "Where are we?"

"A boat."

Good. Locations were good. "Yours?"

"No."

"Mine?"

"Not that I'm aware of."

All right then. She nodded. "Phone?"

"I don't keep one on me. Makes me feel like I'm wearing a leash. It's good to get away from the day job, don't you think?"

She gave him her best *shut up* glare, perfected on her four siblings over the past two decades, and staggered toward a wall. Walls meant doors. Doors meant halls. Halls meant communications devices of some kind. Boats had phones, or computers, or radios, something like that. Her sum knowledge of boats was they were supposed to float, holes were bad, and boats talked to other boats. Ergo, help and warm clothes were just down the hall. And possibly up a flight of stairs.

"Where are you going?" the shadow asked.

"Help. Got to get help." She huffed on her cupped hands to keep them warm. There was a pop behind her as the heating blanket came unplugged from the hall. How inconvenient.

The shadow bent down and plugged it back in. "Sit down. I'll go find a phone. And some clothes."

A real gentleman would have offered his coat. Not that her mysterious rescuer seemed to have one. If he was who she was beginning to suspect he was, he didn't need one. Ghosts didn't need anything to keep the chill off.

Delilah sat on a vinyl bench and looked at the city skyline through a narrow rectangular window. Willis Tower was lit up for the holidays, bright, festive, and a beacon of hope north of her. So, 31st Street Harbor. Good. The cab could be here in a matter of minutes. She leaned back.

"Got a problem here," said the shadow as he entered the room. "The clothes are a bit big and these shoes..." He held up a pair of bright pink satin pumps in a lady's size twenty. Both her feet could have fit in one with room left over.

"Everyone needs a hobby." The words came out clearly between her chattering teeth. "Phone?"

"Nothing. I guess whoever comes here likes their privacy."

"Fine. I'll walk. Give me the clothes."

He held out a matching pink-sequined dress that was too big, bright, and cheap to ever be in her wardrobe.

"And here I thought I'd have to join the circus to wear something this tacky." At least the sleeves were long. Too long. Like an over-sized sweater made in the middle of a sequin explosion. "Thanks for the lift. It was nice not seeing you. Enjoy your evening." She pulled the heating blanket's plug deliberately this time, folded the blanket neatly, and made a mental note to send one of the interns down to the docks with a small remuneration and the dress for the owner.

"Mind telling me what you were up to tonight?" The shadow followed her down the creaky hall.

"Chasing bad guys, busting drug deals, getting evidence. You know, do-gooder stuff."

"You think you're a superhero?"

Ha. "Nope. You are though, right? The Spirit of Chicago, our city's favorite son. I saw the news segment you did in the graveyard last year. No record of birth, no name, no physical body, although you've just demonstrated your ability to lift things up, so I have to wonder how much of that was staged."

The shadows where his face should have been changed, shading to mimic the expression of a surprised man. "Says the woman who impersonates Harry Houdini as a Christmas Party trick." He sighed. "What's your name?"

"At home?"

The *Rosencrantz and Guildenstern* reference flew right over his head. "On your Company file."

"Locke." She smiled sweetly over her shoulder. "But I'm not listed as a superhero."

"The villain?" He swore so softly she would have missed it if she weren't expecting it.

"That's me."

"What are you doing chasing drug dealers? Did they cut you out of something?"

Delilah rolled her eyes. "No, I was chasing them because you suck at your job. Your ability to catch actual criminals is matched only by your ability to stop time and speed up the harvest. You've never done anything but haunt people." She leaned against the rail. "Do you know what time it is?"

"Hot date?"

"No." Her date was lukewarm at best, and being stood up for the third time. Hopefully the mayor's right-hand man would get the point. Every time she ran into him, she fought the urge to stab his eyes out of spite. Alan Adale was the snake of Eden walking around in the body of a fallen angel. He had asked her if she was free for dinner tonight in front of people. There'd been no way to wiggle out of it without losing her standing. Besides, the local tabloids already had them pegged as Chicago's next Power Couple, as if that was something to be proud of. She was pretty sure Adale was up to his handsome neck in whatever was going down. "Time?"

"Quarter to eleven. You missed *Doctor Who*, but you should be able to catch a rerun of the *Firefly* reboot."

"Unlikely. I need to catch a plane. My intern is flying in," she elaborated when he tilted his head.

"Super villains have interns?"

"Well, superheroes have the whole sidekick thing pretty well wrapped up. I guess you could call him a minion, but since he's being paid instead of exploited, I went with intern." And if she missed his flight and left her sister's favorite student of all time stranded at O'Hare airport... Angela had doted on the boy even before he'd shot her in the arm. When he'd come to Angela's wedding over the summer, he'd mentioned he was having weird pre-monitions. Like called to like. Delilah'd asked some questions and, sure enough, Big Sis's favorite kid was a genetic freak too. His powers were minor, premonitions of when people were going to die and the ability to heal a little faster than normal humans. It wasn't enough to win him a spot in The Company as a superhero, but it would be enough to earn him a visit from their silencing squad if they ever found out about him.

Delilah and Angela's family had closed ranks around the boy, herding him in like they had Angela's husband and brother-in-law. Travys was safe. And once he'd enrolled in the University of Chicago, she'd pulled a few strings to get him a place as her intern for a few months. It was the only way to train him to survive.

The shadow sauntered closer. "Where do you need to go? I can drop you off at home."

"I don't take boys home on the first date, or ghosts home ever. My ride will be here shortly."

An icy breeze fluttered her hair. Behind the shadow a man in a tight blue suit landed, face covered by a sculpted mask that horribly disfigured the handsome man beneath. Not the ride she'd expected. "My ears are burning. Were you talking about me?" the man asked with a smile.

She could picture Ty raising an eyebrow behind his mask.

"Cute dress," her brother-in-law said. "Angela will be jealous."

"Long story. How'd you know I needed a lift?"

"Frederick called to tell us you were out of communication. I came out and waited. Who's the new boyfriend?"

"The Spirit of Chicago, and not my boyfriend." She walked over to her brother-in-law, waving careless fingers over her shoulder. "Toodles."

The shadow gave her a lazy salute. "Some other time, perhaps."

"Perhaps."

Ty moved fast, dropping her at the apartment and flying her to the airport once she'd changed. He hovered in the shadows. "You sure you're fine?"

"I'm perfect. No lingering affects except an abiding desire to get home and snuggle under my quilt with the heater turned up to eighty. Freddie is bringing the cab around. I'll drop Travys at his dorm room and go straight home. Which is where you should go," she added firmly. "Your home. Drop the camera off with Daddy on your way, please."

He laughed. "You need to go get your own errand boy."

"I have twelve minions and an intern who eats like a horse."

"Why don't you co-opt that shadow dude? He's here, why can't he work for us?"

Delilah smiled wryly. "Us being the good guys who fight the other good guys for a chance to fight the bad guys?

There is no 'us', Ty. Maybe you and Angela have California tied up, but the Midwest isn't going to suddenly see the light and flee the strangling embrace of The Company. I'm not sure the Spirit of Chicago could. He's supposed to be the ghost of someone who died in the Chicago fire."

"He looked solid to me."

"Yeah." To her too. "I'll worry about it later. Kisses to Angela, tell Aaron I say hi."

"No more adventures before Christmas," Ty said. "Angela's been sleeping poorly enough as it is."

"Oh?" Delilah glanced up, although Ty's masked face gave no hints.

He shrugged. "Nightmares about what happened with Jacob. She wakes up screaming about fires. Not frequent, but between that and the stomach bug going around it's been a rough week."

She nodded. "No more adventures. Promise. I will not do anything thrilling, heroic, or risky for the next two weeks. Girl Scout's honor." A plane rumbled overhead, coming in to land. "That should be Travys. Have a good night." She smiled and walked into the lobby before Ty could remember she'd never been a Girl Scout.

The warm, stale air of the terminal was almost comforting. Still, she shivered. Nightmares were the bane of her existence. First her mother's memories of the time she was kidnapped and mind-raped in Colorado, and now her sister's memories of the man she couldn't save. She'd unlocked those, stolen them in unguarded moments, and they'd become part of her even though they weren't her experiences. A midnight swim in Lake Michigan just couldn't compete. So she tucked the fear out of the way, and moved forward. A super villain's work was never done.

CHAPTER TWO

Dear Dad,

I need a new watch for Christmas. Waterproof. Possibly with a miniaturized Agree-With-Me ray attached. You know, for the days when I run into trouble. I also need new boots. Mine got wet.
Your daughter who is glad she took swimming lessons,

Delilah

THE SPIRIT OF CHICAGO leaned his head against a cold brick wall and stared out over the dark harbor. That had gone as badly as he could have imagined anything going. Delilah Samson. What a gal.

In the city's complex world of politics, crime, and money, he'd had her pegged as a lady on the lowest rung. He knew her, of course; Subrosa Securities was a big name in private safety and Delilah Samson the beautiful treat they trotted out like a show pony for all their affluent clients. She'd even run point a few times, hovering near various Subrosa clients at charity balls and holiday mixers with a slightly detached expression, while the men tripped over themselves to get her attention. Gorgeous. That's all anyone ever remembered. Delilah Samson hadn't been born, she'd been carved from alabaster. Her eyes were luminous topaz, deep, dark, and radiant. Her dark chocolate hair fell in waves to her hips, begging men and women alike to imagine her lying in their beds with a sated smile.

Or maybe that was just him.

He'd known she was involved with that idiot Ivan as well, if involved meant they sometimes traded cool glances at the dry cleaners. He was willing to strangle Ivan for that alone, stealing her time and favor—and then tonight. The one night he'd felt reasonably certain Miss Samson would be safe, she wasn't. His plans for the evening had gone to hell in a burning hand basket when the little radar he'd illegally pinned on Ivan's car met with the one on Boris Lugchevka's car. Boris was a thug with a list of petty convictions stretching back to his childhood in the late nineties. Ivan was the brains, maybe even a major player in the criminal underworld, it was hard to say. He had no arrest record. No proof he'd ever done anything wrong. But he was always on the fringe of criminal activity, and if Ivan didn't commit crimes, he certainly wouldn't hesitate to egg Boris on.

The Spirit had arrived at the dock in time to see Delilah fall into the water. Searching the dark lake with nothing but hope and the faint impressions left by shadows was not the way to conduct a rescue operation in the dead of winter. He'd thought he'd lost her.

That was why he'd made so many mistakes. Bringing her to the nearest yacht seemed safe enough. She'd looked so helpless, dark eyes huge and filled with fear, her long hair tangled by the lake water, so he'd stayed to offer help. A normal woman would have been too shaken to do anything but thank him. Not Delilah. No, she noticed he picked up a towel. She'd identified him. She was evaluating him.

A beautiful, brainy woman.

She was going to be the death of him.

He sighed and ran his hands through his short hair as his physical body reformed around him. For thirteen years he'd kept his secret safe. Everyone, from The Company superheroes to the local media, accepted the fact that The Spirit of Chicago was a ghost. After all, why not? When the evening news was filled with accounts of a man who could turn into an eight-foot giant with bark for skin, a ghost seemed downright normal.

When he'd first approached The Company, a seemingly typical reckless and angry teenager, he'd been wary. He'd been scared of what they might do with him if they knew his name. So he'd lied. The United States government's clandestine superhero control unit didn't know his real name or what he looked like. They were content believing he was a ghost, an incorporeal man without the ability to touch, pick up, or manipulate anything. He watched people. Sometimes he frightened people. But really he was an informer, a Company spy.

And because he'd picked up a towel, Delilah Samson knew more about him than anyone in thirteen years.

The real question was: What else did she know? Could she guess from his voice who he was? Would she guess? And if she guessed, what then? Blackmail? Vows of secrecy? A kiss to thank him next time they met wearing their business faces?

His heart raced, half agony, half hope. Maybe he could find a way to tell her without losing the life he'd so carefully cultivated since escaping the hell of his childhood. Integrate her. Convince her to ally with him and keep Chicago safe.

Wishful thinking, he admitted as he walked into his apartment and locked the door. They'd barely exchanged half a dozen civil words with each other and he was ready to name the date, the kids, and the hypothetical dog.

Tossing his watch on the kitchen counter, The Spirit of Chicago stalked back to what he liked to call The Lair: his apartment's spare bedroom retrofitted with bulletproof glass, heavy curtains to keep out prying eyes, and an entire wall devoted to visualizing the dynamics of Chicago's power players.

Mayor Marco Arámbula occupied one pyramid of power. Chief of Police Brian Wyte owned his own pyramid too; he'd gained ground in the last year and the next election was looking like it might be a run-off between Arámbula and Wyte. The crime syndicates were smaller blobs formed under a big question mark. Ten years ago the individual gangs still had power—some, at any rate. The police force whittled that away and into the power vacuum a new player crept. The gangs and the Outfit had become mere feeder streams to the one big boss.

There was no name to go with the question mark. Not yet. But he'd have it soon enough. He needed the name before the criminal element in Chicago became too organized and efficient to break without going to war.

The Spirit of Chicago traced a finger down the pyramid of power under Wyte. Subrosa Securities worked in happy harmony with the police force, so he'd put Delilah Samson right down at the bottom with the other peons. Only—his finger paused—she wasn't there. Huh.

He checked his desk drawer and after a quick search found a magnet, purple for a reason he couldn't fathom, with a black and white image of her face glued on it. Hesitating only for a moment, he placed Delilah on the third tier under Chief Wyte. She wouldn't report directly to him, but her boss had to know.

Subrosa had a good deal if she really had superpowers. They could offer her protection from The Company and other less pleasant groups that might want to take advantage of someone with super mutations, and she had free license to use her skills. He grabbed a scanner and read the barcode under her picture.

He turned his computer on to read the cross-referenced files. *Let's see...* Delilah Samson, age twenty-six, height five ten, born in 2007, hired by Subrosa Securities in the spring of 2029 at age twenty-four. He scrolled down and stared at a blank page.

Nothing.

Delilah Samson sprang into being five years ago? He doubted that. Logic said she had a family somewhere, a history, school records. People left tracks.

He pulled up the Subrosa Securities website first, scrolling through their list of employees all for hire as discreet service or to set up your next security system. How embarrassing. As if security guards were some kind of accessory you picked to match your shoes in the morning.

Three pages in, he hit the end of the Bodyguards For Hire and still hadn't found Miss Samson. He checked the personnel listings for secretaries, hostesses, and other office minions. Not a trace of his delinquent Delilah.

Grumbling in frustration, he pulled up the president's information. Wilford Andrews, a bespectacled and impossibly fit man with gray hair and dark skin stared sternly back. Andrews was the regional president and head of Midwestern operations (USA) for Subrosa. And there, under the title 'Vice President', was Delilah Samson, resplendent in a blood-red jacket and skirt. She should have looked like a bellhop, but instead her flat stare seemed to oscillate between a come-hither invitation and the cold warning that she would not hesitate to put a bullet in your head.

He loosened his collar and opened up Andrew's file. Yale graduate, law school, served in the army JAG for twenty years before retiring to the civil sector and joining Subrosa fifteen years ago. Delilah? Nothing. No background, no schools listed, no experience.

No super villain alive had such a weak cover story. Most the ones he'd met had not just one backstory, but several alter egos with the paperwork to prove who they were. And super villains didn't play the role of neighborhood vigilante. That was strictly a Good Guy thing.

So, what? She was FBI maybe? CIA? Some other black-ops government group who needed a plant and thought no one would check her cover story? Homeland Security might try to pull something like that. Or the DoD. Although they could have at least made some effort to make sure her history passed a cursory inspection.

Unless she wasn't meant to pass inspection. Maybe she was bait.

His head started to hurt. Would it kill people to just tell him the truth? A little up front honesty was all he wanted. "Hi, my name's Delilah and I was trained by assassin monks in Antarctica to fight the hordes of rabid polar bears descending from Canada."

Or not. He shut off the computer as an email popped up on his work account. That could wait until morning. Right now he needed to wash the reminder of Lake Michigan—and Delilah Samson—off his skin.

CHAPTER THREE

Dear Daddy,

Yes, I have every intention of visiting the 'Splendor of Gems' display at the museum when it comes to town. There's an event there tonight, coincidentally. Or not: I suspect it's because of this fact that you emailed me while you should have been lecturing the freshman of the University of Texas about the dangers of uncontrolled experiments.

I'll ignore the news headlines about the rocket your students made last week if you ignore my social life, or lack thereof. Deal?

Busiest,
Delilah

"YOU LOOK BETTER," TRAVYS said as he walked into Delilah's office carrying a shoebox and kicked the door shut behind him. "And you don't smell like sewage."

"I told you, I fell in the lake."

Her intern looked skeptical and slightly thuggish in his Chicago Bull's leather jacket.

"We need to get you a trench coat."

Travys pursed his lips and shook his head rapidly. "Chicago Gangster is not a good fashion on boys from the hood."

"Neither is a leather sports jacket that looks like you stole it during a fan frenzy."

"I like it." He stroked the sleeve and pouted. "The red brings out my eyes. Gem tones always do."

She paused, then raised an eyebrow at his mocking tone. "When did I say that?"

"When you had to go to the fall harvest ball thing in a red dress like some overpriced assassin."

Delilah leaned back. "Oh, the Dior. I looked amazing."

"Yes," Travys agreed with a very masculine smile, at odds with his still-boyish face.

She wagged a finger at him. "None of that. Baby brothers are supposed to play with LEGOs and cars, not ogle girls."

"I'm not formally adopted," Travys protested.

"Don't argue semantics with an expert, kid. As far as the Powers That Be are concerned, you're my baby brother and I shall treat you as such. No girl will ever be good enough. Your room will never be clean enough. And I will question your personal style on a thrice-weekly basis."

"Thrice?" His eyebrows rose. "Thrice? Really? Thrice?"

Delilah shrugged. "It's the appropriate word."

"Yeah. I bet. You know, my English professor at the college is single. Want me to find out if he's available for New Year's Eve?" Travys gave her a grin that bordered on a leer. "Maybe you could 'thrice' each other a bit."

She picked up the hot chocolate on her desk. "You see this? My aim is amazing." She gave him a warning look and sipped the cocoa. "So, what's in the box?"

"Uh-uh," Travys said with a shake of his head. "Tell me why you weren't out with Alan 'Mister Amazing' Adale last night. The date was on your calendar."

"I skipped it to play footsie with some hoodlums. What's in the box?"

"What's wrong with Adale?" Travys persisted. "Is he a skanky-manwhore? Does he have a disease?"

In town for less than twenty-four hours and already he was scrutinizing her social life. "Did my sister write this script for you? Because for a second there, I could have sworn you were Angela."

Travys rolled his eyes.

She exhaled, setting her mug down. "He's too good to be true. I dated a boy like him in high school. Halfway through our second date I slipped a little. I wanted him to tell me why he liked me and since I was sixteen and could make him be honest... he was."

"How bad was it?"

Delilah tightened her grip on the mug. "He asked me out because I was almost as hot as my sister, and he heard I was easy." She shrugged as if it didn't matter anymore. "I don't need a repeat experience."

Travys eyed her thoughtfully. "What if Adale actually likes you?"

Delilah laughed. "What if Neptune is made of green cheese?" She shook her head. "Men are not attracted to me for my personality. They think short skirts mean I'm open to the idea of a one-night stand. Forgive me for being a little gun-shy. Now, what's in the box?"

"Some of my mom's stuff. A couple of bills from after she left, a note from my grandma, an invite to the school's parent night." He pushed the shoebox across her desk until it bumped into a pile of papers.

"How'd your dad take your visit home?"

"He's not my dad," Travys said as he sat down. "He's a loser. A dick that stood up for me once in his entire life." He glared out her window for a minute, then shrugged. "He's back in jail. He got caught with some dime bags. Stupid. I mean... dime bags? He makes trash look classy."

Delilah didn't contradict him. Chris Freeman was the kind of man parents prayed their child would never meet: charismatic, abusive, and self-centered as a spinning top. His motivation lasted right up until he had cash to burn, and then he was gone. Travy's mom had kept them from living in the street by working double shifts at a hair salon and sometimes picking up temp work at the call center for New York's cab companies. She'd been missing since spring of 2032, when Chris had gotten out of jail and Travys had tried to commit suicide.

Angela, Delilah's older sister, had saved Travys' life and taken a bullet to her arm for the trouble. But Travys was a bright kid; he'd finished school and graduated with a GPA that earned him a full ride scholarship to the University of Chicago.

"What are you doing with the house?"

He twitched a shoulder. "Nothing. I'm not sure who even owns it, so I just cleared out my stuff and Mom's. Chris can make the payments if he wants to keep it." He scuffed his foot on the ground. "She's not coming back."

"Who? Your mom? No, I think at this point it's safe to say she isn't planning to return to New York." Delilah lifted the lid of the box and placed the contents in front of her.

"She's dead," Travys said with absolute certainty in his voice.

Delilah looked up at him questioningly. "What makes you say that?"

"Same thing that told me Wiley Johnson wasn't going to make it through high school alive. Every time I saw him, I couldn't see it. I couldn't picture him in the cap and gown, you know? He was the nicest guy, super smart, funny, everybody liked him. And then some drunk hit him walking home from school. Three in the afternoon. Bright light. Crosswalk. The driver ran over him like he was a speed bump.

"It's the same thing now. I can't picture my mom coming back to me. I'm never going to see her again. Never." His voice caught, the edge of a sob peeking out.

"I'm sorry."

His eyes narrowed. "Did you know?"

"I guessed." She sighed. "Travys, your mom is a wonderful person. I have utmost respect for her, but she's also the perfect victim: alone, scared, vulnerable... Female," she added. "She was on the run, and no one knew where she was. Isolation makes a person an easy target. The fewer people who know where they are, the fewer people will notice them missing."

He frowned, lips trembling as he bit back more tears. After a minute he said, "Do you think—do you think she wanted to come back? She didn't, like, make herself stay gone?"

Delilah tried to catch his eye, but Travys was staring resolutely at the wall behind her. "You filled out your mother's personality profile yourself, and your grandma verified it. She didn't have the mentality to be a suicide. If she was going to do something like that, she would have done it years earlier. No." Delilah shook her head. "I think she ran home to Atlanta to get help, planned on coming back for you, and something unexpected happened. Right now, all we have is conjecture. Who knows? Chris going to jail could be the best thing to happen. If she's out there, she might finally feel safe enough to try to contact you again."

"She's dead," Travys said flatly. "I know it."

"In that case, we'll find the person who killed her and make them pay." Delilah shifted into his field of vision and waited until he made eye contact. "You're family, Travys. We will make them pay."

There was a knock at the door and her boss walked in. Wil looked between them. "Am I interrupting something?"

"Travys misfiled a client folder," Delilah said with a dismissive wave. "Typical new-intern troubles. I'm telling you, we should have a boot camp for them. Make Margo in the front office run them through alphabetizing and stapling practice before we unleash them to touch my files. It would save me so much trouble."

Wil shrugged. "Margo doesn't like the interns any more than you do." He tossed a padded tablet onto her desk. "Addison Mayfield called, she's back in town and wants priority security at the soiree she's attending tonight. Go check the venue. I'll arrange the team."

"Am I running point again?" Delilah asked as she opened Addison's folder. The spoiled socialite didn't need security, she needed a babysitter. Possibly a muzzle. Addison attracted trouble like flowers attracted bees.

"You'll be inside with Emerret, Dylan, and Emelia doing perimeter. Chad will have a three-man crew in the comms van. If the intern's free," Wil said, pointing to Travys, "you can take him along. He can shadow Dylan for most of the evening, get an idea of how these things go."

Delilah turned to Travys. "Can you do that, or do you need to study?"

"I'm good. The only final I'm taking is in English, and that's next Thursday." He grinned. "Where we going?"

"A place where you'll need a suit and proper grammar." Delilah smiled up at her boss. "I'll have the walk through done before lunch and be waiting for Addison to arrive at eight."

"I knew you'd be happy about this," Wil said.

Delilah let that one slide. Private security was the bread-and-butter of Subrosa Security. Addison might have been spoiled, but for a security team this large she was shelling out over a quarter of a million dollars for six hours of work. The salary was good, and the commission for working one of these jobs made it possible to buy all the finer things in life. "Come on, let's head down to the museum."

"The where?" Travys asked, following her out the door that swung shut and locked without being touched.

She picked her coat off the office coat-tree. "The Field Museum. They're opening a display of the world's largest gems tonight with a charity fundraiser. Tickets start in the five-hundred-dollar range. Dinner and drinks are another thousand. With the mid-term elections coming up, there will be a lot of schmoozing."

"I like schmoozing," Travys said agreeably.

Delilah cut him a look. "They won't be schmoozing us. We'll be the polite backdrop and stay out of the way." She checked her watch. "Can you meet me there in thirty minutes? I have a little errand to run now that the dry cleaner is open."

"Sure thing, boss."

Rolling her eyes, Delilah left Travys to find transportation for himself and took a cab over to Way Quick Cleaning, proprietor Mister Lee Way. The cab driver hunched over in his seat, a large flat cap covering his bulbous head. "I won't be a moment," she told him as she stepped out, not bothering to pay.

Having a super villain as a daddy came with certain perks. Freddie, the cab driver, was one of them. Her favorite minion, he was a five-foot-tall frog crossed with who-knew-what-else, made in her father's lab. Completely dependable, able to drive, and good for tossing people around when she needed some muscle, the whole not-paying-cab-fares was a welcome bonus.

Mr. Way looked up from his e-print subscription tablet as she walked in. "Good morning, Miss Samson. Do you have something to drop off?"

"I do." She held up a long, thin envelope. "Remember Ivan, the tall Russian with the dark hair?"

"The one with the bunged up nose?" Mr. Way frowned. "I'm not getting caught in a lover's quarrel."

"It's nothing like that. Just business."

"I don't like that any better," he said, refusing to reach for the envelope.

"All I'm asking you to do is stick this in his pocket."

"How do you know I even have one his suits in?"

"Because Ivan's a very particular man, and this morning he would have brought in a slightly damp suit that looked he tried to wash it in Lake Michigan."

Mr. Way's eyebrows shot up in surprise. "How'd you hear about that?"

"It's better if I don't go into detail." She pushed the envelope across the counter. "Tuck this into his pocket, please? And don't bother mentioning it to Ivan. It's nothing important." Before Mr. Way could object, Delilah laid two hundred-dollar bills on the counter with a wink. "Have a good day, Mr. Way."

CHAPTER FOUR

Dear Daddy,

*No, I won't bring you home any gems as a party favor. Not even
the emerald.*

Tsk tsk,
Delilah

DELILAH LEFT ADDISON MAYFIELD surrounded by
a crowd of gawkers and circulated around the room. As a
rule the Field Museum had excellent security, decent
catering, and plenty of exquisite objects that made her itch
for a little larceny. If she had somewhere to stash a T. Rex,
Sue's skeleton would already be in her apartment. As it was,
she'd already bought the limited edition miniature Sue the
museum was selling to fund whatever it was they'd been
funding. Her eyes had glazed over at that point of the
welcome speech.

These nights were all the same. Come in, spend cash,
meet other rich people, talk shop, and drink moderately
cheap wine. Eleven o'clock couldn't come fast enough.

It was strange that the research gene had skipped her so
thoroughly. Daddy and Gideon would have been absolutely
enraptured listening to someone yammer endlessly about a

new expansion to the labs. She'd been more distracted by the sparkling exhibits in the Hall of Gems. In one corner the Moussaieff Red glittered near the Agra diamonds. The Heart of Eternity sat beside the Millennium Sapphire, beautiful blue-toned rainbows dancing around them. The star of the show sat in the center of the room on a lit plinth: the faceted, twenty-five pound emerald called Teodora.

Large as a watermelon, the Teodora certainly had an eye-catching quality. Delilah circled it lazily, keeping half an eye on Addison while admiring the craftsmanship that had gone into refining the giant stone. Flawless, time-consuming work. A galaxy of lighter colors rifted through the dark green inside of the gem. Mesmerizing.

Other people started filing in, champagne glasses in hand. Without turning from the emerald, Delilah looked for the telltale bulge or crease in a jacket that would give away a concealed weapon.

"The first protestors have arrived," Chad whispered over her concealed earpiece. "None of them are on the watch list for the client."

Delilah nodded, certain that Chad would see her on the cameras. The price of discretion was leaving her voice pickup with Travys for the evening. He was under strict instructions to come find her at the first whiff of trouble.

Protestors weren't trouble, though; they were simply the accouterments of Chicago politics. Half of them were probably paid to make a mini-riot for the evening news and would leave within the hour. See and be seen. Stir up some interest, stir up some cash. The politicians would use the attention to woo new backers for whatever pet project they wanted funded next.

If anyone else had been paying attention they would have guessed the political structure of the city in less than ten minutes. Although Mayor Arámbula was conspicuous in his absence, his snake-eyed second-in-command, Alan Adale, was present and making the rounds. The moment she made eye contact he moved in like a heat-seeking missile.

She walked around the plinth, avoiding eye contact. The first time they'd met, Delilah had carefully filed him away as Too Dangerous To Handle. Lucifer had probably cried hot tears of envy when Adale was born. He had a sculpted masculine perfection and confident swagger that made everyone want to fall to their knees in worship, and one close encounter had been enough to send her scrambling for safety. She'd canceled every date, evaded him at every turn. But, like the devilish predator he was, he kept circling.

Pretty soon she'd need to whip out the big guns and flat out break his heart. Tease him on a little, then drop him like a rock. Dent his ego so he never bounced back her way again. After all, breaking hearts was far more fun than finding out she was just another anonymous booty call.

Adale stopped next to the display case, not completely immune to her 'Don't talk to me' glare. He feigned interest in the cushion-cut American Golden Topaz, glancing at the gem then up at her. Caught staring, Delilah turned away and focused on the Teodora. Lines of lighter green seemed to be moving in the smaragdine depths, rolling like waves before coalescing into spheres like eyes. Two large, bulbous eyes, blinking out at her from inside the Teodora.

Delilah almost gasped. The size of the gem was right, but the color was unusual, as was the texture. Minion eggs were traditionally more gelatinous. Comfy, too. She'd used an egg mass as a reading chair one summer in high school.

The black and bronze display tag said the Teodora had been discovered in Brazil, cut in India, and had a cloud of rumors surrounding its authenticity. In the end, it had been donated to the Smithsonian by the beleaguered owner.

Brazil... Brazil... Daddy had taken them down there one summer when she was six or so. He'd done a week of guest lecturing at one of the universities, and they'd spent another month exploring the humid country while avoiding a cold snap in Texas. All she remembered was a blur of spontaneous decisions that spoke volumes about her mother's unwillingness to sit through a Texas ice storm.

Considering the haphazard nature of life in the years after her mother's kidnapping and return, it wasn't hard to imagine Daddy losing an experiment. Or even leaving it behind on purpose. He probably thought it would be a fun joke.

"Beautiful," said a low, very masculine voice behind her.

Delilah spun on her heel, professional smile firmly in place. "It's a stunning gem."

The deputy mayor looked down at her with cool green eyes. "I wasn't talking about the stone."

A fission of fear climbed up her spine. It was uncomfortable being the center of his focus. Most people were lazy; they chatted and grew distracted and never seemed to be really watching her. Adale's emotionless gaze focused on her like a searchlight, stripping away the layers of deceit she used for protection. It was terrifying. He definitely had a future with the mob if the whole political career thing didn't work out.

"You're too kind." Delilah took him by the arm and steered him away from the Teodora. "Have you been enjoying your evening?"

"It's been uneventful so far. I missed having dinner with you last night."

"An emergency at work. I did leave you a message."

His hand covered hers. "Nothing terribly taxing I trust."

Her pulse fluttered as his eyes filled with concern. "It left me with a bit of a headache, but I survived." She wanted to unleash her skills on him there and then, drown him in the need to tell the truth and end the charade. But the political fallout of an honest evening would turn Chicago into a battleground. So she ground her teeth and kept the battle inside, reminding herself that she couldn't trust him no matter how genuine he seemed.

"I didn't bother rescheduling the reservations," Adale said, removing his hand from hers. "Your work seems to keep you busy at every hour I can invent. Although, I confess, seeing you here improves my day considerably. This would be a dreary party without you."

His smile cut through her like a laser. She shot him her own, full of knives. "Oh, I doubt that's true. You were dancing attendance on Perri Lang earlier this evening." Perri Lang, modern-day Lucrezia Borgia, whose father's chemical plant and research labs only avoided closure because he greased palms throughout the city. Where money didn't work rumor held his daughter's attentions did.

Adale grinned self-depreciatingly. "Yes, I spoke with her. It was even less educational than usual, but I'm glad you noticed."

"I didn't notice."

He raised an eyebrow as they stopped in front of a display of rings. "You said you saw me with Miss Lang."

"I'm here with Addison Mayfield. Miss Lang and Miss Mayfield are..." Delilah search for the right words.

"Rivals?" Adale suggested.

Delilah exhaled. "More like two cats in heat fighting over a tom. Keeping them in the same county is a recipe for trouble. If I can keep them from causing a scene tonight, Addison's father will pay me a bonus." She fought the impulse to roll her eyes.

"How mercenary of you. Tell me, will the bonus be enough to allow you to take a week's vacation? Maybe linger over a meal or two?"

"No." She glanced back at the Teodora and the eyes watching her. Minion biology wasn't her specialty, but if she recalled the development correctly, eyes appeared in the week before hatching.

Adale sighed. "You seem distracted. Am I boring you?"

"Hmm? Oh. No." Delilah stopped scanning the room for security cameras. There were still three hours left of the party. Give the crew a few hours to clean up, and she could be back here by three in the morning. Walk in, break the glass, grab the emerald, run out... No, she probably needed to cut the power to the cameras first. Infuriating.

"It's all right. I understand if you're not interested. Perhaps you like dark-haired men? I think the head of Alrosa is here, the Russian diamond company. He might be your type. Let's see. Ah, yes, over there in the corner."

Delilah scanned the room and spotted the mustached Russian with Ivan Petrovich at his elbow. If looks could kill, Ivan's would have put her in an early grave.

Adale leaned a little closer. "Why is that gentleman glaring at us? Jealousy, perhaps?"

Ivan's eyes narrowed as he ran a hand down the line of his suit jacket. The very same suit he'd worn the night before. He must have gotten her note.

She winked at Ivan. Time to move the party downstairs where there were more exits. It didn't matter if the deputy mayor looked like a cold-blooded hit man, he wasn't. There would be serious repercussions if she let her two lives cross streams.

Delilah turned to beam at Adale. "Who wouldn't be jealous of me? I have the most handsome man in the room at my side. Let me buy you a drink, to make up for shamefully neglecting you last night."

Adale's smirk threatened to turn into a smile. "I'm being used, but I don't know what for."

"Enjoy the attention while it lasts," Delilah said, steering him out of the room. Dylan and Travys passed her, casually chatting as they followed Addison.

"Problems?" Chad whispered in her ear.

Delilah nodded, which drew Adale's gaze.

"Something wrong?" he echoed Chad's question with bland amusement.

"Not at all." They walked down the grand staircase like Prince Charming and his sinister Cinderella. Everyone watched. For the first time in her life, Delilah felt like actual arm-candy. Alan Adale had enough force of presence that people looked at him whether they intended to or not, and she was his decoration of the evening.

Miss Lang's ears were probably steaming with rage.

As they approached the open bar surrounded by gossiping socialites, the caterer's door burst open and Detective Morrow stalked in, a man on a mission.

"Deputy Mayor," Morrow said as he made a beeline for them. "I need to have a word with you."

"Detective." Adale gently untangled his arm from Delilah's. "What an unexpected pleasure."

"Can we step outside for a minute?"

Delilah grabbed two glasses of alcohol and followed. No one had specifically forbidden her from coming along. That made it practically an invitation. The door swung shut behind her and she stopped short as she heard Morrow's voice.

"The mayor is dead."

"Are you sure?" Adale sounded as shocked as she felt.

In the dark, Detective Morrow shook his head. "Alive people have more face left."

CHAPTER FIVE

Dear Daddy,

I need the book on minion hatching and rearing that Hert wrote. I'd also like to see your field and research notes from every trip to Brazil. There's a slight possibility you left an invasive species near an emerald mine. Does that ring any bells?

Don't ask,
D

DELILAH FLOATED THROUGH THE crowded gem room toward Addison with a polite smile frozen in place. Dead mayors, protestors, and hitmen all at the same party was more than her contract covered.

Ivan stepped in front of her. "Miss Samson."

"Hello. Goodbye." She stepped around him.

He followed her. "You need to leave."

"Working on it."

"Town."

Delilah stared up at him. "Excuse me? Was that a threat?"

The couple nearest them turned around. With a brittle smile, she grabbed Ivan's arm hard enough to leave a bruise and pulled him into the corner. "You don't threaten me.

Ever. I'm a little too busy to pay you back for last night, but I promise, it's coming."

She turned to go, and he caught her arm. "Delilah." It was a whisper meant for her ears alone. "Trouble is coming to town. A hunter who likes big game. Subrosa doesn't have the resources for this."

With a soft smile that could have melted the coldest hearts, she whispered back, "Drop dead, Ivan. It'll save me the trouble of getting another pair of boots dirty." She batted her eyelashes.

With a few quick strides that stretched the clingy skirt of her gown to its limits, she caught up with her quarry. "Addison, darling, come with me a moment. There's someone you simply must meet." She brushed away the various sycophants and snatched Addison's glass from her hand. The fumes rising up explained Addison's wobbly walk. "Did you bring a flask of vodka again?"

Addison giggled as Dylan and Travys fell in line.

Delilah shoved the glass at her intern. "Drop that with one of the wait staff and meet us at the back door."

"What's going on?" Dylan demanded.

"The blond man in there? That's Ivan Petrovich, a known mob operative. The client's father is rumored to owe them money, and she'd make lovely ransom bait." Grabbing Addison by the shoulders, Delilah steered her to the back door. "We're moving out now. Alert her overnight team. Tell them to meet us at the house."

Addison smiled drunkenly at her. "Kiss me?"

"You're still not my type," Delilah said.

Travys ran up to them carrying everyone's coats. "I grabbed them from the jacket claim," he explained.

Delilah held Addison's coat by the shoulders. Addison stuck her arm in the sleeve on the third try and Delilah zipped her up. As she turned Addison around, Delilah slipped a hand into the coat pocket and palmed the phone she found inside.

Their party made it to the waiting vehicle without trouble, but as soon as Addison sat down she reached for her phone. As everyone else buckled up, Delilah watched the drunk girl check each pocket three times over.

"Problems?" she asked when it was clear Addison had run out of places to search.

"My phone." Addison pouted.

Dylan sighed and rolled his eyes. "It probably dropped out at the coat claim." He reached to unbuckle himself from the front passenger seat.

"I'll get it," Delilah said, holding up a hand. "Go on ahead. I'll be a few minutes behind you."

"I don't like that," Chad said in her ear.

Dylan nodded at Chad's comment. "We shouldn't split up. Addison can wait until morning for her phone, right?"

Addison gasped as if she'd been slapped. "No phone? All night? Are you crazy?"

"It won't take me more than five minutes to find the phone. I'll be right behind you." Delilah waved away Dylan's next argument. "My call. It's okay." She took her earpiece out and tossed it to Travys. "I'll see you in thirty minutes, give or take a stoplight." With a flash of a smile she stepped back into the bitter winter cold.

The car wheels were turning before the door locked. Delilah watched them drive off. In her pocket, she thumbed Addison's phone off. The last thing she needed was the GPS tracking her every movement. The cab which had followed Addison's car pulled up, cabbie hidden by an upturned collar and an oversized flat cap.

"Where to?" Freddie asked as she climbed inside. He turned down the police radio built into the dashboard.

"To wherever the mayor was shot."

* * *

304

Snow crunched under Delilah's boot as she stepped out of the cab on East Jackson Drive. "Park down by the university," she told Freddie as a voice on the police radio confirmed an ambulance was en route to collect the final remains of Mayor Arámbula.

Buckingham Fountain was beautiful, even late on a winter night. Past the skeletal trees, golden lights illuminated the sparkling water—though the strobe of blue and red from the waiting squad cars rather ruined the romantic affect.

The cab pulled away. Delilah walked through the fresh-fallen snow, drifting across the icy sidewalk with the calm demeanor of someone exactly where they belonged.

At the edge of the square, one of the officers noticed her. "Ma'am, can I help you?" he said stiffly, shining a flashlight at her face.

"No."

He squinted, trying to make out her face under the black top hat she wore. "Did you hear anything? See anything?"

"I didn't." She watched as the ambulance pulled up and paramedics hurried to the body. They lifted the dead mayor onto a stretcher and a scrap of paper fell out of his pocket. The wind caught it, lifting the paper up out of the snow and blowing it toward her.

"Hey!" one of the officers shouted. "Somebody grab that! Gelphi! Catch that!"

Delilah snatched the paper out of the air with a gloved hand. "Here," she held it out to the policeman she assumed was Officer Gelphi. Three barely legible words scrawled across the paper: Kalydon - 77 Wacker.

"Thank you." Gelphi took the paper back with obvious hesitation. "Ma'am, I'm going to ask you to move along. This is a crime scene."

"Of course." News vans were already parking on Lakeshore Drive and she didn't need to be on camera. "Have a good evening." Pivoting on her heel, Delilah strolled back along the snowy streets until her nose was numb. Seventy-seven Wacker was an office building that had been on the market for several months. It wasn't somewhere the mayor would have gone for a party, but a black market business deal? That sounded plausible.

A warm breeze alerted her to company. "Fancy meeting you here," The Spirit of Chicago said.

Delilah stopped, watching him from the corner of her eye. "How did you hear about this?"

"I have friends at the police department. You?"

She shrugged. "I know all the good gossips." She turned to face him, or as much as there was of him. The festively lit streets twinkled through his gossamer body. "Where were you tonight, superhero?"

"Where were you, do-gooder super villain?"

With a grimace, she shrugged again. "Busy. I have an airtight alibi. Over a hundred people saw me flirting with a handsome man tonight. We didn't get as far as drinks. Disappointing, overall. Your turn."

"I was trying to attract the attention of devastatingly beautiful woman."

Delilah almost laughed. "Oh? How'd that work out for you?"

"She looked right through me."

They turned side by side to watch the paramedics cover the late mayor's body. A chill that had nothing to do with the temperature and everything to do with the muted pallor of death wound its way up her spine, leaving her feeling isolated and angry. The ripples of this would spread far and wide, destroying the peace she worked hard to maintain.

The Spirit of Chicago solidified a little more, filling in enough space to cast a shadow of his own and whistling the first few bars of 'All I Want For Christmas'.

Delilah sighed and shook off her malaise. "I guess that's our social plans canceled."

"Ours?" the Spirit asked. "My invite to the cookie swap must have been lost in the mail. I was going to make snickerdoodles."

"There's a man dead and you're joking?"

He held up a translucent hand. "Ghost?"

"Who can swim and grab towels?" Delilah raised an eyebrow. "Let's try the truth. You're alive and well but you can phase in and out of places."

It was his turn to shrug. "Physics is not a class I really understood."

Delilah watched the news crews and police for a moment longer before walking away.

The Spirit of Chicago kept pace with her. There were no footprints, something she should have found more disturbing than she did.

"Are we sharing information?" he asked.

"If I find any, I might be persuaded to share. There's no profit in this kind of crime, and I'm vexed beyond words that someone would invade my city like this," Delilah said.

"Yours?"

"I'm very possessive." Delilah hit the call button hidden in the folds of her coat, summoning Freddie.

The Spirit stood beside her, staring up at the sky. "How will I find you?"

"How do you usually find me?"

He eyed her sideways. "I show up at a scene of a crime and you're there waiting for me."

Delilah smiled as the cab pulled up. "Sounds like a plan. I'll see you at the next crime scene, then."

CHAPTER SIX

Dad,

Something's being brokered in Chicago this week. Things have been quiet. Too quiet. And I've been told a hunter's coming to town. I don't know what's going on, or if the mayor's death is related at all.

Help me figure out what I'm looking for, so I can deal with it ASAP?

D

THE SPIRIT OF CHICAGO drifted through the walls of the late mayor's office. Bookshelves lined two of the walls, another was occupied by a window overlooking marble columns to the street below, and the last was covered a detailed map of the city. No personal objects on display; the family photos had come down a few years ago when Mayor Arámbula and his wife had separated.

The Spirit of Chicago reached out and tapped in the security code on the keypad. For a few minutes at least, he was free to look around.

All the books were in their places. They were the first things he remembered. Very early in his career, Arámbula, then a city alderman, had invited him over to see the house. There was a duplicate library. The mayor bought two of every book, one for home and one for the office, so he never had to worry about forgetting something.

People had underestimated Arámbula. He'd been a force of nature, a bombastic man who steamrolled his competition and naysayers. He was loud, larger than life—almost immortal.

The Spirit of Chicago frowned as he surveyed the room. Everything was eerily normal. He half expected Arámbula to come charging down the hall like a small locomotive, bellowing rage as he shook one of the increasingly rare print editions of the Chicago daily paper.

The police were going to pin the murder on either family trouble or political enemies, but that didn't feel right. Arámbula was rumored to be involved in half a dozen scandals on any given day, but The Spirit of Chicago knew he wasn't. And the divorce had been amicable. Elsa had a new husband, and Arámbula had walked her down the aisle. Privately, he told his friends he was hunting for someone a little younger. A mid-life crisis wife. It was his idea of a joke.

The Spirit of Chicago nudged the curtains aside, not willing to risk turning on a light that could be seen from the streets outside. Moonlight spilled through the clouds and glittered on a golden apple.

That was new.

The Spirit of Chicago picked it up. Arámbula was not a man who invested in paperweights, and an apple wouldn't have been his style at all. A recreation of a Mycenaean bull statue, yes. But an apple? Apples were for teachers, a moniker no one would have dared use for Arámbula. The Spirit picked the apple up, peering at the smooth surface for an engraving, some hint of where it had come from. The moonlight fractured oddly as he turned it. So many angles. Almost like... He tilted his head and saw a number in the pattern: seventy-seven.

* * *

Delilah growled under her breath and switched the police radio off. All the chatter about the morning commute was distracting her. So, Arámbula was dead. That left a power vacuum at the top of two food chains.

She grabbed Alan Adale's file from her desk. File folders were dinosaurs, and the office staff loved teasing her about her manila addiction, but there were advantages. No one could hack a paper file. No one could search her hard drive and find a copy of this information.

Not that she had much about Adale that wasn't public knowledge. For all his cold, mafia-man appearance, he had a record cleaner than a priest's miter. Normally she liked men without any obvious vices, but this one was getting annoying. Especially since she couldn't seem to give him no as an answer.

There was a shortage of perfect men in the world. Adale was attractive, intelligent... If she compared him to a list of qualities she wanted in a long-term partner, he looked like a winner. But the relationship had one fatal flaw: she didn't want to know what he honestly thought of her. Honesty was the death of infatuation.

"I need a social life," she muttered with a sigh.

"What?" Travys said, freezing in the doorway, his arms once again full of boxes. Luckily for him, one of those boxes was donuts.

"You brought me breakfast?" Delilah asked as she took the donuts and set them on her desk beside a stack of manila folders.

He shucked his bulky winter coat and kicked it carelessly under the chair. Such a boy thing to do. "Hungry bosses are mean bosses."

Delilah smiled and peeked inside. "Boston creams! Now I know you want something. What is it?" She picked up the chocolate-covered pastry and bit in.

"I have a Christmas wish list." His eyebrows bounced up and down in a hysterical attempt at an eyebrow waggle.

"Mmm?"

"Well, I was thinking, since I'm spending Christmas alone—"

"You're not spending it alone!" Delilah huffed around a mouthful of donut in annoyance. "We're doing a family Christmas in Vermont, New England's Winter Playground. I've already rented the house."

Travys looked at her in confusion. "Who is doing a family Christmas?"

"All of us. Angela, Ty, Aaron, Maria, Blessing, Gideon, Mom and Dad of course, you, me, most the minions will be up there. You know, the family."

He picked his own donut out of the box. "At this point we probably need to start putting a capital F on Family."

"Daddy is not the Godfather type."

"Are you sure he's not still trying to take over the world?" Travys asked, his eyes narrowing with suspicion.

Delilah shook her head. "We convinced him to settle for a fiefdom. He has the castle and we own most of Llano County now. It's enough, I think. I mean, taking over the planet in one generation is a pretty ambitious project, and he's retired."

"From being a super villain," Travys said.

"Exactly. His activities are strictly legal right now." She finished her donut and guiltily added, "Ninety percent of the time. Probably. Maybe more like sixty. Still. He's getting better."

Travys rolled his eyes.

Delilah sighed. "Never mind. You're coming with us. Christmas is handled."

"And how am I supposed to get gifts for everyone?" Travys demanded. "Aaron's got his brother's bank account. Gideon has his own company. Am I supposed to go shopping with my intern salary? What's that gonna buy?"

"Do you never check your emails?" Delilah shot back. "Everyone was given a name and twenty dollar gift limit. Trust me. You'll be fine."

"Twenty bucks?" Travys sat down with a frown. "So that's a no to my new car for Christmas?"

"Maybe for graduation." Delilah patted him on the head and turned back to her white board filled with purple ink and power struggles. "I need a pattern to emerge. Does the oracle of Delphi have anything for me?"

Travys shook his head. "Nothing." He closed his eyes. "I can give you a solid bet on who the next mayor will be."

Delilah waved a dismissive hand. "Alan Adale. He's politically hot right now, the press loves him, the people are enamored with him."

"Which is why you're not dating him?" Travys guessed.

She arched an eyebrow. "Adale has every red flag for a user: bad childhood, no significant relationships, and too much money to care about people."

"Have you ever considered that he's maybe not a bad guy?" Travys asked. "It's possible to be devastatingly handsome, have a bad childhood, and still be amazing."

Delilah gave him a look.

He held up his hands in defense. "All I'm saying is that I have red flags all up in my background and you gave me a chance."

"Stop using logic and reason on me. My mind's made up." She uncapped her white board marker with a click. "Help me find my killer. Adale is the best suspect—"

"But he was at the party last night," Travys said.

"Could be a well-planned alibi." She shrugged. "But anyway, I don't think Adale is the killer. I think he's the next victim."

Travys frowned at her. "You getting premonitions now?"

A whisper of ice slid down her spine as she remembered Ivan's words at the party. "No. Just something a little bird told me. Chicago's become ground zero for a hunter who likes big prey."

Travys's eyes widened. "I really hope you mean street rats."

She shook her head. "Serial killers."

"Plural?"

"If my source is accurate, yes. The thing is, they like to know their victims first. Buddy up and give them the choice to join or die."

"Arámbula must have said no."

Delilah rocked back in her chair. "Let's get the mayor's phone records. Then get Adale's, and see if we can tap the police street cams and find him. I want to make a timeline for him from, oh, let's say first of November through whenever we finish this project. Phones, schedule, witnesses, bank accounts. It'll be a fun little side project for you."

Travys gave her a skeptical frown. "Superheroes on TV are way more exciting. No one sits in front of white boards in the movies."

"Sue for false advertising," Delilah advised.

Travys glared at the board. "You sure it was a serial killer?"

"Not yet, but I'm sure we'll find out—" A buzz from the front office interrupted her. Delilah nodded, and Travys hit the button on her desk for her. "Yes?"

"Miss Samson, Detective Morrow of the Chicago PD is here. Are you with a client?" Margo the secretary asked.

"No, I'm free. Please show him back."

Travys raised his eyebrows questioningly.

She shrugged with a frown. "I've got airtight alibis for everything."

"I bet." He stood up and grabbed the files. "I'll go start that file on the deputy mayor."

Delilah opened the door for him. "What else is there to do, right?"

"I have my mom's file. There's a business card in the box that I thought might be a lead." The box was still sitting by the donuts.

"I'll look at it after I talk with the police. Promise."

"Thanks." Travys hurried down the hall, nodding to the gruff police officer coming the other way.

Delilah stayed by the door as she waved the policeman into her office. "Detective Morrow, always a pleasure to see you. Although I doubt you're here for fun."

"I wish," Morrow said. He took his hat off, but remained standing. "This is, officially, a social visit. I came by to invite you and Wil to the annual benefit dinner we're having next week."

Delilah returned to her seat, hiding her internal turmoil and boiling curiosity. "Unofficially?"

"Wil says you sometimes do side projects."

Her pulse skipped. "We all do. A little light body guarding, fieldwork for bonuses. It's all above the board."

Morrow pulled a video stick from his pocket and flipped through the pictures before holding it out to her. "Images from the mayor's office taken this morning by the forensic crew. Notice his desk?"

"Everything seems normal." She touched the screen and zoomed in. "You guys need better equipment."

"We got new stuff last year. Every picture in the office came out distorted until we took the apple out."

She froze. "Apple?" Serial killers with an apple as a calling card. She knew who that was right away, and none of it was good.

"A golden apple paperweight. We think it's bugged, but our tech people haven't figured out how it works yet. They're trying to crack it open."

Delilah was already shaking her head. "Bad idea. Don't do that. They tend to explode."

Morrow let out a breath she hadn't realized he was holding. "Yeah. I'd heard about that. In Atlanta, right?

After the DEA officer was shot?"

Delilah exhaled, rubbing at her forehead. "Last October. This spring the Wooden Wonder had an apple on him when he was killed." She met Morrow's eye. "Apples are not a good thing. Though the warped images is a new twist," she added.

He perched on the edge of the spare seat. "What information can you give me?"

"Lots of guesses and no names, alas." Delilah tapped the video stick in her hand. "The apples are the calling card of a serial killer, or group of serial killers, who call themselves The Golden Hunt of Atlanta. Possibly a reference to the city, possibly a reference to the mythical Atlanta. I think they started as a normal hunt club, going after deer and foxes, but someone at the top isn't right in the head."

She stared at her white board, the hastily written names blurring into abstract art. "They started hunting humans. Picking off the weak, the forgotten. They prey on the most vulnerable."

"Like wolves?"

"Like vultures." Rage simmered beneath her calm facade. One day she was going to find the leader of the Hunt, and then God have mercy on his soul, because she wouldn't. "I've linked nearly twenty deaths to the group. Some of the kills are straightforward, like Arámbula. The more dangerous they consider the victim, the more they like to toy with them. The Wooden Wonder was a superhero, nigh on immortal as we would understand it. Almost nothing could hurt him, but they burned him alive."

Morrow had settled back in the chair and was taking notes. "Why? What's the motive?"

She stared at him, eyes cold. "Survival of the fittest, detective. They are Darwinists. Except they take it to an extreme only Hitler could appreciate. They believe they are superior, and the rest of us are just animals. We're prey." Delilah smiled, but she knew it didn't soften her features. "I have a transcription from the one caught in the DEA case." She pulled it up on the computer.

"Did the guy go to jail?"

"He died three hours after booking. The arresting police officer died in a traffic accident the same night."

Morrow frowned at her. "How'd you get a copy of the interrogation?"

She shrugged. "My tip led to the arrest, and I was with Officer Kimley when it happened. Out of habit, my recorder was on. I wanted evidence for court. Emmet Grear babbled like a brook. He told us all sorts of things, some of it utter nonsense, but the Atlanta PD couldn't take the case any further. The perpetrator was dead."

"But he had someone on the outside," Morrow argued. "He had someone mess with Kimley's car. Right?"

"That's always been my suspicion, but I could never collect enough evidence to move on it. They're cagey. They like anonymity. The apple is for the victim. They want them to know they're about to die. They want them to run scared."

Morrow shook his head. "That's just sick."

"It's a troubled world, detective." She held his video stick out. "I'll send you all the files I have."

"Send it to Gelphi, he's handling the investigation."

"Are you sure you don't want copies?"

Morrow pulled his hat on. "Officially, no."

"I'll send the files to your private email then," Delilah said, softening to a real smile. "Along with a question about the dress code for the benefit dinner."

He winked at her. "You're the best. Don't let anyone tell you otherwise."

"I never will."

CHAPTER SEVEN

Dear Maria,

Where the hell is our baby sister? I tried emailing Noah and, lo and behold, his military address no longer works. Did you know he wasn't active duty anymore? I didn't even know you were allowed to quit! You don't think he's in trouble, do you? He would definitely call someone if he was in trouble. He'd call Blessing, right? So where is she?

Call as soon as you can,
Delilah

GOLDEN APPLES. THE SPIRIT of Chicago balanced his chair on two legs and put his feet up on the table. He'd snuck into Chicago's main library after hours to see if the book he remembered from childhood reading forays was still in circulation. It was, and now he was ensconced on the eighth floor of the Harold Washington Library Center, reading the old mythology book like he was twelve again.

He flipped through the weathered pages, ripped and torn by thousands of careless hands over the years—and repaired with great patience, no doubt. Golden apples. He couldn't shake the feeling that it meant something. There were the Golden Apples of Discord, used by the goddess Eris to start the Trojan War. For Kallisti, the fairest.

Well, he doubted anyone had needed to convince Helen to leave her aging husband for a younger man. That happened even without meddling goddesses. There were golden apples of immortality in several mythologies.

A beguiling idea, but that didn't seem right for a serial killer, not unless he thought killing people would bring him immortality. And there were the golden apples of Atlanta, thrown during a foot race to distract the goddess. That sounded almost right. Distractions...

He shelved the book back where he'd found it and drifted through the library. From his pocket he pulled a page from Arámbula's day planner, the unofficial one no one was supposed to know about. The ripped page had been crumpled in the jacket the mayor had left in the office after the meeting. There was a partial date on the corner.

Three numbers and a hunch wasn't much to go on, but it was a start. He stepped through a wall into the shadows, and out into the snowy Chicago night.

* * *

No one at Sub Rosa Securities knew about Delilah's alter ego, the super-villain-by-default Locke. They'd hired her at the Blackhat conference in Las Vegas when she was still playing around as LockPick and earning good money finding holes in people's security systems. Subrosa offered her all that and healthcare. She'd signed once they added a rider to her contract that kept them from asking too many personal questions about life before they hired her.

During her three years in Chicago, no one had ever questioned her results. Legal methods turned up plenty of dirt; her methods turned up more. But Wil had never once asked why. She was pretty sure he wouldn't believe her anyway, even if she swore on a stack of Bibles.

Still, over the years she'd found fewer and fewer reasons to pull out her steampunk suit with its clocks, copper curls, and a top hat. There were better ways to curb her curiosity. But tonight she needed Locke. She needed to have something for people to look at, if they looked at all, because Kalydon hadn't left traces on the computer.

Three hours of gleaning every grain of information from the web had resulted in a pitiful biography. Edgar Kalydon had been an average son of a blue-collar family until a lottery ticket on his 18th birthday had changed his life. He'd dropped out of school, found himself an accountant, and enjoyed his life living off the interest.

There was no record of drug abuse, and although he'd gone through four wives in under twenty years and any number of girlfriends, there was no abuse reported. His major vices seemed to be a stubborn self-centeredness—something Delilah didn't find herself quick to condemn—and a passion for hunting. He'd been a big game hunter in his younger years, and an avid skeet shooter well into his sixties. Now, nearly eighty-five, he seemed to have settled down.

Maybe it was paranoia that made him so cagey. Or maybe he was a victim of the hunt too, being stalked like Arámbula had been.

"Hudson? Thames?" Delilah called over her shoulder as she shrugged a Kevlar jacket cut in Edwardian style on. Four points of red light lit the dark hall—eyes, although not the sort most people liked to see. Hudson and Thames were gargoyle-style Minions, genetic marvels created in her father's lab to guard her in the big city. "Fly over to the Wacker building. Do a preliminary scan, and settle down to watch. I want reports coming into base in thirty-second intervals, and instant alerts if Kalydon arrives. Do you have all the information you need?"

There was the sound of stone scrapping against stone as Hudson opened his mouth. "Yes, ma'am."

"Good. I'll be there in twenty minutes." She finished dressing and strode to the control room. When she had originally bought the apartment, the realtor had waxed poetic on how nice it would be to have a second bedroom, how big it was, what a nice nursery or guest room or workout room it would make. Delilah had nodded noncommittally; the poor woman's nerves wouldn't have handled hearing her real plan, which was to make it a windowless safe room with a super computer that made everything they had at Langley and the Pentagon look slow.

Fortunately, the computer drew power from a kinetic energy strip she'd installed in the subway system and didn't affect her power bill.

Her minion-in-chief glanced up from one of the terminals as she entered. There was no denying that Freddie was a warty, bulbous affront to nature and the good reputation of frogs everywhere, but he passed for a short human in a trench coat and fedora, so she'd never complained. "Kalydon left the building ten minutes ago, ma'am."

Delilah nodded. "Is there anyone else on the premises?"

"Two desk clerks sitting in the lobby. They alternate rounds on the main floor every two hours, checking locks and stuff. It's all for show," he said laconically.

She nodded again. "Should be easy enough. What's the angle of entry?"

"Building across the street. Subrosa has security there." He passed her a tablet with the building layout.

"I know this one."

"We can create a window for seven minutes. Long enough for Thames to tie a zipline on, or fly you across."

Delilah scooped up a handful of tiny golden buttons from a bucket near the computer. One of them buzzed. When activated, they were pinky-nail sized bugs capable of flying and attaching themselves to her chosen victim. In the unlikely event that Kalydon had no security in his apartment that would detect them, she'd leave a few of the snoops behind.

"What do normal girls do on a Tuesday night, Freddie?"

"I wouldn't know, ma'am."

"Neither would I. Pull the car around. I'll be down in a moment." With a perfunctory bow he left the room, webbed feet flapping on the tile. Her other minions, all miniatures of Freddie, continued with their work, bat-like ears twitching as they listened to the Minion Midnight radio station that was tuned too high for her to hear.

There was probably something unethical about creating a sentient species and immediately putting them to work for you. Probably. But his lack of ethics was what made Daddy a successful super villain—and she couldn't help but think that it also contributed to his success as university professor when he left his life of crime. Grad students and minions had a lot in common, including, cold, clammy hands.

Delilah shuddered and left the room to check the mirror one last time. The trick to an effective disguise was to wear something that could pass as commonplace without being everyday wear. The steampunk community in Chicago was legendary, ever since the Affair of 2017. Teenagers wore gear-worked backpacks to school, painted their nails rustic copper colors, and read H.G. Wells on e-readers covered in Gail Carriger stickers.

Most nights of the week it wasn't uncommon to see groups of 'punkers traveling around, usually en route to their role-playing guilds. Even in the dead of winter they were out.

Delilah's outfit blended in with them: a heavy, black-wool coat with brass buttons, a top hat with gears and turkey feathers, and a Daddy-modified pocket watch that was probably breaking the Geneva Convention just by existing. The corset was something she'd picked up at a Ren Fest, along with the leather britches. The boots were from a thrift store, and the copper curls were from her metalworking class in high school. Her teacher had been less than thrilled with the sharp-edged wig, and after some thought, Delilah had rounded the edges so she didn't slice her throat open tossing her hair.

Satisfied that she could pass as just another disaffected college student rebelling against the social norm, Delilah headed downstairs. Freddie was waiting in the underground parking garage in her cab. "Seventy-Seven Wacker, please, Freddie. There's work to be done."

CHAPTER EIGHT

Dear Blessing,

I have a ticket for a flight out of O.R. Tambo International in Jo-burg for the twentieth. If you can't get to South Africa in time, let me know, and I'll send a charter flight to anywhere but a warzone. I know you loathe checking your email, but please, respond!

If it helps at all, Noah is stateside again. The house we're renting for the holidays is less than an hour from his parents' place.

Totally bribing you,
Delilah

INSIDE 77 WACKER, DELILAH leaned against Kalydon's apartment door. The old wood was cold and smooth beneath her fingers. She let out a breath and a part of her travelled with it, seeping into wall and the wood, flowing between the molecules, searching for the break between the wall and the door.

Theoretically she could simply break the bonds between the molecules in the wall and make her own entrance, but that was always a tricky proposition. She'd tried it once or twice, at home in Texas where large explosions went unnoticed by the cattle and jackrabbits. Molecular bonds packed a lot more energy than a twelve-year-old could anticipate though, and she'd accidentally burned a large hole in the Hill Country trying to take a tennis ball apart. Over the years she'd learned to control the energy release, take it into herself or displace it somewhere nearby, but it still tended to be messy.

Delilah's senses crept outwards. A line of metal divided the wood of the door from the wall, but that was it. No real door—and absolutely no lock to pick.

In the corner of her vision, something moved. Delilah pivoted, looking across the hall at the dark, blank windows. Forty-eight floors up with no ledges, and no escape. She touched her earpiece. "How are things outside?"

"All quiet," Hudson reported.

"Nothing to see," Thames agreed.

Freddie cleared his throat. "Control has Kalydon in the building, but no eyes on."

Delilah shook her head. "Not good enough. I want eyes on Kalydon right now."

"Tricky," said a lighter alto voice that was one of the gem-series minions in the control room. "The theater has live security, and isn't readily hackable."

"So send in the pixies."

Various minions swore in a mixture of French and Spanish. The pixies had been made for her youngest sister, Blessing. If you combined reptiles, dragonflies, carnivorous plants, and pure hatred into a flying nightmare, you got a minion who was short-lived, loyal, and perfect for aerial patrol in places where no one noticed three-inch flittering bugs. Her father often referred to them as one of his greatest laboratory disasters, right after the sea monkeys.

Delilah sighed. "Remember—" A scream from the control room cut her off. "...They bite."

"They squish very easily, too," one of the gems said. "Six pixies now en route to the theater."

"Ma'am, there's someone in that hall with you," Hudson said. "I see a shadow."

"No one's come in or out of the building. Front lobby is clear. Both guards are on post," Freddie reported.

At the very edge of her peripheral vision she caught sight of the intruder, a smear of black against the dark windows. Someone started whistling.

Delilah bowed her head and smiled, pulse settling. "Are you whistling 'Hey There Delilah'?"

The Spirit of Chicago swirled closer, becoming almost human. Insubstantial arms wrapped around her waist. "That is your name, isn't it?" he whispered in her ear.

"I can neither confirm nor deny that rumor." She tucked her chin down to hide the smile.

"What are you doing this evening?"

"A little light breaking and entering. You?"

The Spirit of Chicago released her. He seemed solid, although she knew her hand would pass through him like smoke. "A little light prevention of theft and crime."

"I'm not committing a crime."

"Yet."

Pulling a glove off, she fished a piece of paper out of her pocket. "I thought this conversation might come up."

The Spirit of Chicago picked the to-do list from her hand. "Let's see... Pick lock for apartment seven. You know, I'm not a lawyer, but this is something that might be considered incriminating evidence in court."

"That's only a concern if I'm arrested," she said, "and I notice that you left your handcuffs at home."

"Locked to my bed," he said off-handedly.

"Dirty boy."

He leaned against the wall next to the door. "Item two, seduce a superhero. Ah, now I see the problem."

She leaned closer to the door, trying to find the missing lock. Something was barring her way and none of her senses could pick it up.

He winked at her. "You're doing this backward. Why don't you start with seducing the superhero?"

"Because I made the list by priority. I can't jump around higgledy-piggledy. There needs to be some structure." She gave up on the lock. "Are rocket launchers legal in this city?"

"No."

"Do you think you could change that?"

"No."

Locke scowled. "Some date you are."

"This isn't a date. I'm catching you in the process of breaking and entering."

"I haven't broken or entered anything," she grumbled.

He shook the list at her. "Why don't you seduce the superhero first, and then I won't need to arrest you for anything, because you won't be doing anything illegal."

Delilah quirked an eyebrow. "Seducing you is only important if I need to distract you. Which, at this juncture, I don't."

"So unlock the door and kiss me so we can get on with our evening."

She ran her hands along the door again. "Therein you have found the crux of my problem. There isn't a door here."

"What's this?" One barely-solid hand shook the door handle.

"A false door." She eyed the Spirit speculatively. "What's on the other side?"

The glimmer of green light that made up his eyes winked off and on, his version of a blink. "How should I know?"

"Because it's dark in there and you can go in?"

"That would be breaking and entering, the thing I came here to prevent you from doing."

"So?"

"So, no. I won't go in there without an invitation. Not unless you have proof that there's something illegal behind these walls."

326

Delilah glared at the Shadow to no effect. "I bet you we'll find some if we go in there."

"And then, maybe, I'll help you. Not before." His hand, warm, solid, covered in a black glove, encircled her wrist. "Let's leave. We don't need to be here."

"We have movement on the elevator," Control reported as she stumbled into the wall.

She tried to shake the Shadow loose, but his grip only tightened. "Control, repeat that. Who came into the lobby?"

"No one," Freddie said. "All known entrances are quiet. Neither of the guards have moved."

She looked up at her gray-faced captor. "Did you bring someone as back up?"

He shook his head. "You have a sidekick?"

"Minions. Super villains get minions. Superheroes get plucky sidekicks."

"I don't have a side kick and you have minions and an intern," he muttered as the elevator dinged. "That's not fair."

Not good. Not good at all. She licked her lips and hoped she had enough of the family charm to talk her way out of this. "Listen, if anyone asks, this is a costume."

"What?"

Delilah was already walking towards the service elevator and the back door. She punched the lift button and hummed tunelessly as she waited for her exit. Beside her the glass windows reflected frosty light. Tempting, but she was too far up and too unprepared for that kind of exit.

The Spirit of Chicago followed her. "What's going on?"

She turned back as an elevator dinged its arrival and the doors opened. A figure swept out in a heavy, black trench coat. There was an inarticulate squawk as if the sound came through water. The man had a gun. Damn! Damn! Sick with fright, her arms leaden with shock, she grabbed for her watch. Too late. And then the Spirit of Chicago was there, standing in front of her like a smokescreen.

Delilah focused her energy on the pocket watch, praying to whatever god cared for small-time crooks that the magnetic shield would protect them both.

It didn't.

The bullet slammed into the all-too-solid shadow and he fell, his weight pushing her into the elevator. The attacker fired a second round. The bullet splintered the doorframe as she hit the button to close the door.

"Freddie, get a lock on my position and pick me up. I have..." She examined the very-human superhero lying in the elevator beside her. She rubbed her forehead. "We need to get to the hospital."

The cab pulled up in a splash of slush as Delilah opened the delivery door and carried The Spirit of Chicago out over her shoulders. "Get this scene cleaned up. No blood. No tracks," Delilah ordered Thames, who stepped out of the car to help her load the fallen hero. "Freddie. I need you in the back with me."

Hudson climbed into the front seat as Freddie scrambled into the back. "River or hospital?"

Delilah doubled checked the Spirit's pulse. "Hospital, he's still breathing." For now. "Stupid man decided he was going to rescue the damsel in distress." She took her hat and wig off, tossing them into the front passenger seat. "Go dark, Hudson, I don't want anyone harassing the cab companies trying to find us after we drop him off." She gulped down another ragged breath and tried to will her heart to stop racing.

So, she'd almost been shot. No big deal. It happened. She'd survived close encounters before.

But never with casualties after. Victimless crime. Stealing from thieves. Never delivering more bodies to the morgue.

"Are you all right?" Freddie asked.

She nodded, shoving the fear aside. "I hate to be cliché, but who was that masked man upstairs? Did we stumble into the Golden Hunt?"

"Control has pixies quartering the building," Freddie assured her. "We're doing everything we can to find him."

Delilah studied the man in the ski mask bleeding across the back seat of her cab. The right side of the Spirit's black shirt was sticky with blood. "Hand me the first aid kit. We need to staunch the bleeding. Do The Company records say if he's fast healer? Can I let him sleep this off in a hotel somewhere?"

Freddie handed her the kit and helped move the Spirit's arms so she could cut away his black polyester suit. "The Company has no record of him being able to form a corporeal body. They also have no known alias, address, or any other information on him. He's a ghost."

"He's a human who lied to The Company," Delilah said as she dug in the kit for scissors. "Ghosts, as a general rule, don't exist. He's probably like Maria, able to make illusions and control light or something. Maybe be in two places at once." She cut his shirt free and winced in sympathy. The bullet had torn a hole in his abdomen.

"It missed the lungs," Freddie said. "He might still live."

"Yeah." She stuffed sterile gauze in the wound and tried to wrap it. "Take his mask off. I want to see who he is."

Freddie tugged at the black ski mask and revealed a blond man with a face that she would have said reminded her of the better Greek gods if he didn't look exactly like Alderman Adale.

"Merde."

Freddie hissed, as close as he ever came to swearing. "This isn't good."

"You're telling me. We can't let him die. Three superheroes in a year isn't coincidence; it's targeted racial violence."

"Two dead mayors in less than a week is also a noticeable trend."

Delilah touched Adale's face. Still warm, thank all the lucky stars in the firmament, but when she forced his eye open he showed no signs of waking. She shook her head. "Okay. Game plan. We need to create a crime scene outside Adale's apartment." As an afterthought she turned her earpiece on. "Control, did you copy that? Crime scene at Adale's place. I want shots reported to the police. Get someone on the radio, I want to know when the shooting at the Clousson building gets reported and what they say."

"Copy that," Control chittered.

"Freddie, give me your clothes, we need to get Adale dressed as something other than a second-story man. If The Company doesn't know what he is, I want to keep it that way." She'd flirted with Alan Adale. Had he guessed? When he approached her at the Field Museum a few hours ago, had he been trying to tell her he knew? "I can't believe I killed my first date in years."

"He's not dead yet," Freddie said, pulling his jacket closer. "And outing him might prove beneficial for our long range plans in the city."

She held out her hand. "Revealing the pro tem mayor as a super-powered freak is going to throw the city into chaos and make him the target of every big game hunter out there. Atlanta's Golden Hunt is already working in Chicago. For all we know, the shooter was following Alan." That made her stomach leap. What if they had been following him? "I need a background check on Adale finished. Everyone he's talked to. Every meeting. Every hour accounted for. Start a file on the mayor and start cross-referencing everything he did with what Adale was doing. Find all the points of connection."

Her minion-in-chief frowned, bulbous eyes protruding further than usual under feathery eyebrows. "What are you thinking?"

"I'm wondering if Adale wasn't the target all along. Maybe someone knew who he was after dark, and Arámbula was just collateral."

"It's coincidence," Freddie insisted.

She shook her head. "That was a well-timed encounter. Too well done for my comfort. Now, stop arguing and hand me your pants."

Freddie grumbled under his breath. "Aren't you going to look the other way?"

"What? What are you trying to hide? You're part frog, part plant. You don't even have genitalia!"

"I have modesty!"

She rolled her eyes and faced the window, watching the Christmas lights dance on the snow until she felt Freddie's pants slap on her hand.

"Hand tailored, I'll have you know. Custom made just for me!"

"By a minion we keep at the castle," Delilah shot back as she loosened Adale's belt. "This is so awkward." A hot blush crept up her neck and she giggled. "See, you mentioned modesty and now I feel bad about stripping an unconscious man."

Hudson laughed in the front seat, sounding more like an avalanche. "We're about to kick the guy out bleeding into the snow and you feel bad about seeing his undies?"

She turned to Freddie for help. He was laughing at her too. "Shut up! This is not enthusiastic consent! I don't want to... molest him."

"Just shut your eyes," Freddie said. "I'm genderless, no reproductive organs, so I can't molest anyone. Right?"

"Right." She shut her eyes firmly. No peeking allowed.

"What kind of underwear is that?"

Ha! She peeked. "Those are running shorts."

"Fond of black, isn't he."

"Shut up and put the pants on him. And," she said, noticing the bandage was soaking through, "get him some more gauze."

"Someone is going to notice he's stripped and treated. Shouldn't we... You know... Leave him for the doctors?"

"Gauze!" She pulled the soaked dressing away. A hard lump gleamed sullenly in the cab-light. "His body expelled the bullet. That's good, right?"

"Coming up on the hospital," Hudson said. "There's two police cruisers at the ER door and an ambulance unloading."

"Pull up, we'll push him out on the far side so they don't see in. Freddie, you better switch with Hudson when we slow down, we'll need to evade like the very devil was on our tail."

"Ya think?"

"Less snark, more minioning!"

Freddie snorted.

Hudson slowed the car. "Switch... now!"

Freddie threw the door open, helped Delilah shove Alan Adale into the snowdrift, and hopped into the seat Hudson was hastily vacating. They sped off, leaving the alderman bleeding in the dirty snow.

CHAPTER NINE

Dear Daddy,

Freddie says he needs more pants. His measurements are attached. Don't ask. Just... don't ask.

D

BRIGHT SUNLIGHT WAS OBSTRUCTED by the blocky body of Detective Morrow. Alan turned away and tried to make sense of the pain. Machines. Beeping. Squeaking wheels. Nothing he associated with home.

"How are you feeling?" the detective asked.

"Sore. Confused. Um... This is a hospital, isn't it?"

"John H. Stroger Junior," Morrow confirmed.

Alan nodded and instantly regretted it. Bright lights twinkled in his vision, gradually fading to black spots. "Home sweet home. I wonder if the nurse who named me still works downstairs." He blinked the last of the spots away and found Detective Morrow's eyes. "Pertinent question, why am I here?"

"Someone shot you."

"What?"

Morrow sat down beside the hospital bed. "Last night, around eleven thirty, you were shot outside your home."

"Shot? In Chicago? No. No, no-no. We have the lowest incident of gun crime in the country. People do not get—" His words slurred. What was in that IV? "People do not get, shot," he enunciated clearly.

"Uh-huh. How you planning on explaining the bullet hole that ripped your side open?"

Alan looked down at his aching right side. "Um..."

"You were shot." A notebook appeared as if by magic.

"Cute trick."

"I do parties," Morrow said, pulling a pen out of his jacket pocket. "Now, what do you remember about last night?"

A cluttered mess of colors and shapes gabbled for attention in his mind. "There was a"—not a girl, couldn't say girl, that sounded too young—"a woman. At the apartment. We talked." Flirted. Most assuredly flirted. "We talked."

"Do you remember what you talked about?"

Lock picks. "Stuff."

"And did she have a gun?"

"No. No." He shook his head against the pain. "She didn't hurt me." The fragments of the night before started piecing themselves together. Locke in the hall with her steampunk gear. Flirting. An elevator. A man? Probably a man, stepping out of the elevator with a gun. "How did I get here?" he whispered to himself.

Morrow leaned forward. "What?"

"How did I get here?" Alan asked, louder. "I don't remember that part."

The detective cleared his throat and pulled out an electronic file pad. "According to the nine-one-one report, two calls came from your area reporting the sound of gun shots. First call was at nine-twenty-seven, the second at nine-thirty-one. The second caller reported that they saw a gray sedan driving fast down the street. A traffic camera in your neighborhood picked up a gray sedan doing seventy at nine-thirty-three. Indiana plates. We ran it, the car was reported stolen two months ago. No joy there."

"I was kidnapped?" That didn't work. Delilah had no reason to help him. No reason not to expose him.

Not unless their flirtation meant more to her than she was letting on. The drugs were clearing out of his system fast now that he was awake and focusing. "I hate to ask, but what was I wearing when I was brought in?"

"Same thing you wore to the party last night; black slacks, dress shoes, no shirt. Someone took it off and tried to bandage you up. The pants were ripped at the hem."

His eyebrows went up. "Is that the usual MO for an attempted murder? Wouldn't it be easier to let me bleed to death?"

The detective shrugged. "The running hypothesis at the station is that it was a case of mistaken identity. Most of our violent crimes are related to domestic violence now. The girl you were with, she's not married is she?"

"No, not that I'm aware of. No ring or anything." He'd checked the first time they'd met, and every time since. Delilah wasn't Chicago's most eligible bachelorette, but she was in the top ten and making the boys in town work for her attention.

"Can you give me her name so I can check it out, just in case?" Morrow asked.

"Um..." There wasn't a good answer to that. "We aren't... We weren't... This was not..."

Morrow rolled his eyes. "You're a politician, Adale, not a saint. Just spill already."

"She doesn't want to be in the spotlight. We weren't going public with the relationship yet. It's too early. I don't want people harassing her." Close enough to the truth. Probably closer than the truth would sound. But Morrow didn't look like he was buying it. "I'll call her when I get home and see if she'll talk to you."

A familiar face poked around the corner.

Morrow turned and frowned. "Chief Wyte, good to see you." The detective glanced over his shoulder at Alan. "Do you want visitors? He was out in the foyer when I came in this morning."

Alan nodded to the chief of police. "Hello." Wyte had been one of Mayor Arámbula's poker buddies. He was always around when you didn't need him, always subtly putting down the people around him, always ready to schmooze his way into power and money. "Coming to check on the walking wounded?"

"I'm just being neighborly." Wyte patted Morrow on the shoulder as he walked past. "Great job, Detective. Why don't you take a break while I chat to my buddy here?" The snake oil all but dripped off him.

Morrow peered over the chief's shoulder and waited for a nod from Alan before he left. The detective was good people.

"Chief," Alan said, refocusing his attention. "I wasn't expecting you to stop by."

"Really?" Wyte put a hand to his chest as if he were hurt. "Come on, Alan. We've been friends for how long and you didn't think I'd come out to check on you?"

"Have we ever spoken without Arámbula around?"

Wyte sighed. "You wound me. I know you like put on the Man of the People act, but come on, Adale. We're cool, right?"

There was a knock on the door and Alan's side burned when he sucked in his breath.

"Delilah Samson." Wyte moved in like a heat-seeking missile.

The steampunk Locke was nowhere to be seen in the perfection of Chicago style that Delilah wore as her day costume. Her dark hair was pulled up in an elegant twist and her flawless skin was framed by a tailored purple suit so dark it was almost black. He coughed to hide a snarl when Wyte reached for her.

"Chief Wyte," Delilah held out her hand like she expected him to bow and kiss her fingertips. Wyte almost did. That woman could wrap men around her finger like nobody's business. "I heard you were here."

Alan scowled. Delilah's gaze flickered to him and she winked. It was enough.

"What can I do for you, Miss Samson? Name it, and it's yours."

She fluttered her eyelashes, the little coquette. "Can you make rocket launchers legal in this city?"

"Um." Wyte stumbled over the request, but Alan could see the wheels in his head turning as he tried to think of a way to make it happen. "Well..."

Delilah laughed. "I'm teasing! All I need is to borrow a few plain-clothes police officers for Addison's New Year's Eve party."

Alan rolled his eyes. Petty jealousy was not attractive, he told himself firmly. And he wasn't jealous. Delilah flirted with people. She probably did it without thinking. It wasn't her fault Wyte was tripping over her like some under-sexed pimply teen waiting for his first kiss.

"Will you walk me to my car?" Delilah asked the police chief.

"Of course!"

Of course. Alan ground his teeth together.

Delilah hit him with a dazzling smile. "I did bring a little something for you, Adale. A get well card from Subrosa Securities."

"Trolling for clients?" Wyte teased as Delilah left a small white envelope on the nightstand beside Alan's bed.

Her smile was deceptively calm when she turned away. "Subrosa has always made the safety of Chicago's prominent citizens a top priority. You can't have your police everywhere, but I can put a team anywhere in this city in under five minutes." The words were innocuous enough, but there was a hard edge to them that offered the promise of swift retaliation if things didn't go her way.

Alan waited until they'd left before he opened the envelope: a generic get-well card and Delilah's business card. On the back, in a careful hand, she'd written, "Do not trust Wyte."

That put a slightly sinister spin to Wyte's visit. And Delilah's. Was she tracking him or the police chief?

A nurse came in with a tray of what he was certain was nourishing but bland food. "How are you feeling today?"

"Fantastic. I could run a marathon," Alan said. "When are they releasing me?"

"After a gunshot?" Her dark eyebrows climbed. "Honey, you ain't going nowhere for at least seventy-two hours. Eat your lunch and get comfy."

Alan smiled politely and took the food. The nurse nodded approval and closed the door behind her.

Nine minutes later, he ghosted out of the room leaving nothing behind but a memory and a plate of rubbery scrambled eggs.

CHAPTER TEN

Daddy,

Thank you for the watch! It's absolutely perfect, and it even matches my new necklace. See you next week.

Lovingly,
Delilah

DELILAH CHECKED HER WATCH, then looked up at the McCormick Tribune YMCA. It wasn't nearly as dingy as she'd anticipated. True, the rows of neat two-story houses were all closing in on their century marks, and the cars parked along the street were not the newest models by any stretch of the imagination, but everything seemed well kept. Christmas lights adorned the trees. Wreaths hung in windows. Wood smoke and snow filled the air with a wintery perfume. All that was missing was a wintery soundtrack and some mistletoe, and she'd be in a bad made-for-TV holiday movie.

"I told you it wasn't the bad end of town," Travys said from the depths of his hoody and jacket. "Perfectly safe."

"Remind me again how I got roped into this," she said as Travys opened the front doors of the YMCA, hot air and the smell of sweat swamping her.

Travys smiled. "I have to do community service as part of my social awareness class. You are here because you need to leave the office occasionally."

"I'm work oriented." There were a million and one things she needed to do tonight, but the minions were still trying to trace the late mayor's last hours. So rather than pacing the apartment and grinding her teeth, she'd come here. To play basketball, because Travys told her she had to.

"You're a workaholic who's going to die of a stress-induced heart attack at thirty if you don't watch it."

"What are you, my mother?"

"Locker room is over there," Travys pointed.

"I see the sign."

He grinned like a shark who'd seen a seal pup. Poor boy. The chance to school his boss on the court was giving him delusions of grandeur. She hadn't played since college, not competitively, but a girl didn't grow up with four active siblings without learning how to play one-on-one everything like a demon bent on the conquest of hell. Delilah changed, tightened her shoelaces, and stretched. A little physical activity was good for the soul. Especially—she snickered—if it left her favorite intern trembling in terror whenever she mentioned sports.

The YMCA had multiple courts laid out side by side. Several games of pick up were going on, and in one corner a middle-aged Hispanic woman was coaching a co-ed little league team with polite English and a few earthy curse words in Spanish. The kids were eating it up. One even made a basket.

Very few of the players turned to look at the new girl. Skinny, white, ponytail... Nothing to see here. If Angela the Hollywood starlet had walked in, people would have turned. If it were Maria, with her dark-tan skin and emerald-green eyes, people would have stopped. If Blessing walked in, pale curls framing a face with lavender eyes, people would have gathered around her faster than she could blink. Even

Gideon, their baby brother, would have caught someone's attention. But of all the Smith children, Delilah had to admit she was the average one. Average height. Average weight. Average looks. Average everything. Even her super quirks didn't do enough to set her apart from every other brown-haired, brown-eyed human walking the planet—and she took comfort knowing she was part of a vast majority. Stealth was far, far easier when you had a forgettable face.

Only one person acknowledged her, a muscular blond man shooting hoops with some teens on the far side of the gym. Probably another coach. He nodded to her with a smile, and then made a three-point basket.

"Hey," Travys said, dribbling a ball like a Harlem Globetrotter. "Ready to see my Skillz?"

Delilah snorted. "You did not just put a Z on the end of that."

He laughed and tried to run past her for a lay-up.

Delilah stole the ball, pivoted, and made a basket. "Oh, wait," she said, cocking her head. "Who took her college team to conference championships? Was that me? It was, wasn't it?"

Travys looked at her in mock outrage. "Oh, no. No, this is not happening. I'm young and viral."

"Virile," she corrected as he made a shot, and it bounced off the rim. "Okay, maybe viral."

They played a quick game that Delilah won by a point before the group across the gym broke up. "I gotta check in with my people," Travys said.

Delilah raised an eyebrow. "You have people?"

"Quinton. He's a good kid. I'm sort of mentoring him. The Y has a tutoring program, and I'm helping him with math."

"You dragged me away from work to play basketball so we could check that this kid is doing his homework?" She rolled her eyes. "I have minions for chores like that."

Travys's wide grin returned. "Yeah, so do I. You."

She wagged her finger at him. "You are getting coal for Christmas!"

Travys laughed at her anger and pointed out a scrawny kid badly in need of new sneakers and a couple of 2000-calorie cheeseburgers. He was... maybe a size twelve mens? Maybe thirteen. She'd have to get Travys to steal one of his sneakers so she could get the size and replace those shoes.

"I need to cut him out of the herd," Travys said. "Isolate him."

"I'm glad you've been paying attention in biology class."

Travys bumped her with his elbow. "Go be my distraction."

"What?"

"Go flirt with his coach or something."

Delilah widened her eyes and pretended to be outraged. "Flirt with a random stranger? What are you, my pimp?"

Travys rolled his eyes. "Just go in and do your girly thing with his coach, so I can get Quinton alone. Please?"

Delilah's eyes narrowed. "What 'Girly Thing'?"

"You know, the flippy-hair pretty-girl thing you do right before you emotionally disembowel people and leave them socially dead. You do it at parties all the time."

"I don't emotionally disembowel people!" Delilah protested as Travys pushed her toward the other side of the gym. "I just speak my mind."

"Trust me, it's the same thing."

Delilah stopped walking when the coach turned. "Alderman Adale." She looked over her shoulder at Travys who made a shooing motion and then pretended to ignore her. Some days, the universe really was against you. She turned back to Adale. "Hello."

"Hello." Adale smiled.

Quinton shuffled at the alderman's side as Delilah debated what to do. Well, what the hell. Why not? She smiled perkily and tilted her head. "Hi! I'm a distraction! Want to shoot some hoops?" She grabbed Adale's arm and led him away from Quinton so Travys could go in for the kill.

"A distraction?" Adale asked. "What are you distracting me from?"

She fluttered her eyelashes exaggeratedly. "I'm supposed to leave Quinton isolated, so his math tutor can talk to him. I'm not sure if Travys is issuing death threats or trying to convince Quinton that a higher GPA is the only way to meet the University of Chicago cheerleaders. We're supposed to act like we're interested in talking to each other," she added when Adale turned back to the boys with a frown.

"Right, of course." His smile was warm. "How are you?"

"Better than you are, I imagine. How's your side?"

He gave a one-shouldered shrug. "I've been worse. Want to kiss and make it better? Or are you going steady with Wyte now?"

She laughed. "What is this, high school?" She bounced the ball before adding more seriously, "I have reasons to be cautious around Wyte, as do you. Leaving him alone with you while you were wounded seemed like a bad idea."

"So you rushed to my rescue?" Alan teased.

It shouldn't have been funny, but Delilah laughed at the absurdity of the thought anyway. "I hardly think of it as rushing to your rescue after you took a bullet for me. How are you really? Should you be playing basketball a day after being shot?"

"By the time the hospital triage team got to me I was only grazed."

Delilah relaxed. "Here's to fast healing."

Alan caught her hands with a gentle touch and finessed the ball from her grip. "Want to play a quick game of twenty-one while your intern practices his Spanish Inquisition routine on my boy? I promised Quinton's mom he'd be ready to leave by ten."

"He'll survive," Delilah said as she circled around, waiting for an opportunity to steal the ball back. Hot or not, no man who'd just walked out of the hospital was beating her on the court. She feinted in for the ball but Alan twisted, leaving her nothing to do but slap his hip.

"Are we playing or not?"

Delilah raised her eyebrows. "Half-court, poison points at eleven, no tips, no free throws?" They'd shoot only at one basket, each player trying to make twenty-one points with a combination of two-point and three-point shots. Eleven was the poison point; if a player had eleven points and missed their next shot, they reset to zero.

"And here I thought my math days were over."

Delilah shrugged. "I'd love to stay longer, but I have plans tonight and I need to drop Pumpkin back at the dorm before I hit the club scene."

Alan dribbled the ball. "I'm telling Travys you called him a Pumpkin." He feinted left, pivoted right, and still came up against Delilah blocking his way to the net.

"Come on, Adale. Aren't you going to show me some moves?"

He stepped back, dribbling as he watched Delilah. This time he drove left; Delilah swiped the ball out of his hands, pivoted, and made a three-point shot.

"Come on," she taunted. "You have to want it."

He caught the ball as it bounced between the nets. "What are we playing for?"

Distraction. "Fun?"

"How about a kiss for the winner?" He shot her smoldering look that promised hot and dirty things if she wanted them.

Picturing him naked wasn't necessary—she'd gotten a good show last night. "How 'bout you buy me dinner?"

"Winner gets a free dinner?" Alan sounded doubtful.

"I get a free dinner," Delilah clarified, "because I'm going to win."

Alan shook his head, turned, and did a lay-up. "Maybe you'll have to buy me dinner."

Delilah took the ball. "Mmm, hmm." She stepped closer, invading his personal space, keeping eye contact. Alan's eyes widened. She could hear the hitch in his breath as she brushed against him. She smiled, and shot the ball over his head into the net.

Alan caught her around the waist, and her heart raced as her cheeks heated. "That's cheating!"

"No it's not." They were close enough to kiss. Tempting. So tempting. She tore herself away from his gaze and stepped back. Shooting him a flirty smile she sent the ball flying over his head. Nothing but net. "Five to two."

He shook his head and retrieved the ball. Ten points flew past for each of them. Alan jumped and grabbed, pivoted, and scored two more points.

"You're not going to hit twenty-one like that." She shot another two-pointer that sailed over his head. "Oh, wait, that puts me ahead! Nineteen to fourteen, me."

Delilah bent over to pick up the ball, making sure Alan got an eyeful of her hind end while she adjusted her tank top. A little tug down was all she needed.

His eyes widened when she stood up. "That is cheating."

"What?" She batted her eyelids innocently. "A little cleavage wouldn't distract a big, tough politician like you, would it?"

"On anyone else? No. On you? Make a couple baskets already so I can kiss you."

Delilah took an unopposed shot as Alan devoured her with his eyes. "Oh, come on. I know you aren't that tired!"

"I'm recovering from a gunshot!" he protested. "And that was a free throw. One point for you."

"What!"

He smirked as he leaned close to steal the ball. "Twenty to fourteen." Smiling, he shot a three-pointer.

Seven sweaty minutes later Delilah scored her final two points. "I win."

"Right," Alan agreed with a cocky smile. The ball bounced away, forgotten, as he caressed her face. "You win." His lips brushed over hers, warm and tempting.

The list of pros and cons burned to ash at his touch. Love always brought a risk. Relationships brought a risk. But something that felt this good couldn't be wrong, could it? She tilted her head, deepening the kiss. Alan wrapped his arms around her and the kiss became something more, almost desperate. A thousand unspoken words silenced at hundreds of chance meetings fueled their collision.

Movement on the edge of her peripheral vision was the only thing that pulled Delilah away from his embrace. She cleared her throat as Alan wiped lipstick from his mouth. "Well. Hi."

Travys raised his eyebrows. "Hi."

"Are you done?" Delilah asked nonchalantly.

"Am I interrupting something?" Travys asked.

Yes. She made eye contact with Alan. Yes, he'd definitely interrupted something. She just wasn't sure what yet. "I was distracting him. That's what you wanted, wasn't it? Ready to go?"

"Whenever you are," Travys said, frowning at Alan.

"Good night, Alderman." She smiled brightly and walked away, low-grade panic jangling in her chest.

Travys ran to catch up with her. "What was that?"

"I don't know."

"Didn't you say you didn't trust him?" Travys asked, stopping short of chasing after her into the woman's locker room. "I swore that's what you said."

Delilah threw her hands up in frustration. "The situation has changed, okay? I need to go home and think."

Travys let the door swing closed with silent disapproval.

Well, that had not gone as planned. She leaned back against a cold metal locker and stared unseeing at the wall.

She had to get that background check finished, it was the only way out of this mess. Either Alan could be trusted, and she was safe to fall in love, or she'd just kissed a man she was destined to kill.

CHAPTER ELEVEN

Dear Maria,

I know you're busy with the elections and everything else that's coming up, but I do need an RSVP for Christmas. It's my year to set up the holiday fun and twist arms. This is Phase One of the arm-twisting. Mom wants everyone home for Christmas. I will beg, bribe, and threaten you with physical pain and the destruction of all you hold dear to make sure you are there.

Let's start with the bribe. I know that in your free time you happened to cross paths with a certain dark-eyed wonder boy who goes by the name of Kon and controls the weather.

I also happen to know that The Company has a very extensive file on him. Sorry, had. Until this morning when I accidentally smashed their firewall to smithereens. The file is now in my possession. And my, but it makes fascinating reading. I may have to give this cowboy a call, see if he likes bareback riding.

Don't even trying to hack my system. The data is on a reserved hard drive and not connected to anything you can touch, kept in an undisclosed location that even my best minions won't divulge.

RSVP or else.

Your evilest sister,
Delilah

ALAN DRIFTED THROUGH THE shadows of the alley to the dead drop, memories of Delilah still keeping him warm. He'd spent all day wondering whether or not he should call her. Twice he'd composed emails. Ads for floral arrangements had teased him, but he wasn't sure if Delilah would like flowers. And, if she did like flowers, she probably wouldn't like them delivered to her office. Peace of mind was out of the question until he could figure out exactly where their relationship was.

Which wasn't going to happen until after this meet-up.

When he'd originally joined The Company, he'd been a distrustful teen who was unwilling to give them too much power over him. Eighteen years of other people picking everything from his name to the food he ate to the clothes he wore had left a mark. He liked the freedom of adulthood, and The Company's standard contract was too restrictive for his liking.

The dead drop had been the compromise. A Company operative left him messages that he'd read and leave untouched in the forgotten space between boarded up buildings. There'd been a dearth of communication since the death of the Wooden Wonder, but last night there'd been a message.

Two women stood under a broken street lamp, one rather elderly with an uptown style and primly pinned gray hair. The other wore a leather catsuit with a slash of red that matched her matte lipstick. Katrina, The Company boss, and the superhero Lead Feather who often acted as Katrina's bodyguard. The Wooden Wonder had once said Lead Feather could kill with a touch, turn people to stone, and stop superpowers from working. It was probably office gossip, but he made a point of avoiding her all the same.

"Katrina." He stayed a shadow, hovering in the darkness out of reach of human touch.

She turned to face him with a scowl. "The Spirit of Chicago? You're exactly how I imagined you."

Lead Feather's fingers flexed in black gloves. "I expected more."

"I'm sorry to disappoint you," Alan lied smoothly. "How may I be of service this evening?"

Katrina glanced at Lead Feather, a sidelong expression she probably didn't intend him to see. "We need to know the city is safe."

"As safe as I can make it."

"And you know of no other mutants here? No rogues or villains?" Katrina asked.

"I've encountered none on my patrols."

"Very good. If you find one, trap them and hold them until we come. The Company has lost too many operatives in recent years. We're to the point where we have to offer even rogues a second chance of safety with us."

"Are fewer mutants being born?" Alan asked.

Again Katrina shared a look with Lead Feather. "We believe so. Super powered humans can't breed. Every experiment and attempt to provide us with another generation has failed. I fear the time will come when you are alone, Spirit of Chicago. The only one who remembers us and our noble purpose."

He and all of Delilah's family, if he'd understood Delilah correctly. "There are rumors of others—"

"We know," Lead Feather cut him off with a snap. "That's why we're here."

Katrina held up her hand for silence. "We're aware of the Russians."

That wasn't what he'd meant, but Alan didn't correct her. Better to leave Delilah's family out of this, though he suspected that if they were anything like Delilah they could take care of themselves. "You want me to follow them?" he guessed. The only Russians in Chicago were not super-anything that he was aware of, but if The Company knew something different, he wanted some skin in the game.

"No," Katrina said. "Tomorrow night you'll come with, unofficially. Once we have the location, I'll place it in the dead drop."

"You can't fight," Lead Feather said in a bored voice. "You can't open doors or repel bullets, but you may be useful in other ways."

"Agreed," he said. "What are we meeting the Russians about?"

"They are rumored to have a black market toxin that is fatal to even our fastest healers," Katrina said, but the way her eyes darted away told him it was a lie. "We need you to watch them. Possibly follow them back to their hide out."

Warning bells sounded in his mind, a sixth sense that something wasn't quite right. "If you wish. I will be as silent as a... ghost." That was essentially the truth. Ghosts were known for rattling around, moaning, and generally causing a raucous when no one wanted them to, and that's exactly what he had in mind.

Fading out of their sight, Alan watched. Curiosity and dead cats and all. There was no logical reason for them not to have an extra person with them unless they were trying to limit witnesses.

"Do you think—" Lead Feather began.

Katrina waved her hand for silence again. "Not here."

They walked nearly a mile of city streets before getting into a plain black four-door sedan. Alan ghosted into the darkness behind the seats, a pool of shadow hidden from sight.

"Do you think the ghost will listen to you?"

"He's not a ghost and I doubt he'll listen entirely, but he's been reasonably good at following directions before," Katrina said as she started the car.

Lead Feather buckled her seatbelt with more force than necessary. "You should have let me take him out. Any super being not under our control is a threat to our existence."

"No," Katrina said. "The ghost is expendable enough, but not yet."

"Do you think Locke will try to recruit him?"

"She's taken others like him. Amber Gris in Maine? That had the thief's fingerprints all over it. And the one in New York last year, the school teacher."

"Rage?" Lead Feather asked. "She only escaped for a few months."

"Long enough to put our operation in jeopardy. We lost Arktos trying to bring her in."

Lead Feather snorted. "He's not lost."

"He's useless if he can't fight or fly."

The superhero snorted in disagreement. "If you thought he was useless, he'd be six-feet under by now."

"He's momentarily useless," Katrina said. "Once we have the Grecian formula we'll be able to bring Arktos back to the fold, and make ten more like him if we want."

Alan slid out of the car; he'd heard enough. He'd always harbored a suspicion that The Company wasn't exactly on the side of angels; this was the confirmation he'd been waiting for. The seller with the Grecian formula was more of a concern. There wasn't an outfit in Chicago that wouldn't like a super powered freak on their pay roll. If he didn't get the drug off the market, Chicago was going to be Ground Zero for World War III.

Brooding, he walked down the dark and empty street to the train station, his body reformed around him. His phone rang. "This is Adale."

"Mayor Adale, this is Chasten Huntley from the office. I was Mayor Arámbula's social secretary," he added in case Alan had forgotten the hyper young man rushing around the office like a fruit fly on a bad dose of meth.

Alan sigh with resignation. "I thought you headed home at five."

"Well, I was, but I came back because I... ah... forgot something and then Mister Kalydon called."

"Kalydon?" Alan searched his memory for the name. "He's an older gentleman, isn't he? Not a native."

"That's him," Huntley said. "He's a major player in the financial sector of Chicago. You probably didn't meet him as an alderman, he's a bit of a recluse, but he's decided to make some time for you."

"How generous of him." Alan rolled his eyes.

"Great, then I'll tell him you'll stop by the club for dinner at eight."

Alan stopped walking and stared at his phone. It was already after six. Factoring in time for dinner, he had less than five hours before he needed to leave for the meet site. "Listen," he said, resuming the conversation. "Tonight isn't going to work for me. Tell Kalydon I appreciate his invitation, but I can't accept. If he's upset, remind him I'm only the temporary mayor. After the voting in January, if I'm elected, I'd be happy to meet him."

"Mister Kalydon is very influential," Chasten wheedled. "I'm sure he could be of great use to the mayor's campaign."

Alan pinched the bridge of his nose. "I'm going to forget you said that. Any meaning would be unethical. I'm not in the business of buying votes."

"S-sorry, sir. Would you, um, be willing to stop by the office again tonight? If you can't meet him for dinner, Mister Kalydon could stop here. Or meet you at your home."

The last thing Alan wanted was a stranger in his apartment. "I'm a couple blocks from the office. If Kalydon can be there in the next twenty minutes, I can meet with him."

"He'll be here, sir. I'll see to it personally."

Alan checked his phone, then turned it off. Kalydon... Kalydon... The name bounced around his head as he walked through the slush to the nearest pedway entrance. Chicago's underground passages, once used for bootlegging, were now the warmest way to move around during the winter. He jogged down the cement stairs to the crowded underground.

An Apple billboard toting the latest in home computer equipment caught his eye. Ah ha. Kalydon was the man who lived at 77 Wacker where Delilah had been scouting, the man Arámbula had gone to meet the night he died.

Alan walked into his empty office twenty minutes later. Everyone was gone for the night except for Chasten Huntley, who was hovering out in the foyer in anticipation of their guest. He'd made a mental note to check into Huntley's background when he had some free time. The boy was way too eager to please, and inferiority complexes were a liability in politics.

Chasten knocked on the doorframe. "In here, sir."

An elderly man followed him into to Alan's Spartan office. Kalydon was an octogenarian who looked a breath away from natural mummification. Wisps of white hair brushed across his liver-spotted scalp. The tatty suit he wore was several decades out of style and sewn for a younger, more muscular, man. He wore rings, thick bands of gold and silver, but nothing else. No glasses, no cane, even though his stride was uneven. His eyes were filled with burning hatred.

"Mr. Kalydon," Alan said, "it's a pleasure to meet you."

Kalydon sat and lifted his chin. "You're a liar. A pretty liar, but still a liar." Chasten stationed himself behind Kalydon, broadcasting his loyalties loudly for those who cared to notice.

Alan nodded. "Right. It's good to know where we all stand. Why are you here, Mr. Kalydon?"

"To see matters settled. I'm moving to Chicago, and I was working with Arámbula to make sure my needs are met."

"I'm sorry, I don't follow. Why do you need the mayor for this?"

Kalydon creaked as he leaned forward. "I have more money than God. I can make you. I can break you. Give me what I want, and we'll be friends."

Alan shook his head. "I'm sorry, what are you looking for? Tax breaks? A license to kill? Introductions to a golf club? I'm very sorry that Arámbula misled you, but that's not what mayors do."

"You can get the superheroes out of my way," Kalydon said. "That'll be enough."

Alan hid his thrill of nerves with a raised eyebrow. "I don't think Chicago has superheroes."

Kalydon sneered at him. "That's what book learning does for you. Makes you think you're smart when you're stupid as a pig. There's at least two in the city right now, maybe more. Monday morning I want you to draft some papers kicking 'em out of the city."

Alan raised an eyebrow. "I'm not Hitler. I won't pin the proverbial Star of David on anyone so you can be happier. And I certainly won't knock on doors to ask people if they're mutant freaks. As long as they're living the laws of the land, I don't care what they do."

"So change the laws," Kalydon said. "Or watch your back. Your choice." He stood up with Chasten's help. "I expect you'll see reason soon enough. If not?" He shrugged. "Politicians are cheap in Chicago."

CHAPTER TWELVE

Delilah,

I'm not going to make it up to surprise Blessing for Christmas like we talked about. There's a mission I need to run. Something last minute. I'm sorry. Tell Blessing I'm sorry. She'll understand. I'll be home by New Years.

Blessing's gift is being mailed to you. Please make sure she gets it on Christmas. Tell her I love her.

Respectfully yours,
MJR Noah Cobb
5 SFG(A), 2nd Battalion
Fort William Henry Harrison, MO
Office: (408) 555-2152

ALAN STOOD IN THE cold, staring at the light shining through his apartment window as snow flurries fell around him. Getting shot had been a very bad idea. Getting shot again because an assassin was waiting in his living room sounded even worse. Two press conferences in twenty-four hours was something that should be banned by the Geneva Convention. And keeping Chasten Huntley on staff was definitely against the eighth amendment. First thing tomorrow he and Chasten were going to have a little chat about acceptable political behavior, and then Chasten could check out with HR and go find a new job. Preferably a long way from Chicago.

But that was a problem for tomorrow.

Frowning, Alan typed in the passcode to get into his building and took the private elevator to the seventh floor. All three of his neighbors were the married-to-work types who saw apartments like this as a place to sleep when in town and nothing more. Alan felt he fit right in.

He unlocked the door and waited for the sound of movement. The light stayed on. Alan pushed the door open and the scent of Chinese food wafted out into the hall.

Delilah sat on the couch reading, legs curled up, high heels lying neglected by the front door. It hurt. The pain of wanting was staggering. How many times had he dreamed of this? Of coming home to something other than a cold, empty house?

Delilah glanced up, smile warm and engaging. "Are you all right?"

No. "Yes."

"You look a little pale."

"Long day at the office." He couldn't seem to convince his feet to move. Everything he wanted was just across the threshold and he couldn't take the step. Delilah stood, long limbs stretching like a ballerina ready to dance. The way her hips moved as she walked toward him was mesmerizing. Every curve begged to be touched. Caressed. And oh, how he wanted to reach out and hold her. But he couldn't.

She stopped in front of him. "Alan? Are you sure you're not hurt?"

"No worse than I was." She took his hand in hers, and the warmth broke the spell. He shook his head. "Sorry. Tired."

"Shock," she said with the authority of one who had seen it before. Delilah tugged at his arm and brought him inside. "Let's sit down and eat."

Alan took his coat off and tried to reorder his thoughts. She wasn't doing this on purpose, he was certain of that. At least, ninety-five percent certain. He'd been on the receiving end of seduction before and it usually involved less clothing on the part of the seducer. One girl had gone as far as to wait for him in his dorm room wearing nothing but a bright blue thong. Delilah was still dressed in her suit from the office.

"Alan?" She laid the plates on the table with efficient ease. "What's wrong?"

"Nothing."

"You're shaking." She came to him, hands brushing his arms. "Are you cold? Sick?" Concern and fear filled her dark eyes. "What happened?"

"Nothing." He stepped away, retreating to the familiar comfort of his overstuffed couch. "It's... silliness. I'll tell you after dinner."

She raised a questioning eyebrow. "It's really hard to partner with someone, or guard them, if they're keeping secrets. I find it particularly annoying." The muscles around her eyes tightened with anger.

He sighed in defeat. "It's been a bad day and to come home to this..." The words trailed off as he choked on the rest.

She sat down across from him. "I didn't think I'd scare you. I didn't even think about how shocking it must be to get shot like that. I'm sorry. That was thoughtless of me." She shook her head in disgust. "You weren't here at eight and I didn't want to sit on the landing while the food grew cold."

"It's not that." He licked his lips as he tried to think of a way to explain. "I'm not good with emotions I guess. It's getting shot, the press conference, Arámbula's viewing, police reports, there was a lot of emotional stress today. Other things. I came home on the defensive. And then you were just here. Sitting here."

"I'm so sorry." Delilah stood up and slipped on her shoes. "Try to eat, please? And I'll, um, send you a text or something if I hear anything about our mutual friend."

Alan spun around in confusion. "What? Where are you going?"

Delilah stood frozen by the hall closet, coat in hand. "Home?"

"I thought we were going to eat dinner together. Catch up. Talk."

"Not when you're already stressed out." She pulled her coat over. With a sweet smile she walked over and kissed him on the forehead, a virgin-saint blessing the sick. "It's not a big deal. This can wait until you recover."

"I'm not stressed!" Alan protested.

"Then what's wrong?"

He sat back, staring at the curtain-covered windows. "I was happy."

Silence filled the room with an unwelcome chill.

"I've never had someone waiting for me. Never had someone care if I was sick, or late, or dead." Old pain stabbed at his heart. "I've never come home to a hot dinner before."

"Well, it's not like it's home cooked or anything," Delilah said with the brittle laugh of someone desperately trying to escape the deep end of the emotional spectrum.

He nodded, still refusing to turn around. A hot meal made him tear up? Very manly. Very romantic. He sighed and waited for the door to creak open as Delilah left.

Her coat flopped over the back of the couch beside him.

"That wasn't a guilt trip," he muttered, vaguely ashamed. "I wasn't trying to make you stay."

"I was going to leave because I thought you needed space." She sat down beside him.

"And now?"

"Now I think you need someone here. To be a friend, if nothing else."

He glanced sideways at her. "What if I wanted more than a friend?"

Her smile turned seductive. "Hmmm." Delilah leaned toward him, hand resting suggestively on his knee. "I'm sure that could be a topic of discussion." Her lips were a breath away from his. "I do have a weakness for brainy blonds."

Alan leaned in to steal a kiss.

Delilah ducked away. "But remember the To Do list. Unlock the door, then seduce the superhero."

"Ah, see, there's our problem. Right now I'm a pro tem mayor, not a superhero. And at the very top of my to-do list is seducing a world-class rogue and security operative."

"Is it?" Delilah gasped with mock surprise, hand covering her delightful lips. "Dear me! Whatever shall I do to protect myself from your wicked blandishments, Mister Adale?"

The thick southern accent she served up made him laugh. "I think Southern belles are supposed to swoon at my dashing and romantic nature and kiss me passionately."

"Really?"

He nodded. "Pretty sure. Read it in a book once."

"Must not have been a Texas southern belle." Delilah stood up, all playfulness gone. "Dinner first. You're still recovering."

"A kiss would make me better."

She arched an eyebrow. "Would it stop with one kiss?"

He paused. "It could."

Delilah didn't seem convinced.

"We should try it. For the sake of science."

She rolled her eyes but came back to him. "For science?"

"Mmmhmm."

"That's your best pick up line?"

"My best pickup line is, 'Hello, what's your name?' But when I used it on you, you gave me a look that promised a painful death and walked away without a backward glance. I remember it quite clearly."

Delilah shrugged. "It'd been a long day and I didn't need another bad boy in my life."

"But I'm not a bad boy," Alan assured her as his hand slipped around her waist to pull her closer.

"You're not a boy at all. I like that in a man."

Delilah's lips were soft, gentle, teasing... like a dream dancing just out of reach of memory. He pulled her closer, wanting to catch hold of the magic she brought with her.

Her fingers caressed his cheekbone. A moment later she was straddling him on the couch and he was lost in her touch.

Delilah pulled away. He whimpered in dismay, and then the whimper became a groan of lust as hot lips trailed kisses up his neck.

"We. Need. To. Eat," she whispered in his ear.

Alan caught her wrist. "Food is overrated."

"If we don't eat, how will we have energy for anything else?"

The promise of more was a drug, a seductive lure with poison inside. Alan narrowed his eyes. "Now you're teasing me."

"Yup," Delilah said as she stood up, pulling him with her.

He shook his head, feeling like a fool. At least that was familiar territory. She wrapped him in knots, played him like a yo-yo, and when she smiled all he could think of was winning another kiss. "You are a wicked, wicked woman, Delilah."

Her eyes sparkled with secret mirth. "Me?" She fluttered her eyelashes innocently. "You seduced me with your suave demeanor and reckless charm."

"Reckless charm?" He propped himself up on one elbow. "If you were enjoying that as much as I was, why are we stopping for dinner?"

"Because you're healing at a superhuman rate, and that takes more energy than you think." She kissed him again, leaving his head spinning. "You're shaking," she said softly. "I stopped because I don't want to see you hurt. Let's eat dinner. Get you healed. And then we'll talk about everything."

* * *

In the study, Delilah held her carton of Chinese food in front of her like a shield to protect her somewhat tarnished virtue. That butt! Alan stretched again, slacks cupping a grade A rump as he rearranged his player board. This wasn't how it was supposed to work. Every storybook said she'd kiss her crush, no sparks would fly, and she'd learn her lesson. It would leave her jaded and better able to focus full time on her work. A kiss to tease the hero wasn't supposed to leave her so hungry for more that Mongolian beef wasn't hot enough to burn away the memory of his touch. She sighed.

Alan turned around. "Are you okay? Am I boring you?"

"Um..." Telling him she'd stopped listening ten minutes ago was going to cause all sorts of problems. "They skimped on the chili flakes," she said, waggling her half-eaten box of dinner. "It's bland."

His lips quirked up in an endearing smile. "I'm so sorry. Do I need to get you some hot sauce?"

Was that a pick-up line? Delilah tried to think of a good reply. I've got your hot sauce right here. I like it hot and saucy, and I'm not talking sriracha.

"And that concludes the boring portion of our evening." Alan coughed and tucked his notes away. "You know all this already, don't you?"

"The board? Yeah, I've got the same one at my place. Great minds and all." She abandoned her dinner on Alan's desk. "The only major difference is here," she tapped Alan's picture off to the side, "here," she tapped her own in the midlevel-hoodlum-management level, "and here," she tapped Ivan's surly mug. "I had you and Arámbula tagged as major criminal players."

"His wife was. Her family is very old, very dirty, and has lots of money."

Delilah nodded. "I figured that out. But I'm still not here, and I think you've got Ivan too high."

"Ivan runs contracts for Vtoraya Volna—Second Wave—they're Russia's answer to The Company, if The Company ran guns for Serbian terrorists. Ivan's American born, Russian raised, and good at not being there when the outhouse hits the fan."

"I noticed that about him."

"He's one of their captains. Not likely to go any higher, but he's not a low level flunky."

She raised an eyebrow. "Which begs the question, 'What is *mon capitaine* doing in Chicago?'"

"Your captain?" Alan gave her a quizzical look. "You and Ivan have a thing?"

"We exchange punches on a regular basis."

"Right. Well, now I'm irrationally jealous of a thug." Alan shook his head in disbelief. "You ditched dinner with me for Ivan."

Delilah laughed. "Not intentionally."

"Uh huh." Alan cornered her against the desk. "You turned me down or canceled every date. How long have I been chasing you? Over a year now?"

"I had perfectly valid reasons." She tossed her hair. "I thought you might get hurt."

"Hurt?" Alan smirked.

Delilah shrugged. "It was a valid concern. If you weren't a superhero you'd still be at the hospital nursing the world's worst stomach cramp."

"So, you're saying I should have led with the superhero thing?"

"Oh yeah." She nodded.

"Because you like superheroes?"

She wrinkled her nose. "I like you. Let's not push any of the other details." She scrutinized the board once more. "Where does Kalydon come into play? He owns the Wacker building. Is he part of this, or no?"

Alan shrugged. "I don't know. Up until today I would have said he's a businessman, older, semi-retired, and all I know from his private life is that he likes hunting. He's a Good 'ol Boy with a chip on his shoulder."

"What changed your mind?"

"He came to my office tonight to make demands. Vague ones. He wants the superheroes out of the city, then said he knows there are two here. He finished by telling me politicians are cheap. I don't know if he meant we were bribable or replaceable."

Delilah frowned at her empty take-out container. "Does he know we're the supers he wants gone?"

"Probably not. He might not even mean us." Alan grimaced. "Which leads to my other piece of bad news for the evening. The Company is in town on a shopping trip."

"They go near Travys and I'll kill them," Delilah said without hesitation.

He shook his head. "No, they're trying to get a formula of some kind. Katrina thinks she can make new superheroes. I don't even know if it's a real thing though."

"There's nothing like that on the market now, but there's always been rumors. I'll have my research team look into it."

Alan shot her an amused smile. "Research team? Who are you, Bruce Wayne?"

"Mmm, more like Batman's beloved and well-financed daughter."

"Lucky girl." He squared his shoulders. "I'm supposed to meet The Company operatives at midnight. Want to tag along?"

Anything The Company could dish out, she could handle, but it didn't seem like Alan was trying to set her up for a take down. "I have other plans tonight."

"Would I make your life easier if I wrote down the GPS coordinates for the meeting?"

"It would save me some legwork."

He smiled. "Then I'll leave the address somewhere easy for you to find on the way out the door. But, first, is there any chance of a kiss good night?"

CHAPTER THIRTEEN

Dear Mom,

Random question of the day... When you first met Dad, how did you know he was The One? Was there a flash of light? Did he take your breath away? How'd you know he was perfect for you, or was it just a lucky guess?

All my love,
Delilah

DELILAH BALANCED THE TEODORA on one hip as something at her other hip beeped.

"Want help with that?" Alan leaned over her shoulder, arms encircling her as he gently lifted the Teodora out of her grasp. "Now you can answer your phone."

"Give it back." She reached for the gemstone with one hand as she pulled out her phone. "I have a really good reason for taking that home with me."

"Uh huh," Alan said. "Like you have a really good reason for skipping out on our date again? I thought we were meeting to watch the buy."

"I was on my way and remembered I needed to pick something up that I left here after the party."

"A giant emerald?"

She glanced at her phone. A blue light on her phone's map of Chicago showed Travys in the wrong part of town. "I need to get it out before it hatches and eats everything. They're ravenous when they first emerge."

"Hatch?"

"Yes, hatch. It'll eat the other stones, and most of the fossils, and possibly the building. We can leave it at the zoo if you want, but it's not safe to leave here."

"Hatch?"

"What? You thought I actually wanted a twenty-five pound emerald? What would I do with it? Green is not a flattering color on me." Delilah grabbed Alan's wrist and dragged the Spirit after her. "I've got to go get Travys." He slipped through her fingers like smoke.

"What's wrong with Travys?"

She watched the tracking point of his phone. "He's gone and done something stupid."

"You're tracking your intern's phone? Isn't that illegal?"

"It's a family phone." Locks on the cases around them cracked open. Delilah rubbed her forehead, trying to contain her emotions. "Angela is going to kill me."

"Family? What, you're in the mob now?"

Delilah froze halfway down the staircase, where the winter moon threw odd shadows across the darkened museum. "What are you going on about?"

Alan came down the last few steps so he stood on eye-level with her. "You don't look like you belong to a crime family, but..."

"Family; as in Mom, Dad, Brother, Sister. Travys is sort of my adopted baby brother. Sort of. It's weird." She waved his next question away. "Do you know how amoebas roll over and absorb everything they touch? My family is like that. They steam roll and assimilate everything in their path. Travys got caught in it one day, but he's a good kid and he didn't have anyone else, so we dragged him into the clan."

"Why?"

"My sister used to be his math teacher."

Her boots echoed on the tile floor of the atrium and Delilah realized Alan had stopped. "Hello? You have my egg. You need to keep walking."

"You know, I never had a family of my own, but when the other kids in foster care talked about loving home environments they never used terminology better suited for a biology class."

"They probably didn't have a family like mine," Delilah said. "Even by our own lax definitions we're a little weird. Every family is, I imagine."

"I wouldn't know. I never had one."

She pivoted, walking backward so she could watch him. "Did you ever try to look them up?"

He shrugged. "There never seemed to be a reason to."

The lights flickered as the secondary generator cut back in. A siren screamed and she sighed. With a touch of her finger she turned the coms unit on. "Freddie? Meet me at the side entrance. And open the pixie cage."

Alan's footsteps echoed on the floor behind her.

Delilah pulled out her whistle as a voice yelled from the third floor for them to stop. Brightly colored lights flitted past and she barely had enough time to grab Alan's hand as he reached. "Don't touch. They bite."

"What are they?"

"Pixies. Don't ask." She held the door open and shooed him toward the car. "How'd the buy go? Did you see the seller?"

"It was a preliminary meet up with a voice recording on a tape recorder. The thing had to have been forty years old."

Delilah whistled again to call the pixies back before climbing into the vehicle. "And the voice on it was warped?"

"Noticeably." Alan frowned as he pulled his seat belt on. "But I recognized it anyway. Remember Kalydon?"

"The man who said politicians were cheap? Yeah, he sticks out. Freddie?" She tapped the minion on his shoulder as he merged into traffic. "Slow down, or the pixies will never catch up and they'll freeze to death."

The car picked up speed.

"Freddie!" The car slowed and Delilah stripped off her gloves. "Did Kalydon say what he was selling?"

"Whatever it is, he wants one million in unmarked bills and a donor from anyone interested." He shifted the Teodora. "I... just stole this for you, didn't I?"

"Yup."

He closed his eyes. "You are so bad for my moral integrity."

"But a vast improvement to your street cred." She smiled.

Alan didn't smile back.

"It's an egg! Look." She pulled a flashlight from her bag on the cab floor and shone it into the egg. The deep green ribbons rippled, rolled, and two riparian eyes blinked at them. "My father forgot this one when we were on vacation one year. It wasn't incubated at the right temperature and it's only dumb luck the poor little thing didn't die. If it had hatched in the museum there would be all sorts of problems."

Alan dropped the Teodora on the seat between them. "Your father tinkers with a lot of genes, does he?"

"Not officially. He's a professor in ethics. Now." She squirmed. "He was a little bit wild as a kid."

"How wild?"

"America's Most Wanted Super Villain wild?"

Alan seemed to consider this. "I thought the Most Wanted Villain in the world was Strike, and last I checked, she was a woman."

"Is a woman. Yes. My father was a super villain, then he retired. Gave up the life of crime almost completely when he married Mom."

"I feel like I'm missing a story here."

Delilah shook her head. "You have no idea how true that is. Freddie, turn left up here." She turned back to Alan. "Are you coming with me to pick up Travys, or am I dropping you at home? I know you have a city to run in the morning."

"Are you going to need rescuing?"

"That's always a possibility."

* * *

Alan fastened his seat belt and smiled brightly at Locke—she was Locke right now, from her shiny metal curls to the top hat to the thigh-high boots that kept dragging his attention down to where it was not supposed to be. "I'm not leaving."

She rolled her eyes. "Fabulous. Freddie, head after Travys. We don't have time to waste."

"Travys works security with Subrosa. He's probably at a party. You realize that, right?"

Her glare made the wind chill feel warm. "The Company is in town and while Travys isn't going to be a superhero any time soon, he's got enough precognitive powers that he might draw unwanted attention. While there's a threat, he's supposed to stick to routes I have surveillance on. Right now he's out of sight, and I'm worried."

Alan frowned. "I didn't realize he was anything out of the ordinary."

"Most people won't, but that doesn't mean The Company doesn't have someone who can pick him out." Locke shrugged, her copper ringlets tinkling as she moved. "Angela had to protect him. It's really not complicated. If you stay around us long enough, you're either one of us or you're dead. I don't think we know any other way to live. Travys needs people to take care of him, to make sure he's eating right, to..." Her voice trailed off. "Are you all right?"

Belatedly he realized his tightening shoulders had rounded until he was hunched up and folded in the corner like he was three again. "I'm fine."

One eyebrow went up in question. "I can make you tell the truth," Locke threatened.

"I'm fine. It was a stupid reaction." He sighed, forcing himself to relax, and looked out the window at the Christmas lights. "When I was little, that's all I ever wanted: a big family and the postcard-perfect holiday. Candy canes, hot cocoa, sledding down the hill and then running inside to spend time with a huge throng of people who all loved me."

"You never had that." Delilah's voice was flat.

He shrugged. "I was abandoned at the hospital when I was a few hours old. It's not the start of a story that ends with happily ever after."

"You never know," she said as she took off her top hat and wig, once again transforming into Delilah. "Maybe if you're very good, Santa will bring you a family for Christmas."

Smirking, Alan turned back to her. "Right. And what is Santa bringing you?"

Delilah shrugged dismissively. "A pony? I don't know. I don't want things. Anyone can buy things, or, well... Anyone born into a wealthy family like I was can buy things. What I can't buy is safety for my family, or an end to my mother's nightmares. If there was a way to buy that, I would."

Alan leaned forward, interest piqued. "What happened to your mom?"

"She was kidnapped when I was five. The Rainbow Dane had this mad idea that he'd kill all the children of super villains and he was going to get my mom to help because she can move at super-speeds and fly. She wasn't going to, but he used a lotus serum to strip her freewill away. It was rape, but not the physical kind. Everyone thinks she's fine, but people can't lie to me. That's my talent—utterly useless as it is; I can make people tell the truth. So when I caught her crying one day, huddled in the back of her closet during the middle of the day when I was home sick and everyone else was gone, I made her tell me the truth. And she did." Tears sparkled in Delilah's eyes. "She hates herself. She hates everything about herself, because that's what put us at risk. And I can't do a damn thing about it."

"Did you tell anyone?"

"Daddy knows. I think he knew all along. Mom tries to act like it's not a big deal, because the fact that she is getting better is the only thing keeping Daddy in check. But it's going to break down one day. She'll fall apart, because you can't live like that forever, and then Daddy will retaliate and this little cold war we currently have will turn into something that makes World War Two look like a picnic." She pressed her lips together in thought, and then said, "My dad's a little scary when he's angry."

"Good to know." Alan reached for her hand, their fingers entwined. "I'm sorry I brought that all up."

She shrugged. "Someone needs to know, in case I ever go crazy. Keeping secrets... Sometimes it feels like everything is on my shoulders. I know too much to be happy. I know what's wrong with everyone and what they want and why they want it, but I don't know how to fix it."

"That's the secret," he whispered, giving her hand a squeeze. "You don't have to fix everything."

Delilah laughed, light and airy and winsome. "You are definitely not a Smith."

"Your surname is Samson."

"Because I legally changed it at eighteen. I was born Delilah Minerva Sorsha Smith, which is an unholy mouthful with more geek references than any sane person deserves."

"Could be worse," Alan said with a shrug. "I was named after one of Robin's merry men because the nurse on duty that night happened to be watching some old BBC show and thought it was cute. Cute it may be, but it's definitely not modern or stylish."

"Were you teased?"

"Horribly!"

"You would have been teased worse if you were Robin." She flashed him a smile that erased the old pain before turning to the front. "Freddie, how close are we?"

"Another block, ma'am," said the warty thing driving the car.

"Is that what the Teodora is going to hatch into?" Alan murmured.

"Maybe. Possibly." Delilah grimaced. "Honestly, I haven't a clue. Daddy likes to tinker with things. You never know exactly what you're going to get."

The car slowed outside a gated community. "I believe the young gentleman is inside, ma'am. Would you like to go through the gate?"

"No, circle the neighborhood once and we'll find a place to get out. Why a gated community? I was expecting an abandoned warehouse or a brickyard. Something a little more traditional."

Alan frowned at the cookie-cutter houses, all neatly lined up behind shoveled sidewalks. "Maybe he's meeting a friend."

"Maybe he's doing some after-hours snooping. Freddie, stop by those bushes," Delilah ordered. "And get a team working on those gates. I want electricity cut in five minutes." She picked up her phone. "Let's go hunting."

CHAPTER FOURTEEN

SOS - D

DELILAH CURSED THE SNOW under her breath. They were going to leave a trail a blind hamster could follow.

"Where are we going?" Alan whispered in her ear. In his shadow form there wasn't even a hint of warmth behind her.

"See the pretty blue dot on my phone? I'm trying to figure out where the pretty blue dot is in relation to all these over-priced homes. Tacky, turn-of-the-century cookie-cutter homes in a gated community. It makes me weep for humanity. Ugly, ugly architecture."

"Do you always critique your surroundings like this?"

"Yes, it's one of my many failings."

Gentle arms wrapped around her. "Hold on, I think I know where your pretty blue dot is."

Shadows swallowed her as the air turned frigid. Her heartbeat echoed in her ears, and then they were standing beside a house with plastic siding. "Why didn't we go inside?"

"They don't have any shadows. That's why I picked it. Who else would light up every corner of their home?"

She glared up at the windows covered by curtains. "I don't see any light."

"The windows don't go inside the house, they're built into a layer of the wall, like a safe house."

"Charming. For the record, I don't approve." She tapped a fingertip against her chin.

"I didn't think you would."

They stalked around the corner, quietly opening a chain link fence to sneak into the backyard. "It looks so normal." Snow, dead branches sticking up like the skeletons of spring, the winter perfume of wood smoke and... Delilah inhaled deeply. "Do you smell lotus flowers?"

"I don't even know what they smell like."

She inhaled again. Under the scent of wood smoke was a hint of rain forest, sweet and a little fruity with the promise of jungles and exotic locales. Definitely not the usual scent associated with Chicago suburbs in the dead of winter. "It's like orange blossom. You don't smell it?"

Alan shook his shadowy head.

"I hope I'm wrong. The Company hasn't started using chemicals to control their super-slaves, have they?"

"And I would know that how, exactly?" he whispered as she approached the back door.

She took off her glove and gripped the cold metal as she tried to reach the lock. But like Kalydon's apartment, there was nothing there.

"Problems?"

"Too many to count. This isn't an entrance."

"Probably fake like the windows."

"And there are no shadows inside?"

"Not unless you want to appear inside someone's clothing."

"How many people are in there?"

He closed his glowing green eyes and his lips moved. "Six? Maybe seven. Counting the shadows inside clothes is not an exact science."

"None of them are on this end of the house, are they?"

"All the small shadows are in the basement."

"Fine." She released her power. The metal doorknob shook under hand, burning and melting before the door exploded with a sound that made her eardrums sore. "Knock, knock?"

She stepped into a stripped room with bright photography lights hanging every few feet, planted in the walls, strapped to every corner. "I guess they knew you might be in town."

"Looks like."

Voices filtered through the house's cold air. Delilah followed them, anger growing as the smell of lotus blossoms became ever more distinct. Damn them all to the seventh hell. If they'd poisoned Travys the way the Rainbow Dane had poisoned her mother, she'd see them all burn. The basement door exploded before she even touched it.

"Calm down," Alan whispered in her ear. "You can't kill them."

"Yes, I can," she bit off as the stairs shuddered under her steps.

"Okay, but you shouldn't kill them."

The door at the bottom of the stairs was heavy and metallic. "That has yet to be determined." The door disintegrated. "Travys?" she called, amazed her voice wasn't shaking. Tears filled her eyes. That smell! That horrible, horrible smell! The one her mother had puked all over the car when they'd driven away from Colorado and the superheroes who'd wanted her family dead. It was etched in her brain with the worst form of emotional acid. "Travys, you find the kinkiest hide outs." She stepped into the basement and saw Travys strapped to a chair and stripped to his tighty-whities. An IV tube hung from his arm, dripping blood onto the floor. "Travys!"

Alan reached him first, removing the IV needle and covering the wound with his solid hand. "Shh," he said. "Do you have a first aid kit?"

She took a shaky breath and nodded.

"Take care of him. There's a tunnel. I'm going to follow them," Alan said.

"Don't get caught."

He turned to a curl of smoke in answer.

She stepped to Travys's side, holding his injured arm with one hand as she dug through her bag. On cue, the lights died. "Control? Do you have me?"

Nothing.

"Travys? Travys, come on. I need you to wake up now." She flicked her flashlight on, put it between her teeth, and bandaged his arm. Travys groaned. "That's a good boy," she said indistinctly around the flashlight, saliva trailing out of her mouth as she tried to talk. "Come on." She held the ropes, letting them unlock in her hands before dropping them in evidence bags. Detective Morrow was going to kill her. This case was one serious SNAFU after another. A known killer, but not enough evidence. Evidence in the form of a kidnapped college student, but she'd ruined it.

Travys's head lolled to the side.

"Hey, hey, come on. I need you to wake up." She checked his pulse; it was slow but steady. Why the hell would anyone want his blood? "Kid, if this is some weird initiation rite for a frat that you forgot to tell me about, you will never hear the end of it. Didn't you ever watch the classics growing up?" she asked the unconscious Travys as she slung him over her shoulders in a fireman's carry. Stumbling through the dark, she found her way to the stairs. "If you'd seen even one episode of Buffy you'd know what a bad idea wandering around town alone is. Or Veronica Mars. I'll make you watch that," she huffed. "You can learn all about the dangers of not communicating with people. Was one phone call too much to ask?"

She sank to her knees half way up the dark stairs. "Hey, Delilah, I'm going to this place. Can you do a background check? And I would have said, 'Why, yes, Travys!' And, 'Don't go, Travys, it's full of vampiric suburbanites.'"

"You talk too much," Travys muttered.

Delilah forced herself up, climbed the last few steps, and rolled him off her shoulders to the floor.

His teeth chattered, but his eyes opened. "Why's it so cold?"

"No one thought to install a heater." She took her coat off and laid it over him. "Stay right there, I'm going to see if I can find anything else upstairs."

Travys lifted his head off the floor. "'Lilah?"

"It's okay. I'll be right back." With a forced smile she headed upstairs, hitting her comms unit. "Hello? Control?"

"Ma'am?"

"Freddie! Lock on to me. Get the car here now. Make a scene. I want the cops crawling all over this place by dawn."

"Yes, ma'am."

The upstairs was much like the downstairs, heavily lit and stripped of everything that might make it homey. No paint on the sheet rock walls, no windows, nothing to indicate that someone had once lived here, although they obviously had. The outside was too tidy to be an abandoned home. Details from the outside filtered back in her mind. She'd seen curtains like that before, a hot cranberry color that was an offense to Mother Nature. Sadly, it was popular this year. So, new curtains and a cut lawn, but a stripped interior. Chicago Tribune's front-page headline for tomorrow was already written.

None of the rooms held anything; even the bathroom was torn down to a faucet and yellowing toilet. On impulse, she went to the attic. There probably wasn't anything but insulation up there, but she'd feel better having checked everywhere.

"Almost to your location, ma'am," Freddie said over her comm. "We'll need to leave in a hurry. The gate guard was less than polite."

"I can't imagine why." She found the attic door and watched it drop to the floor as her powers eased the locks open. "Travys is in the kitchen, go around back and load him into the car. I'm checking the attic. There's a heavy lotus smell." And the dusty attic door reeked of the potent flower. It took two tries for her to jump high enough to grab the rim of the attic opening and pull herself up.

As she'd expected, the attic was lit with the same heavy-duty lamps found throughout the house. It seemed like a huge investment just to keep the Spirit of Chicago at bay. Why not pick a smaller house to use if you were going to light it up like this? Why do it at all? There had to be better things to do with your life. Delilah walked the perimeter of the attic, stopping where the window should have been. Nothing. Time to go, then.

A bulge in the insulation caught her attention as she turned. From any other angle it was virtually unnoticeable, but from that spot... Lucky find. She put her gloves back on and pulled the pink insulation away, mindful of the fiberglass spines, and pulled out an ornate box with drawings carved on it. No, she amended, tracing her gloved fingers over the box, not drawings. Hieroglyphs. Something she could translate with enough time.

"Ma'am, the police have arrived at the gate," Freddie reported. "We need to leave."

She needed to leave the box. Detective Morrow needed the evidence. Her fingers clenched it tightly. "Gimme three minutes." She pulled a camera out of her bag and began photographing every angle. She was still there when the police pulled up outside.

CHAPTER FIFTEEN

Dear Maria,

Hypothetically speaking, if I needed bail money and a place to hide for a few years until the statute of limitations expired, I could stay at your place... Right?

Delilah
P.S. Can I borrow some cash?

"HOW COULD YOU DO this to me?" Detective Morrow demanded.

Delilah sat in the uncomfortable interrogation chair, resolutely silent. They'd found Travys, handcuffed her, and now the lunch hour was toiling past with nothing to show for a hungry morning.

"Damn it, Delilah. How many times have I looked the other way? How many times? All you needed to do was call us. That's what the police get paid for, you know that, right? You know I earn my bread and butter chasing down criminals? While you earn your paycheck installing security cameras. Which is not what you did last night."

She closed her eyes, ready to relent, when there was a knock at the door.

"Hello?"

Delilah twisted in her seat, wide-eyed and furious.

The man in the doorway wore a tailored three-piece Dior suit. There was a touch of silver at his temples, and a charmingly smug smile on his face. "Detective Morrow?" Her father held out his hand. "I'm Miss Samson's legal counsel."

Morrow crossed his arms. "Really? Here I thought she'd done nothing more than tamper with evidence and interfere with the scene of a crime."

"She didn't do that," Doctor Charm said with easy reassurance.

Morrow's bulldog face wrinkled in confusion, but he started nodding.

"Miss Samson went to rescue her intern only moments before the police. She has no ulterior motive."

"No ulterior motive," Morrow murmured. He shook his head, trying to shake the effects of Daddy's Agree-With-Me-Ray. Since it had never worked on Delilah, she couldn't say she sympathized, but it had a similar effect on the boys she'd used it on in high school. Daddy had read her the riot act after that little stunt.

"If you bring us the evidence, we can sort everything out and be on our way. Miss Samson doesn't need to stay here any longer."

"Evidence. I'll go get that." Morrow walked to the door nodding like a concussed chicken.

The handcuffs dropped to Delilah's lap with a metallic clink. "Daddy, I think you're over doing it," she said as he sat on the table.

He looked down at her with dark eyes that struck fear into law enforcement everywhere—the untouchable villain, the one who always got away. "What in the Sam Hill do you think you're doing?" The Texas twang was faked, but it made her giggle. "I drove by that nut house on the way through town. What are you mixed up in?"

"Nothing. Travys left his dorm at a weird hour so I followed. I've no clue what was going on, but if you can get my phone back I have pictures."

"This isn't about the Golden Hunt, is it? Your mother will have bovine-producing fits if you're nosing around them again. We've only just managed to get the FBI to stop calling, asking for your phone number."

"Was it Jake?"

"It was Jake."

She winced. "I'm so sorry. I really did not mean for him to get so attached. All I did was collaborate on the arrest. We never even had a meal together."

"Smith women are very easy to obsess over," her father said sympathetically. "Look at me, I met your mother once and couldn't stop thinking about her."

Delilah rolled her eyes. "I know. I've only heard the story a few thousand times."

"And one of these days you'll have a very similar story to tell. Some gentleman who captured your attention, or you, depending on the scenario." He stood up and straightened his tie. "Put the handcuffs back on, the detective is headed this way."

"Talk fast and don't melt his brains. Or ruin his career! Detective Morrow is a good resource and I like him."

Her father raised an inquisitive eyebrow.

"Not like that. He's a friend."

"Who you shared no information with and who doesn't consider you a friend. My darling daughter, you are getting a dictionary for Christmas." But he did touch the watch with his Agree-With-Me ray in it, so at least he was going to dial down the mind-to-Slurpy rays.

Detective Morrow came in with a large box. "Phone, bag, and this box you were holding when we arrived."

"I'd only just found it," Delilah said. "I found Travys tied up in the basement. While I waited for the ambulance, I walked around the house searching for other victims."

"What ambulance?" Morrow demanded. "The one you didn't call because you didn't report anyone missing and didn't call 911?" He slammed the box on the interrogation table. "I repeat, what the hell, Delilah?"

She crossed her arms.

"I think you might be a little out of your league," Doctor Charm said. "Do you have evidence gloves, detective? This isn't something I'd touch lightly."

"You recognize it?" Morrow asked.

Delilah frowned at the box in confusion. Hieroglyphs and languages were not Daddy's department.

"A number of years ago, when I was fresh out of law school, there was a bizarre kidnapping case in Colorado."

"The lotus blossom smell!" Delilah burst out.

"Precisely. I wouldn't be surprised to learn this once belonged to Lady Grimoire, matriarch of a significant branch of the superhero family tree back in the day. That was before The Company started pruning things to the point of extinction. An odd policy, I always thought. Very anti-superhero."

"Ahem." Delilah cleared her throat and kicked her father in the shin. "Back to the task at hand. Can I be released? I'm starving, and tired, and I'm very late for work."

With a grave smile her father turned to the detective. "Naturally. Detective Morrow, I think you will need the expertise offered by Miss Samson. This is not an ordinary case."

"I need to know what happened," Morrow said.

"Miss Samson will write a statement, you will release her. I will liaise between the two of you until the killer is brought to justice."

"Killer?" Morrow looked at her. "What killer? I thought this was about your intern getting kidnapped."

"Travys was helping me review the mayor's case." Delilah shrugged. "He must have found more than he let on. Maybe he thought he could solve the case by himself. Too many movies about teenage spies and investigators I suppose. How is he doing? You've purposefully failed to mention his health this entire time."

Morrow grimaced in response. "He's fine. They gave him a pint of blood at the hospital, but otherwise he's fine. No drugs in his system, nothing that some bed rest and a few steaks won't fix."

"Tell me," her father said, "is blood theft a common crime in this area?"

"No." Morrow shook his head. "I've been on the force for over thirty years and I've seen some weird sh—stuff." He shuffled his feet a little at the slip up. "But this is new."

"An overly aggressive blood bank, perhaps?"

"Maybe." Morrow sighed. "All right, Delilah, I'll bring you the forms. Once the statement is filled out, I'll let you go. But that better be the most thorough document you've ever written. The chief is ready to eat me alive. You're our best contract worker and you screwed with a crime scene. Rookies aren't even that dumb and they can barely tie their own shoes."

* * *

Delilah walked out of the precinct two hours later in a huff. Half the day wasted and she was still hungry. Lunch, or an early dinner, that was the first course of action. Then she'd book Daddy Dearest a hotel, or a flight home, and check on Travys.

Then maybe she'd have time to search for a new job in the Help Wanted section before bed. It didn't matter what Wil said over the phone, she was sunk in Chicago. All that time carefully building a relationship with the police, growing her contacts list, making a place for herself... Gone. Straight down the loo. All because she trusted a handsome man not to abandon her.

Well, Alan Adale could keep his cold bed and shadowy hands to himself.

Superheroes and villains... Maybe it only worked if the girl was the good one. Her mom had been a superhero before marrying Doctor Charm, but her mother also had the kind of body that made men trip over themselves to please her. The best compliment Delilah had ever been offered was that she was regal. Most people called her stern. Or aloof. Or cold.

Cold seemed to be a favorite. Or the old stand-by: heartless.

Well, she tugged her gloves on and bit her lip, it happened. There were only so many times a girl could hear her date confess he asked her out for sex alone, or because he wanted to date her sister, but Angela was hard to talk to. Angela looked like Mom, and was sweet as honey and happily married, and—Delilah reminded herself firmly—it wasn't her sister's fault all males were born with only two brain cells and a couple ball sack's worth of stupidity. A het woman just had to roll with their infantile fascination with balls and accept the inevitable social gaffes.

Being a lesbian was growing more attractive by the hour.

"Delilah!" Alan's voice made her turn. "Are you crying? What's wrong? What's going on?"

She wiped her eyes and threw her head up. "I had something in my eye. What are you doing here?"

"I came to talk to Detective Morrow because I heard you were arrested."

"Yes, I was pulled in at four this morning. About five minutes after you left, actually. Convenient timing. But everything's fine now." She gave him a bright smile and tried not to think of stabbing him. Her New Year's resolution was going to be to date every blond man in the city. One by one she'd pick off the herd and break their hearts. It would be a cathartic exercise to complete before her passport arrived.

Hmmm. Passport.

She changed directions and headed for the nearest post office. An official passport would make life so much easier. Muddle the trail a bit. And she could switch names; Cassandra More, Ellie Fine, maybe Ann. Ann the librarian.

No, not a librarian. The temptation to get a job in New York would be too strong. She needed something that kept her out of the country a lot.

Alan caught up with her. "Where are you going?"

"Why do you care?" She stopped and glared at him. "Oh wait. You don't. Funny thing that."

"I do too and you know it."

She waited for the brutal cold that came with hard lies. Nothing happened.

"I got back to my office at ten, dealt with a ton of... Never mind. I'm sorry I didn't come back for you right away. The tunnel went all the way down town and I wanted to keep Kalydon in my sights. He and the Hunt went to somewhere off Lake Street. It's a mess. I need—"

"You aren't lying," Delilah said, interrupting.

Alan stared at her in confusion. "Why would I lie?"

"Because everyone tries to lie to me."

"I haven't."

Her heart raced as she tried to remember all their many conversations. Alan had never lied. There were implications there she wasn't quite ready to explore.

"Delilah?" Alan stepped forward.

And she stepped back.

"Hi, sweetheart." A heavy hand landed on Delilah's shoulder. "Am I interrupting anything?"

She looked up at her father. Replacing Alan would be as easy as finding another green-eyed blond with the body of Adonis and a dry sense of humor Terry Pratchett would envy. Replacing Daddy was infinitely more difficult. "Aren't you supposed to be somewhere? Catching a flight? Talking to Detective Morrow? Anything at all?"

"Nope. I was going to go buy you lunch and talk to you about all this. But it seems I'm going to make an awkward third wheel. Who is the nice young man?"

"Someone who is neither nice nor young," Delilah muttered, shooting Alan a glare that would have turned a lesser man to ash.

Alan frowned. "Delilah..."

"He knows your name?" Doctor Charm asked, reaching for his watch.

Delilah grabbed his hand to stop him. "Doctor Smith is a recent expert in strange languages like the one found on the box at the crime scene."

"What box?" Alan asked.

She ignored him. "Alderman Adale is Chicago's deputy mayor, the pro tem mayor under the circumstances. He's following the whole case very closely." The muscles in her shoulders tightened until she thought bone might break. "Don't you both have jobs? It's the middle of a work day!"

Alan raised an eyebrow. "Smith?"

"Yes."

"Then I assume I have the immeasurable pleasure of addressing the one and only Doctor Charm." Alan nodded his head in a semi-bow.

It was a terrible twist of fate that gave her the ability to unlock things but not break the earth apart to swallow her whole when she most needed it.

Daddy's eyebrow went up as he turned to her. "Where do you dispose of bodies in this town, sweetheart?"

"You can't kill him." She floundered for a second. "I don't have a reason why you can't kill him, but you can't. Dad, you need to go home. Right now. Leave town. Alan, you need to go to work. And erase my phone number. I'm going to lunch."

They both started following her.

She spun and faced them. "Alone! I am going to lunch alone." To think.

She stopped at the first hole-in-the-wall Mexican place she found and ordered the house special. After a glass of horchata and more guacamole than she strictly needed, the locks on the cupboards stopped popping open.

This needed to end. Tonight.

Alan said he'd chased Kalydon down the tunnels to the lake. There was a lot of ground to cover there. Plenty of places to enter the old bootlegging tunnels. The property on Wacker Street probably had a subterranean entrance, something the owner paid to keep off the public records.

Tonight, she'd find it and make them pay.

CHAPTER SIXTEEN

Dear Mom,

Can you remember to pack an extra stocking for Christmas? We might have a surprise visitor and I want to make sure there's enough to go around.

Love,
Delilah

WHITE WINE SWIRLED AROUND the inside of a crystal glass. Alinea had been known for its avant garde menu for nearly two decades, and the debonair Doctor Charm had danced past the maître d' as if there wasn't a two-week waiting list.

"Do you drink?" the doctor asked.

"No."

He put his glass aside. "So you are a superhero. It seems alcohol and mutations don't mix."

"Maybe I'm Mormon."

The doctor smirked. "I doubt it. I've met a few, and there's nothing in your background to suggest religious affiliation."

"You checked?" Alan asked, only mildly surprised.

"Wouldn't you check on the potential bachelors in a

town your favorite child was moving to? There's a very short list of acceptable men out here."

Alan pretended to be interested in the menu. "Having children isn't a problem I have."

"Oh, do you have children already?"

He stopped reading, eyes widening in horror. "I meant I don't have any children to worry about!" Alan folded the menu in exasperation. "Why are we here?"

"I'm trying to help you," Doctor Charm said.

"How?"

The waiter stopped to refill Alan's water glass. "Are you ready to order, sir?"

"The Winter Sampler for two, please," Doctor Charm said. He paused while the waiter walked away before saying, "We have two options. One, I erase your memories of recent events. You won't remember your time with Delilah, but you won't have the heartache either."

Alan sipped his water. "Difficult to do, erasing nearly eighteen months of memory. The gaps would be noticeable."

"You haven't been close to Delilah that long."

"Not that you know of."

"My daughter keeps me apprised of what's happening in her life."

"Somehow I doubt she's always truthful. Delilah likes her secrets."

The doctor pursed his lips as the waiters delivered a terrarium of salad greens, accented with mushrooms houses and some unidentifiable food shaped into a red gnome hat. Frowning, he poked at the greens. "We should have flown to Paris. They know how to make a decent lunch there."

"But the customs wait would be too long," Alan quipped.

"Indeed, although there are numerous ways around that." He sighed and set his fork aside. "You seem like a very nice young man. But you don't realize how much trouble a woman can get you into. You think it will be all flowers, and cupcakes, and sex, and the next thing you know you're changing the oil in cars and rocking colicky babies to sleep at three in the morning. Liking her long legs isn't enough to build a relationship on."

"You think the only reason I care about Delilah is how attractive she is?"

Doctor Charm shrugged. "You wouldn't be the first."

"I'm not like those men."

"In that case, you're going to need a better arsenal. Tell me, do you have a bulletproof vest?"

* * *

Raw earth, cement, old brickwork... Delilah ran her hand along the tunnel wall deep under Chicago proper. It was like a dark fantasyland. The ghost of jazz music flitted through her mind, a memory of a simpler time.

Or perhaps not. Perhaps superheroes were only the next evolution to it all. Kalydon was the new Al Capone, the shady business baron dealing magic elixirs in the dark. And she was Elliot Ness, the untouchable, incorruptible dealer of justice.

The thought made her grin in the darkness as her flashlight panned ahead of her, looking for security cameras and doors into the Wacker building overhead. Something rat-sized moved in the shadows ahead, shuffling and digging, but not moving away. It twitched, then fell still as she walked closer. The toe of a heavy work boot pointed upward, the edge of a leg of denim pants barely visible through a layer of heavy mud.

For a moment her mind couldn't quite grasp what she was seeing. And then it all clicked. Someone was buried alive under the muddy floor. Or, at least, they had been alive when she'd started walking toward them.

Stretching her hand over the packed dirt, she tried to

loosen everything. But the dirt wasn't locked per se, it was just there, and she hadn't thought to bring a shovel for breaking and entering.

A hand clawed through the mud. Delilah grabbed it, pulling the hapless victim out of the grave. The mud-covered face was barely recognizable as Ivan with a broken nose. "You?"

"Me." Delilah squatted down and looked him in the eye. "What happened?"

"They decided I was expendable."

Focusing on Ivan, Delilah loosened her grip on her talent. His pupils dilated even wider than before. He stared at her with a glazed expression.

"Tell me everything," she said.

"The Mégisti formula gives normal people superpowers. Flight. Strength. Health. The seller proved it to us. Shot one of his men, gave him the formula and healed him in front of us. Said he needed money and a volunteer."

"And you got volun-told?" Delilah guessed.

"Seller said I was wrong. His guy punched me. It was like being hit by a car. I woke up choking on dirt." He paused, reaching for his still buried legs. "I think I broke a bone."

Delilah blew a stray hair out of her eye. "Where's the entrance?"

"Don't know. Wasn't conscious when they brought me in." Ivan rocked back as his eyes returned to normal. "I hurt."

"Can you wait twenty minutes, or should I call the police?"

He stared out into the darkness. "Got an extra flashlight?"

She took her phone out, turned on the GPS, and put a lock on it. "Here."

Ivan turned it over in his muddy hand and grinned. "You're going to leave your phone here for me to hack?"

"Yeah, that's exactly it." Delilah rolled her eyes. "You unlock that and I'll buy you dinner." The Pentagon couldn't unlock her phone and she'd sold the prototype for the lock to them when she was in college. Good educations weren't cheap. When people asked about her sudden surge of wealth, she told them a rich uncle had left her money in his will.

It made you despair, it really did. Her entire life's history had been available if anyone had wanted to look, but they never had. Not a single person had considered her worth a full background check. Yet they'd given her the keys to every room on campus because she did work-study as an early morning janitor. The minions had done the cleaning, but still, they'd handed over the keys! Humanity.

Walking along the broken wall, intensely aware of Ivan watching her, she wondered why she thought the keys had mattered anyway. Doors were just bigger keyholes.

A flutter of warm air caressed her hand through the chipped mortar. Somewhere on the other side was a heat source. She focused, and the wall crumpled to dust under her fingers. With a quick smile at Ivan, she stepped through the hole and into a section of the Chicago pedway illuminated only by emergency lighting.

Odd, for this time of day. The pedway closed at five but there were usually lights on down here, homeless people, and all the other little joys of subterranean Chicago life. She sniffed the air, inhaling dust and bleach.

Taking the handheld GPS out of her pocket, she pinged the satellite quickly and confirmed her suspicions; she was under 77 Wacker Drive. Someone had boarded up this area to use as a private entrance to the mostly-abandoned building.

Turning the GPS off so it didn't attract unwanted electronic attention, she found the signs for the exit and followed the concrete stairs upwards. Three flights up the stairs changed, wooden doors dividing the bare concrete from padded floors covered in a rich tapestry carpet with maroon and gold accents. There was a lock on the door. Relying on the tech gadgets she'd borrowed from her father to handle any unseen security, she swept past it.

The hall didn't feel lived in. It smelled like a mausoleum, all death and dust and forgotten dreams. Maybe in some ways it was. If Kalydon was behind this—and she had no reason to believe he wasn't—then he was running out of time. Money couldn't buy him immortality. She wasn't even sure why someone would want to buy immortality. Death wasn't frightening. It was simply there—like the night sky, or the ocean, or a mountain.

An old man bent and broken by the indelicacies of age should embrace death. It was a release of pain, a final farewell to every sorrow. But maybe that was only a young person's point of view. Perhaps, after a few more decades, life would become such a terrible addiction that she too would view death with fear.

If she died today her mother's fury would bring her back to life long enough for a harangue that never ended.

Two more flights of stairs and Delilah found herself looking at a row of basic conference rooms with windows in the doors and a few computers—old boxy machines that were new when her parents married, but computers nonetheless. At the very end of the corridor was a different door, white with the black number nine hanging in the center, like one would find hanging on the front of house in any urbanized area. Like Atlanta, to pick a not-so-totally-random example.

Delilah quirked her lips in a smile, tugged her black leather gloves on, and opened the door.

She waited for a minute, watching the interior gloom to see if anything moved. No sirens screamed. No lights flashed a warning. Everything was deadly quiet.

Stepping inside as she closed the door behind her, she flicked on her flashlight. The carpet continued here and pictures hung on the wall, none of them spectacular. Hunting prints for the most part. Cheap posters of green tractors, bird hunters, and deer standing under autumn leaves, all in expensive frames. Dusty bookcases with leather-bound books, covers dirty and cracking from age, lined the wall.

A deer head hung on one wall next to an overstuffed red chair. In another corner she saw a stuffed grizzly bear. Kalydon liked trophies, but she suspected those were from his younger days. The rooms flowed together to another set of stairs, another lock she snapped open, and another set of lavishly appointed rooms in the same dark red plush and velvet.

There was an air of opulence here, but not of cultivated taste. It was as if Kalydon had seen a picture of a wealthy home and bought everything out of a catalog. Or maybe she was biased because red velvet was so very 1970-something.

It was an interior apartment with no obvious windows, but even in bright sunshine this room would be gloomy. The furniture was all heavy wood stained black. The fabric on the rugs and the curtains framing a black-and-white image of the New York skyline pre-9/11 were all deep red, almost crimson. Bookcases covered a wall in here too, but a cursory glance told her these weren't normal books. These were in shades of sand and earth, mixed with an eclectic choice of statuary. The bust of a woman carved out of a black stone with a gold skull erupting from her face was the focal point.

Delilah leaned forward and sniffed at the books. Without a lab it was impossible to tell, but they looked suspiciously like examples she'd seen of auto-anthropodermic bibliopegy from the seventeenth century: books bound in human skin. The grotesque practice had fallen out of favor fairly quickly, but these didn't appear to be all that ancient.

Shivers of apprehension crawled up her back like an icy spider walking on her spine.

There was another door, this one with a combination lock, and for most lock picks it would have presented an interesting diversion for several hours. Delilah opened it with a glance and stepped into the room she'd been dreading, but knew all along she would find. It was no bigger than a jail cell on death row, ten feet by ten feet perhaps. There was one chair, a match to the one downstairs, a fake fireplace that was turned off, and a rug of pale leather. Bare skin... Human, unless she missed her guess completely, although the hair and fingers rather gave it away.

Revulsion and bile filled her mouth. She wondered which of the faces on the wall once belonged to the rug. She recognized several of them. The Wooden Wonder and Mayor Arámbula were on one wall with clippings from the newspaper taped next to their pictures. On another wall she saw street photos, men and women Kalydon had stalked perhaps... But no. Up at the top was a row of smiling faces.

The Hunt.

The Golden Hunt of Atlanta was pictured with their victims tallied below them like some sick scavenger hunt. She pulled out her micro-camera and started snapping pictures. As she zoomed in on a familiar face, something else tore her attention downward.

Travys's mother. Thinner than when she'd left New York. Haggard. But unmistakably Travys's mother, walking through the Peachtree Plaza in Atlanta. Up above was the late mayor's toady, Chasten Huntley. Even his name fit.

She took a few more pictures and then stepped out, fusing the door shut behind her by unlocking all the molecules and letting them melt together. Kalydon didn't seem like the sort of man who understood subtle gestures. That was fine. What she had in mind was about as subtle as a jackhammer.

There was only one last place she wanted to search: Kalydon's bedroom. People of his ilk kept what they loved close. The kill room was a toy room, really. Some people had places to watch TV, and sociopaths kept rooms full of tokens stolen off their victims. It probably balanced out in the scheme of things. But Kalydon had been raised in the Deep South and in deep poverty, which meant money in the mattress and a gun safe in the bedroom.

After several false starts she found the bedroom. It wasn't hard to see how deep Kalydon's roots were. Under the expensive coverlet was a set of plaid flannel sheets. It seemed like a waste. All that wealth and ambition wrapped up in the brains of a chicken. She pulled a hunting print to the side and glared at the gun safe. It swung open, revealing an array of guns that would keep a small dictatorship in power for at least a year, and a row of test tubes with a glowing blue liquid. Bingo.

Delilah scooped the test tubes up, wrapped them in a pillowcase stripped from the bed, and put them in her bag. Now, how to let Kalydon know what she wanted? Maybe something written in red...

CHAPTER SEVENTEEN

Noah,

You better get your butt back safe and sound or you will never hear the end of it. If you make my baby sister cry I will move Heaven, Earth, and Hell to make sure you pay. There is nowhere on this planet or in near orbit that you can hide from me. And you know you can't fight me because your mother will ground you if you hit a girl. She won't care how old you are. So keep that in mind. Merry Christmas.

Come home safe,
Delilah

A SURLY IVAN WAITED for her in the depths of Chicago's tunnels. "About bloody time you got back. I thought you were gone for good."

"I ran out of lipstick and had to go buy more."

His face contorted into a horrified grimace. "What would happen to me if you died?"

"You'd be motivated to unlock my phone," Delilah said as she squatted beside him. "Figure out the code yet?"

"Hmph." He rolled his eyes and held the muddy phone out. "It's not a phone, is it?"

"It's a phone, but it's my phone, which is why it's customized."

"Voids the warranty if you do that," Ivan muttered.

She scraped the mud aside so he could see the insignia. "This look like a brand you know? I doubt it."

"You make your own phones? Don't you have any life at all?"

"I don't make my phones. I own stock in a small company that makes custom phones for wealthy professionals."

Another eye roll.

"How are you feeling?"

"Both legs broken, maybe a rib. You going to drag me out of here or call the police to come pick me up?" He was the very picture of stoic despair, the beaten villain brought low.

Delilah smirked, an expression he doubtless didn't see in the darkness. "That all depends." She pulled one of the vials out of her bag. "Do you know what this is?"

"The Mégisti formula, Greek for great or something like that." Ivan shrugged. "My boss wants it. Seller had it. But the deal went south." He paused and frowned. "How'd you get it?"

"I took it out of the wall safe."

"Out of..." Ivan spluttered in frustration. "Do you know what I've done to get my hands on that in the past two weeks? I've tied myself in knots! Begged. Bribed. Threatened. Cut throats." He switched to Russian for a good long tirade. "Bloody woman! How'd you get the safe combination? Tell me!"

Delilah raised an eyebrow. "Combination? Why would I do that when the doors all unlocked for me?"

Even in the darkness she could see him flushing red with rage.

She held the formula out. "What happens if you ingest this?"

"According to the seller?"

She nodded.

"It's a magic potion that heals you, gives you super strength, superhuman speed, flight. There was something about distilling proteins from blood of freaks and finding the right balance of whatever. I don't know." Ivan shrugged. "Sounds like a lot of nonsense to me."

"Did Kalydon try to use this on you?"

Ivan's brow wrinkled in confusion. "Is that the seller's name? I didn't know." But now he did and there was more than a hint of retribution in his tone. "He didn't offer it to me. He wanted blood."

"And not as in revenge?"

"Nah, two of his thugs grabbed me as soon as my boss dropped me off. Popped a needle into my vein like I'm some damn junkie." His shoulders hunched over at the memory. "But something went wrong. I wasn't right." He shook his head.

Delilah shook the vial. "Drink up."

Ivan scowled at her.

"It might heal you. It might kill you. But I'm leaving now, and this is your one chance to get out of here."

"What? You're leaving me? I thought we were friends! We had this whole villainous rapport with each other. Witty banter was exchanged."

She laughed. "You really are delusional. Drink up. If you survive, you can rescue yourself."

"And if I don't?"

She shrugged. "I'm sure someone will find you. Eventually."

* * *

"Rescue me!" Travys shouted as soon as Delilah entered the room. "You have to get me out of here. There's nothing on TV but shows about house hunting and bread baking."

Delilah's four-inch heels clicked on the hospital room linoleum. "Those are useful life skills."

"I'm going to die of boredom. Also, I'm going to die if I miss my finals and can't play basketball because my grades are too low."

"You'll also die if the Golden Hunt of Atlanta finds you," Delilah said. "Which is why you're leaving the city."

Travys's jaw dropped.

"Your doctor is signing the release forms as we speak, and your luggage is packed."

"You can't do that to me!"

She lifted her chin with a small smile. "You'll find there's very little in life that I can't do."

"Delilah, you can't," Travys said. "I'm so close to finding my mom. I know the answer's here. That guy knows."

"Yes. And now the police know." She let that sink in. "It's over. All that's left is the wrap up."

He narrowed his eyes. "If it's over, why do I need to go anywhere? I'm safe."

"This isn't a police show on the television. Sometimes wrap-up takes more than five minutes. People run. People fight. You have already been injured and I won't let that happen a second time."

He slammed his head back into the pillows, making the hospital bed quake. "She's dead, isn't she?"

"Yes."

He stared at the wall. "Why don't I feel anything?"

Delilah sat on the edge of his bed. "You've suspected this for a long time. Maybe you've already done your grieving. Or maybe it will come later. Or maybe you never will. Sometimes, when we can't handle an emotion, it's like a phantom limb. You feel the pain and it never goes away."

"I knew she was dead last year." He turned away to look out the window. "The guy who did it?"

"Dead."

"Good." Travys nodded and turned back to her. "So which relative are you foisting me off on? My aunt? My cousins? Maybe Chris is out of jail and we could have some dick-son bonding time over the holidays."

"Don't be ridiculous. You're going to California to stay with Angela, Ty, and Aaron."

Travys gave her some serious side eye. "For real?"

Angela, as always, had perfect timing. She walked in, wearing flip-flops totally unsuitable for the snowstorm outside. "Hey! How's my favorite student!"

Travys chuckled weakly. "Hi, Miss Smith. I'm good. I'm doing real well on my math..." He turned as pale as a boy with ancestors from Zambia could get. "Son of... My math final is tomorrow! Miss Smith, ya gotta let me stay! My final is tomorrow!"

Angela smiled and smoothed his hair back. "Handled. I went and talked to the dean about everything today, then spoke with your teachers. They're going to let me proctor the test at home. You can take it as soon as we get to the house if you want."

Travys grimaced. "That's going to be what, three in the morning? No offense, Miss Smith, but I'm not ready for a test after a plane ride."

Delilah covered a smirk with her hand as Angela stared at Travys in utter confusion. "Arktos doesn't need a plane," she said softly. "But I do need to get going. It's after eight and I've had a long day."

Tyler Running-Fox, once the most eligible bachelor in America and still considered by most to be the handsomest man in the world, stepped into the room with a bevy of nurses floating in his wake.

"Oh, joy, you brought gawkers." Delilah frowned.

Ty shrugged. "I had to show them my ID to get in. What did you want me to do?"

"Lie," Delilah said. "Remind me to make you a fake ID sometime. How do you feel about being Carlos Manoso?"

"Leave my favorite books out of this," Ty said, pointing a warning finger at her. "I am man enough to admit I like funny books."

Angela and Delilah shared an exasperated sister look. No one else could possibly understand the pain of their mother's obsession with a clumsy bounty hunter from New Jersey who churned through cars faster than Daddy did through first-generation minions. Some people went door-to-door selling religion; Mom was a zealot bent on sharing the wonders of nineties romance novels cum noir detective tales.

"I hold you fully responsible," Angela said. "If you hadn't left them alone while I was getting changed to go out for dinner, Mom never would have handed him the book."

Ty leaned over and kissed Angela's forehead. "It's just a book. Let's get the kiddo out of here. We still have a party to go grocery shopping for."

"Party?" Travys perked up. "I like parties!"

"Aaron's having an end-of-semester bash with some of his school friends," Angela said with a slinky cat-that-ate-the-canary grin. Oh, yeah, Delilah's big sis knew the way to make men do what she wanted. "Ever heard of DJ South?"

"The singer?" Travys's voice hit a high note in excitement.

"That's her. She lives next door, so Aaron invited her to drop by for the pool party tomorrow. She's already confirmed she'll be there."

Travys held out his arm with the blood pressure monitor. "I'm ready to go."

CHAPTER EIGHTEEN

Alan,

The Hunt has captured Travys again. I don't know how they got him out of the hospital, but they did. I'll call as soon as I know anything.

Love,
Delilah

DELILAH PULLED HER KEVLAR under-armor on and strapped a knife to her leg. It was on the small side, but it was all for show anyway.

"I don't like this," Freddie muttered.

"It doesn't matter," she said as she pulled her black dress on. She turned in front of the mirror, watching to see how the skirt fell. Perfect.

Freddie handed her a red wool coat with silk lining. "You should have asked for backup, not sent the one ally you have on a wild goose chase."

"And how would Alan help, exactly? He can't do anything to hurt the Golden Hunt. He can't risk exposing who he really is. It would be political suicide at best. Telling him Travys was kidnapped again keeps him safe." Worse, the Hunt was waiting for the Spirit of Chicago. In her gut she knew they were hunting him. But he was hers now, and they could have him when they pried him from her cold, dead hands. Sending him on a wild goose chase to the south of town had been the best she could do, but it should keep him safe long enough for her to deal with the mess.

"Why aren't we calling the police and getting a SWAT team in there?" Freddie asked.

"One, because at least one of Kalydon's minions has taken the Mégisti formula and has super speed, so any normal human would be killed, and two, because they hurt Travys. He's one of the family, and people who hurt the family don't walk away from me."

Freddie snorted.

"I watched Ivan after he took a drink," Delilah continued. "Two broken legs working in minutes, and he moved faster than any human could. Even Mom doesn't fly that fast. The only way I can take the Hunt down is if I get them to sit still, and you get more flies with honey than vinegar. Kalydon fancies himself a made man, attractive and wonderful. He wants me now."

"Because you vandalized his apartment."

She waved a dismissive hand. "It was a note written on his mirror."

"And who is to watch to see that no one else interferes with this take down?" Freddie asked. "The Russians haven't abandoned their course. The Company might still be in town."

"I'm counting on it." The Company had hurt her family too, but that was the beauty of her plan. If everything went according to her script, she'd be able to pay The Company back tenfold. "Let's go."

The drive over was silent. Freddie kept giving her hurt looks in the mirror.

"Go home," Delilah ordered as she stepped out of the cab. "I'll be back within seventy-two hours."

"And if you aren't?" the minion demanded.

"Then, and only then, may you call in the cavalry." She slammed the door shut. Anticipation warmed her like nothing else could. Too long the Golden Hunt had prowled her city, hunted her people, hurt the ones she loved. And now it was time for a reckoning.

* * *

Alan's phone screamed with a ringtone he hadn't programmed in as he steered the car smoothly through the traffic. He hit the call button on the dash. "Delilah?"

"No."

It took him a moment to place the gravelly voice on the other end of the line. "Freddie?" he asked in disbelief.

"Yes, sir." There was a silence. A very obedient silence, as if Freddie was trying to fill it with all the things he wasn't supposed to say.

"Where's Delilah?" he said, dreading the answer.

"I'm so glad you asked, sir," Freddie replied. "She's gone for a drive up town to meet a certain huntsman I've been specifically forbidden to talk about. While I can't name the bastard, I can say that my mistress is visiting him at his Chicago domicile and nowhere south of Lake Michigan near the address she sent you."

"How circuitous," Alan said as something to say while his brain raced. Delilah was going to meet Kalydon. Alone. In Chicago. And she'd sent him out of the city on purpose. "Where is Travys?"

"I have been specifically forbidden to mention the young gentleman's whereabouts, or the fact that a certain family member stopped by late last evening to collect the young gentleman's coat that he had left here inadvertently."

Alan snorted. "I like how that forbidden bit keeps you from saying anything. Very effective."

"I was programmed for loyalty, sir, not stupidity," Freddie said primly.

"Delilah is going to have your ears when she realizes what you've done." Alan took the highway exit and stopped at a light so he could get back on 90 North.

Freddie was silent for a moment. "Miss Delilah may very well be upset, but within the parameters of my programming and understanding, I'm not sure. She may have anticipated this phone call. It's the only reason I could call."

"She forbade you to call but you think she expected you to call me anyway?" The light turned green and he drove under the overpass.

"There's a twenty-three percent chance that my mistress anticipated this phone call and your return at the right moment."

Alan's gripped tightened on the wheel. "Wouldn't it have been easier for Delilah to tell me when she wanted me to show up and save the day?"

"I couldn't say, sir. The mistress's mind is a mystery to me."

"Me too." Alan sighed. "I'll be there in about forty minutes if the traffic stays steady."

"Sir, if I could be so forward, I would recommend breaking a few of the more pedestrian traffic laws. Miss Delilah entered the building over ten minutes ago, and I didn't call until the building sealed itself. We're unable to reach her, sir." Worry underscored Freddie's words.

Alan's foot flattened the accelerator. "I'll be there in time." Even if he had to ditch the car and ghost his way to Chicago.

* * *

"Miss Samson, what a pleasant surprise." Kalydon's voice dripped with contempt as she stepped inside the shadowy room. He moved a wrinkled hand and she heard the door seal behind her with a smothered thump.

Delilah looked around the room, matching the faces visible in the gloom to the pictures on Kalydon's Kill Wall. "My, my, my, the whole gang is here." She smiled. "What? No chair for me?"

"You volunteered yourself," Kalydon reminded her. "Your blood for the city of Chicago."

"And names in exchange for the formula," Delilah said, stripping off her gloves. "Thankfully I'm young enough that senility and dementia haven't set in yet."

Klaydon growled at the insult.

Her smile grew sweeter.

"Blood first," said a woman's voice. She stepped out of the gloom, revealing obsidian black skin and a shimmering gold dress. Her hair was white and tied up in a hundred small braids. "Do you know me?"

"Ayo Naiabi," Delilah said. "I know your reputation. Child soldier in Africa, brought to England by an international charity group, suspected of your boy-friend's murder in college but you were found not guilty in court."

"Murder is between equals," Ayo said. "One such as myself can never murder a human, only exterminate them."

"Yet you cried on the stand and declared you loved him," Delilah mocked softly. "Such love, you said. Such devotion."

"Like a dog." Ayo shrugged. "He was my pet, and when he became unruly I put him down."

Kalydon thumped his cane on the ground. "Enough. The blood, Miss Samson. A donation to our work."

"To your longevity you mean? That is what you use this serum for isn't it, Kalydon? You keep the Grim Reaper at bay with these injections, but they're not working as well as before." She brushed past Ayo to sit down in the empty chair. "That's why the murders have become more frequent, isn't it?"

The old man glared at her. "Nonsense."

"Perfect sense," Delilah countered. "The formula first became available in 1985, a product of a villain called Lady Grimoire. She produced small amounts using her own blood as part of the Eden Project. Of course that was before she considered a villain, wasn't it? She was plain, ordinary Marjorie Thayer, single mother and biochemist, when she worked for Kalydon Industries."

"I don't know what you're talking about," Kalydon said stiffly.

"Liar." Delilah winked at him and relaxed. "Marji was one of your little failures, wasn't she? You mentioned her in an interview once. A brilliant scientist who spurned you because your wealth wasn't enough to blind her to your other failings."

"I have no failings!"

"Hubris being chief amongst your faults," Delilah continued as if he'd said nothing. "When The Company was formed and Project Eden was taken away from her, Marjorie quit. She left you, went rogue, became a villain. Her black market formula for superpowers created dozens of one-shot villains. Angry men and women who thought a single dose would make them gods. What's funny about people who want to become gods is that they're never happy with that first elevation, are they? No one with power is content. We all want more. I want stronger powers to be like the other superheroes." It was a plausible lie, especially to someone like Kalydon who lived with the More Is More mentality. "You wanted superpowers to prove Marjorie, and everyone else who mocked you, wrong. Ayo wants revenge. Chasten Huntley," she waved to the mayor's social secretary, "wants attention. I bet we could ask everyone here if they want more power and they'd all say yes."

Ayo shrugged. "So? We are the pinnacle of evolution. We are the wise ones. The brave ones. The warriors."

"No, warriors fight for a cause," Delilah said. "You're power-hungry fools."

Kalydon stood. Rage radiated off him like a perfume as he shook. "How dare you," he said between clenched teeth. "How dare you challenge me? I have laid low your protectors of humanity, your so-called heroes. I have hunted them like the animals they are!"

"And?" Delilah asked calmly.

"I am better than they are!"

"Because you pulled a trigger?"

"Yes!"

She clapped ironically. "Bravo! You are a tool-using monkey! What a smart monkey."

Something moved behind her, grabbed her arm and twisted it up. "Do you know me?" an angry voice asked.

Delilah scanned the room and picked the missing name from the list. "Winda Leverick? From Boston?"

"Yes." He pushed her arm to the point of breaking. "Guess what I took a dose of this morning?"

"Oh, hmm. Let me guess. Mégisti?"

"That's right. I can rip your arms from your body, run faster than a train, fly like a bird in the wind. Can you, little girl with a big mouth?"

Delilah laughed. "Do I need to? I'm exactly where I want to be."

"Gag her," Kalydon ordered. "Get the machine out here. I won't waste any more time with her talk."

Leverick held her wrist tight enough to bruise, but the Megisti formula had its flaws. That's why notes mattered. That's why old records about dead people were worth reading. The serum numbed the nerves of the skin; it was the only way for a normal person to move at high speeds without writhing in pain. Someone born with super-powered flight or speed wasn't using muscle, they were using magnetics, a fact Delilah learned all about from her mother. But Lady Grimoire's potion numbed the pain receptors and pumped extra oxygen into the muscles to allow a person to move at inhuman speeds.

Which meant that Leverick didn't feel the heat rising in the room until it was too late.

Kalydon wiped sweat from his forehead. "What is that? Who turned on the heater?"

"I feel nothing," Ayo said.

"Are you feeling well, sir?" Chasten asked, moving at a speed he wasn't born to.

Delilah smiled as the floor under her sagged.

"You!" Kalydon shoved an angry finger in her face. "What are you doing?"

"Unlocking things," Delilah said with a laugh. "That's my talent, didn't you know? The ability to unlock things. I can open doors. Make people tell me their secrets. It's a small, worthless, unimportant talent. Not very grand. Not very showy."

Ayo screamed as the floor under her collapsed.

"What are you doing?" Kalydon demanded.

"Unlocking the bonds between atoms."

She wasn't sure Kalydon had time to register what she said. It was possible he didn't even know what she meant. But he saw the results. One controlled atom bomb going off in his secret bunker on Wacker Street. After that, he probably didn't see very much at all.

CHAPTER NINETEEN

Dear Mom,

No matter what you hear, don't worry about me. I'm fine.

I love you,
Delilah

BRIGHT LIGHTS SWAM IN Delilah's field of vision. First little sparks, then pale yellow, then a strobing red and blue. A fireman in yellow pulled a rock aside. "Are you alive, miss?"

"I'm fine." Bruised, possibly with a fractured ankle, but fine.

Police cars swarmed the scene. She almost wished she could call them off. There was nothing left to find. The Golden Hunt hadn't been bombed, they were the bomb. In time, hopefully, someone would find the bunker with the kill wall. She'd done her best to keep the heat away from the room, but explosions were such an imprecise science. At least, done her way they were an imprecise science. A gifted arsonist could probably have left the room wholly untouched.

In the muzzy-headed way of the lightly concussed, Delilah knew this was an unproductive line of thought.

There were people. Soon there would be questions. It wouldn't hurt to have a doctor look at her ankle or her head. But all she wanted to do was lie in the rubble and take a nap. Curl up around the still-warm chunks of concrete and sleep for a good twelve hours. For the first time in over a year, she relaxed. Everyone was safe. The Hunt was gone.

The fireman was carrying her to a waiting ambulance. News reporters flocked around. It was all a lot of fuss for one little girl from Texas.

"Delilah?" Detective Morrow pushed an EMT aside to get to her. "What were you doing here?"

"Following a lead." She managed to keep the smug self-satisfaction out of her voice.

Morrow folded his arms across his chest. "You okay?"

"I'm not dead," Delilah said. "Just tired."

"Don't go to sleep!" Morrow said at the same time as one of the emergency responders.

An EMT stepped forward. "Could be a concussion."

"Maybe one of the falling rocks hit me," Delilah said.

Morrow frowned. "Were you in the build—"

"Stop!" An elderly woman in white high heels picked her way across the rubble, a black wallet with a badge in it in hand. "Homeland Security. This is my witness."

The EMT smiled genially. "Sure thing. Let me get her checked out and we'll turn her over to you."

Detective Morrow looked like a fish out of water. "Homeland Security? I thought you guys disbanded. We don't need you here. A building collapse doesn't make it federal jurisdiction."

"A terrorist bombing does," the woman said with a snide smile. "It was a bomb, wasn't it, Miss Smith?"

Old memories of a darker time invaded Delilah's peace. "Katrina?"

The woman's smile grew sharper.

"You need to update your files. The name's Samson, not Smith."

"Either way," Katrina said. "You're coming with me."

Delilah weighed her options. Morrow would stop this if she objected. The EMT could be dealt with, and he undoubtedly had something in his kit that would make her head stop aching. It was the sight of a green-eyed blond on the other side of the police cordon that stopped her from making a fuss. Alan.

Freddie must have called him in. Either that or he'd ghosted to the national park address she'd sent, found no Travys, and come back to Chicago to find her. Katrina was reaching for her handcuffs. Things were a hair's breadth away from escalating.

The handcuffs clinked together and it was all Delilah could do not to laugh. Across the wreckage, she sent Alan a very firm glare. Hopefully he'd do the smart thing and stay away.

Katrina didn't get the joke though. She cuffed Delilah's hands behind her back and pushed her towards a waiting car. Delilah snickered quietly. Things couldn't have gone better if she'd written this script herself.

* * *

"Would you like some water?" The woman asking Delilah wore a black leather catsuit with a red slash down the left side and used a tone of menace that turned a drink of water into the promise of death.

Not that Delilah was going to eat or drink anything The Company offered, but even if she hadn't known Lead Feather's affiliations, she would have given the woman wide berth. "I'm fine. Thanks for asking."

Lead Feather sneered at her. "It's going to be such a pleasure to wipe that smile off your face."

"I'm sure you'll enjoy trying." Delilah relaxed in the uncomfortable chair. Her head was better, although her ankle still twinged. Running was out of the question, but

The Company wanted to talk and she wanted to get some answers. It was a win-win scenario at the moment. "Are you going to take these cuffs off?"

"You wish," Lead Feather said. "Enjoy your new bracelets. They'll be a permanent feature in your life."

The interrogation room door swung open and Katrina, Company boss, stepped inside. "Lead Feather, what are you doing here?" she chided. "Get to cleaning up."

"Yes, ma'am." With one last death glare, Lead Feather stepped out of the room.

When Delilah's mother was a young superhero working for The Company under the name Zephyr Girl, Katrina had been a hard-nosed woman with power suits and a Margret Thatcher haircut. In the decades since Zephyr Girl had 'died,' very little about Katrina had changed. Her dark hair had gone steel gray, she'd lost weight, and wrinkles had appeared, but on the whole she was very much like the woman Delilah had grown up seeing pictures of.

If you ever see this woman, you come get Mommy or Daddy right away. Do you understand, Delilah? Don't talk to her. Don't follow her. Don't unlock things near her. Her name is Katrina, and she is dangerous.

Some children grew up with the bogeyman; the Smith children grew up knowing The Company was lurking in the dark to kidnap them. Facing her childhood nightmare now, Delilah wanted to laugh. A chicken-boned woman with a smile like a ruler wasn't scary. She was pathetic. Delilah grinned like a shark. "Katrina, I've heard so much about you. I'm so glad you could fit me into your busy schedule."

Katrina's eyes narrowed into dark gimlets of fury. "Where's the formula?"

"Which formula?"

"The one that makes superheroes. The one Kalydon was peddling and that you were trying to steal when the bomb went off. It's out there. Six vials were sold at auction yesterday, but Kalydon said he had more."

Delilah leaned as far forward as she could. "Did you buy those six vials?"

"No. We're negotiating for the purchase of the formula."

Delilah's gaze fell on the window of bullet-proof glass and the empty offices beyond. "So it's true. The Company is losing superheroes."

"Like a sieve," Katrina confirmed. "It's the only reason you're alive. Twenty years ago we had over three hundred superheroes in the Midwest alone. Now there's one."

"That's a pretty high rate of retirement."

With a wintry smile Katrina said, "Superheroes don't retire. They die."

"No more heroes. No more mutant babies. No more Company?" Delilah guessed. "Maybe you should convince the super villains to switch sides."

"We tried," Katrina said through gritted teeth. "There's fewer of them every day too."

Delilah shrugged. "Have you ever considered the fact that there are superheroes out there, they just aren't signing up to do their patriotic duty? Maybe they don't like Company policy."

"Nonsense." Katrina either didn't know what Delilah's talent was, or hadn't taken precautions against it. She rambled on. "My daughter was born a superhero. I've done everything to keep her safe. Do you see grandchildren?"

"Maybe you were playing it a little too safe. Can't have the grandbabies if she's using a condom."

Katrina's death glare put Lead Feather's to shame. "I'm going to bring you some paper. You will write a full confession. You will detail every skill you possess. I will read it. If I think for a minute you've left anything out, I'll bring my mind-raper in. You may not have met one before. The Company doesn't keep one on staff, but the Russians loaned us Boris as a show of goodwill. I'm sure you and he will get along like a house on fire."

"There'll be nothing left?" Delilah smiled.

"Quite." Katrina stepped out, leaving a manila file folder with Delilah's information next to a blank sheet of paper and a pen. It was good to find a kindred soul who appreciated dead-tree documentation. Such a shame Katrina was a hubris-riddled fool.

The minute the door swung shut the handcuffs dropped to the ground. Delilah scribbled the word GOODBYE on the paper, took her file folder, and collapsed a bit of tile floor. Dropping into a supply closet was sheer dumb luck, but Delilah wasn't one to question providence. The locked door swung open at her touch, and she sauntered into the winter sunlight a free woman.

CHAPTER TWENTY

Delilah,

It's been a week and I don't know where you are. I miss you. There isn't an hour that goes past that I don't want to call you. I don't know if you'll ever forgive me, but please, let me know you're safe. If you get this email... let me know.

All my love,
Alan

ALAN SHOVED ANOTHER PILE of paperwork to the side. If he kept up this pace he might be able to find an end to the mess before the New Year rolled around.

The door opened and shut. He kept reading, scribbling his signature over highlighted portions and flipping pages as if his life depended on it.

The person who'd entered finally cleared their throat. "Boss?" It was Jesse, the office manager hired to replace the late Chasten Huntley.

"Yes?" Alan turned away from his computer reluctantly.

Jesse raised an eyebrow. "You do realize it's Christmas Eve, don't you?"

"Yes."

"Are you trying to be Scrooge?"

Alan blinked in confusion. The reference seemed to have no meaning. A vague recollection of a Muppet movie floated past. "You want to go home?"

"Everyone wants to go home, boss. Except you, and you're wearing the suit you wore yesterday."

Alan looked down at his shirt. "I changed my tie."

Jesse sighed. "Is this about the girl from the news?"

Delilah. Thinking about her in handcuffs made him want to run. To rescue her or to run away, he wasn't sure which. The Company had hauled her off while the building was still smoking and he'd been useless. Absolutely, infuriatingly useless. "It's not about her," he lied. "I just like to work."

"So it has nothing to do with the flowers that got returned from her office, or all those phone calls where no one answered?"

"No."

Jesse squinted at him. "Yeah. How'd you make it as a politician? You can't lie."

Alan shrugged. "An honest politician in Chicago? People voted for me because I have novelty value. It's like being the only unicorn in the petting zoo. Everyone thinks I'm pretty."

"I've got bad news for you, handsome. Unicorn or not, no woman is going to give you the time of day when you act like this. Go home, shower, sleep, order some Chinese food tomorrow and watch reruns of Christmas specials until you feel like puking. But don't come back to the office until the third."

"The third?" Panic took over. "What am I supposed to do with that much free time?"

"Sleep?" Jesse suggested. "Go grocery shopping? Scrub your sink? I don't know, what do single people do when they have time off? Get a hobby. Take up crochet, or something." He crossed the room, snatched up Alan's pen, and pointed at the door. "Time to call it a night, boss."

"Are you allowed to order me out of the office?" Alan asked as Jesse fished his coat out of the small office closet.

"That's what you pay me for. It's right in the contract, subsection B12: Make sure the office environment is healthy, safe, and pleasant for everyone. That includes monitoring overtime hours and making sure people don't kill themselves for the greater good of the city."

"I like the city," Alan protested feebly.

"And the city likes you," Jesse reassured him in a calm voice usually reserved for small, frightened children. "But it's not worth dying for."

No, only losing the love of his life for.

He let Jesse usher him out. Everyone else had gone home, limp garlands from the party he'd missed hung on the walls, another sad reminder of all he'd given up. Because he was a superhero. Because he was a freak. Because... He stepped outside into the snowy street. Chicago at rush hour on a holiday was never empty, but it felt that way. It was already getting dark and the snow was piling up. Alan trudged through it, kicking the slush in front of him.

The lobby was empty. He rode the elevator up alone. The silence wrapped around him and he walked to his front door like a man approaching the gallows. For a brief, shining moment he'd almost had everything he wanted. There had been the promise of a real holiday in front of him. He let the dream image of Delilah sitting with him by a Christmas tree surface in his memory once more. It was so real that for one sparkling second, he could almost smell her perfume as he fumbled for his keys.

The door fell open.

Delilah stood by the console table wrapped in a heavy black coat, lit only by the lights from the city outside, her hair and makeup a flawless shield. "I wondered how late you were planning on working," she said without preamble.

His mouth dried out. "How..."

She raised a perfectly sculpted eyebrow, her face an emotionless ivory mask. "They had me in handcuffs, Alan. How do you think I got away?"

Handcuffs... "Oh."

The faintest hint of a smile tugged at the corners of her mouth. "I'm glad you had the sense not to come rushing in. For a moment, I worried you'd think I was helpless."

"I did. I just didn't know what to do."

Delilah shrugged it away. "No matter. The Company gave me the information I wanted, so it all worked out on that end. You were the last loose thread I needed to take care of." She tapped a white envelope on the console table. "Your Christmas card. Happy holidays." She made eye contact, cool and deliberate and dismissive, and then swept past his reaching hand as if he was the least of her worries.

He probably was.

Alan sat in the dark as the scent of her perfume faded into the chill air. Christmas alone. Again.

He leaned against the console table and took a deep, shuddering breath. It hurt. It hurt almost as much as the time when he was six and thought that one family might actually adopt him. They'd been so nice, so sweet, and so generous. There'd been a mountain of toys bought and wrapped—and then on Christmas Eve the department of child services took him away. His adoption hadn't gone through.

He'd waited for them to come back, but they never did. They'd found another adoption agency, another little boy, and his one chance for happiness was gone without a trace.

His hand clenched around the envelope, and he felt something hard. Quickly, Alan flipped on a lamp and ripped the envelope open. A Christmas card with a horse-drawn sleigh and carolers slid out. Inside, there was a round-trip ticket to Vermont, a printout of a car reservation in Vermont for Christmas morning, an address, and a key. He held his breath as his heart raced.

She couldn't have...

She wouldn't...

The idea was too large to think of in one piece. Could she have found his family? Delilah, with her quick fingers and her seemingly endless list of resources. Even if he asked her not to look, wouldn't she? Always prying. Always hunting for answers. That was Delilah...

He took a deep breath.

No, he'd said he didn't want to know them, and she would have known that he meant it. So... He turned the key over in his hand. An airplane ticket, a car, and a house key. Invitation or threat? Or... challenge. She was going to drag him kicking and screaming out of Chicago after all. At least for a few days. He checked the dates on the flight again. There was no way he was going to sleep tonight, and maybe if he arrived early the airline could bump him up to an earlier flight. It was worth a shot.

CHAPTER TWENTY-ONE

Miss Samson,

I owe you. Come to Toronto if you ever want to collect.

—I

THE CAR SWERVED DANGEROUSLY on the icy road. Alan fought the wheel and managed to bring the rental car to a stop next to a snowdrift. Flat tire. It figured. Heavy snowstorms had threatened to close O'Hare airport overnight, so he'd flown out early, not wanting to risk getting snowed in and missing Delilah. But every step since then had been fraught with trouble. The rental agency didn't have cars. When he was finally given a tiny, blue two-door POS, the onboard GPS couldn't find the highway he needed. Then the GPS talked in Swedish for five miles. And now there was a flat tire.

Movement out of the corner of his eye made Alan turn. The little red sedan that had followed him since town had stopped behind him and the single occupant, a blonde woman wearing a sweater and jeans, was picking her way through the snow to him. She was thirty, maybe a few years older. Alan rolled down the window. "I'm fine. You can keep going."

"And how are you going to get anywhere with a flat tire?" the woman asked. Fine lines appeared around her eyes when she smiled and he bumped his estimation of her age up an extra ten years.

"I'll be fine. I can call the rental company. Get a tow truck." Be late. Hopefully Delilah would forgive him.

"Do you have cell reception?" the woman asked.

Alan pulled out his phone to check. No signal.

His face must have given her the answer. "Why don't you come with me?" she asked. "Our cabin's five miles from here, and we have a land line."

"I don't know if I should leave the car," Alan said. "My girlfriend—uh, friend..."—my something—"paid for it. I don't want her to get in trouble."

"I hate to break it to you, kiddo, but no one's going to steal that car. People in rural Vermont aren't that desperate for bad transportation."

He smiled. "Yeah, I don't even know why it was on the rental lot."

"This girlfriend's breaking up with you?" the woman guessed.

"I hope not. They told me they had someone break into the lot last night. All the fences were broken. This is probably the rental agent's car." And he'd given it a flat tire driving on the icy, bumpy, rural road.

"Pop the trunk," the woman said. "I'll take you to my place and you can call from there. Come on. I don't bite!"

Alan felt the blood rush to his cheeks. "Thanks, um. Miss?"

"Missus," she said as he climbed out of the car, "but I'll take the compliment. You can call me Tabitha."

He grabbed his carry-on bag out of the trunk, locked the little car, and climbed into the tropical warmth of Tabitha's car. "So, you're not a native New Englander?"

She laughed. "Is it that obvious? Actually, I was born as far away from New England as you can get on the East

Coast. Born and raised in Coral Gables, outside Miami. Beautiful place. I hate it."

"Um? That's a little..."

"Harsh?" Tabitha waved a hand. "It was miserable. My parents ignored me and even paradise gets lonely. But that's old news. I got married just after college, had five babies who are all grown up, and life is pretty darn perfect now."

Alan laughed. "Wow. Um, okay. I don't know what to say, sorry. I'm not a family person, I guess."

"Only child?" Tabitha asked as they wound through the scenic pine forest.

"Foster child. No one wanted me." Except Delilah. Maybe. He drummed his fingers on his knee.

Tabitha leaned forward, blue eyes sparkling. "So, this is me being a nosy future grandma, but are you ever going to be a family person? Is this girlfriend The One? Are you going to settle down?" She waited a beat and asked, "Are you going to run screaming because I'm asking?"

"Are all potential mother-in-laws like you?"

Tabitha's smile split into a cheery grin. "Of course not! You don't meet a girl like me every dynasty." When he didn't respond quickly enough she nudged him with her elbow. "You need to brush up on your Disney references." The car turned down a street lined with feathery pine boughs that bent under heavy snow to form a dreamlike tunnel. "Ah, there we are. Home sweet holiday rental home. I wanted to stay in Texas, but my second daughter got to pick the location for Christmas this year and she decided we needed a rustic retreat. Or so she says. I think it's because Major Cobb's family lives nearby."

"Who?" Alan asked as the car pulled to a stop outside a stone mansion that could only be considered rustic by someone who thought Chicago was a cute little town. Delilah would have loved it.

"Major Cobb? He was our neighbor years and years ago. My youngest daughter has been engaged to his oldest son since kindergarten. She's usually in Africa, my youngest daughter that is, so getting her to leave work for a week was like pulling teeth. We bribed her with having the Cobbs nearby."

Alan followed her inside to a cozy living room with a roaring fire and a towering, undecorated, Christmas tree. "Did you guys just get here?"

"Last night," Tabitha said. "Here, make yourself comfy. I bet there's cookies baking."

"Isn't it dangerous to leave the stove on while no one's home?"

Tabitha tilted her head in confusion. "Oh. Yes. It would be. But there's always someone at home. We don't have minions for nothing!" Her eyes widened. "I meant kids. Not minions. I don't have real minions. Who would? That's a super villain-ish thing, and I'm obviously not a villain. Or a superhuman. Or anything. And if I were, I would totally be a superhero with a very cute outfit. But there are kids here. My son and baby-son-in-law and my extra-son are downstairs playing video games. One's natural birth, one we had by marriage, and the other we had by adoption at gun point."

The clock ticked loudly as he stared.

Tabitha frowned. "Sorry. Is that over-sharing?"

"No, no, it's just, I..." He almost said he knew a family with minions, but that way led to awkwardness and more stunned silences. Tabitha would probably think he had a concussion. Normal people did not take genetically engineered minions for granted. "Sorry. Why..." He shook his head. "I don't know how to frame this question."

"I look so normal, so why am I not a member of the two-point-five WPF club?"

He nodded uncomfortably.

She grinned. "Because two-point-five kids is very hard to arrange for, I always wanted a big family, and white picket fences don't go with castles."

Alan dropped his bag on the kitchen table. "Castle? Did you say castle?"

"It's just a little one," Tabitha said as she checked the oven for cookies. "In retrospect, I shouldn't have told my husband to have a house picked out by the time I left the hospital with our youngest. But I didn't want to go home to the house he'd set on fire—"

"Fire?" Alan shook his head again, wondering if he'd heard correctly. "You're joking, right?"

Tabitha pulled a tray from the oven and flipped cookies off with a spatula, shaking her head. "Oh, no. Evan's a wonderful man, practically perfect, but he doesn't cook very well. He gets distracted, and it turns out grilled cheese is flammable. No one was hurt, but I did let him do the house hunting while I was in the hospital with complications."

"Buying a castle seems a little extravagant."

"Oh, no, he got it for a steal." She brought the cookies over. "Have a seat, you're not in a rush are you?"

"I should call the rental company and get out of your hair," Alan said, reeling a little.

Tabitha waved his suggestion away. "Nonsense. You look like a young man who's had too much stress and not enough food lately. Eat a cookie and tell me about this girl of yours."

"She's not mine," Alan said reluctantly as he sat down. "We're kind of complicated at the moment."

Tabitha smiled, a warm, genuine expression that wrapped around him like perfect acceptance. "All relationships are complicated. What's she like?"

Alan bit into his cookie and tried to come up with a good answer. "Amazing? She's so self-assured. Confident. I'm used to working with drama queens and people who melt down over every little thing, and she's always so calm. She's intelligent, beautiful, fun to be with. I can relax with her, joke around..." He trailed off. She was Delilah. How else could he say it?

"Sounds like love," Tabitha said before taking a bite of her own cookie.

"Is it?" Alan asked. "I liked her for ages but she kept turning me down. Sometimes I think it's all a daydream."

Tabitha brushed cookie crumbs off the table, avoiding eye contact. "Why'd she turn you down?"

"Bad first impression. She says I look like a hitman."

She met his gaze at that. "Are you?"

Alan raised his eyebrows. "What sort of question is that?"

"An obvious one," Tabitha said. "You aren't from Wyoming, are you? Because it would be really funny if you were."

"Because you know a hitman in Wyoming?" Alan guessed. "No. I'm from Illinois and I'm in politics. Local, not national."

Tabitha sighed. "Well, I suppose a reunion was too much to hope for."

"How does that tie in with hitman?"

"I knew one, back in the day. He's dead now. Punched his pregnant girlfriend and a passerby broke his head on the concrete for it. The son's much nicer from what I hear. Lives up in Wyoming with his grandparents. I always wondered if he'd follow in his father's footsteps." She shrugged. "Do you want another cookie?"

"That's not a normal segue."

This time her grin was impish as she waggled her eyebrows at him. "It is in this house."

Alan leaned back in his chair and watched as Tabitha plated more cookies and poured milk. "You look very familiar."

"I get that a lot," she said. "If I was wearing a white sweater you'd get it right away. It's become something of a signature color for me."

He tried picturing her in white and the image fixed in his mind. "Zephyr Girl."

Milk sprayed across the table as she coughed. "Excuse me?"

"Zephyr Girl. You look like Zephyr Girl." Killed in a fight with Doctor Charm according to rumors. Although, since he'd had lunch with Doctor Charm, maybe Zephyr Girl was still flying around somewhere. Hard to picture a superhero baking cookies though.

Tabitha's eyebrows bounced skyward. "Really? I usually get Pacifica from *Fractured*. The TV show." She paused. "You've never seen it? My oldest daughter played the superhero Pacifica on the TV show and she looks just like me. Younger, of course, and a bit firmer all around. But that's age for you."

He shelved the budding daydream of meeting a childhood hero. "Sorry, I'm not familiar with the show." Watching TV took time that he could never seem to squeeze into the day. Especially once he'd started chasing after Delilah.

"Really? It's popular with the superhero-believer set."

Alan shrugged. "I'm not sure I believe in heroes, super powered or otherwise. People are just people. They make good choices. They make bad choices. At the end of the day all you can hope is that you did more good than harm."

An alarming grumble shook the house and Tabitha sat up, eyes bright. "What's that?" Alan asked.

"The garage door. The conquerors have returned. I hope they remembered the onions for the soup."

He cleaned up his seat at the table. "I'll go step outside and call the tow truck. Happy holidays."

"What?" Tabitha frowned at him. "There's no need to rush off. Sit down and try to act suitably rescued. If I start dragging eligible bachelors home, I'll be accused of having Mrs. Bennet Syndrome. This needs to look completely accidental."

"It was accidental." He laughed. "You couldn't give me a flat tire!"

She didn't laugh along.

Suddenly the kitchen air was too thick to breath. The whole conversation had been slightly to the left of normal, and now Alan wondered if he hadn't wandered into much more dangerous territory. Maybe Tabitha was an ax murderer. Maybe the onions were for fresh politician soup.

"Mom!" a young man's voice shouted from the basement. "Mom, Blessing threw me in the snow!"

Tabitha smiled. "Aren't kids adorable?"

"I... Uh..."

"Mom?" A far more familiar voice said as light footfalls ran up the stairs. Delilah turned the corner into the kitchen and halted. "Alan."

"D-Delilah. Hi. I... Uh... I just... My car got a flat tire." He forced his hands to stop moving.

She tilted her head—just like her mother. He knew he'd seen that gesture before! "You're not supposed to be here for another six hours!"

"I got an early flight ahead of the snowstorm."

"I had a red sweater all picked out!" Delilah cried. "I don't even have make-up on!"

He swallowed. "You... You look great." And hopefully she hadn't heard the raw desire she'd inspired in his voice.

"He's right," Tabitha added. "You look amazing without makeup. You're father's genes, I think. No one in my family has eyelashes like that."

Delilah turned on her mother. "What is he doing here?"

"Sweetheart?" Doctor Charm turned the corner, hands full of groceries.

Alan's shoulder blades hit the wall behind him. But it was far too late. The whole family was crowding into the kitchen to see what was going on. A blonde woman who could only be Tabitha's oldest daughter was holding hands with someone who resembled Arktos from L.A. too closely for it to be coincidence. Travys was in the back with two other young men, one who looked like Delilah and the

other like Arktos, along with two other women Alan
assumed were Delilah's other sisters.

He panicked and slipped into the shadows.

What had he been thinking? Big family holiday? Had he
lost his mind? Families had to start small! You added one
person at a time! You didn't just pick up the deluxe edition
wholesale one afternoon.

The chill of the outside brought Alan back to his senses
and he leaned against a pine tree for support.

"Alan?" Delilah's voice echoed across the yard. "Alan?"
She ran to him, scarf trailing behind her. "What's wrong?"

He stared at her.

"Alan?" She stopped a few feet away. "Are you okay?"

"I wasn't expecting the whole herd at once."

She glanced over her shoulder at the house. "Yeah,
I meant to break them to you slowly. I did say I had a
big family."

"You didn't tell me that's what was waiting in
Vermont!"

Delilah shrugged. "You said you wanted a big family
holiday. This is the only family I have." She caught his
hand. "Come on. Come inside and meet them. Once you
get to know them, they aren't so scary."

"Your mother is Zephyr Girl and she told me over
cookies about how a hit man she knew got killed!"

"But she left out the part about how she's the one that
killed him. That's progress."

"That's scary."

Delilah leaned in close, pressing herself against him. "It
could be worse?"

"How?"

"They could all be normals."

He let that sink in. Then he raised an eyebrow. "They're
all superheroes?"

"Mostly villains, but a few of them are heroes." She
wrapped her arms around him. "Come on, isn't this better?

They all know how you feel. They all know what it's like to not be like everyone else. You'll have someone to sit with and discuss chasing criminals, or having a secret identity. How many in-laws could you do that with?"

Alan held her tightly. "And what happens if they don't like me?"

"Why wouldn't they like you?" She squeezed him. "You aren't six any more. No one is taking you away from me. If this is too much, we can go do Christmas by ourselves somewhere else. We can find a hotel, or fly back to Chicago."

Visions of Christmas alone flashed through his mind, followed by images of what he and Delilah could get up to alone. He swallowed again. But... She'd brought him to meet the family. That had to count for something, didn't it? "We can stay," he said at last. "I want to meet your family. Really. I just wasn't prepared for this. Flat tires don't usually lead to your future mother-in-law interrogating you."

"Mother-in-law?" Delilah laughed. "Aren't we skipping a few steps?"

He blushed. "Potential mother-in-law. Mother of the woman I am dating. You know what I mean."

She kissed him gently. "Come back inside and I promise not to tease you about that slip up too much."

He took her hand, holding it just a little more tightly that he should have. "Okay," he said. "Okay."

CHAPTER TWENTY-TWO

To: Delilah
With Love: Alan

DELILAH CURLED HER LEGS up on the big comfy chair and watched Alan ease into the deep waters of Smith family living. He'd lost the deer-in-the-headlights look over dinner and was playing video games with the younger boys. Now all he had to do was defrost enough to talk to her sisters.

Maria collapsed in the sofa beside her. "Do you know how hard it is to lose an election?"

"Apropos of nothing," Delilah murmured toying with the necklace Alan had given her for Christmas. "No. Is that where you've been?"

"Yes! And it's not going well."

"Does it concern a certain superhero who thinks he's a god?"

Maria scowled at the ceiling. "I'm not answering that."

"You like him."

Her sister glared. "So what? At least I'm not engaged to a boy scout! He's so squeaky clean he makes my teeth hurt."

Delilah watched Alan, who was talking with Ty about something involving hand gestures. He noticed her staring and smiled. Delilah smiled back. "I like him. And we're not engaged. We're dating."

"You brought him home," Maria said bluntly. "Let me list the guys who have been introduced to the family: Noah, Tyler, and Alan."

"And Travys and Aaron," she said, adding in their adopted sibling and Tyler's little brother. She sipped her hot cider. "And Martin."

"Dad only met Martin because he had to come post bail for us," Maria said tartly. "It's not the same."

"You would have brought him home eventually."

Maria rolled her eyes and sat up. "Maybe. But I was young and stupid then." She glared at Alan. "Do you really think he's good enough for you?"

"Do you really think he's not?" Delilah challenged her.

Alan stood up and walked over to them, folding his arms over his chest. "Do you really think his hearing's that bad?"

Maria's eyes narrowed. "If you hurt my sister..."

"They'll never find my body," Alan finished for her. "Yes. I think I caught the gist of that threat the first time." He reached down and twined his fingers with Delilah's. "Do you know, you have a very over-protective family, Love. I swear the only person who was excited to see me was your mother."

"He's cute! We should keep him!" Mom chimed from across the room.

Delilah put her cup to the side. "Let's go for a walk."

She pulled Alan away from the festivities and out into the winter darkness. Starlight glittered on the diamond-and-topaz necklace he'd had given her. For him, she'd bought a pair of season tickets to the Bulls games. It didn't meet the agreed twenty-dollar limit, but then again, neither had his. And it wasn't her only present for him, either.

The snow crunched under their boots as they walked away from the house.

"It's beautiful out here." Alan sounded wistful, as if he still wasn't convinced that it was real.

"I thought so." Vermont was picturesque. Not a place she'd want to live permanently, but worth visiting from time to time.

He laced his fingers with hers. "We're not planning on retiring here, are we?"

Delilah laughed. "We?"

"Family Christmas, exchanging gifts, I don't know. I'm feeling a bit we-ish." He looked sideways at her with a smile. "I like being part of a We."

His joy was radiant. She leaned against his shoulder and he moved so she was in front of him, his arms wrapped around her waist, chin resting on her head. After a moment, she reached into her coat pocket and pulled out the thick white-gold ring she'd bought several days before. "What do you think about making the We a permanent thing?"

There was a stillness behind her and she gripped his hands to keep him from running away. A barn owl's distinctive call shattered the deathly silence around them.

"Do I need to get down on one knee?" she added, laughing because it was the only way to keep from crying. If he said no... Well, she wouldn't be a Smith if she didn't have a contingency plan for that kind of disaster. But she'd like not to need it.

Alan took the ring from her. "I don't have one for you."

"We can go shopping when we get home." He was playing with it. Turning the ring around so it caught the moonlight. But he wasn't saying yes.

Delilah's heart pounded.

"Where will we live?"

She shrugged, keeping her voice utterly neutral. "Your house. Mine. Neither. Both. Somewhere in Chicago, but I'm not picky." But she'd appreciate it if he would hurry up and answer, because in a second she'd forget how to breathe.

His gaze flicked up and met hers, and he softened into something much gentler than a smile. "Yes," he said. "I love you."

He slipped the ring on, and Delilah remembered how to breathe. Everything was perfect. She stretched up and kissed him under the winter stars. After all, even villains could have happy endings.

Sharp-eyed viewers spotted some shiny swag on Chicago's newly elected mayor. During the city council press conference, several people noticed that Mayor Adale was sporting a swanky new ring on his left hand. The new mayor later confirmed that he and Delilah Samson of Subrosa Securities had gotten engaged over the winter holidays. Although Chicago's infamous gossip mill has long had the two paired together, this is the first public confirmation of their relationship. The couple plans to marry this spring and hold a public reception for family, friends, and well-wishers at the Chicago Field Museum.

ABOUT THE AUTHOR

Liana Brooks was born in San Diego, California. Years later she was disappointed to learn that The Shire was not some place she could move to, nor was Rider of Rohan an acceptable career choice. Studying marine biology so she could play with sharks seemed to be the only alternative. After college Liana settled down to work as a full-time author and mother because logical career progression is something that happens to other people. When she grows up, Liana wants to be an Evil Overlord and take over the world.

In the meantime, she writes sci-fi and SFR in between trips to the beach. She can be found wearing colorful socks on the Emerald Coast, or online at www.lianabrooks.com.

For all the latest news, subscribe to Liana's newsletter at:
http://www.lianabrooks.com/p/newsletter.html.

THE DAY BEFORE
Jane Doe Series #1

A body is found in the Alabama wilderness. The question is: It is a human corpse... or is it just a piece of discarded property?

Available from all major ebook retailers.

Now available in paperback!

www.lianabrooks.com

SUPERVILLAINS ANONYMOUS
Superheroes Anonymous #2

For years, the villains kidnapped her. Now Gail Godwin is one of them. …Sort of.

Available at all major ebook retailers.

Hostage Girl to Hero to Villain. See it all:
www.dunnewriting.com

www.ingramcontent.com/pod-product-compliance
Lightning Source LLC
Chambersburg PA
CBHW030646120726
47905CB00001B/82

THANK YOU!

Dear Reader,

Thank you for taking the time to read this book. I hope you enjoyed reading it as much as I enjoyed writing it.

The best way to support books you love is to spread the word: word of mouth still sells more books than any other method. If you'd like to see more *Heroes and Villains* books, please consider leaving a review at the outlet where you bought this book.

And of course, don't forget to say hi either on Twitter (@lianabrooks), on Facebook (Liana Brooks), or on my blog (www.lianabrooks.com).

Liana